Mark Macrossan grew up in Brisbane. Previous occupations include barrister (Sydney) and film extra (London). He currently lives in Sydney.

Dark Oceans is his first novel.

He can be found online at www.markmacrossan.com.

Φ 

DARK OCEANS
or The Geometry Of Chance

Mark Macrossan

ANTIMERIDIAN PRESS

First published by Antimeridian Press in 2018
This edition published in 2018 by Antimeridian Press

Dark Oceans

ISBN: 9780648313649 (e-book)
ISBN: 9780648313656 (paperback)

Cover design by Jonathon Eadie
www.eadie.biz

The epigraph extracted from the poem "Relic" by Ted Hughes (published in his collection *Lupercal*) is reproduced with the permission of Faber & Faber Ltd

Publishing services provided by Critical Mass
www.critmassconsulting.com

To Lisa

The deeps are cold: In that darkness
camaraderie does not hold: Nothing touches
but, clutching, devours.

from *Relic* by Ted Hughes

Author's Note

All characters appearing in this work are fictitious and any resemblance to real persons, living or dead, is purely coincidental.

Or would be, were there such a thing as a coincidence.

Prologue

(Wednesday 16 October 2013)

1. Western Australia

[Great Sandy Desert, W.A. (-19.7333, +121.7111), 16 Oct 2013, 12.30PM]

The Nissan Pathfinder was heading, rocketing, in a geometrically-perfect straight line across the desert plain. A plume of dust like a jet's vapour trail stretched out behind it, an emphatic proclamation that it was coming from somewhere and going somewhere else.

Suddenly the vehicle began to slow down, almost to a stop, and just as the pursuing dust threatened to engulf it, the Nissan turned off its line, to the right, and ambled south for about two hundred metres. And then it pulled up completely with a small, final jerk.

A solid man with distant eyes, wearing brilliant, sea-ice white, Bermuda shorts and navy topsiders, stepped out of the car into the dissipating bubble of swirling dust, and looked around. Scanned the horizon in every direction, slowly, as if he needed a pair of binoculars. A fair-skinned, blonde woman in a loose-fitting white cotton dress did the same thing, emerging from the passenger's side. It was a searingly hot, cloudless day and the sky's blue was washed out to a hazy topaz. The red of the earth was overwhelming. There was hardly a landmark in sight, with the exception of a few low shrubs, the odd tree, and a slightly raised mound of soil and rock about half a kilometre away – the bulk of it was possibly a hundred metres long and looked like a plinth that had lost its statue.

'This has to be it,' Aleks said, looking up from the ragged map he was clutching. It had been folded and unfolded so many times, holes had begun to appear where the creases intersected. This, like many things, disappointed him. 'That must be the hill, surely.'

'Not too many to choose from,' the woman, Lydia, remarked. They were both speaking in Russian.

'So where is it?'

Lydia just shrugged.

'So where.... is it,' Aleks said again, but to himself this time.

'You still haven't heard anything I suppose.'

'Who from.'

'Africa. From our woman—'

'Africa? No.'

'You don't think Lena might have...'

Aleks stared at her for a moment. 'I would put nothing past that woman. You tell me, she's your friend.'

Lydia sighed and looked away.

Aleks took off his cap and sunglasses and with his upper arms, he wiped the sweat from his eyes. Those distant eyes, they were topaz too, the same as the sky. He looked around again and cursed under his breath. 'Maybe we passed it. There was another hill... a bit like that one, but it was miles back. I knew we should have stopped.' He looked at his silver divers watch – it was reflecting a blinding ray of light into his face like a second sun. 'Who knows how long it'd take to find it again. And then if it's not the right one, we have to turn around and... Before you know it, the sun's gone.'

'Wouldn't be the end of the world,' Lydia said and took her own cap off to fan herself. 'There's always first thing tomorrow morning.'

Aleks stared at her. 'You want to spend the night here? Is that a joke? Do you know how cold it gets here at night?'

'Cold? Here?' She shook her head, meaning she either didn't know or didn't believe him. Put her cap back on and stretched. 'Anyway. It's nice to be outside for a change. Good for that tan you promised me.'

'OK,' Aleks said eventually. He was nodding. 'OK. Let's take a closer look.'

And then they were back in the Nissan again, stirring up some more dust.

Aleks's dream, which he'd woken up to that morning, hadn't been the perfect way to start the day, and at first he wondered if he shouldn't have been reading something into it, the fact it'd been so distressing. He never remembered his dreams, not as a rule, and this one had been no exception. He knew he'd had a nightmare and that he and Lydia were in it, that was all. But as soon as they found what they were looking for, the bad feeling he woke up with vanished like the morning mist.

Because praise the gods, there it was. The galleon.

Lydia saw it first. It was in a place where the red soil had ceded ground to low dunes of paler-coloured sand. The shifting sands, which for so many years had concealed the vessel – enveloped it, swallowed it whole – had now, in their eternal impatience, shifted again. Looking more like a dead tree, part of the ship's mast, snapped off down low, was now visible. Just. And beneath that, remnants of what appeared to be the top of the ship's once-glorious stern.

'Over there,' Lydia said and plonked the binoculars down on the dashboard, a habit that had begun to get on Aleks's nerves. But she was worth it, he kept telling himself. There was only one Lydia. And right now, he'd forgive just about anything.

It hadn't seemed so long since they were standing together, holding hands, looking out over the vast, cold expanse of the Southern Ocean, with its whitecaps stretching all the way to Antarctica. He loved her then and he loved her now, in the heat, near another ocean altogether.

Aleks threw the wheel to the right and in a great curving arc of dust, he steered his own 'ship' – which was how he thought of the Nissan, their loyal fellow-voyager – towards their new discovery, this reclining old lady of the sea. Towards the most beautiful pile of old wood imaginable. Lydia kissed her new GPS and tossed it down on the dashboard as well, next to the binoculars. Aleks hardly noticed.

Thirty seconds later they pulled up again, this time in a skid.

They were still a reasonable distance away, just in case. So as not to disturb anything. From where they were parked, due to some slight undulations in the terrain – as if they were in the middle of an ocean – they could no longer see the ship, but Aleks had seen enough on the approach. It was her, all right. He fumbled for the door handle, uttered what would best be described as an excited little squeal, grunted and cursed, and then stumbled out of the Pathfinder, falling over completely.

Bit the earth for a second, dirtied his white shorts and scraped his face on the hot, gravelly soil. Jumped up again, wide-grinned, unfazed. Lydia didn't stumble, was already over the rise and got there first, racing to touch the timeworn oak of the stern, where the words *Destino En Distancia* were, now, more or less discernible. She threw herself on the ancient warrior queen and rubbed her hands over the letters in "*Distancia*" until her fingers were peppered with splinters. But she obviously didn't care – and probably didn't even feel them – because she was in love. And so for that matter was Aleks. They'd found her.

He pulled at Lydia's shoulder and made her turn to face him. They giggled like children. He cupped her small face in his hands. All that history. He kissed her, she kissed him back, but she was too excited to keep her mouth still, or any part of her, she was trembling all over. He slipped his hand under the hem of her cotton dress, on her thigh, and up, between her legs. She pushed him away but he persisted. 'No...' she began to say, but despite her splinters and despite the sand and the heat and despite Aleks, she didn't care and gave in to him...

But Aleks was frozen, like he'd been shot. His pale blue eyes were staring over Lydia's bare shoulder, past the edge of the *Destino*'s stern...

'What is it?' She straightened and turned to see what he was looking at.

And then they were both staring. In the distance, an approaching trail of billowing dust was rushing towards them like a lit fuse.

'You don't think... it could be him, do you?' she asked, but it was a question which didn't want, let alone require, an answer.

'Aleks,' she said, speaking softly now. 'I think we should get in the car. I think we should go.'

'It might not be him.'

'If it's not...' Lydia's words trailed off. She probably wasn't fully trusting her eyes, or wasn't wanting to, because it was now apparent the erupting cloud of dust was preceded by a red vehicle. Which meant there was a good chance it was the Porsche. Good chance? *Bad* chance.

'They're in one hell of a hurry to get here,' Aleks said. 'Whoever they are.'

'Can we please get in the car?'

He stared for a few more moments. 'Yeah. You may be right.'

They scrambled back, scuttling like desert prey, over sand and rocks and red earth.

'Quickly,' she said once they were in. 'Start the engine.'

He was still staring though, his door still open.

'What are you waiting for?'

'I just want to...'

'*What*?'

'Make sure it's him. It could be—'

'The moment we make *sure*, it's too *late*. So for the love of Christ can we please *go*?'

'OK, OK.'

When Aleks turned the key in the ignition, the approaching vehicle was still about a kilometre away. It was really starting to look like the Porsche now. The red Porsche Cayenne. Not too many like it in the whole of Australia, let alone this insignificant corner of the Great Sandy Desert. Lydia looked like she was beginning to panic. As for Aleks, it felt like the time he got caught in his first 'rip', swimming at the beach two years earlier. He'd been sure he was about to die.

He was trying to start the engine – it kept ticking over, no problem, but it wasn't catching. He swore. He'd fumbled around with his keys before trying to start the car, and now this.

'Have you flooded it? Is it flooded?' Lydia spat her words at him like she was throwing them.

'It's just a heap of fucking junk, that's all.' He glanced up at the red SUV – and it *was* a Porsche – maybe three hundred metres away now. Like a mad dog racing towards them, he thought. A mad, red dog from hell.

This wasn't meant to happen.

At that instant, when a small cloud flirted briefly with the sun, the desert around them seemed to turn a deep shade of crimson.

Aleks looked at Lydia, but she didn't look back. She was staring at their visitor.

The Porsche slowed to a halt – smugly, it seemed – about twenty metres away. And all Aleks could think was how it wasn't meant to be like this. Because there he was, mostly hidden behind the reflection on the windscreen, hidden except for his smiling, white teeth. There he was, the Korean who'd confronted them in Perth four days ago. The man who'd been calling them. Who'd been following them.

Mr Song had arrived and his was a tune that Aleks, for one, was not looking forward to hearing.

*

About two hours later, purely by chance because it wasn't the route they usually took (due to inexperience, they were both from 'out of town'), a couple of sweat-soaked geologists in a Jeep spotted a Nissan Pathfinder, next to an old watercourse, just over sixty kilometres from the present day coastline – and drove over to investigate.

The occupants were nowhere to be found. And because they didn't know what they were looking for, and because they were pressed for time anyway, the geologists didn't explore the area thoroughly, and didn't get to see the *Destino*'s broken mast and stern poking out of the sand about fifty metres away, over a small rise. If they had, and if they'd ventured inside, they would have found a white cotton dress, lying on its own, in what had once been the captain's quarters, a place in times past replete with royal blue velvet and glints of gold, but which was now little more than a dark and stifling sandy prison.

2. Jon

What do you call a near-fatal accident: good luck or bad?

OK, and what if it keeps happening? What do you call that?

The concept of luck and its ramifications – probability theory in other words, the odds, the chances – had never previously figured greatly in Jon's world. He'd never been a gambler and generally speaking, as far as he was concerned, you made your own luck. He never questioned that any success he'd achieved in his life might have been due to anything other than his own talent and hard work. Fortune only *appeared* to favour the brave, as indeed the saying implied – in reality, there was no such thing as good luck, just good management. And bravery.

But that was before.

The fact of the matter was, in Jon's unsuperstitious, *post-luck* world – a world of reason and consequences – there was no easy way to explain the events that had begun to befall him. And "befall", was that even the right word? Were they falling on him like random raindrops? Or were they being launched at him like bolts from some malevolent crossbow?

And as he sat there in his barrister's chambers, looking out through dirty windows at a cold, monochrome London outside, he wondered what, if anything, these things had to do with the money? Or Emerald?

His desk calendar reminded him it was

Wednesday
16 October

and that these incidents had been happening for a week now. Although it was hard to believe only seven days had passed. It certainly felt like more.

Sabine – pronounced *Sabina*, she was German – was too young for him, he'd always really known that. It wasn't so much her age – she was twenty-six after all, so no child, although by the same token, exactly two thirds of his age, so nothing to be proud of. Pride didn't come into it, of course; far more relevant was the fact that she was a young twenty-six and Jon was an old thirty-nine. He'd been aged and matured by years of work, she'd been preserved by her lack of it. He was a velvety, red burgundy wine to her exuberant non-vintage champagne. She wasn't so much too young for him as too young at *heart* for him. And as such, it was never going to work.

Correction: *would* never have worked, it was already over, she'd left him for good this time. For good and, it would appear, for another man. Meanwhile he'd left her for singledom. Now for a thirty-nine year old living in London, being single was not exactly a shocking hardship it had to be said, but it did entail saying goodbye to their perfect little flat in Notting Hill. Seemed the right thing to do though, give Sabine some space, and as luck (or otherwise) would have it, the owner was re-taking possession anyway. So why Sabine? Why her in the first place? The obvious answer, you'd have to say, was his failed marriage to Romy, his writer/journalist ex-wife. But life was rarely so simple that it could be explained by the obvious, and anyway, that was unfair to Sabine. She lifted him in ways he doubted he would ever be 'lifted' again.

It had been an interesting episode in his life, but really, the whole thing was, had been, ridiculous. There'd always been, if he was honest with himself, more than just an air of unreality about it – like, perhaps, some sort of bizarre dream which occasionally bore a vague resemblance to the real world.

So in a sense, when the incidents began, he shouldn't have been all that surprised. They were really just a logical extension of his personal life.

Except there was very little that was logical about it.

'Jon Marriner,' she said, sounding pleased with herself, or her life, or most probably both. It was Sabine, ringing him. So she still cared.

He asked how she was going.

'Oh yeah, no change... Yeah. Hey listen. I just wanted you to know that...' She paused.

He thought he knew what she was going to say, but as it turned out, he didn't. He was waiting for the anticipated recantation – he'd already mentally prepared his response (cold-hearted and best for everyone involved) – when he heard a giggle on the other end of the line. As if it'd been suppressed, and not done into the phone but directed elsewhere. She had company.

And then she was back.

'You left your... I don't know, really, what you call it... a file of some kind. Legal, maybe?'

So later that day – Wednesday the ninth – Jon dropped in to their Notting Hill flat to pick up his file, which was when the first accident happened.

It was one of those spectacular autumn days that London occasionally managed to produce, with the sun and the sky making one final effort, and Jon felt bombarded by beauty: the day, the architecture, the girl.... they all looked gorgeous. Everything was exuberant and sparkling – the sun, the blue sky, her eyes. She was wearing a.... But it doesn't matter what she was wearing, because he'd already been handed his file, they'd finished with the small talk, and he was leaving.

'See you,' he said as the heavy, black-painted front door closed, aware of the irony, because "seeing" her was exactly what he wouldn't be doing. That poignant, inexorable feeling of finality, while no doubt destined to be short-lived, was unexpectedly acute. He stood there for a moment, clutching the file she'd given him: it was part of an old brief, no longer of any use, but it did represent the last of his things. As for her things, he'd noticed that some were, even now, already in boxes, in preparation for their eventual move to Sabine's new flat over in Primrose Hill in a few weeks' time. New flat. Bought by her father. Sabine's father lived in Hamburg and part-owned a small shipping line – probably not strapped for cash in other words. Funnily enough, it was only now that the thought occurred to him: was one of the reasons she was attracted to him in the first place because his surname was Marriner? He pondered this as he stared at the brass numbering on the closed front door.

He turned and made his way to the street and imagined he could feel the mild October sun on his back and its featherlight caress. Or maybe it was a push. He passed the squeaky gate at the top of the stairs to the neighbours' basement flat one last time, stepped onto the unforgiving concrete footpath he knew so well, and headed off down towards Holland Park tube station, passing a pretty girl with red hair in a bright green dress who smiled at him. He turned the corner into Lansdowne Rise and then, for some reason, before he stepped out between two cars to cross the road, he happened to notice a bird – his favourite, an orange-breasted robin, a bit out of place, you didn't usually see them in the street like that – and, just as unusually, it was standing on the roof of the car right next to him, unfazed, just staring at him. He stopped and stared back. Moments later there was a deafening crash as a car, that had silently appeared from nowhere on the wrong side of the road, flew past down the hill like a ghost, narrowly missing him, slammed into a parked car, and continued on its path of destruction before eventually jolting and grinding to a scraping halt.

The bird flew away.

As for the offending car, there was no-one in it. Unbelievably, it had, apparently of its own accord, come careering down the street and almost, so very nearly, taken him with it.

A bird's stare from oblivion.

And thus, it had begun.

Ascribing times and dates was easy. The real question was *what* had begun?

3. Dark Oceans

11.50pm South African Standard Time (21:50 UTC)
Wednesday, 16 October

Tiny points of brilliance – quartz-white, emerald-green and silver – sparkled under the overhead light, bright respite from the sombre hotel room, from the foreign night outside.

This fine scintillation, it was reminiscent of a quartz-white and an emerald-green from earlier that day, in the Aquarium: sunlight on kelp. And the silver, too, recalled the silver of the fish, darting between the shadows, from light to dark and back again. *Just like me.*

It was, as always, a pure, oceanic dream, sitting there, but then *he* had appeared again and the spell was broken. The Aquarium, a sanctuary no more.

And this thing, this inexplicable prize, the cause of all this, what was it really? Other than a mystery? This thing with its beauty and its crooked lines and patterns, with its hundred oceans – some shimmering, some dark.

Old friend or destroyer of worlds?

Or both. It felt like both.

Part One – Jon

4.

It's not as if his life hadn't been complicated or unusual enough to start with. London had always had its fair share of madness posing as sanity, and on top of that, the life of a barrister, by its very nature, lent itself to strangeness. So the life of the average London barrister was, *ipso facto*, doubly odd and that was without anything out of the ordinary happening. Not that Jonathon Marriner would ever have described himself as an average London barrister, but then again, what London barrister ever would?

Barristers (or attorneys, trial lawyers, advocates, whatever one chose to call them) – those skin-of-their-teeth lawyers who frequented courtrooms, often in those outfits, and those *wigs* – had carved out an interesting niche for themselves over the centuries, which to a large extent explained, and justified, the strangeness of these undeniably abnormal members of humanity. Sole practitioners in many jurisdictions and in London, too, they practised alone, yet operated out of a set of chambers with other, similar-minded colleagues, sharing outgoings. And conversations. Working shoulder to shoulder with their friends and, technically, their competitors. A big ego was a prerequisite. And as a general rule, a sense of humour.

A sense of humour though was always going to be subject to the vicissitudes of life and liable to erasure either in whole or in part. "Vicissitudes" being the operative word.

After the runaway car incident in Notting Hill, Jon decided he'd spend the rest of the day working from 'home' and headed back to his hotel. The hotel was, putting it mildly, a few notches below his usual standard, but at least it was close to work. And the Covent Garden Travelodge in Drury Lane was only seven minutes walk from Gerrard Street, Chinatown, and all that went with that. A lot of roast duck, for a start. Let's hope, he thought, the ducks never get the Bomb, never get their beaks on weapons-grade uranium. Robins, for example, seemed capable of empathy, and amenable to round table discussions. But ducks... There was too much water under the proverbial bridge. Putting it bluntly, he'd simply eaten too many of them for the relationship to be savable.

In the evening, it was the usual: a quick meal, consisting of Peking duck, fried rice and a glass of white wine in his favourite restaurant whose Chinese name supposedly meant "Lucky Day", and then back to his room to watch another episode of something on his laptop. His temporary new life.

As soon as it was clear that he was about to become an ex-resident of Notting Hill, he decided to find a place to rent. Quickly too, as the novelty factor associated with staying at the Covent Garden Travelodge was rapidly fading, helped in no small measure by his neighbours' loud arguments, not to mention a strange odour which he couldn't quite pin down (and didn't want to). He did own a cottage in Wiltshire and an interest in a house in Chelsea, but commuting from Wiltshire was out of the question, and he shared ownership of the Chelsea property with his ex-wife Romy who still lived there. As attractive as the idea was of telling Romy where to go, he still had a soft spot for her, and in any event, it was really only because of Romy's family that they were able to afford the Chelsea house in the first place, so he was hardly about to turf her out or force a sale.

So he'd signed a lease on a house in West Kensington and was due to move there in a few days. Not his first choice of areas but it put some space between him and Sabine. It felt like a good idea at the time.

The next day Jon was back in his chambers, 29 Lincoln's Inn, and chatting to the floor clerk, Tiffany. She looked happy. He told her of his close shave. She noted that he still looked a bit shaken up.

'You could have Post Traumatic Stress Disorder.'

'I'm fine.'

She still needed some convincing and was strong for both of them. 'What doesn't kill us…' she offered.

'That's right.'

'These things do make us stronger.'

Jon nodded and smiled. Tiffany loved clichés, it had to be said, loved their authority. They were like a religion to her.

'And just remember,' she added, 'there's nothing you can do to stop this stuff. When your number's up…'

'Your number's up, that's true. And it wasn't. Thanks to that bird.'

'Sabine?'

'No, the… Never mind.'

Jon was leaning against the doorframe at the entrance to Tiffany's office, the interior of which was plastered with dozens of photographs, most of them of creatures with four legs, all of them her pets (she lived in Barnes). But he wasn't looking at the photographs. Nor was he looking at his untiringly enthusiastic clerk, kitted out today in her favourite dress: a slinky navy-blue number with an eye-catching décolletage. Jon wasn't usually all that narcissistic – or at least not for a London barrister, he was well aware as a class they weren't exactly known for their humility – but on this occasion he happened to catch a glimpse of himself in the glass door of a bookcase and in the flattering, half-light of the reflection, he couldn't help but admire what he saw. Not just his tall frame, nicely athletic torso, not too stocky, not too thin, but his not unpleasant face too, framed, as it was, by his well-trimmed black hair and cold, blue eyes. He didn't see himself as a cold person at all, but girlfriend after girlfriend said as much so he supposed it had to be true. An occupational hazard, he told himself, but deep down he knew it went way further back than his first days in a courtroom. He had to admit though, everything considered, he'd been blessed, at least physically. He could still see his toes for a start: not bad for a thirty-nine year old. He guessed though that sooner or later he'd need to begin a regime of exercise more regular than his weekly boxing classes and twice-monthly games of tennis. Maybe swimming? If he could find a clean pool somewhere. Not the gym, though, where everyone seemed to be middle-aged and desperate – desperate to find a way of jumping off the express train to the grave. You can slow it down, Jon thought, but you can't get off.

'What are you two plotting.'

Greg Burnham QC. Corporate and commercial law specialist, and second-most senior barrister in the chambers. Booming practice and a smile – and a mouth – to match. 'Hope you're not offering this rogue any of *my* briefs, Tiff.'

'Not likely,' she said. 'Your briefs? They seem to be popping up all over town as it is.'

'Oh yes?'

'So I hear. Falling into all sorts of strange hands. Female hands.'

In fact Greg was a notorious pants man. And the pants only came off in the presence of a highly select few: females under the age of forty with large breasts and/or any female under the age of thirty. Which would be fine – each to his (and her) own, live and let live, it's a free world, etcetera – except Gregory Nathaniel Burnham was fifty-eight, newly divorced and exceedingly unattractive. Luckily for him he had a taxable income of two million a year. Made it easier for him to sound like he meant it when he offered a new acquaintance a week's holiday in the Maldives...

It wasn't so long ago – when Jon's practice wasn't as healthy as it was now, and when it suffered from a serious lack of activity – that Greg's success, and that of others like him, provided Jon with a constant reminder of where he should have been but wasn't. Moreover, he still hadn't fully let go of a habit, acquired at the time, of maintaining a certain degree of secrecy. Because if he'd learnt one thing at the Bar, it was to never divulge the true state of play, never suggest things weren't going anything other than gobsmackingly brilliantly. Because as Tiffany might have said: loose lips sink ships.

It obviously paid off because Jon's was a ship that was well worth keeping afloat. At last, he was raking it in. He was turning down briefs on account of being virtually fully booked. He had little free time and he was saying no to clients. Real clients and genuine briefs.

Half an hour later, Greg was striding off down Serle Street towards the Royal Courts of Justice and another court engagement, his black robes billowing behind him – like they were unsuccessfully trying to keep up with this man on so many missions – while Jon, about thirty metres further back and out for a breath of fresh air, was ambling along at an easy pace, a man on one mission only for the moment: coffee.

And as he ambled along – after being forced to cross the street to avoid a closed section of footpath – he took in, on a semiconscious level, the dark brick walls of the building across the road, housing various barristers' chambers and shielding New Square behind it, and then, beside him on his right, the orange and beige stonework of the old Land Registry building. For some reason he looked up, and he noticed, perhaps even for the first time, the beauty of the building's Dutch gables, decorative cornices, mullioned window bays and the polychromatic banding so typical of Victorian architecture...

He wondered where his mind was trying to take him and wrenched it back to the far more important issue of how to stay fit. He had to do something. Whereas thirty-nine was a pretty good age for a single male, he was nevertheless on the wrong side of thirty-five and from now on, for the rest of his life, he would have to remain vigilant. For the rest of his life...

It was with these superfluous, vain and melancholic thoughts in mind that he happened to notice, walking towards him, pounding the pavement in a gleaming battleship-grey pinstripe suit, the perpetually self-satisfied, *consistently* happy, Martin Nevers. Or, to be precise, Sir Martin Nevers, Lord Justice of Appeal and, lately, hotly fancied to fill a forthcoming vacancy on the Supreme Court, the highest court in the land. Sir Martin was a man who always seemed on top of the world. As if his horse was always winning, his case was always finishing, his children were always coming dux of their class. Maybe they were, all of those things. And, Jon had to admit, Nevers always seemed to go out of his way to be friendly. To Jon in particular, that is. Was he gay? Jon doubted it, he'd seen him ogling (and for that matter manhandling) too many attractive women over the years: if he was gay, it would've had to have been one hell of an act. Nevers was, perhaps, just one of those people who had no use for rudeness. They did exist, such people, although mostly they worked in churches and homeopathy practices. They did not, however, as a rule work in courtrooms, where rudeness was frequently regarded as a skill rather than a character flaw.

Tagging along with him today though, like a sucker fish, was the worst of legal sycophants, the barrister Tony McCroogan who wore a navy suit a shade too light and the trouser hems two inches too short revealing M&S socks bearing a playing cards emblem (the suit *du jour* was, it would appear, clubs). McCroogan was one of the few barristers Jon truly despised, he was as bad tempered as they came. What was he doing with Nevers? The two them were chalk and cheese – or sweet and sour, speaking of Chinatown – although today, together, they looked more like Batman and Robin. Nevers didn't look happy though, for once, and this made a certain amount of sense at least. In fact the closer they drew, the angrier Nevers appeared. It was all very strange indeed. Jon even heard a snippet of their conversation. It was just one word, a name: "Irwin".

They were moving quickly, even faster than Burnham (who'd already swept past them in a whirlwind of dust and other, no doubt, poisonous detritus), and just when they were almost upon him, Nevers looked away from McCroogan and straight at Jon. A nod of recognition, and then a smile. So there's my smile, Jon thought. It was a relief, in a way. The sun would rise in the east again after all.

'Lord Justice,' Jon said, nodding back at him.

He'd barely walked another ten paces when everything seemed to explode.

His first, fractured thought: a bomb under the footpath. Maybe improvised. Or someone had simply lobbed a grenade in front of him.

It was an explosion of stone. Leicester red clay brick and Derbyshire Stancliffe sandstone to be precise, the composition of the old Land Registry building next to him. The blast though was not caused by any explosion in the usual sense. There were no explosive materials involved, but simply gravity: a large gargoyle-sized chunk of masonry – a cornice possibly – had chosen that moment (or that moment had chosen *it*) to plummet from the top of the building, downwards and slightly outwards – it must have hit a ledge – towards the middle of the footpath below. It was a miracle no-one had been underneath it. It was certainly a miracle Jon hadn't, it must have missed him by a matter of feet and inches. Even the pieces of exploding brick and sandstone shrapnel managed to miss him despite scratching, denting and, in one or two cases, embedding themselves into the paintwork of a shiny, Vapour Grey XJ-series Jaguar parked nearby, self-evidently in the wrong spot.

What was that? he wondered. A miracle? Or something else?

He quickly crossed the road, to the relative safety of the dark walls of the New Square building – the orangey-brown clay of the London stock bricks had long been discoloured gunmetal grey by the sooty air of a lost era. Almost history himself, his heart was pounding in his chest.

The next thing he knew Nevers was back, at his side, in his shiny suit, resting a friendly hand on his shoulder and talking to him about "luck".

And then he was gone and Jon was continuing his journey past the dark bricks, turning the corner into Carey Street. He looked up to see a sight that he saw nearly every day of his life but had hardly ever registered, a sculpture of a learned-looking man carved into the white-grey Portland stone, along with words commemorating the martyrdom, in 1535, of Sir Thomas More, the faithful servant of both God and the King...

And then it occurred to him. That made twice. Twice in two days.

He figured that if he didn't already have a stress disorder, this was as good a way as any of acquiring one.

5.

The next one was worse. It happened the following Monday.

The runaway car incident had happened on the Wednesday, the falling masonry on the Thursday. On the Saturday, Jon moved to his new place in a quiet part of West Kensington. A cul-de-sac, in fact. It was a house this time – a character-filled (true, for once) turn of the century extravagance – and with five bedrooms, a study, a large living room and a gigantic kitchen it was way too big for him, but he was in a hurry and after the emotionally-charged air of the Notting Hill flat, he was treating himself, excited by the idea of *space*. And anyway, he could afford the rent without too much difficulty, so why not.

Mind you, West Kensington was no Notting Hill. West Kensington was, for that matter, no Kensington. West Kensington was in fact West Earl's Court. Because West Earl's Court was both where it was, and what it was. (Although that wasn't being completely fair: there were some grand houses and streets in West Kensington, albeit with a jaded, crumbling-Empire feel about them.)

The house had a name, too: *Qui Vive*. "Qui vive?" – literally "who lives?" but really "long live who?" or "who goes there?" – was the call of French sentries, and in English, being "on the qui vive" meant being on the lookout. Jon had chuckled to himself about it at the time, when he'd signed the lease. Now though, four days after moving in, he wasn't finding it all that funny.

On Monday, Jon caught his usual train to work. His *new* usual that is, the first time from his new home. It was still an easy trip, much like the last one from Holland Park: a short walk to the tube station, and then just the one District Line train, from West Kensington to Temple. Nine stops, twenty minutes.

Different line, but otherwise everything much the same as before, much like the *old* usual. Same uncivilised level of crowdedness. And as usual, Jon staked out his claim to his favourite air pocket: next to the doors, which not only provided him with good light for reading, but also an occasional view of sorts, helping with the mild feelings of claustrophobia. He was actually thinking about the sameness of it all as the train rattled up to top speed between Gloucester Road and South Kensington stations.

Which was when, without warning, the door he was leaning on sprung open.

At first it all seemed to happen so quickly – mainly because of the surprise factor – and he had no time to wonder how the doors could do this, or how they could do it so quickly or even how fast the train was going. All he had time for was one desperate lunge for something to hold on to before he disappeared into space.

And then it all ground down somehow – a common experience in sudden emergencies, everything seemed to be happening in slow motion. His left arm flailed wildly outwards in a desperate arc, but encountered just emptiness and disappointment. His right hand, his last hope, let go of the paper and thrust itself back towards the interior of the carriage and the other passengers. His immediate neighbours though, in this deathly sluggishness, were starting to recede into the distance, partly due to a natural recoil reflex on their part and partly due to Jon's movement in the opposite direction. He was beginning to lose touch. A pole, a doorway edge, he thought. Anything solid…

But it was all too far to reach; it was as if the whole train itself was stepping back from him, disowning him, already washing its hands of this particular passenger. This one passenger too many.

So this is what it's like, Jon thought. This is what it feels like when the process begins. The process of falling out of a train.

6.

His head had begun to turn downwards, towards the blur of sleepers two metres beneath him. It would have been the last thing he ever saw.

And then a hand, out of nowhere like the hand of God, snapped around his wrist, and before he knew it, he was being pulled back in. Time sped up again, he was back in the carriage, saved by the man with the reflexes. Saved by the guy wearing the uniform of the builder's labourer: dirt-encrusted shorts and thick, concrete-flecked boots. Besuited city workers with briefcases looked on bemused, almost embarrassed. Some managed, at best, to raise a frown at the open doors, while others just looked away.

The train thundered into a tunnel, sending a wall of air thudding through the open door into their carriage. A couple of people with iPhones looked up with expressions of annoyance on their faces. And then the door closed again, but slowly, hissing all the way like a furious serpent. As if it knew it'd been beaten. *This* time.

Thissss....

As Jon continued his journey into work, he was already, in his head, penning his letter of complaint to London Transport. But then he thought, what about the falling masonry? And the runaway car? And at once the letter began to look like a waste of time. He clearly had more important things to think about.

Three in a week, for example. Three near-fatal accidents. Was it just bad luck? Just an unfortunate coincidence? Or was there something more insidious at play? Was it some sort of self-fulfilling prophecy? Was he somehow jinxing himself?

He decided it was simply a run of so-called bad luck. All you had to do was understand the odds. Just as throwing heads on a coin was unlikely to happen three times in a row, it didn't mean there was anything sinister behind it if it did. Or to look at it mathematically: one chance in two of throwing heads once; one in four of managing it twice; and one in eight of doing it three times in a row. Not so outlandish, when you thought about it. Strange things happen, unlikely things happen, that was how Life organised itself. Or rather *dis*organised itself. Things didn't just happen regularly, according to the odds. They grouped themselves into clumps of good, and clumps of bad. Clusters of the beautiful and the ugly. That was all.

Still. It felt like he was going to be having to watch his step for a while, however he reasoned it.

By the time he'd made it to his chambers building in Lincoln's Inn Fields, he was feeling rather philosophical about it all. It was pretty funny, really, when you thought about it. And yes, he'd probably send the letter off to London Transport after all. He had a duty, for the protection of others, as much as anything else.

In the meantime, a gym workout would do him good, clear his head.

He walked around to High Holborn where his gym was located. The building was a particularly uninspiring example of post-war architecture (and that was saying something, there was a lot of competition): layers of white-grey concrete alternating with layers of brown encasing dark, rectangular windows... A concrete lasagne. Passing a Waitrose, he strode in through the building's foyer to the row of lifts and pressed the button, which then obediently lit up. Behaving, in other words, as you'd expect it to.

And why shouldn't it?

The lift area gradually filled with a small collection of people, all waiting, like Jon, for the next lift, about half of them kitted out for the gym. A secretarial type in a short leather skirt and high heels clip-clopped her way over to the button and pressed it unnecessarily, as it was already lit. She pressed it rapid-fire as well, an AK-47 to a normal person's handgun, but she was obviously someone who didn't mind a bit of attention. Jon was toying with the thought she was on her way back from seeing Greg when another girl walked in, about twenty-eight years old, in neck-to-toe black Lycra, anything but petite, but not an Amazon either: with a body that exuded only tightness – pure meanness – she looked like she was made of steel. Her hair was drawn tightly back, and she was clearly ready for a good workout. She upstaged the secretarial type completely and utterly, immediately stealing whatever lascivious attention was going.

The lift arrived and began to fill. The secretarial type stepped in first, winning a consolation prize of sorts – the girl in the black Lycra let an old woman go in ahead of her, perhaps out of politeness, or perhaps allowing two young men in suits, who were hot on her heels, a better look. Jon stood to one side, but it wasn't courtesy, something else was holding him back, although he wasn't quite sure what...

He pushed through this strange moment and was about to step into the lift when some joker (the one you always get in a group) made a crack, at his expense. It was someone he knew although not well, it was another barrister.

'Oh no, not you. *Nowhere's* safe!'

And Jon just stood there. Someone motioned for him to join them, an older woman with a gym bag and too much lipstick, saying there was plenty of room. But he mumbled an "it's OK thanks" and smiled and backed away. Watched the lift doors close. Watched the indicator show the lift ascend and stop, ascend and stop, all the way to level two and beyond.

And that was when he knew he was beginning to lose his nerve. Which, as he was soon to find out, was more than justified.

The next day, Tuesday, the wind was whistling through the cracks around his windows and rattling the panes. It didn't last long, this gusty little hurricane of angry air, but it hurtled in from Essex like a headlong hens' party, and created havoc in the city, targeting anything loose and not tied-down. Like me, he thought, with a wry smile. He could see the people down in Lincoln's Inn Fields below battling its effects – there were miniature wind-tunnels and whirlwinds popping up all over the place. Pieces of paper and other rubbish tore down the street faster than the black BMWs. Even the birds were finding the going tough flying sideways. He wondered if they felt stupid doing that, or just frustrated. Or maybe it was a bit of fun, adding drama to their lives. Or were humans the only animals who liked drama?

Whatever. It was the wrong moment to be leaving. He couldn't speak for the birds, but when he watched all the upheaval, it made him nervous. All that turmoil, all that atmospheric discontent.

Delaying his trip home, he plucked an old New Yorker magazine from the pile of miscellaneous paper items on his desk and flicked through it, casting an eye over the articles, and looking at the cartoons. Found it hard to stay concentrated for any length of time, so the cartoons were perfect. Or should have been: in this week's edition, most of the cartoons seemed to deal with sudden death in one form or another. Maybe they always did?

By the time things had started to calm down half an hour or so later, Jon decided he may as well make his move. He'd had no calls, and received no new work – which wasn't surprising, given he hadn't been actively seeking any. And he'd finished his New Yorker by then, including skimming through a story about the murderous implosion of the royal family in Nepal. More support for Tolstoy's much quoted aphorism about unhappy families all being unhappy in their own way.

He was just about to close the door to his room, when the phone rang on his desk. It was Sabine.

'I found something else of yours,' she said. Typical Sabine, straight down to business, no time-wasting pleasantries.

'Great.' There was no point in mentioning the car incident, she wasn't the sympathetic type. No sense of drama, either: in her book, near-misses were the same as misses, which were the same as never-happened. 'What is it?'

'The sheets.'

'For the bed?'

'No, for toga parties.'

Her sarcasm barely registered with him anymore. 'Haven't you been sleeping in them?'

'Of course. But I just realised they're yours.'

'It's OK, Sabine. You keep them.'

When he got off the train at West Kensington, it was just after 6pm. It being mid-October, the sun had only just set. The earlier winds had all but disappeared, or moved on, although there were still remnants, roving around causing trouble, and every now and again, there'd be a sudden gust, rustling the upper branches.

After he left the station – on the crest of the latest wave of commuters – he crossed North End Road, and just as he'd done the previous evening, turned down the first street he came to, in order to escape the bustle and chaos of the high street. And, as previously, he was accompanied by the sound of his and his co-passengers' collective footsteps fanning out into the surrounding streets. Today though, unlike yesterday, there were leaves and branches everywhere – spread out like a ragged carpet over the road and footpath – and mindful of the nasty events of the previous few days, and in particular, of the possibility of falling masonry, he steered clear of the older buildings, and even crossed the road at one point.

An hour later, he found himself heading out again, retracing his steps, walking back up towards the station, with the intention of catching a train to South Ken for a quick meal. The wind had not only died down, there wasn't even a breeze. No air movement whatsoever, it was dead calm. It was dark now too, and the only sound was the sound of his own footsteps, and as he listened to them beating out their steady rhythm in the vacuum of the still night, he gradually became aware of a dull discomfort. Like a rising sense of dread. As if there were someone watching him, someone close…

And then he heard another sound, strange, unidentifiable, like a sharp click. He stopped walking and held his breath, straining to listen. But there was only silence.

And then a crack.

Moments later there was a ground-jolting shock, accompanied by a loud bang and a tumult of branches and leaves.

A massive branch, the size of a tree trunk, had crashed to the ground five metres away. Indeed it was more than just a branch: a good quarter of the large tree it had come from – a sizable London Plane tree – had split away and slammed into the footpath in front of him.

Five metres away. One car had really copped it, a black Peugeot, its alarm was going crazy, as if it were crying out in pain. And it wasn't the only one: a number of other car alarms went off at the same time, seemingly in sympathy, like a flock of birds. Above this cacophony, while Jon was backing away, horror-struck, and beginning to ponder the unsettling mathematics of the equation that presented itself (distance, his speed), he managed to catch the sound of a second set of footsteps vanishing into the night. Or he thought he did. He really didn't know anymore.

7.

On the floor of his chambers, the lift indicator light pinged, and the doors opened, and he stepped out, along with a couple of others – solicitors or clients, arriving for their morning conference, presumably on time. Jon, on the other hand, was running late. Or rather, later than he wanted to be. Did it matter? Yes it did. These days, everything suddenly seemed to matter, and he had no idea why. All he knew was that everything mattered because, somehow, everything was linked. As if the world had been sucked into a black hole and the totality of its contents had been crushed to the size of a pea.

Christ, he was sounding like a geek, he'd have to slap himself.

On a brighter note...

Tiffany was dressed in all white and seemed to bathe her office in a radioactive glow – from her suntan or sunbed tan, Jon wasn't sure. Or fake tan, but if it was, it was the only thing fake about her. She was what was commonly described as 'the genuine article'.

Would he go there, to put it crudely? He'd thought about it more than once, if truth be told, but he was, if he were honest with himself, a little ashamed of the thought, it'd only been three weeks since he'd broken up with Sabine. And yet... how long was the period of mourning supposed to be? He'd never been one to mourn, when it was over it was over. A friend once told him he had a revolving door policy and maybe, unconsciously, he did. So, back to the original question: would he go there? Not a question he should try to answer, was the answer, he knew. And anyway, he needed his clerk. Or to be more accurate, he needed his clerk to be his clerk.

Her bright eyes smiled at him. Which prompted a second question: should he tell her? About the incidents? He wanted to. She'd always been his confidante – she'd always been his eyes and ears, regarding the various goings-on at the Bar. His eyes and ears, yes, and also, to be blunt about it, his thighs and cleavage too, given Tiffany's physical assets and her effortless ability to break down defensive barriers (in men, certainly, but also, counter-intuitively perhaps, in women as well). Which was how he learnt for example, before anyone else, about Martin Nevers being the latest hot tip for the Supreme Court.

And it was a two-way street, he did what he could to keep Tiffany filled-in too – breaching the strictest duty of confidence was no barrier if it was something he thought she needed to know. He could talk to her about almost anything. But even so, if he told her about this latest business… However he framed it, she'd think he was losing it, or at the very least losing his edge – and he very well may be – and that wouldn't do. Not at all. Clearly, on this issue, he was going to have to confine his discussions to just one person: the Killer.

'Big night?' she asked, somewhat cheekily, but always in that radiant, wholesome way of hers. And, yes, he'd had better mornings.

'Not big in any good way.'

'Uh-oh.'

'It's not what you think.'

She delivered a crumpled, disbelieving grin, before brightening again. 'Well I just might have another brief for you.'

'Oh yes?'

'The Thames Water inquiry.'

'Well that should go forever.' Inquiries crossed pages out of your diary – in *bulk* – so they were lucrative. And fun. All facts and no law. They were, basically, a paid holiday without the long-haul flights.

'Exactly. Look, it's only a long shot at this stage, but… I should know by this afternoon.'

'Great, Tiffany, thanks. Fingers crossed.'

Tiffany was as optimistic as she was rumoured to be adventurous in bed. In other words, he could forget about the inquiry. And he knew should probably forget about Tiffany too, for the sake of both his practice and his sanity.

In any event, he had more pressing concerns.

'Well they do all involve gravity, in a sense.'

He was in the room of another barrister in his chambers, Ryland Pugh – also known as the Killer – who was explaining his theories about what was going on with the incidents. Everything about the Killer was short, including his height (five feet six inches, at best), his hair (crewcut) and, reputedly, his temper. Despite claims to an aristocratic lineage, he had the face of a nineteenth century convict – it was both brutal and mischievous – or some sort of satanic pixie, the sort of face you might see in an old political cartoon. Jon couldn't attest to how many loaves of bread the Killer had stolen, but he had a formidable record as criminal defence counsel. He was also the most generous person Jon knew.

'When you think about it. Runaway car… falling bricks…', the Killer was counting them out on his short, dangerous-looking fingers, '… the murderous train door… and…'

'The tree,' Jon said glumly.

'The fucking *tree*. Exactly. Gravity. And also… all, somehow, so incredibly banal. Not even remotely newsworthy. *And…* all in… when was the first one?'

'A week ago. Today.'

'Four in seven days. Has anything happened today?'

'No. Not yet.'

Ryland went quiet for a moment.

'So what are you telling me Ry,' Jon said. 'It's the Universe. I'm a prisoner of Quantum Theory.'

'Hmmm. It's a bit of a bizarre… *concurrence*, isn't it, all of this.'

'A bit? It's ridiculous. What are the chances?'

'The chances,' Ry nodded. 'Probability theory can be a little complex. You could calculate it, but look, flukes and coincidences, they do happen you know. The most improbable of things. Life, for example.'

'Life.'

'Originating as it did in the primordial soup. A bunch of chemicals finding each other in the right combination etcetera, etcetera, I read somewhere the chances of it all coming together the way it did... About as unlikely as a tornado tearing through a junkyard and randomly throwing together a jumbo jet.'

'Yes, well, with a bit of luck I'll be spared the tornado at least.'

'Luck, yes, and that's kind of the point,' Ry said, suddenly animated. 'The wildest improbabilities do occur. And far too often, people attempt to ascribe meaning to them when they shouldn't. When it's really just a random throw of the die... so to speak.'

'So why has this lotto-win-from-hell fallen on *my* head? Why me?'

'Well that's the way it...' Ry began.

But he'd stopped, frozen in time and space; he was staring at Jon, looking through him though, not at him. It either meant Ry was thinking, or the arrow of death from the fourth dimension had missed Jon and killed the Killer.

'What.'

'Of course,' Ry said, finally, 'there's another way of looking at this. Anything as improbable as this series of so-called accidents is more likely than not to have a rational explanation... a link, if you like. Goes without saying.'

Jon just looked at him.

'No, I mean,' Ry added, 'just because you can't see the link, doesn't mean there isn't one.'

'Right. Aren't you contradicting yourself?' Jon looked out the window, keeping one eye out for malevolent weather. This wasn't helping, it was time to go. Time to move on. He'd only really been looking for someone to tell this to, to complain to, and someone who wouldn't think he was mad, and so the job had fallen to the maddest person he knew. He was reminded of why he was called the Killer: because all his ex-girlfriends had so comprehensively disappeared after they'd broken up with him that everyone reasoned he must have killed them. It certainly put to shame Jon's 'moving-on process' (for want of a better phrase, there was no process, let alone time period, just the 'moving'). It should be said that Ry, who was Jon's age, was no longer being accused of these particular crimes – he'd married a nice solicitor seven years ago, and now he had two nice little boys and a nice twelve month old baby girl to juggle and hold him well clear of any temptation to plunge back into his earlier life of villainy.

'I mean, OK,' said Ry. 'As things stand, there's no evidence of any connection, no demonstrable link. That you know of. That *you* know of. Right?'

It was a rhetorical question – like nearly every question Ry ever asked – so Jon just stared at him and said nothing.

'So the filth. Have you spoken to them?'

'The cops? I'm sure they have better things to do. And anyway, say what? Check the tree doesn't have a criminal record?'

But Ry didn't smile at this. He was deep in thought.

'To check…,' Ry said eventually and not just a little enigmatically, 'to check they really were, in fact, all *accidents*.'

All Jon could do was shrug. Shrug at the question and shrug at the whole situation.

'What about…,' Ry continued. 'What about the footpath being closed.'

'In Serle Street.'

'Exactly.'

'You think there could be a connection? Like someone paid off the police to close off the whole of the… eastern side of the street just to make sure I walked under their brick booby-trap on the western side? Gee, I didn't think of *that*.'

'I'm not sure sarcasm would be my first weapon of choice in your position Jon, but there you have it.'

Jon sighed. But Ry had a point.

'OK,' Ry went on. 'Leave aside *how* you think these things might be connected. The how is the hard bit. The *why* might be easier of the two to answer.'

'Why what.'

'Why someone might want to… I mean… Why are you so sure that there's no-one who wants you dead?'

A great help he was, the Killer. A great help, that is, if Jon was trying to find any solace, which of course he wasn't. Not solace, but he was however looking for a rational explanation, and it did get him thinking. *Was* there a "why?" Was there any reason someone would want to kill him? And then something emerged from his subconscious, rising up out of that stagnant swamp of memories, something that had been there all along. He'd been blanking it. He'd been ignoring the money.

And as everyone knows: it always comes down to the money.

8.

He didn't know why he hadn't thought about it before. He must have been 'blocked' in some way, because it seemed so obviously relevant now, now he came to think about it. Two years ago, almost to the day, an extraordinary thing happened. Extraordinary, in the true sense of the word.

It was a Monday morning and Jon had just arrived at his chambers. He wasn't due in court, and yet again, had no conferences in his diary either. This was back in the days when his practice had taken a bit of a downward turn, indeed *spiral* if one were to be frank about it: after a promising start at the Bar, there'd been a serious hiccup, never really explained, although it coincided with the deterioration in his marriage to Romy, so there was your answer right there, he supposed. In any event, things were quiet, and he was doing "paperwork", as hanging around in Chambers with nothing to do was euphemistically called (in other words, reading the paper). On this particular morning he'd set about doing some internet banking, paying bills, that sort of thing. He logged in and cast an eye over his accounts summary before moving some funds out of his savings and into his general account. Which was when he noticed something wrong. It had to be a mistake. His net position – which should have been around twenty thousand pounds or so (not including a quarantined tax debt of about thirty thousand) – was over a million pounds in credit...

One *million*.

After the double-take – and the triple-check of the number of digits (and the positioning of the decimal point and the commas... all those commas!) – he looked at his account more closely and ascertained that a total amount of one million, sixty-six thousand, nine hundred and thirty pounds (£1,066,930.00) had been directly transferred into his savings account over a period of five days the previous week: £250,000 each day from Monday to Thursday, then £66,930 on the Friday. The transaction details were unhelpful – they were all made from different, unnamed bank accounts, none of which he recognised.

Did a rich relative die somewhere? Not that he knew of. No doubt there were a number of obscure relatives of his out there, but if any of them were rich enough to be bequeathing this sort of money he would have heard about them.

Obviously there'd been a mistake. He hadn't been expecting any payments of anything like this. About the most he'd ever been paid at any one time was around a hundred thousand pounds and even that had been a rare occurrence – he made sure he billed his solicitor clients at the very least monthly as a rule and it was pretty hard for all but the most senior of barristers to manage to accumulate fees of that magnitude, attributable to a single client, over a thirty day period.

He was fairly certain the five payments had to be connected, despite the different bank accounts, or the coincidence would be too great. It was most probably due to some sort of daily limit, particularly if no more payments came in after the smaller Friday payment (they didn't). Of course a daily limit alone didn't explain the different bank accounts, but there was, no doubt, some similar reason behind that too.

So a *million*, it simply had to be an error. Undeniably, the only thing to be done was to immediately notify the bank.

On the other hand...

There was the state of his practice, which was definitely approaching 'endangered' status, and of course, in the meantime, his bills were mounting. Including that nasty tax bill which he couldn't otherwise cover... In short, he badly needed an injection of funds.

And here it was, apparently.

Still, he held off for a while, to see what would happen, who would claim it. But nothing eventuated. No-one came forward. Two weeks later, and the money was still sitting there.

Off the top of his head, he knew that as a general rule, moneys paid by mistake could be recovered – the payer could successfully sue for them if the payee refused to pay them back. However he also knew that this wasn't necessarily the case if the moneys had been spent, particularly where the payee honestly didn't realise they weren't his...

Normally Jon would not have done what he proceeded to do, but he was, it was no exaggeration to say, becoming desperate. Desperate to pay his bills, and not sink beneath the waves as he'd seen happen to so many others. Times were tough. So he made up his mind to spend the money and be damned. Spend it, he thought, and let them sue me. And if I lose, they can bankrupt me and I'll be no worse off. They're probably up to no good themselves anyway, whoever they are.

So after nearly three weeks of waiting for the call that never came, he started spending. It was his shout. Stretched resources, British reserve and simple greed ensured no-one questioned *why* it was his shout. (The provenance of the cash, he kept to himself: as far as his friends were concerned, he'd simply been having a good year.) From impromptu drinks beating around the bush with envious colleagues (always in the same humble pub, the Lamb, in Lambs Conduit Street), to boozy meals in flash, celebrity-ridden restaurants in Mayfair and thereabouts (Scott's, the Wolseley, Le Caprice) with small groups of thirsty, grateful acquaintances to celebrate some new baby or flat or job. There were weekend flights to Corsica, and Cádiz, not to mention a week in Paris sharpening his French and making new friends. He had the most fun he'd had in years. He even made space for a bit of downtime exploring the property market, resulting in the purchase of a five bedroom 'cottage' in Wiltshire. The rustic, green sandstone hideaway in a garden setting complete with two majestic oak trees was a bargain at £490,000 (the owners had their backs to the wall, something Jon knew a little about). And on top of all that, he got to pay off his debts and buy some expensive new furniture for work.

After a whirlwind three weeks of excess and countless hangovers that almost, but not quite, merged into one, he splashed water on his face one crisp and clear autumn morning and the thought suddenly occurred to him: if his unwittingly generous benefactors, whoever they were, were indeed up to no good then why was he assuming they were going to be polite about recovering their money? Why was he assuming they were going to do it the *legal* way? Sure, it wouldn't necessarily be all that simple for them to get the money back if they murdered him outright, but presumably they had their ways.... In any event, he decided, should they come knocking, it'd be far better for his health and general wellbeing if he could pay them back straight away, no questions asked.

Trouble was, now he'd gone and spent a decent-sized chunk of it, roughly half – enough to look like a large rat had got at it, in other words. Of course, he could invest the rest, and earn it back, but that would take time, particularly in the current climate, and if he was going to be receiving any nasty house calls, it was likely to be soon. And then he got an idea.

After making a number of overseas telephone calls, he left work one Friday evening, caught a Piccadilly line tube to Heathrow Terminal 3, and boarded an Air China flight for Beijing. His ultimate destination was Macau. He had no desire to draw attention to himself any closer to home.

Three films and sixteen and a half hours later, his Air Macau jet touched down in the dark, China night. He had no need to wait for his baggage – it was a hand-luggage-only trip – and so made a beeline for the taxi rank, and headed straight for the *Venetian Macao*, the largest casino in the region and one which had indicated to him it would be willing, on a one-off basis, to take a bet of the kind he wanted to place. After checking into his hotel room and introducing himself to the relevant casino managers, he bought the equivalent of five hundred and thirty-five thousand pounds sterling in casino chips, representing a touch over his total expenditure to date out of his recently acquired treasure chest (including paying off his tax debt). He then took up his prearranged seat at one of the roulette tables there, and placed all his chips on black.

It came up black.

(As to what he would have done if it had come up red, there was no plan B, not for Macau at least. It was only ever going to be the one bet. The million restored or the million lost, that was his preferred scenario. Good, stark choices made for easier decisions. Luck – and Chance and Chaos for that matter, and the likelihood of the silver ball falling in the right slot, 48.65 % – was irrelevant. Events had unfolded; at any given moment you have to work with what you've got.)

Jon calmly exchanged his chips – which had now, so very suddenly, doubled in size – for a cheque the weight of a feather, convivially said his goodbyes to the casino managers who were all wearing smiles about as genuine as the Canaletto paintings behind them, and made his way back up to his 3,800 square foot *Cielo* suite, the "complete royal retreat". In kingly fashion then, he rang room service and ordered one, no, make that two bottles of *Billecart-Salmon* vintage champagne. By this stage he definitely wasn't feeling himself, as it were, and he continued the trajectory of his evening by doing something he'd never done before (or rather, never admitted doing before) and he rang an escort service and ordered a girl. Then he thought to himself, don't be ridiculous and rang the escort people back and changed his order to two of them as well.

He knew he was no angel, but after all, wasn't this supposed to be a "royal retreat"? Since when did any great king, or emperor, ever behave like an angel?

And anyway, the person experiencing this was not him. It was his double, his doppelgänger, leading this strange second life that was somehow being constructed around him.

The champagne arrived in ten minutes. The girls in thirty.

They were so similar, he could have sworn they were sisters. Maybe they were. One was called Tina, and the other Tracy. He'd already opened the champagne and the girls said yes to a glass each although neither of them ended up drinking very much. On the job and all that, he supposed.

And business it was. One of them – Tina? – came up behind him and lifted his shirt up over his head and then stopped and held it there, so he couldn't see. For a horrible moment, he wondered if he hadn't made a terrible mistake and his debt was going to be repaid after all. He was pushed down onto the bed, and another pair of hands began undoing his belt – possibly to strangle him with: he realised it was eminently possible that a Triad organisation was responsible for the mistaken payment and he'd walked straight into the lair. Behind enemy lines. (He'd acted for them once too, in his one and only case in Hong Kong, but why was he only remembering this now?) Other equally grim thoughts began to form, and then a cold pair of hands was removing his underpants and a mouth was closing around him and his conclusions were lost in the ether.

An hour later, after he'd failed to persuade Tina and Tracy to stay for more champagne and then sadly watched them leave, he noticed for the first time, on top of one of the television sets – the one facing the bed – a little red light that he was sure hadn't been on earlier.

He amused himself with the thought that there was a hidden camera and smiled at how disappointed the blackmailers were going to be when they realised he didn't have a reputation – or a wife and family – to worry about losing. Or even any money he could properly call his own.

The following evening, with a surprisingly clear head and a relatively well-rested body, he took the four minute taxi ride back to Macao International Airport and boarded his return flight to London which delivered him there on time at 7.15am on the Monday morning and enabled him to comfortably make it into chambers at an eminently respectable hour.

So he was back to square one. But not really. It was getting on for a month since he'd received the funds and still, nothing. Not a word from anyone. No sign. He decided to start being a bit smarter about it all. He'd done well – and, yes, been 'lucky' up to a point – so now was the time to consolidate. In fact it had been on the plane home, in his first class seat, just out of Bangkok, relaxing into a viewing of *Margin Call* over a glass of yet more French champagne (it was the only alcoholic drink you could never have too much of, it was impossible) and a packet of Thai Airways mixed nuts. He'd congratulated himself for his coolheaded approach and for not placing another bet, and for realizing his luck or whatever you wanted to call it would run out eventually (it was one of the inescapable laws of Probability, as he remembered noting at the time – and oh how ironic that seemed now). And it was then that it had become blindingly obvious to him that all he had to do was invest the money wisely: a five percent return would supplement his earnings from the Bar *and* he'd still be in a position to pay them back reasonably quickly, if they showed up, whoever 'they' were. They could hardly expect interest as well, especially with U.K. interest rates being so low they were virtually non-existent.

Totally obvious and totally simple, and how often did the two go together?

So he got to work as soon as he returned and spent the following week targeting shares and real estate and the following month acting on his hunches and investing most of the million pounds. It was a healthy amount, enough to more than supplement his now modest and fast-shrinking income at the Bar. He could get by, in other words, even without his practice recovering. And then it occurred to him that he may as well create the impression he had a busy practice, even if he didn't – he could have quite a comfortable time of it while he waited for things to improve. It was a perfect set-up, if he could keep it going. If no-one came to collect what was rightfully theirs.

And no-one did.

And for a while, with nothing compelling him to improve his practice, nothing changed. Dand the longer nothing changed, the more he realised he needed to hide that fact. He needed to continue the impression of a busy practice so that his *real* practice still had a chance of rekindling. And thus his temporary double-life began in earnest, and for a while he found himself proactively constructing this new, fake practice, complete with fake briefs, fake solicitors and fake clients. It was tiring, but necessary (and it paid well!). In the meantime, he could tell no-one the truth. Not even Tiffany. Barely even himself.

Eventually, his plan worked. People are attracted to success; confidence is the best kind of come-on. And so genuine briefs began to trickle in, solicitors he'd never heard of began to call him. The trickle turned to a flow. The flow became a flood and his double-life was over. He was, at last, a successful barrister. He no longer needed the million pounds of investments and he gradually forgot about them.

He should have followed it up with the Bank at the time. He should have been upfront about it. And assuming it wasn't the result of a rich uncle's demise, which it clearly wasn't, he should have directed that the moneys be returned to whomever had transferred them. It was obviously too late now.

One of the reasons he'd forgotten about the whole business with the money was that he'd treated it as being all in the past. He was wrong though. Because your past was never truly in the past: it was never fully *passed*. It was as much a part of the present as the dark clouds out your window.

And now, had it caught up with him?

9.

About an hour after speaking to Ry, something very odd occurred. Jon's desk telephone rang: it was Belle, on reception, telling him his client had arrived. But he didn't have any conferences scheduled, he told her. Who was it? Hang on, Belle said, she'd check. And then moments later: she's gone. Who? Who's gone? The client, Emerald. Emerald? But he didn't have any clients called Emerald. Emerald who? And where has she gone? Just Emerald, and Belle had no idea where she'd gone, she'd just gone.

'Also, she's…' Belle began, but trailed off.

'She's what.'

'I don't know how to put it.'

Very illuminating, so he left it at that.

And then about fifteen minutes later, he saw her. He watched her as she walked into reception – he'd been talking to another barrister, Greg Burnham as it happened, and as if they both had the same radar system, they turned their heads simultaneously. Her eyes were what he noticed first, and as soon as he saw her, he knew it was the mystery caller, Emerald. There was something out of the ordinary, something not quite real about her. And not just because her eyes matched her name, but she even *walked* as though she were acting a role. As if she were auditioning for something. So was he the director? Or the audience?

She had straight black hair that was so shiny it looked as though she'd stepped out of a shampoo advertisement. But it wasn't her hair that had him spellbound, it was those bright green eyes…

After confirming her identity with Belle – Belle had a glint in her eye that said *See what I mean?* – he walked over to where his visitor was seated.

'Emerald...?'

She looked up and didn't smile, just nodded and gathered her things, she was down to business immediately. Or *acting* like it. When she was standing – she was almost as tall as Jon – she held out her hand and introduced herself.

'Emerald Strand. Could we speak in private please?'

She had an accent of some kind, although it was difficult to place: maybe German, or even Spanish, but he really had no idea.

She hadn't yet taken the seat that he'd shown her to when they walked in, she was just standing, looking out the window. What on earth was she looking at, the grey solitude of the sky? Or the miserable citizens below, going about their quotidian routines? Perhaps she was seeing problems in the clouds? If so, the problems, were they hers or someone else's? Was she looking into the past, or into the future?

'Ms Strand...'

She turned and looked at him, and shot him a steely stare – an icy reception, if ever he'd experienced one. And he'd had some pretty tricky clients in his time.

'Please. Have a seat.'

Finally, she sat down. As she settled in, he looked across his desk at her. She was possibly thirty years old. She had Eurasian-shaped eyes, and yet they were green. Straight hair that was jet black, yet as light and silk-like as if it were blonde. The features of a northern European, but with the dark complexion of a honey-skinned Brazilian. Combined with her accent, she was one glorious contradiction.

'It's Miss, incidentally,' she said.

'Right—'

'But call me Emerald.'

'Emerald. Perhaps you'd better tell me what this is about.'

She looked at him as if he'd just said the most ridiculous thing she'd ever heard.

'I have to tell you,' he went on. 'I don't normally take on cases without a solicitor attached and it may be better if, to begin with, you were to see—'

'This is not a *case*, Mr Marriner.'

'Or advice. Same thing. You'll need to do this through a solicitor.'

She was silent for a moment. Regrouping, he assumed.

'Yes, well,' she said. 'I'm not here for your advice either. I'm here to advise *you*.'

'Advise *me*. OK. That certainly makes it easy. So what is it that you want to advise me?'

There was another awkward pause, as if this woman was trying to work out what she wanted to tell him. Or was in the process of making it up...

'It's about your sister,' she said, finally. 'In part.'

'My sister? I don't have a sister. Maybe there's some mistake here...'

'You are Jonathon Marriner? The barrister? There aren't any others are there?'

'No. But I'm telling you. I have no sister.'

She didn't respond, and there was a sadness about her. As he looked into her green eyes – now more deep-sea dark than gemstone bright – he was momentarily overcome by a feeling of vertigo. It was strange, like everything else about this woman. Strange and beautiful and rare.

'Perhaps,' he said, 'it might help if you were to tell me a little bit about yourself. You know. Just the basics.'

'The basics.' She smiled, but it was *at* him, he felt, not with him.

'Not your life story or anything, just...' She wasn't making this easy. 'Your name I know, so... Can I ask what you do for a living?'

'I am Danish. Courtesy of my father. Hence the surname, Strand.'

'OK. And what about your—

'Also courtesy of the fact that I was born in Copenhagen Although I can tell you, I haven't lived in Denmark for a very long time.' She nodded, by way of conclusion.

And that, for now, appeared to be all he was going to get.

'Great,' he said. 'You don't *look* Danish by the way.'

'You can thank my Ukrainian mother for that. I grew up in Kiev, for what it's worth, but you know, I'm not sure how relevant it is what I look like.'

'No, I didn't say it—'

'Looks are what get most people into trouble, one way or the other, when you think about it. You would do well to remember that.'

'I'll try. Now listen. What I need to—'

'No *you* should listen Mr Marriner. *You* need to learn how to listen. You guys never do enough *listening* because you are always *talking*.'

She was right about one thing. Looks got you into a whole lot of trouble, and evidencing the fact, here he was, unable to take his eyes off this woman and unable to show her the door when they were precisely the two things he knew he should have been doing.

'Can I call you Jonathon?' she said, in what he took to be a welcome change of tone.

'Sure. Just don't call me before ten.'

'Is that supposed to be funny?'

Jesus. 'No. Yes. Listen… Emerald… I don't know what sort of advice you've got for me, but I have a conference starting in half an hour, so unless there's something that's…'

'Unless it's urgent? Because yes, you could say it's urgent. It's definitely *important*. Like breathing. Urgent and important. Unlike breathing, though, this will require some explanation. Some of your time, Mr Marriner.'

There was an awkward silence.

'I see. Well I'm sorry, but…'

He knew what he had to do, but he was having trouble doing it. His reluctance to end their meeting was despite the not insignificant issue of the woman's sanity. He toyed with the possibility (or probability) that she'd escaped from somewhere she shouldn't have (her home, *a* home, a hospital, the police…), not to mention the very real prospect of there being some connection between her visit and recent events. She may have been mesmerizingly good-looking, but he'd have to try harder. Because beauty was one thing and death was another.

'Can I at least deposit something with you?' she asked.

'What kind of thing?'

'A will.' She pulled a folded document from her handbag.

'Ah. Now that most definitely *is* a matter for your solicitor. You'll have to leave it with him, I'm afraid. Or her.'

She threw him a look of pure exasperation. Resignation.

'I'm sorry,' he said. 'Is that what you came here for?

She just shook her head. And then:

'May I use your bathroom please.'

He hesitated, and then pointed her in the direction of the female toilets down the corridor. She'd taken her handbag, but left the will on his desk, face down. Had she done it intentionally or was it just an oversight? He assumed the document was the reason for her visit. He turned it over and read the cover. It was the last will and testament of one Martin Lemar Nevers.

Was it the same Martin Nevers? Sir Martin Nevers, Lord Justice of Appeal? How many Martin Nevers could there be? He was dying to open it up and read it. What was she doing with the will of the next Supreme Court appointment?

'Don't forget your will,' he said to her once she'd returned, handing her the folded document.

She stared at it a moment, transfixed, as if under a spell of some kind.

'I couldn't help but notice,' he added, 'that it appears to be the will of—'

'Are you telling me...?' She didn't finish her sentence though, just continued to stare at the document. Was she in a trance or just thinking of what to say?

'I thought it was going to be *your* will, but... clearly not. Is this Martin Nevers the judge?'

She ignored him, and slowly touched the document as if it were three thousand years old, straight from a pharaoh's tomb. He could have sworn her eyes *glowed*.

'Emerald?' He was getting worried now. Was she ill? On drugs? He sighed a nervous sigh, looked out at the people in the square below, people hurrying along from A to B, did they have problems like the ones he had? Like the additional one he appeared to be acquiring? Because this document had a definite smell to it, and it was the tang of trouble. Not to mention the pugilistic attitude of its most unusual bearer...

'Have you read it?' she eventually asked, fingering the corners.

'No of course not. Just the cover.'

'You opened it.'

'No. No, I *nearly* did though. Given it seems to be why you're here.'

She was looking at him – intently – and now her green eyes weren't just bright again, they were burning. He could see the flames.

'I mean,' he clarified, 'to seek advice on it.'

'Why would you think that? I wasn't clear enough before?'

'Well I assumed that—'

'Do *not* assume *anything* Mr Marriner. Please. Do not *assume... anything.*'

'OK,' he said, raising his hands. 'OK. Just tell me what you want me to do.'

'What I want you to do,' she said, looking at the document again, 'is not possible.'

'And what might that be?'

'*Unread* it.'

'Unread it.'

'Forget it completely. Forget I was even here.'

'That shouldn't be a problem,' he said. 'I have an excellent short term memory, but a pretty rubbish long-term one. Alzheimer's probably.' He smiled, a last ditch attempt at lightening things.

'You think this is a joke?' she said calmly. 'Because it's not.'

And with that, she picked up the document, elegantly slipped it into her handbag, and walked out. Simple as that.

A spell of some kind had been cast, perhaps. Because the moment he closed his eyes, she was there, opening hers. They were a deep green, now, her eyes, and they held his gaze. She was trying to tell him something. What was she saying? But her lips, with their beautiful curl, they weren't moving. She said nothing, just smiled at him. Looked down. And there, although he couldn't see what it was, he knew there was something important. Emerald, he said. Emerald, listen to me, what is it? But she just kept looking down, her glistening dark hair falling forwards in sections....

And so there he was, shaking off cryptic daydreams and looking out through his chambers' dirty windows that fateful day –

Wednesday
16 October

as his desk calendar was insisting with a clamour (these things only stick in the mind later) – taking stock of the previous seven days and philosophizing about luck and provenance and things beyond our control. And Emerald. And the more he thought about it all, the further it seemed to drag him from an answer, so he decided, simply, that it was time to head home. Time to give his head a rest. From now on, he'd just take things as they came. After all, that was all we ever did, wasn't it, we humans?

10.

By the time he'd stepped out of the West Kensington tube station and plunged into the torrent of humanity that churned up, down and around North End Road – pedestrians, cyclists, buses and cars – he was in another world. He'd forgotten, for the time being, about his mysterious visitor called Emerald, and had almost forgotten about the incidents.

Almost, but not quite.

As he crossed at the pedestrian crossing, he caught, out of the corner of his eye, a double-decker pulling up abruptly at the red light, inches away, as though stopping were an afterthought, and for a split second he thought being run over by a bus was going to be the completion of the sequence. It was, however, just normal bus behaviour. And as he approached the corner he'd rounded the previous two evenings in order to escape the buses and the busyness of the main road, he realised it was the street with the trees. The tree branch was still there too, like a body on the footpath, waiting to be removed.

He changed his mind and kept walking straight ahead down North End Road.

A black guy with a posturing reggae air about him stared and smiled. Smiled right at him and almost laughed too, in fact *did* laugh, a loud sneeze of hilarity, all eyes and teeth. Jon chuckled back, although immediately regretted it, as there was clearly nothing funny going on. Nothing funny ha ha, that is. Plenty funny strange.

A few steps further on, he looked up and a girl was approaching him on a bicycle, cycling in his direction, looking at him, but not smiling, not like the reggae guy was, she was just staring. She looked familiar too. No. She looked *really* familiar. She had red hair… Where had he seen her before?

A loud police siren startled him and broke his train of thought. When he looked back at the girl again, she was gone.

Next thing he knew he was in Tesco buying smoked salmon, and eggs, milk, apples and steak. And wine. It was like there was something in his head, something important which he couldn't access. Didn't have the password. Didn't have the key.

The self-service checkout machine seemed to glare at him when he approached, and sure enough, twenty seconds into the process a message flashed up: "Unexpected item in the bagging area". His heart almost missed a beat, he didn't need any more of the unexpected. And just to put the boot in, when he tried to pay, the rogue machine first rejected his money entirely and then, in a parting shot, spat out his change in a fistful of coppers.

Copper. The word reverberated in his head. It was something to do with the police. But what was it?

He looked over, made sure the unsmiling checkout woman from the subcontinent wasn't watching, and gave the machine a good hard kick in its guts with the heel of his shoe. The tin monstrosity rattled and juddered and to Jon at least, his lightning *coup de pied* felt exquisite. He smiled a question mark at the Tesco woman frowning at him, calmly picked up his unexpected items and left the store.

He gave up trying to think. The weather was clearing, and strolling the last couple of blocks home, he simply admired the sky. The sky and the sunset, but it was no ordinary sunset, there were a myriad variations on the theme, sundown orange and all its relations: rose and coral, crimson and cherry, burgundy, fuchsia, vermillion and pink. Salmon and ruby, russet and copper and red.

Copper and red.

It was the red-haired girl, that's what was going on in his head. The one he'd just seen near the tube station: he'd seen her a week ago in Notting Hill, he was sure it was the same girl. Just before the car had nearly hit him. Was she following him?

Or was he just cracking up?

He continued on home through the lonely West Kensington streets – they were treeless in this part, looking more like a Pompeii or a Herculaneum before the calamity, long rows of ivory-coloured terraces with their Romanesque columns, dignified against a classical sky, like a painting by Claude Lorrain. There was no-one around. Even Bertie, his neighbour's cat, didn't bother to come out and greet him. Wouldn't deign to do the civilised thing.

There was, clearly, something wrong.

The feeling that something was wrong continued all the way home to his cul-de-sac in its quiet corner of West Kensington. *Qui Vive*, Who Goes There, what sort of name was that for a home?

Qui Vive stood out, which suddenly seemed like a bad idea, but there was no denying it. It was a lovely house. As his footsteps echoed against lesser walls (and still no sign of Bertie, where was Bertie?) and the proud white building ahead of him gradually swelled, occupying an increasingly greater portion of his field of vision and eventually dominating it completely, he couldn't help but admire the place. It was a dignified two storeys, in contrast to the three of its neighbours, and had large angled bay windows, a moulded string course with a cornice and parapet, and its white bricks were set off with a Klein blue trim: it was a happy-looking abode if ever he'd seen one, as well as being all very noble somehow, in a castle-like, French Foreign Legion, Saharan fort sort of way, with a touch of Greece thrown in... A kind of I-am-but-I'm-not way of thinking. He liked it, it reminded him of himself or at least how he'd once been.

He passed the wrought-iron, fleur-de-lis railings and gate, walked over the mosaic compass design built into the entrance path, and ascended the three steps to the front door. The words above the door, *Qui Vive*, asked him the question and he gave the house his silent reply. The mail slot in the door reminded him of a mouth, especially now because it was stuck half-open: there was something lodged in it. Mail, it looked like – a bundle, for the owner, or possibly the previous tenants. When he pushed it through, the bronze flap nipped his fingers like a hungry dog.

He put his key in the front door – it was stiff and difficult to turn (had he noticed this before?) – and when it opened, it straightaway seemed to hit something. It couldn't have been the bundle of letters that he'd just pushed through. This was nothing that would fit through a mail slot, it was solid and immoveable, like a heavy bag or a sack, or a body.

A body? What was he thinking?

He pushed harder on the door and it gradually gave way – as if the obstruction was being shoved, inch by inch, across the floor inside – and eventually the gap was big enough to be able to squeeze through.

As it turned out it was nothing, just a section of carpet which had buckled and become stuck under the door.

And himself, he had to stop worrying over nothing.

He closed the door and stood there for a moment, taking in the smells of his new home. Musty, as you'd expect, there'd been the recent rains but there was something else. Like a soap or a scent, a perfume or aftershave he wasn't familiar with. Remnants of the previous tenants' perhaps, evidence of their existence, but again, why hadn't he noticed it before?

The living room, at least, was the way he'd left it that morning with its clutter of velvet sofas, and paintings, and bookshelves filled with histories. A skylight revealed the deepening colours of the low sky above.

It was all perfectly quiet.

He lay down on one of the sofas for a moment and stared out, through the glass or plastic or whatever it was, to the heavens beyond. A passing jet, thousands of feet up, was heading, rocketing, in a geometrically-perfect straight line across the firmament, with a vapour trail like a plume of smoke stretched out behind it, an explicit statement that it was coming from somewhere and going somewhere else. The gradually expanding streak of white was lit by the last rays of the sun and added another dimension to this majestic sky. The wide blue yonder. Beyond it there were stars but in London at least, they tended to remain hidden, as if out of shyness or calculation. Like his pursuers perhaps.

Pursuers? Bodies? Why did his mind continue with this folly? There was nothing. Just a series of accidents. Flukes.

He sighed and his sigh seemed to echo, and linger past the fading of his breath, feeling the walls, testing them...

What was that? It sounded like a clicking noise. He jumped to his feet, silently, from his prone position, not breathing, his ears straining to hear whatever came next. But nothing did. In the extreme distance, a muffled car horn. But the house remained quiet. His ears hadn't deceived him though, he'd definitely heard it. It had been crisp and distinct. And it had come from downstairs. It had come from the kitchen.

He crept across the living room, relieved the house was carpeted and silently made his way down the stairs, past framed architectural drawings from the seventeenth century, another London. Another world, really.

A tinkle. Another sound, and there was no doubt, it had come from behind the door at the bottom of the stairs, the door to the kitchen.

There were only two ways to enter a room when you wanted to catch a potential adversary off-guard: either as quickly as possible or as slowly. He chose the former. He gently enclosed the door knob in his hand and tightened his grip, remembering which way it turned and on a mental count of three, threw the door open, ready to duck.

The intruder was a wide-eyed, orange, confusion of fur.

Bertie was completely taken by surprise and for a split second stood frozen, his paw stuck in mid-air, before he jumped straight up off the floor, all legs and tail and big eyes, and then torpedoed across the kitchen floor and through the closed door. Through the cat flap.

He hadn't even noticed he *had* a cat flap.

He was relieved, but he still conducted a thorough search of the house while his heart rate returned to normal – or as 'normal' as it was going to get, after the last seven days.

Around nine that evening, his ex-wife rang. It was just after he'd finished his dinner and a third glass of red. He was feeling relaxed, finally, for the first time in days, so the phone call was well-timed.

'Jon?'

Romy was a journalist and a writer and their short, two year marriage had produced no children – just incendiary arguments, moments (to be honest) of great sex, and some good ideas for Romy's writing. But really, nothing much else to speak of. They were both unquestionably happier apart; their respective hearts had grown fonder but not more desirous. Indeed the positive effects of absence had easily outweighed the negative ones, and had done so for about two years now and neither of them saw any reason to change that. There was, however, still a level of affection there that never seemed to fade. He was pleased to hear from her.

'Romy!'

'So you've moved.'

'Well... yes. How did you find me?'

'Sabine told me.'

'So, what, are you two hanging out these days?'

'I don't hang out, or in, or *anywhere*, for that matter, these days. I'm too busy to hang. I called your place. Your old place.'

'Why didn't you just call my mobile?'

'I tried to,' she said.

He looked at his phone on the table in front of him. Dead, out of juice. He'd have to charge it again. These new phones, unbelievable.

'So what's going on?' she continued. 'Sabine didn't give much away.'

'You know. The music started and stopped. And here I am.'

'*Where* are you. She said Kensington. You're not in a palace by any chance, are you?'

'*West* Kensington, in fact, so no. Not quite.'

'So it's all over. Again.'

'It happens, as they say. So anyway, enough about me, how are you.'

'Thought you'd never ask. I'm pregnant.'

A lengthy silence followed while he collected his thoughts. A portion of his life flashed before his eyes, namely, two and a half years living with Romy in their modest 'abode' as she insisted on calling it, in Carlyle Square, just around the corner from the Chelsea Arts Club. His vision of their future life together had never really extended past Friday evenings getting drunk with Romy and her friends in the Arts Club garden and it certainly didn't include children or pregnancies or anything of that ilk. What's more, as far as he knew, there was no-one 'special' in her life, so this latest piece of news came to him somewhat as a shock.

'Jon? Are you still there?'

'Yes, sorry. Congratulations. Of *course* congratulations.'

'Well. Thanks, but there was nothing to it, really.'

'Oh I'm sure you deserve at least some of the credit.'

'It could have been you, you know,' she said. Her tone was serious. *She* was serious.

'Never saw it as being your thing exactly, Romy. Children I mean, as opposed to the bit where you pretend to make them.'

'Was I good at that do you think?'

'Very good.'

'Well as I say,' she said. 'It could have been you, but it seemed that the attractions of all things German were destined to win out...'

'Well, not all things.'

'... although as it now appears, not. Shame. Just when I was thinking they won the war after all.'

'Who's the lucky fellow, then.'

'Oh...' She sounded dismissive. Maybe she didn't know who the father was? 'Just a journo.'

'Anyone I know?'

'Doubt it. Writes for the Independent.'

'Right.'

'I think,' she added. Was she seeking his blessing? Commiseration? Forgiveness for being a bitch? Requesting him to be the father of her unborn child, tell the kid the truth when he's twelve?

'So you rang our Notting Hill flat,' Jon said. 'Were you wanting—'

'Just to say hi, really.'

She never would have rung Notting Hill, not if there was a chance Sabine would have answered. Whether his mobile was dead or not. What the hell was going on?

'Let me know if you need anything,' she added.

'Of course, thanks. Are you sure you're...' But he didn't know how to finish his sentence. He did his best though, soldiered on. 'I mean... I hope things, um... go well for you.' An awkward silence. 'And please Romy, I'm sure your, um, man, whatever his name is, actually what *is* his name? I do read the Independent sometimes you know, aim for more of a spread these days, so... ' But she remained silent. 'OK, that's fine, but if you need anything, you tell me, all right? I mean it.' Still no response. 'Romy?'

Just silence. No breathing. Not even background noise.

'Romy?'

She'd gone, But there'd been no disconnection tone. No click. Nothing, But she was definitely gone. Vanished, seemingly, into thin air.

How completely odd, he thought. And when darker thoughts crept in, like a shadow over a sunny sea, he quickly dismissed them. She obviously had an urgent call. Probably said something while he was talking... So why was the line still open?

'Romy? Are you there?

He hung up. Tried redial, but just got her voicemail. Left the usual, perfunctory "we got cut off, great to hear from you, speak soon" kind of message.

Maybe he was reading too much into it, but he knew Romy and it didn't make sense, didn't feel right. For every benign, logical explanation, there was a disconcerting one. And at the very least, how unfortunate. How annoying that such a welcome phone call from an old friend, just when he needed it most, should turn out in such a weird, unsettling way. To use a card game metaphor, he just couldn't seem to take a trick these days. It was one thing after the other.

These thoughts, though, soon dissipated like teardrops in an ocean and by the time he'd finished a further glass of wine and saluted the almost full moon that was now visible (majestic, radiating a cold, brittle light) and by the time he'd said goodnight to the bookshelves and sofas, tapestries and Persian rugs, stuffed animal (just the one, the macaw from Peru) and to the paintings and the rest of the eccentric contents of *Qui Vive* (he was fortunate to have a landlord with such, apparently, meagre storage space at his disposal), and set off up the stairs to his bedroom and gone to bed and turned out the light (leaving vividly before his eyes the image of the last thing he saw, a rustic painting of a golden, Cotswold stone cottage, brought to life by its rustling trees and smoking chimney), his thoughts were already as light and airy as dandelion seeds on a summer breeze. Perhaps it was the fact that Romy still cared, or he still mattered to her or perhaps it was the house itself, but he went to sleep with a peaceful look on his face for the first time in weeks...

... And he woke up choking to death.

Choking and coughing, in pitch darkness. As hard as he tried to suck in air, nothing would come. He sat bolt upright, threw off his bedclothes, grappled for the bedside light which went tumbling off into the murk. The light from his radio alarm clock was barely visible, the room was full of dense, acrid smoke, reeking of burning plastic. Industrial. No clean air, nothing for his lungs, just this suffocating black fog like a bag over his head. He fell to the floor, his limbs no longer obeying commands, and in this way Jonathon Marriner slowly, slowly lost consciousness, and the last thing he thought of was a headline, a headline in the morning paper, and on television too, a news item about the death of a man in a house fire in *West* Kensington, not Kensington...

Part Two – Dark Oceans

LEE.   Do you ever get a sudden dark feeling about something?

MALKINA.   Concerning a deal?

LEE.   Concerning anything.

MALKINA.   I don't know. But I could imagine that my dark and your dark are different darks.

(from the screenplay *The Counselor* by Cormac McCarthy)

11. <u>24° 40' 4" S 14° 29' 22" E</u> (Southern Atlantic, off the Skeleton Coast, Namibia)

Two months earlier. Tuesday, 13 August

It had been an unusual day, but then again, every day on the *Diamond Moon* had a tendency to be unusual.

For some reason, no matter how many times he did it, the headcount kept coming up as one too *many*. There were supposed to be only ten of them – including himself – so it shouldn't have been difficult. And now there were eleven. Better than being one short, of course – bad news for any scuba group, everyone's heard about *those* incidents. But one extra? How did that happen?

Bertrand ran a hand through his long, wet locks and counted one more time. But there was no doubt. Eleven. Including the Japanese girl who came on her own and had to be buddied by Bertrand himself. Eleven and for the life of him, he couldn't work out who was here now that hadn't been here earlier. There was no-one who looked unfamiliar... Speaking of the Japanese girl – he'd suddenly forgotten her name – where was she? (Had he counted her in the eleven? If not, that would make twelve, that was all he needed.) He asked one of the others. But Gerhard, a fifty-five year old German with a weathered, mahogany face, just shrugged.

So what was going on? Maybe he was suffering from a touch of nitrogen narcosis. *Rapture of the deep.*

Possibly number eleven was the new guy, the ex-fisherman or dockworker or whatever he was, from Marseilles, he could see him right now, chatting to one of the women. Arnaud, that was his name. Dark-eyed, he was a strange one, always lingering in passageways like a bad smell, possibly a little simple. Was Arnaud not included in the original ten? No, he was, definitely. (What had he done with the list?)

Today was going to go down as one of the strangest days Bertrand had ever experienced.

First, there was the white shark. Not a great white, but a shark that was actually *all white*. The whole group had been underwater, diving at a depth of about forty metres, and this... vision... glided past. Everyone froze of course, and stopped breathing too, judging by the absence of bubbles. And as quickly as it had arrived, it departed, vanishing into the underwater gloom, its gigantic pale tail waving them all goodbye.

And if that wasn't strange enough, by the time they arrived at the wreck, Bertrand's compass had inverted itself – north was now pointing south and south, north. He knew this because the bow of the *Prospero's Dancer*, an old British clipper from the early nineteenth century, pointed east, and according to his compass, it was now pointing west. The ship, half-buried under the sands of the sea floor, could hardly have turned around one-eighty degrees – the currents could be pretty wild and powerful in this part of the world, but not *that* powerful – so his compass had obviously had a fit.

And then, in the wreck itself, there wasn't a single fish to be seen. It was normally teeming with them. *Teeming*. And today, not a single one! It gave Bertrand the creeps, as they explored around and inside the ship's skeleton, and he couldn't get away fast enough.

And now this, a mystery passenger. Or two! He couldn't wait for the day to be over, when he could finally put his feet up, crack open a Kronenbourg, and watch the sun setting over the ocean.

Still the day hadn't been without its high points. Finding the wreck in the first place was one: his boss, Dominique Drayle had been over the moon, so to speak. Everyone had.

And then finding the metal case – "the decagon" as Drayle called it. The *Isfahan decagon* in fact, if he'd heard him correctly. Drayle was keeping things under wraps though – no surprise, Bertrand was no fool, these dive tours for the adventurously inclined were a blatant front for Drayle's illegal salvage operations – and Drayle rarely told Bertrand anything directly. Again, no surprise there either: Bertrand was pretty sure these salvage operations weren't the only thing Drayle was up to, and frankly, the less Bertrand knew about all that the better. (He'd heard Drayle speaking Russian on his satellite phone on more than one occasion – unusual as no-one on board spoke anything other than French to each other, and maybe the odd word in English to a customer – and as far as Bertrand knew, Drayle didn't have a Russian bone in his body.)

So, yes, the less he knew the better, *except* when it came to the articles they recovered, because lost treasure was his thing, and his experience with underwater salvage was why Drayle had hired him in the first place.

And the fact that he'd been the one to find the decagon, that was definitely a feather in his cap. Now if only he could work out what exactly it *was*. It was certainly beautiful, but supposedly it had some particular significance that he wasn't yet privy to. He'd overheard some talk about a connection with an even older ship. A galleon? It didn't really make sense, but one thing was clear: Drayle appeared to be even happier about the discovery of this decagon than that of the *Prospero's Dancer* itself.

12. <u>22° 56' 35" S 14° 30' 9" E</u>
(Walvis Bay, Namibia)

Wednesday, 14 August

A remarkable thing happened the next day, aboard the *Diamond Moon*. For Bertrand though, "remarkable" wasn't really the word: things took a distinct turn for the worse.

They'd sailed overnight and arrived at Walvis Bay at dawn, where they were now moored. During the morning, Bertrand had managed to do a pretty good job at cleaning up their much-prized, recent discovery.

The *Isfahan decagon* – which seemed to be some kind of metal container – was unlike anything he had ever seen. It was about thirty centimetres across, and it was ten-sided (hence its name) which made it appear almost circular, despite there being not a curved line on it. The metal itself was silver, but it was heavily inlaid with hundreds of gemstone tiles covering all twelve surfaces. The tiles were cut into shapes outlined and separated by an intricate, rectilinear network of joining and intersecting silver lines.

The decagon was undoubtedly an object of superior refinement and style, and demonstrated an extraordinarily high degree of craftsmanship.

There was a hinge on one of the sides, and a keyhole, although the lock itself had rusted away, and the decagon was easily opened. There was nothing inside – or not anymore at least.

But it was in remarkably good condition for something that had been imprisoned beneath the ocean for the best part of two centuries: there was barely a single tile missing and very little cleaning was required. This was, Bertrand decided, due to a combination of factors, including the temperature and mineral content of the waters in that part of the Atlantic; the fact that the metal was silver; the fact that the decagon had been enclosed in a larger container; and the quality of the article's construction.

A closer inspection revealed the majority of the tiles to be green jade and quartz, but there was also turquoise and amber and red garnet, as well as lapis lazuli and obsidian and even emerald. In particular, the mesh or web of silver lines bordering the gemstones formed angular geometric shapes, polygons – including decagons and star shapes, (some of the larger ones being ten-pointed stars) – and patterns, complex and intricate, some apparently repetitive, some seemingly irregular, and similar, he thought, to those seen on Islamic mosques and shrines.

Indeed from his knowledge of art history – and Bertrand was no novice – he estimated the object was around five hundred years old. Fifteenth century maybe. And judging by the name Drayle had given it, it apparently hailed from Isfahan, Persia (now Iran).

The more he looked at it, the more he found.

The silver lines, he could now see, were of two kinds: some fine, and others less so. The latter more prominent set of lines zigzagged across the larger shapes and formed their own, separate pattern. The more delicate lines revealed smaller shapes, all angular, all various types of polygon. On this smaller scale, six different polygons could be identified, including pentagons, kite-shaped rhombuses, and bowtie-shaped hexagons.

And then, surprisingly, a third layer of patterning revealed itself, formed by the outlines of the gemstones themselves, each of which were in the shape of one of the six polygons appearing on the slightly larger scale.

The patterns in the three layers of networked lines contained, to his eye at least, no obvious repetition, or nothing uniform at least. There was repetition of the various shapes, but the design continued to change the further it extended. It was a kind of geometric pattern with no pattern, in other words. Such geometry, he was aware, was something Islamic mathematicians had discovered hundreds of years before Western Europe.

He'd read about this recently in fact. Before they'd set out on their trip, Drayle had suggested he do some research on the topic, and now he knew why.

Islamic art in the period dating from the 12th to the 15th centuries commonly employed so-called *girih* tiling and lines ("girih" meaning "knot" in Persian), which essentially consisted of a changing pattern of jagged lines – or 'strapwork' – in combination with a set series of standard shapes, and was based on highly advanced principles of geometry and mathematics. Examples of the use of *girih* lines ranged from the Gunbad-i Kabud tomb tower in Maragheh, Iran (1197) and the Mustansiriya Madrasah in Baghdad (13th century) to the Darb-i Imam shrine in Isfahan (completed in 1453) and the Topkapi Scroll (late 15th to early 16th centuries). It wasn't until the 1970s and the discovery of 'Penrose Tiling' (named after British mathematical physicist Roger Penrose) that the advanced mathematical concept behind the *girih* patterns was finally recognised by Western mathematicians.

After seeing Drayle's excitement the day before, Bertrand had realized straight away that the decagon's value lay in something other than its precious stones and silver. He now wondered if it had some particular historical significance, beyond its age or its use of fifteenth century Islamic geometry. Drayle didn't excite easily. Historical significance, or was it something else, something intrinsic?

Which is when, all of a sudden, he saw it.

It was gone almost as quickly as it appeared: it was like an optical illusion that you needed to stare at for a while before the hidden image revealed itself. The irregular patterning of the silver lines and stone tiling seemed to morph, for an instant, into a person's face. It was a woman's. In Bertrand's mind at least, it was as clear as a photograph, or a painting, but by the time it registered, his eyes were no longer seeing it. The only evidence of it, frustratingly, lay there, in his memory, the disappearing beauty fading fast, and no amount of effort could bring it back.

But that wasn't the truly remarkable thing that happened. That was coming.

He waved his hand in the air, beckoning, catching the attention of the Japanese girl who had just walked in. She was ambling casually, carrying a fruit juice, looking for something to do. He was pleased she chose his company to find it. And now, just in time, he remembered her name too: Ishiko. He shouldn't have forgotten it, Ishiko meant "child of stone" in Japanese, and he liked that.

'Look at this, Ishiko.' He spoke to her in English. 'Tell me if you can see a woman's face.'

She walked over to him and smiled, and looked at the decagon. When she did, he took in her figure: she was wearing skinny jeans and she looked great in them. Great, despite her legs being a little shorter than he would have preferred. That was the deal with Japanese girls, but it wasn't a bad trade-off, it was a compromise Bertrand was happy to make. She had a pretty face, too. Exquisite, you could even say.

'It is beautiful!' she exclaimed.

'It is that.'

'What is it?'

'Apparently it's the Isfahan *decagon*, whatever that is. We'll need some help on this one.'

'The… *decagon*,' she repeated, following his lips.

Bertrand stood up and made his way over to the other table. He glanced back for a moment, and while Ishiko admired the decagon, he admired his colleague's pear-shaped buttocks and the unmistakable outline of her panties. He then began looking for a book he'd seen, something on Islamic art of the thirteenth and fourteenth centuries, although he doubted it would help him.

He was, in fact, just about to discover that nothing would help him.

13. <u>22° 56' 35" S 14° 30' 9" E</u>
(Walvis Bay)

Wednesday, 14 August

While Bertrand was looking through the pile of books, Ishiko turned around and cast a sly glance back at him. She liked the way he stood – he was tall – and she had a thing for his shoulders and forearms. And his backside, his "ass", as the Americans called it, he had a great ass.

She marvelled at how all of our destinies were already written, long ago.

And then she sprang into action, for the time had come.

She pulled the cord out of the back of her jeans (she'd been wondering whether it showed) and twisted the ends around her hands and wrists. She wasn't powerful, relatively speaking, but she was exceptionally, demonstrably, undeniably skilful.

Bertrand was totally focussed on one of the books now – he was flicking through pages of diagrams and figures. Ishiko felt like telling him he wasn't going to find what he was looking for, not in the time he had, and given his curtailed future, what was the point? And anyway, she was working – she had a job to do. And jobs, like everything else, like the trees and eating rice, were the building blocks of Destiny.

Ishiko imagined his surprise when her pelvis pushed in against his buttocks... a second before the cord flew over his head. She wondered what he was thinking during that second, before the cord changed everything; she wondered what was going through his mind when she was, all of a sudden, grinding him from behind. She knew how much he lusted after her – or she had a good idea – and he must have thought he was getting luckier than he'd ever been before, or else he was dreaming.

And while he was choking there, seconds from the end of his life, a vague feeling of regret passed over her. A feeling that she'd perhaps made a mistake. That this man she was in the process of killing could well have been the sort of man she could have lived with, had children with, got old with. He could have been the *one*. Crazy as it sounded, Ishiko wondered, was it not possible that she'd received a chemically coded signal from his body in those moments? A signal received by *her* body and subsequently decoded and analysed, with the result being a large, green light?

Bertrand slumped lifelessly to the floor.

The green light flickered and faded and disappeared altogether. Just like it always did.

And Ishiko, the exquisite Japanese girl, lapsed fully into work mode again. After first double-checking the body was indeed dead, and then sliding it under the adjacent work bench and covering it with a tarpaulin, she collected the metal case – the *decagon* – and hurried out onto the deck, into the harsh African sun, banishing all further self-indulgent thoughts from her mind.

14. <u>22° 56' 35" S 14° 30' 9" E</u> (Walvis Bay)

Wednesday, 14 August

'Enter!'

At the same time that Ishiko was making her hasty and furtive exit from the *Diamond Moon* (and before her and the decagon's absence, along with the demise of Bertrand, had been discovered), Dominique Drayle was reading. Knowing Drayle, it was probably some obscure topic such as barter-trading with the Peruvian Indians in the sixteenth century, or perhaps, more appropriately, it was *The Rise Of The Russian Mafia*, but Arnaud couldn't see the name of the book because he wasn't close enough. And he wasn't close enough because he was hanging around in the passageway outside because, yes, he was up to no good and yes, he was spying, and yes, it would get him killed one of these days but life was short anyway so what the hell. He got a kick out of it, OK?

Gerhard had just knocked on Drayle's cabin door. Bravely. Because everyone knew that Drayle – who insisted on being called "Mr Drayle" (and not "Monsieur", note) by his crew and other employees, never by his first name, that was a hanging offence – hated being disturbed when he was in the middle of something. After receiving the one-word response, Gerhard had gone ahead and opened the door and stuck his head in. Which is when Arnaud had seen Drayle and his book, whatever it was.

'Excuse me Mr Drayle, I was just…' Gerhard paused at that point, presumably having seen the predictable look of annoyance on Drayle's face. 'I thought you should be informed. That the, er… the Namibians have found out. About us finding the *Prospero's Dancer*. Over the radio just before, we—'

'*How.*'

'Sorry…?'

'*How* did they find out.'

'Well I'm guessing someone said something. When we were last here. In Walvis Bay. So maybe we can expect…' Gerhard's eyebrows were raised as he let his sentence hang there.

There was a long pause this time. Drayle, who notoriously suffered anger management problems (to put it mildly), was probably feeling, once again, the familiar effects of that rising tide of crimson. All Gerhard could do was stand there and watch Drayle's face turn a deep shade of red. Perhaps he said a little prayer.

And then, seemingly, a reprieve. Instead of a tirade of abuse, Gerhard was met with the sight of Drayle taking a deep breath in, and then a long, slow one out. When Drayle finally spoke, his voice was controlled and clear.

'Thank you.'

Gerhard just nodded. He'd seen enough to know when to disappear, but it was now Drayle who seemed to want to prolong things. Gerhard was retreating and closing the door when Drayle spoke again.

'Gerhard.'

'Yes.'

'Get in here. And shut the door.'

15. <u>48° 51' 14" N 2° 20' 48" E</u>
(Paris, *4ᵗʰ arrondissement*)

The present.
8.45am French Summer Time (06:45 UTC).
Wednesday, 16 October

He was chewing his pen again – it was a bad habit and his teeth would pay the price one day, he knew it. But a habit was a habit.

Whatever transpired in the remainder of that conversation two months ago between Drayle and Gerhard, Commandant Laurent Ruart, of the *Préfecture de police* in the *Île de la Cité* in central Paris, will probably never know. The witness to the conversation, Arnaud – the man from Marseilles who had been Ruart's eyes and ears on the *Diamond Moon* – neither heard nor saw anything further after Gerhard entered Drayle's cabin and closed the door behind him. And both Arnaud and Gerhard were now missing-presumed-dead. As for the other person present...

Who knew where Drayle himself was by now, although there had been reported sightings of him about 1,300 kilometres away, in Cape Town, South Africa.

What Ruart did know was that the *Diamond Moon* – a sleek forty-nine metre luxury motor yacht (technically, a "superyacht" and almost a "megayacht") registered in the Cayman Islands, but frequently seen moored on the French Riviera in the summer months – after visiting the wreck of the *Prospero's Dancer* and recovering an artefact referred to (by Drayle at least) as the *Isfahan decagon*, continued its journey south, hugging the desolate west coast of Africa, past Namibia and on to Cape Town, and four men (Bertrand, Gerhard, Arnaud and one other) plus a Japanese female disappeared in the space of two weeks. None had been seen since, with the exception of Arnaud, whose skeleton, it would seem (subject to further forensic testing), was found in a witchdoctor's hut two hundred miles inland, in north-western South Africa, every trace of flesh scraped clean from his bones, by *whom* or *what* Commandant Ruart had, as yet, no idea.

Whatever the *Isfahan decagon* was, too, was fairly unclear.

Clearer was Dominique Drayle's occupation. Despite his French origins, he'd originally been a member (a brigadier) of a Russian mafia group (or *bratva*) with its roots in a district of Moscow. After operating out of Moscow for many years, and taking a firm grip of a sizeable section of the art and antiquities black market, he'd formed a breakaway organization which he originally based in Paris, but which now had no central headquarters. His organization operated cells throughout Europe – including, as well as Moscow and Paris, London, Venice, Bucharest and Istanbul – and outside Europe as well, in Vladivostok in Russia's far east, and even in South Africa (Cape Town). The organization was called *Draylskaya Bratva*, named after him ("bratva" meaning "brotherhood"). It had also come to be known as *Black Star*.

Drayle himself was wanted for questioning in three countries: in France, concerning the rape of two women (on the same night); in Equatorial Guinea, in relation to the murder of two security personnel in Malabo; and in Gabon, over both the theft of approximately one tenth of that nation's annual GDP and an attempted coup begun in the country's second largest city, the isolated seaport of Port-Gentil. He had also dated Ruart's sister, which made things interesting, to say the least.

Commandant Ruart, as it happened, had just bought a plane ticket to Cape Town, although it wasn't going to be travel in any official or state-sanctioned capacity: this trip was most definitely pleasure and not business (his leave had already been approved). Because pleasure was what he was going to get from wringing Drayle's neck. And that was because one of the two women Drayle raped on that evil, moonless evening was none other than Ruart's sister, Constance. It had happened in Paris only six months ago, and so for Ruart the wound was, metaphorically speaking, still particularly fresh.

These thoughts occurred to him in a disconnected fashion as he stared out his south-facing window on the *Quai de Marché Neuf*, with its view over the Seine, and on the other side, the rooftops of the Left Bank. And when he looked in a roughly south-south-easterly direction, directly over the *Petit-Pont*, and the tops of the buildings of the *5th arrondissement* and, in the distance, out through the high-rise blocks of the *13th* on the other side of the *Place d'Italie*, he imagined that he could almost see all the way to the Mediterranean and the coast of Algeria, and then the rest of Africa beyond that, and that if he looked hard enough, he could just about make out Table Mountain and Cape Town itself.

Part Three – Western Australia

16. Lena Was Dangling

[Indian Ocean: off the Kimberley Coast, W.A. (-16.8439, +122.2022), 16 Oct 2013, 2.50PM]

While Commandant Ruart was chewing his biro in Paris, Lena was dangling off the side of the *Seaking*. Thousands of kilometres away from Ruart, but still on the same, sunlit side of the globe, Lena had her legs wrapped around the *Seaking*'s guard rail and with her back against the side of the boat, she was upside down and letting her arms dip into the water every time the boat rolled in that direction.

Diane, who was on the other, far larger yacht, found it a very odd sight, judging from her expression. Brian, not so much. He'd seen her do it many times before – she used to be his wife for starters (briefly) and they'd spent one long European summer sailing all over the Mediterranean. Lena was always mucking about, the usual mischievousness: flinging herself off the boat, nude sunbathing when there were other boats about, sleeping with the crew (usually in that order)... Those Russian women, unbelievable! It was a relief to be out of that relationship, frankly. Diane was wonderfully down to earth and not at all pretentious – maybe a little on the dull side, but after Lena, dull was a wonderful luxury. Come to think of it, dull wasn't really the right word. A little on the *careful* side, was Diane – realistic, reliable and discreet – and Brian loved her for it.

'Let's all go swimming!!' Lena was shouting out. Roy, the captain and proud owner of the *Seaking* and Lena's new 'man' for want of a better description, raised his eyes for what was probably the sixtieth time that day. Poor Roy! Brian smiled to himself. He wouldn't trade places with Roy for all the tea in China (and didn't Diane love her Chinese tea, her always 'glorious' *lapsang souchong*).

'Lena!' Roy yelled. 'Get back on the *boat*, for God's sake!' He'd been about to up anchor, but stopped what he was doing, possibly about to lose his temper? 'Lena!'

'Impressive bait!' Brian shouted out gleefully. 'Fishing for great whites are you?!'

'Coward!' Lena yelled back. 'You know very well there aren't any this far... *aaaayyyyyyeeeeee*!!'

She was cut short.

Not by a shark though, thank heavens. Roy had grabbed hold of Lena's legs and was pulling her back into their boat, ignoring the ear-bursting squeal. It was a miracle her bikini managed to stay on. Brian was just starting to think how much he missed her after all – certain things, anyway. Diane looked like she was sick of Lena already, and in the circumstances, Brian could hardly blame her for that.

They were all on a yachting holiday together – not the Mediterranean this time, but the tropics, around the Lacepede Islands to be specific, off Western Australia's Kimberley coast. Roy and Lena had the *Seaking* to themselves (a fact which was becoming increasingly obvious). Lena's best friend Lydia and her boyfriend Aleks were supposed to have joined them, but they'd had a better offer or something, Brian wasn't completely sure what the story was there. Off on some quest or other – driving up the West Coast, *all* the way up apparently – they were quite the lunatics, Aleks and Lydia, always up to something. It was no surprise Lena and Lydia were best friends. (Brian even remembered one time when there was just the three of them, when they'd hit one Perth pub too many and, well, let's just say, that night at least, Lena and Lydia ending up behaving like they were a little more than merely best friends...! Anyway.)

Meanwhile he and Diane were on Bob's yacht with Bob and his latest squeeze, Peta. She was a beauty too, but Brian wasn't too sure where Bob had picked her up... Réunion was it? The yacht that is, not Peta! (although she wasn't too dusty either, it had to be said). But the *Diamond Moon*, which he'd only just acquired, was really something. It was massive. A forty-nine metre, silver, Italian-made superyacht with aluminium alloy hull, equipped with zero speed gyroscopic stabilizers, maximum speed of almost thirty knots and accommodated ten crew plus twelve guests when necessary – although in this case there were five crew including the skipper, and four guests: Bob reckoned with so few souls onboard it felt like a ghost town (which was a pretty odd way of describing a boat as far as Brian was concerned, but that was Bob for you, he was always coming out with stuff like that). Anyway it certainly demonstrated in no uncertain terms the benefits of owning a W.A. copper mine, although where Bob got the money from to buy *that* was anyone's guess (and guesses, there were plenty of *them* floating around, there was always a new piece of gossip about our mate Bob).

Unlike the *Diamond Moon*, the *Seaking* was a sailing yacht. It was a sloop – with a single mast, mainsail and headsail – and at twenty metres, a somewhat more modest affair. But it was still a rich man's toy (designed to be sailed short-handed with fully automated winches, but could also take four VIPs and four crew, with two luxury double bed cabins and two twin bunk cabins, all fully air-conditioned) and in fact, it used to be *Bob*'s toy. Bob sold it to Roy at mate's rates after he bought the *Diamond Moon*.

Lena had Roy in a koala-hold by now, hugging him to within an inch of his life and, by now, giggling her head off. When she started grappling with his shorts – she nearly managed to get them off, too – he laughed, finally, and so very subtly, Brian thought, steered both of them into the cabin and out of sight.

Brian looked at Diane, the twinkle of lust in his eyes. 'Girls will be girls", he said, trying to admire her body, but realising he'd have to get Lena out of his head *and* find some way of ignoring the fact that Diane had no breasts to speak of. Fantastic legs and a nice figure, but...

Diane caught the look in Brian's eyes and Brian caught her catching it. And she looked, to Brian, as if she was thanking her lucky stars for blessing her with such a manly, no-nonsense, hunk of a boyfriend who, out of all the beautiful girls in the world to choose from, had chosen her.

17. Two Forensics Personnel

[Great Sandy Desert, W.A. (-19.7492, +121.7244), 17 Oct 2013, 11.05AM]

The next day, and a little over three hundred kilometres to the south of the antics taking place on board the *Seaking* and the *Diamond Moon*, two forensics personnel emerged from a Kawasaki Bolkow BK117 helicopter, which had just landed on a dusty red patch of ground in the middle of nowhere.

It wasn't long before they came across the remains of the old ship. While this was a high point – they'd only been expecting a hot, empty car and a few dusty footprints – their day pretty much went downhill from there.

They'd flown in from Perth that morning, and the possibility of not making it back in time for Thursday night drinks meant that their spirits weren't high to start with. They were somewhat placated, though, once they got there, by the realization that despite the discovery of the ship – the *Destino En Distancia* – there was very little for them to do.

Other than sweat.

On the plus side, they weren't wearing the blue jumpsuits that, as forensics, they were usually required to wear. Not that they would have served much purpose anyway, but given the extreme temperature conditions, the jumpsuits were out of the question. It was bad enough as it was, in their casual gear.

The only section of the ship poking through the sands was the stern, containing the captain's cabin. The years, the centuries, had conveniently created a de facto entrance in the side of the ship and it was easy enough to enter, without too much of a strain, the 'cave' formed by what was left of the ship's hull. Inside, though, was not much better than outside. Oven-like was the polite term for it.

They found the one item of clothing – Lydia's white cotton dress – and that was all. Nothing else out of place, no other shreds of clothing material, no footprints or drag marks, no other clues in there of any kind. The desert though, as they well knew, had little respect for police operations.

Apart from finding the ship and the dress, the other highlight of that first hour at the site was spotting a Pig-Footed Bandicoot, supposedly extinct and not seen for over fifty years. An eccentric-looking little creature he was too: the size of a large rat, and kind of a grotesque cross between a mouse and a kangaroo. With rabbit ears and hoofed feet. He hopped out from the *Destino* as they drew near – which was puzzling in itself as they are, or were, known to be nocturnal creatures, and why he was fleeing his dark hiding place in broad daylight was only to make sense some time later.

*

A glistening sheen of sweat coated the exposed skin of the two men – neck and arms – as they conducted one final look-around. The timber inside the half-buried cabin was age-blackened and lifeless, the floor just sand and broken fragments of wood.

Not much to take particular note of, but for one thing.

Carved into one of the cabin walls was some sort of design containing a series of surprisingly intricate geometric markings – unusual, it seemed to them, although they were no experts. The design itself consisted of a series of neatly-fitting, straight-sided shapes – polygons – over which was superimposed a network of jagged lines which formed further shapes of their own. The combination of elements created an effect that was both complex and visually striking. Was it a symbol of some kind? A secret sign?

Apart from the carving though, there was little to catch the eye. Except, perhaps, for the remnants of a couple of small animal skeletons, which managed to effortlessly express the way the two living visitors felt. Their lamps seemed to add to the already overwhelming heat, and they both, independently, experienced the urge to turn them off and welcome the darkness, anything to mitigate this slow-basting torture.

'I reckon that's it for us,' the taller of the two eventually said. He was bald with big eyes and had been pretty much over the idea of this job before it had begun. And after fifteen minutes, for sure, it had become patently obvious to him that this had been one wasted trip. Whose idea was it that they come up, again? It was nothing more, nothing less than two city folk, tourists, whatever, who stupidly left their vehicle, left these ruins and wandered off into the desert. Dingo food, now.

The other one – stocky, with close-cropped black hair – grunted and kept looking around. 'Hmm.'

'Leave it to the History Boys,' the bald man went on. 'They'll be straining on their leashes to get an eyeful of this. Whatever it is.'

'Oh yeah. The archaeologists. If they knew we were in here, they'd be pissing themselves we're gonna step on a skeleton or something. Christ it's hot.' He breathed in deeply through his nose and exhaled wearily. 'It's gonna be big news that's for sure.'

'This, and little *Pig Foot* out there.'

'Mmm.'

'So what do you reckon this is. Some old... I don't know... Captain Cook era, kind of—'

'Actually looks like a galleon to me. And the name... I think it's Spanish. If it's for real... it could be one of the, er... Manila galleons I think they call them. Blown off course, or.... even Portuguese, although that'd rewrite the history books if they beat the Dutch, who got here in, when was it? 1606? *Destino En Distancia*. I'm sure that's Spanish. I'm pretty sure the Portuguese'd use "Em", "e-m", and not "e-n".'

'Yeah? So what's it doing in the middle of the desert? Sixty clicks from the sea?'

The black-haired man stared back for a moment. An intense, laser-look. Right into his eyes. Some serious thinking was going on.

'Most likely the coastline's shifted,' he said eventually. 'This whole area could have been some kind of inlet back then. Or I dunno… Maybe a tsunami did it.'

His bald colleague just nodded. Taking all this in. To the extent he could. In this heat, the brain could barely function. And his brain was normally OK, he had a good brain. Normally.

'Not sure about the name though,' the black-haired man continued. '*Destino En Distancia*. So what's that. "Destiny In Distance"?' He shrugged. 'And doubly odd because they usually named them after saints or something religious. Or… the whole thing's a fuckin hoax.'

'Someone went to a lot of trouble for a laugh.'

'Yup.'

'And I for one ain't laughin'.'

'Nup.'

'And if it was a hoax, why didn't they get the name right and call it the… Santo… Pedro or whatever.'

'*San* Pedro.'

'So… d'you get the… friggin'… social studies prize in grade three or something?'

The dark-haired man grunted.

'You're into this shit though, right?'

'Just a… bit of an interest yeah.'

'Huh. Man. It is so hot in here. So is that it, then?'

'The only other thing is…. the fact that there isn't any other thing.'

'What do you mean.'

'Have you noticed? There's only wood in here. And a couple of rusty iron bolts. Some copper fittings.'

'So?'

The dark-haired man motioned the bald man over and shone his lamp on something. 'See that?'

They were looking at what appeared to be a jagged hole in the blackened wood of the cabin wall. Hot darkness beyond. Hell without the fires, as far as the bald man was concerned.

'Yeah?'

'That hasn't just crumbled with age. Someone's broken through. Recently.'

'You reckon? Bit hard to tell isn't it, with this—'

'I reckon. And I reckon a ship like this... Probably full of gold and silver. Pesos, jewellery, whatever. They were bounteous times you know. No credit crunches. No fucken global financial crises back then.'

'That so.'

'Yep so you never know. Ship's recently been exposed... Every chance it's still here. Or was until...'

They both peered through the gaping hole.

'Well I'm not going in there to check,' the bald man said, aware his bargaining position was somewhat weakened by his lower rank.

'Be a shame. We've come all this way. And anyway there could be something else of the couple's. Could be a dingo's lair.'

The bald man hesitated, clutching.

'I doubt...' he began. 'Look this is, you know... clearly a, er... Health & Safety issue, it's too dangerous. The whole thing could collapse.'

'We have to do it.'

The bald man sighed. Wiped off another layer of sweat. Swore under his breath. Nodded.

They edged closer to the hole.

Which was when they heard something. There was something in there.

18. The *Leaping Lady*

[Indian Ocean: off the Kimberley Coast, W.A. (-16.8847, +122.0675), 19 Oct 2013, 10.00AM]

It had been a beautiful night on the *Leaping Lady*, the night just passed. Roy was sure of it.

Well, almost sure. Hang on...

He remembered thinking it at the time, it was magnificent all right, but... He was on the *Seaking*. The *Leaping Lady* was his last yacht. What was with these brain somersaults?

A wonderful evening it had been though, one of the better ones. Stunning, really, as she bobbed gently up and down, in a rhythmical oscillation, riding the long, gentle swells of the Pacific, a hundred and forty-five kilometres off the coast of Fiji...

No it wasn't. It was Western Australia, off the Kimberley coast. The Lacepede islands. And that was when he realised it hadn't been quite as wonderful as he'd first thought. In fact, things had taken a bad turn...

The last thing Roy remembered was the dazzling full moon, its long silvery pathway stretching to the horizon... and a strange clicking noise behind him. And then turning his head, and seeing something out of the corner of his eye: a giant yellow tentacle rising, in slow motion, out of the black, silken waters. And then, at the same time, suddenly losing all feeling in his arms and legs, so that in seconds, all he could do was watch the long tentacled arm approach him, draw right up to just in front of his face, almost inquisitively, and all he could think of was Rhuna – no, Lena – and what an incredible pity their delightful cruise should end like this, and how upset she was going to be...

But I'm alive, he thought. But why can't I open my eyes?

He tried and tried. It felt like minutes, or hours even, but it was probably only...

But anyway, then he succeeded, and... what was this?

Roy, when he woke up properly, was tied naked to the deck of the yacht, spreadeagled, with the sun high in the sky and Lena, in her yellow bikini, was leaning over him. She was pouring some of her drink on him – it felt fizzy, it tickled the skin of his stomach.

'We might need to circumcise you, Roy. I much prefer a circumcised cock. Yes? OK?'

His head ached, and the mast behind Lena's head seemed to be buckling and straightening with the swell. An optical illusion. It must be the drugs, Roy thought. She's poisoned me. She's going to kill me. It wasn't rape, I didn't rape you...

'But first, I want to say goodbye.'

She crouched down, and took his penis into her mouth – without spilling her drink, it was an impressive trick, from yoga? or Pilates? perhaps – and he was immediately hard, *despite* the dire circumstances.

'Rhu...' His mouth began to work but stopped, gave up. He gave up, and lay back, and just let himself enjoy it, like a prisoner before a firing squad, smoking his last cigarette. Yet his cock was the cigarette and she was the prisoner, it was all wrong, *Jesus*, the drugs, it must be the...

'Rhu...'

She was using a hand now, as well as her mouth, and skilfully, so skilfully, better than she'd ever done before: she had him on the point of coming and kept him there. She was, truly, a virtuoso... virtuosa...

And then suddenly, she stopped, stood up, put her drink down, turned around so that she was astride him, facing the other way, and slowly lowered herself over him, and onto him, pulling her bikini bottoms down as she did so. Took him into her, deep into her, and then rode him, truly rode him, violently, slamming her buttocks down hard on his stomach.

And she screamed a scream so loud it frightened a gull that'd been watching from the top of the mast. The gull flew off with a squawk.

And all Roy could think of was where it would head to now. Where would the gull go now, if not this boat? It's a big empty ocean, a *whole world* of *dark* oceans, out there…

19. A Massive Jolt

[Sydney Airport, N.S.W. (-33.9444, +151.1756), 19 Oct 2013, 1.10PM]

It seemed like a massive jolt – it was enough to wake *him* up which was saying something – but it was just the plane touching down. Touching down? Plane? What was he doing on a plane? And for that matter, touching down *where*?

The truth of it was that Mikkel Backstrom – Mick to his colleagues in the Forensics Division of the W.A. Police Department – was hungover. Wickedly hungover. And it was going to take no small amount of time to piece together what was going on.

He rubbed his eyes and ran a hand over the top of his bald head. Looking out the window to his left, he guessed Sydney airport. He glanced to his right and a short blonde girl in denim shorts smiled at him nervously. He thought of asking some questions but knew it was extremely unlikely his mouth would co-operate. An announcement confirmed his worst fears: *Welcome to Sydney airport, where the time is ten past one in the afternoon.* Checked his watch which was insisting the time was ten past ten. Perth time.

Think. Think. They had to have come from Perth. Arrival 10.10 a.m. Perth time, five hour flight, no, flying east, quicker, just over four hours, so he must've left Perth around… six a.m. Must've got to the airport around five a.m. But why?

Fragments of the previous evening returned. Friday night drinks. With… A long list of friends and pubs and bars flashed before his eyes. Was it a new nightclub he'd never been to before, never heard of? Weren't there a couple of girls, mocking and teasing, but sticking around anyway...? Or was that the week before? All his Friday nights were blending into one.

Mikkel looked down and noticed what he was wearing: fluorescent boardshorts patterned with large, black and yellow squares, and a white t-shirt with some kind of Aboriginal design on it, neither of which he'd ever seen before let alone owned. He had a pair of thongs on his feet (he'd never travel in thongs, or shorts for that matter) and there was a bag under the seat in front of him which he didn't recognise.

He snatched a look at the marble smoothness of the brown legs next to his own and looked away again. Quickly, in theory, although nothing Mikkel ever did was quick, never mind on a day like today.

Out the window an Air China jumbo was taking off for some faraway shore. Mind you, given that he was waking up over three thousand kilometres away, *this* was a faraway shore. Christ. What *happened*?

Deano. Deano was there, now he remembered. Deano, Dean Howard... who he did a job with only two days ago. Which was when it all came flooding back to him. The ship in the desert.

And the rest. The horrible, *horrorful* rest.

20. In The Darkness

[Great Sandy Desert, W.A. (-19.7500, +121.7256), 17 Oct 2013, 12.40PM]

Something was moving in the darkness.

Mikkel and Dean had been staring through a jagged hole in the back wall of the captain's cabin of the *Destino En Distancia*. Dean was telling him they had to investigate. And just as Mikkel was about to articulate an argument that the shorter of the two – Deano – should go in first, something in there moved.

A mouse? A bilby? Another Pig-Footed Bandicoot?

Dean lifted his lamp, directing it into the darkness, and then slowly moved towards the hole. At first the light on the ground only picked up more of the same, pieces of wood, and sand and orange-brown earth. When Dean changed the angle of his lamp though, the light illuminated a tail, then a reptilian body, and then the head of a most extraordinary and frightening creature: it was a huge lizard, maybe two and a half metres long, speckled black and white, its snake-like head side-on to the light so it could watch them.

It was a *perentie* – the largest lizard in the land.

It had been chewing on something, something it held in its claw, but for a few moments it was dead still, just staring at the two men with one large eye – a yellow iris almost completely covered by an enormous black pupil. Unwavering, unblinking. Unpredictable.

If Mikkel and Dean were wondering about its potential for aggression, they didn't have to wait long. In a split second, as quick as a camera flash, the perentie had shot out of the hole and clamped its powerful jaw around Dean's leg. Taken by surprise, Dean leapt and tripped and stumbled over backwards to try to get out of its way, and for an instant Mikkel thought it might go for Dean's throat. But the perentie continued to grip Dean's leg and thrash around, its tail lashing out at Mikkel at the same time. Not that his attempts at rescuing Dean were anything other than half-hearted. By this stage Dean, unsurprisingly, was screaming up a storm.

And then it was gone. Out into the light, into the harsh Australian sun.

It was probably over in a few seconds, although it felt like minutes. All that was left was the sound of Dean's groaning. Which was considerable.

'What the fuck *WAS* that??!!' he yelled, now that he could articulate sentences again. '*Ahhhhh*,' he moaned. 'Was that a goanna or a fucken *crocodile*?'

'A perentie, Deano. Haven't you been to the Perth zoo?'

'A peren... Fuck. Are there any more in there?'

'I'm not about to find out.'

'Hey I'm the one that took one for the team here. Fucken... *check* the *hole* Mick. Check the fucken *hole*.'

'You know those things are venomous.'

'Oh great. Aaaaaargh! Feels like someone's sawing my fucken *leg* off!'

'Seriously, they are. But don't worry. You'll live. Just may be a bit uncomfortable for a while.'

'Oh really? You think? Christ almighty.'

'I think we can give the tourniquet a miss on this occasion,' Mikkel said as he held his lamp towards the hole in the wall and cautiously moved towards it.

'*Aaaaaargh*.' Dean was still complaining.

'Quiet.'

'Just wait til one of these fuckers chooses *your* leg for lunch.'

'Exactly what I'm trying to avoid, can you shut up for a second?'

Despite Deano's huffing and puffing, Mikkel was pretty sure there was no sound coming from the hole. He gritted his teeth and slowly stuck his lamp hand forward into the unknown.

Nothing moving. Nothing speckled black and white. Nothing that looked like any type of crocodile.

Mikkel pushed forward through the hole, avoiding its sharp edges – but there was plenty of room even for his tall frame.

Inside, there was another room, much like the one he'd just been in, only much smaller, no doubt some kind of antechamber. Did they have toilets on these things? But like the main cabin, it was empty. No furniture, no treasure chests, not a sailor's dagger in sight. Just a few animal skeletons and whatever it was the perentie had been chewing on. Mikkel took a closer look.

'Mick? You still in one piece in there?'

He'd been expecting the perentie's meal to be brown, or red, but it was a kind of white-ish-pink in colour...

'And not swallowed whole?'

... and smooth. Furless.

'I'm fine,' Mikkel said. 'but...'

It looked like a piece of flesh of some kind.

'But what?'

With the epidermis attached. The outer layer of skin, in other words. Complete with sweat pores. Which meant it had to be one of two things. It was either the skin of a domestic pig... but as far as Mikkel knew, there weren't too many domestic pigs roaming the Great Sandy Desert...

'But *what*?' Dean repeated.

Or it was the skin of a human.

'Mick?'

*

Decomposition rates of human flesh tend to be faster the warmer the air, yet slower in dry conditions and, especially so if encased in sand. So everything considered, both Dean and Mikkel agreed that in the event it turned out to be human, it was likely the flesh they located in the interior of the *Destino En Distancia* at approximately 12.40pm on Thursday 17 October had been attached to a living human being somewhere in the range of between twelve and thirty-six hours earlier. Obviously further testing would be required and what was left of the perentie's meal was slipped into one of the many ziplock plastic bags the two police officers had at their disposal.

A quick search of the surrounding area – or as quick as it could be, with one of them now walking-impaired – revealed nothing further of any interest other than one thing, something they'd missed on their way in: a third set of tyre tracks, not belonging to the deserted vehicle on site (the Pathfinder) or the geologists' Jeep. Other than the tyres being Bridgestones (possibly Dueler HP Sports) and belonging to a four-wheel drive, probably a large one, a Jeep or SUV, there wasn't much else they could do either: the tracks gradually disappeared when they merged with those of the Pathfinder and both faded away anyway after they hit an ancient stony watercourse of which, in this area, there were many.

They could, however, be reasonably confident they were synchronous with the tracks of the Pathfinder and the Jeep.

Even assuming the item in their ziplock bag turned out to be human in origin, the whereabouts of the owner was still anybody's guess and because they only had so long to comb the Great Sandy Desert in unseasonable forty-plus degrees heat before becoming perentie-food themselves, Dean and Mikkel called it a day and headed back to the chopper. Dean's limp was getting worse anyway.

Their anti-social pilot, Travis Seward, was still where they'd left him: slumped on the ground in the shade of a tree – a majestic Desert Bloodwood – with his back against its trunk. And not just in the same place, but in the same position too. He could have been dead, if they hadn't known him better.

'Travis!' Dean called out.

'Find anything?' Apart from raising his eyes, Travis still hadn't moved; he appeared to talk without even moving his lips.

'My shout if you get us back to Broome by two-thirty!'

It was now just after 1.20pm. Broome was just over 200 kilometres away. The BK117 had a top speed of 250 kph, so an hour's flying time was eminently doable. And if they made it to Broome by 2.30pm, they'd make the 3pm Virgin flight, delivering them back in Perth just after 5.30pm. If they missed the 3pm, the next one that day wasn't until 6.15, which would mean back at 8.45 and that'd be that for their Thursday night, especially as they'd have to deal with the sample they were carrying first…

Travis moved. Lifted his left wrist up a notch, glancing at his watch.

'Yeah that's fine, but… I gotta warn you.' Travis slowly, slowly stood up and brushed the red earth off his trousers. 'I get pretty thirsty on Thursday nights.'

Dean needn't have worried about his promise though, because they never made the 3pm flight. Not even close.

'What happened to you?' Travis said, noticing Dean's limp.

'Lizard.'

Travis raised an eyebrow. And then his body jerked slightly, as a gentle chuckle rippled through him.

*

They'd come in from the north and the BK117 was positioned facing south. When they took off, Travis gunned the chopper forwards at the first opportunity to get clear of the cloud of dust they were kicking up. In doing so, they flew out over the *Destino* itself and drew a long, languid arc over countryside they'd not yet traversed. Their view took in the near-white sands of what looked to be an old riverbed and then, further on and stretching into the distance, the boundless grooved landscape – looking like a vast, orange, corrugated roof – which was dotted with spinifex and bloodwoods, and the occasional desert walnut: compact, dark, and gnarled. There was even a snappy gum, with its white, twisted trunk, startling, almost handsome, the way it stood out against the red earth.

They banked sharply over an area of raised ground that looked – to Mikkel – like a gigantic burial mound. And then, when they were probably just over two kilometres from the *Destino*, Mikkel spotted something out of the corner of his eye, something out of place. It was a bottle-shaped boab tree – odd enough in itself, as far south as this, in country this arid – but there was a bright patch on it. At first it looked like a large, white bird had settled among its skeleton branches (as the tree was not yet cloaked in its wet season greenery)… but it wasn't a bird.

'What's that?!' he shouted to Travis, who raised his eyebrows when he saw it and obligingly took them on a detour.

As they drew closer, the white object morphed before Mikkel's eyes – from a bird, to a white cotton sheet recently blown off someone's line, to a pair of overalls, to a blow-up doll for heaven's sake...

It was a naked woman. A naked, white woman.

She was draped over the upper branches of the boab tree, facing the sky, limbs splayed lackadaisically, staring into the brutal, tropical sun. She was clearly dead.

Dead, and draped over the branches like some horrible Christmas decoration.

To add to it, Mikkel had the uneasy sensation that the body had been positioned for the benefit – for the viewing pleasure – of the airborne, rather than the ground-bound.

Travis put the BK117 down straight away, a respectable distance from the boab so as not to disturb any evidence but not so far that the boys would have to trek to get there. Dean's leg was bad enough as it was. Which was also the reason it was Mikkel and not Dean, the better climber of the two, scaling the tree a few minutes later, after some photographs were taken.

What happened next was a blur, much of it irretrievable – which wasn't a bad thing, given the nightmarish quality of what he *could* remember. There was the climb up into the boab in that terrible heat, besieged by the surrounding red earth that seemed to suck the oxygen out of the air, and seemed, somehow, to threaten to engulf them all at any moment. There were the leafless branches that tore at his clothes. And from that unforgiving, barbed-wire tree, there was the struggle to recover the body, the naked body of the young woman. The body of a girl who once, but no longer, needed his help. There were no protests as he manhandled her. There was no resistance offered as he grabbed her legs, her breasts, her neck, there were no complaints as he battled to get her down. And it *was* a battle, it was all one terrible, interminable struggle: that was what he remembered most of all.

The body was already in a poor state. Which was hardly surprising – especially to him, of all people – but even so, when he thought about it now, it made him want to gag all over again. They estimated twenty-four hours. The body had been decomposing – in that heat – for a day. She'd been alive, in other words, the day before. You'd never have known it though. By the time they got to her, she may as well have been there a week.

Mikkel remembered having a discussion with the others, the men he was with, about what sort of further search they would conduct. But even now, just about all his brain would register, would recall, about that part of the day, apart from flashes of the struggle to get the body down, was the image of the splayed body in the branches. Taken from the air though, not the ground, the view from the helicopter, blown up, magnified, as if it was a photograph, but of course it wasn't, it was a tattoo. A permanent tattoo on the tissue of Mikkel's brain.

There was something else he remembered. As far as they could tell – given the stage of decomposition – there was no skin missing from the girl's body (*Caucasian, blonde, approx. 165cm / 5' 5",* *blue eyes, slight build, no obvious distg. feat.s and no pubic hair –* *prob. waxed, ie., a 'full brazilian'*). With this in mind, it was becoming increasingly likely that the tissue sample they'd found earlier was human, and not only that, but that it came from the (living or, as things were shaping up, more probably dead) body of the missing man.

It went without saying that by that stage, the chances of them making it back to Perth in time for Thursday night drinks were miniscule at best. Proverbial snowball's. And snowballs in hell is exactly what they were, it occurred to Mikkel. It wasn't just the heat, either: he didn't know it at the time, but things were about to get worse.

A careful search was now required, but Mikkel and Travis doubted Deano was up to it. Travis reckoned the perentie venom wouldn't do too much harm, but with the conditions as they were, there was no point in taking any chances and they ought to curtail things. So a quick search was conducted with Dean hobbling around, and to speed things up, Travis pitched in as well.

It might have been quick, but from Mikkel's point of view at least, it wasn't quick enough to avoid making more unpleasant discoveries.

Body parts, to be precise. A hand (*R., male*). A thigh (*R., male, excl. knee*). A toe (*4th(ring) toe?, L?, male?*). And a penis (*male*). All items had been cut rather than torn, and were found not far from the boab in their own shallow graves, thus temporarily preserving them, for the most part, from the likes of the perentie. They only found them because each had a twig or branch sticking out of the sand above it.

Someone had gone to a lot of trouble, not to avoid detection, but to be noticed.

There was one other thing they found. And like the first of their findings, it was on the boab tree. But this time it wasn't a body or a part of one, it was nothing macabre at all, just a little mystery. Something had been carved into the bark of the trunk. Boab markings can last for centuries – Dean pointed out Aboriginals often left symbols on boabs – and this particular one looked just that: centuries old.

It looked like a crude version of the carving in the *Destino*, or at least a part of it. Unlike the more complex carving in the ship, this one consisted simply of a ten-sided figure divided up into a number of different shapes, all straight-sided (or "rectilinear" in Dean's words). It was as if someone had roughly copied a section of the *Destino* carving from memory.

And that's exactly what must have happened, Dean reckoned.

He also said the carvings, especially the one in the *Destino*, reminded him of fractal geometry and its use in Islamic tiling and traditional African culture, and of particular geometric shapes repeated on an infinitely shrinking scale in architecture and seen, for example, in aerial photography of huts in Tanzania. Fractals, he pointed out, was where the more something was magnified, the more the same pattern kept reappearing. Like a snowflake, for example, or even, some would say, the Universe itself.

'You've heard of the Fibonacci Sequence?'

Dean posed the question to no-one in particular, although he was hardly expecting a response from Travis. So Mikkel pitched in.

'Isn't it… a sequence of numbers where each one is… ?'

'An infinite sequence where each one is the sum of the previous two.'

'The previous two, that's right. Zero. One. One. Two. Three—'

'Three five eight thirteen twenty-one thirty-four fifty-five eighty-nine—'

'OK, OK,' Mikkel said. 'Jeez. Another hobby?'

'To cut a long story, it's something that crops up in nature a lot, it's related to the Golden Ratio.'

'So what's that.'

'The Golden Ratio is one point six one eight zero three two seven eight—'

'Got it.'

'It goes on. You see it in classical architecture, geometry, that sort of thing. And divide a Fibonacci number by its predecessor, you get an approximation of the Golden Ratio which gets closer, the further towards infinity you go.'

Mikkel made a point of looking at his watch.

'My point is,' Dean went on, 'the Fibonacci sequence, the Golden Ratio, fractal geometry, they're all related, you find them in nature, you find them in infinity tiling in Islamic architecture, and, well... Some even say it's proof of God.'

And on that note...

They stared at the weather-blasted, time-worn carving on the boab for a few more moments. All very curious, Mikkel thought, but compared to everything else they'd found that dark day...

It was almost three by the time they decided to call it quits. Dean's injury ruled out a more painstaking search, and Mikkel thanked his lucky stars for small mercies.

*

He *thought* he remembered thanking his lucky stars, at least, but it occurred to him maybe he didn't thank them at all. That day – that Thursday – was breaking up in his head, breaking up and fading away into fractals, and fractals of fractals, and...

The flight attendant was smiling at him as he emerged from the tunnel at the arrival gate where the passengers from his flight were pouring out into the terminal building and off into the real world to continue their lives. The bag Mikkel was carrying, the zip-up shoulder bag that had been under the seat in front of him on the plane, turned out to contain clothes he *did* recognise because they were his – a pair of shoes, jeans and t-shirt – and even more than the fact that the contents were all, inexplicably wet, what disturbed him most of all, although he wasn't yet sure why, was that the bag bore the words "*Broome: It's One Pearl Of A Town*".

Was there really a body in a tree? A ship in the desert? Did he even *go* to the desert on Thursday? But of course he knew he had.

What's more, he almost didn't make it back.

*

By the time they'd stashed their gruesome cargo, no-one was speaking. They all just wanted to get out of there. It was nothing to do with Thursday night drinks anymore (they'd missed their flight anyway), but the thought of staying an hour longer suddenly felt like a form of torture. Dean's injury seemed to have plateaued – he hadn't broken into a feverish sweat, but on the other hand he wasn't looking that crash hot either, he was as pale as a ghost.

The landscape seemed full of ghosts: the ghostlike trunks of the snappy gums, not to mention the real ghosts...

As soon as Travis fired up the BK117, Mikkel felt his chest expand, like he could suddenly breathe again. The red earth seemed to back off a little bit, even before they'd begun to move. The sensation of relief – or release – grew even more pronounced as they disconnected from the ground and rose up into the cool, blue sky. Mikkel decided that this time he wasn't going to be the one to give them a reason to hang around – he'd keep his eyes on the horizon, on their destination, and not look down. No matter how many bodies there were down there, dangling from trees.

It happened about thirty seconds after take off.

The helicopter had just finished its turn and straightened out when it suddenly started juddering. It felt like riding a bike over cobblestones, or a corrugated iron roof. Mikkel and Dean looked at Travis who was glancing at his instruments and shaking his head. Shaking his head and cursing, so the prognosis looked bad.

'We're not gonna make Broome,' he said. 'If we're lucky we might make Sandfire.'

The other two nodded – what else could they do? – and Travis turned the craft around again, this time with some difficulty – and nudged them in a new direction: a fraction north of due west, straight for the ocean. Travis was indicating sand seemed to have somehow got into the fuel lines, or something like that, Mikkel wasn't sure, all he knew was he wished he hadn't seen the body in the tree.

"Sandfire" was the Sandfire Roadhouse and Caravan Park on the Great Northern Highway – one of only two roadhouses on the entire six hundred kilometre stretch of road between Port Hedland and Broome, and the closest to their current position. It was, therefore, their closest source of fuel, their closest source of supplies and their closest access to internet and telephone connections. And 'closest' counted for a lot in these parts, especially when your means of transport had a question mark over it.

A question mark, but unfortunately you could now add an exclamation mark as well: the shaking was getting worse – the juddering had upgraded itself from worrying to violent and Dean looked like he was about to throw up. Mikkel was beginning to wonder exactly how lucky Travis had meant they had to be to get to Sandfire, but now was obviously not the time to ask. They were now only flying at about a hundred and fifty kilometres per hour, and Sandfire was over sixty kilometres away, so that meant they had to hold it together for twenty or thirty minutes. Still, Travis appeared supremely cool, and Mikkel loved him for that.

They were flying low, maybe at a hundred metres or so, possibly less, and with all the violent juddering, it felt as though they still hadn't broken free of the grooved, red terrain flashing by below them. As if it was indeed the landscape causing all this. And in a way, perhaps it was, Mikkel thought, and was reminded of the contents of the plastic bags just behind where they were sitting.

It felt like an eternity, but eventually they found themselves flying over the Mandora Marsh, with its paperbark trees and mangroves and waterbirds. And water! all turquoise and white, what a sight that was, what a welcome relief from the relentless ochres and reds of the endless country around it. Like an oasis on Mars.

21. Edge Of Nowhere

[Sandfire, Great Northern Highway, W.A. (-19.7725, +121.0917), 17 Oct 2013, 3.30PM]

A small settlement on the edge of nowhere, Sandfire consisted of a handful of buildings planted next to the Great Northern Highway – an empty two-lane bitumen road stretching almost endlessly in both directions: to the north-east, towards Broome, and to the south-west, towards Port Hedland. The clump of buildings, like the clumps of wiry shrubs and trees covering the flat, red landscape, was sandwiched between the highway and a dirt runway for light planes.

The BK117 obviously didn't need a landing strip, but there was a circular clearing adjoining it specifically for helicopters. Travis steered the vibrating aircraft towards it, and deposited them with a bone-jarring crunch that Mikkel initially put down to the malfunctioning engine.

After the dust had settled and they began to unbuckle, Mikkel looked across at Travis who seemed to have undergone some sort of metamorphosis: all of a sudden he looked shattered. He just sat there, with glazed eyes, his sunglasses now off, staring out through the windscreen at the vista of red earth with its legion of low shrubs disappearing to the horizon – like he was a lookout who'd just spotted an army of overwhelming force.

'Well done Travis mate,' Dean said. 'You're a legend. Great effort.'

But Travis said nothing and didn't move. Mikkel and Dean were happy to do the same, and the three of them sat there in silence until a man in a blue checked shirt, loose-fitting grey trousers, a large straw hat, and over-sized gold-rimmed aviator sunglasses emerged out of the dusty glare to greet them.

'Gedday,' he said. 'You all right?'

Mikkel and Dean got out, but to begin with, Travis remained where he was. Something inside there, in his internal workings, seemed to have snapped. Like the engine of his helicopter. He eventually showed signs of life (barely) and got out and made a half-hearted attempt at joining, or at least appearing to join, the conversation Mikkel and Dean were having with Rod, the Sandfire Roadhouse manager. They explained their need to clean out the engine and refuel and told him they were there on police business. Dean kept things on a need to know basis – in relation to the human remains, he simply commandeered a separate cold storage unit for their use (he'd deal with the health inspectors if it came to that), saying they had "a few items" in need of a bit of temporary refrigeration. Rod eventually acceded to the storage request but under protest. Travis, his sunglasses back on again, stayed out of it.

"Temporary" was a relative term and as it turned out, they wouldn't be heading off again in a hurry. Travis was spooked. He'd lost his nerve. He'd been fine on the flight back – a hero, as Dean put it – but it seemed to have taken its toll. That, and the body, Mikkel guessed. The body and the body parts. But Travis, despite managing to summon the strength to carry out the necessary refuelling and repairs, refused to fly them. He was convinced there was something else going on apart from sand in their engine. He seemed to be under the impression the whole countryside had it in for him, so Dean made an executive decision that they'd spend the night there and head back to Broome the next day when everyone (meaning Travis) had recharged their batteries (meaning recovered their wits). It was the off-season, so luckily there were rooms available.

He might have been stuck in the middle of nowhere for his Thursday night, but Mikkel consoled himself with the thought that he would make up for it the following night, on Friday. (Which is, he was now guessing, exactly what he went and did.)

With Travis a casualty and not much use to anyone, Mikkel and Dean with his limp were left with the job of getting the body and the other various plastic bags into cold storage. Rod watched them with a troubled look on his face, but asked no questions. Any mug could have seen that they were carrying a body (although when they later rang their Perth base, they were told there had already been an inquiry from a worried roadhouse owner, so they figured Rod at least knew they weren't murderers). And as Mikkel and Dean struggled with their "naked lady in plastic" as Deano so helpfully put it, they were observed not just by Rod, and a shirtless guest with a stubby of beer in his hand, but also a commotion of noisy geese, a parade of strutting peacocks and a bored-looking camel. It was the goanna though that freaked Deano out – unsurprisingly perhaps – and he actually dropped the body bag when the docile lizard ambled into view.

A fine old lot we are, Mikkel thought. All this Post Traumatic Stress Disorder, anyone would have thought there was a war on. And in a way, as things turned out, there was.

Later on, when Dean reported in to their superiors in Perth and told them about the body and the other human remains, he also told them about the *Destino*. It was agreed that for the time being, that particular finding should be kept a secret, at least from the media and the general public, until it could be ascertained whether or not it was the real McCoy, and if it was, until the archaeologists or whoever had had a chance to look over it before it was plundered by souvenir hunters. Sure, the location was pretty remote, but you couldn't be too careful. After all, there were plenty of unscrupulous operators out there.

That evening, little was said over their burgers and beers – none of them had the stomach for much drinking, Thursday night or not – and when Mikkel finally retired to his room (air-conditioned thank God) he could barely remember what had happened to the rest of the day. And as he lay on his bed, thinking this very thought, he caught himself staring at a spider in a web in the corner of his room and realised he'd been staring at it for about half an hour. Which was when the heart palpitations began, for no apparent reason, and he didn't get to sleep until after 2 a.m.

*

Dawn occurred around 5.30am, which was exactly the time that Mikkel was woken by a terrible screeching. It was tacked onto the end of a horrible dream and he was relieved to discover the noise was coming from the peacocks and not from whatever it was in his dream that had made him break out into a cold sweat...

When he finally emerged at 8am, the sun was already blazing. The other guests had, for the most part, already gone or were in the process of leaving. Somewhere an engine was running. He caught sight of a curious wallaby, watching him from a patch of scrub nearby. As he strolled between the buildings of the settlement, he caught a glimpse of the helicopter. Travis was next to it, busying himself with something, which struck Mikkel as a good sign. As was the sight of Deano leaving the restaurant, despite the reminder that he could still taste the barbeque sauce from the burger the previous night.

The blue of the sky was already losing its lustre as the sun rose ever higher.

Mikkel greeted Dean and tilted his head in Travis's direction.

'We gonna be right to go?'

Dean nodded. 'We're out of here. Hope you're packed. We're leaving in fifteen.'

'*Minutes?*'

'No fifteen days.'

The thought of staying there, in the Great Sandy Desert or the edge of it or wherever they were, gave Mikkel the creeps to an extent he couldn't have fully explained. He hurried back to his room and grabbed his things. The spider was gone. For some reason that stuck in his mind.

The way Mikkel saw it, there was at least one event in most people's lives, somewhere along the line (be the line long or short), that seems in retrospect so critical, so fundamental in shaping what follows, that the person feels compelled to believe – and could be forgiven for believing – that it was more than purely a matter of chance that caused it to happen. That it was, in some way, either their fault, or their destiny. Or both. (Chance is almost always overlooked as the culprit, people love to blame themselves – what breathtaking egos we all have!). What happened next to Mikkel –

or what he caused to happen, whichever way you looked at it – was shaping up as one such event.

Mikkel and Dean were repacking the BK117 for their flight to Broome. For obvious reasons, they left to last the recovery of the 'items' in cold storage. Their final run involved carrying the body. They were weaving their way through the settlement, past some of the other guest rooms, ignoring the puzzled looks from one of Rod's employees and from a couple of nosey geese when Dean – whose limp had returned – needed a quick breather. They deposited their load temporarily in the shade of a nearby grove of trees, and as Dean wiped the sweat out of his eyes, Mikkel happened to notice, in the red earth of the rough avenue they were following, tyre tracks identical to the unidentified third set they'd seen near the *Destino*. The Bridgestones. Most people wouldn't have been able to tell that they were the same. But Mikkel had always been blessed – or cursed – with an eye for detail and an almost photographic memory when it came to anything that interested him. It hit him with force, like someone had hit a switch and bathed a dark scene in bright light.

In normal circumstances, there would have been no question about what to do next. It was what he was there for, what he was paid to do, and unlike the day before, when he was suffering from claustrophobia and heat exhaustion in the *Destino*, and worse later on, he was clear-headed and feeling fine. But these were not normal circumstances. Just as the thought of spending fifteen days there was intolerable, so was the thought of spending even *one* more day. And that was a real possibility if he drew Dean's attention to the tracks. They'd be obliged to follow the lead. They'd have to do a full job on the whole of Sandfire – the rooms, the books, guest details, the grounds… it didn't bear thinking about. Mikkel decided on a compromise. He'd ask Rod a couple of questions and worry about it later. They could always come back. And in terms of covering his arse: they were all exhausted, so it'd make sense that some things might not occur to them until later…

'So, er, Rod,' Mikkel said a short time later, after they were all packed and ready to go. 'Been many guests over the last few days?'

'Pretty average for this time of year. Last month of the tourist season, so, you know…' and he shrugged.

'I mean, what types? Just the last two or three days for example.'

'Types? Well we've had a couple of guys on a fishing trip. From Perth. Couple of grey nomads. From, er… Brisbane I think.'

'Right.'

'That's about it. Except for the couple still here, the honeymooners.'

Mikkel nodded. He'd fulfilled his promise to himself and now he was keen to go.

'Oh and… yeah,' Rod added. 'We had an Asian guy, left a couple of days ago. Korean I think. Driving this big flash SUV.'

Mikkel could have asked Rod a lot of questions at this point but decided not to. He could have asked more about the vehicle. Where it'd been parked, for example.

'Had some funny name like… Mr…'

Rod had a sudden pained look on his tropical face, which alarmingly erupted in a series of wave-patterned frown-lines.

'Argh!' he said eventually. 'On the tip of my tongue…'

'That's fine, Rod, thanks,' Mikkel said.

And he, for one, didn't give it another thought. Not for a while, at least.

*

They took off to the north-west. The Indian Ocean was only about twenty kilometres from Sandfire and the red earth soon gave way to a sandy flood plain, and then, at last, the ocean itself. The contrast of the indigo blue of the sea with the white sands of Eighty Mile Beach was dazzling. The beach itself stretched far further than its name suggested – almost twice as far – and took the form of an awe-inspiring crescent of sand covering about half the distance between Broome and Port Hedland. Looking in both directions, Mikkel couldn't imagine anything more colourful than that view, floating a few hundred metres up in the air – dangling, as they were, on the tenuous thread of their rotor bolt – over such an extraordinary kaleidoscope.

Travis – who visibly cheered up when they reached the ocean – steered them north along the line of the coast towards Broome, maybe an hour away at their current speed, now that the helicopter was healthy again. Even Dean had sparked up, perhaps because he was off his leg, but whatever the cause, his colour had returned.

Only Mikkel was plagued with doubts and fears. As if the dead red of the interior had stayed with him.

Seemingly embodying these anxieties, he could see a thin, dark bank of cloud covering the whole of the north-west horizon. The beginning of the wet season. It appeared it had arrived early this year.

22. Like A Map

[Mascot, Sydney, N.S.W. (-33.9269, +151.1877), 19 Oct 2013, 1.35PM]

Mikkel's memory was unfolding like a map.

The last forty-eight hours were coming back to him but slowly, section by section.

He was in a cab heading into Sydney and for a moment forgot where he was going. This was happening a lot. Why not back to Perth?

He knew people in Sydney. May as well visit, say hello.

James. Catching up with James Lavelle, that's where he was heading (James, never Jim or God help you). And confirming it, he found James's text, with an address in Newtown.

Mikkel could see there was a storm approaching. This made him feel uneasy, but why? What was it reminding him of? Was it the stormy horizon they saw on their way to Broome? But it was more than that, he felt, it was something else, an actual storm somewhere...

What happened after they landed in Broome? He still couldn't remember the actual landing, but they obviously made it. What did they do there?

And then there was the flight back. Try as he might, there was nothing in his head about a daytime flight back to Perth, or any flight back for that matter, with Dean and Travis. Judging by the hangover he was experiencing, he assumed they – or at least he – made it back for those drinks.

And for some reason he had the year 1929 in his head – so what was with that? The stock market crash, the beginning of the Great Depression?

Industrial estates made way for old buildings and shop awnings and next thing he knew they'd arrived and he was paying the driver. In King Street, and it was busy. It was hustle and bustle. He remembered a particularly big night with James at the Bank Hotel, which he was now staring at. And the Zanzibar across the road, they went there too. Ten years ago, and he could remember it better than yesterday.

James was Mikkel's age, thirty-three, and was an old friend, from their uni days in Perth. He'd been a law student, although last Mikkel had heard he now ran some kind of furniture import business. He lived in Australia Street, up at the Camperdown end, and even though Mikkel vaguely remembered where he lived, it had been years and James wasn't answering his phone. Lucky for street maps and smartphones.

Relieved to be escaping the King Street traffic, he turned up Australia Street: he walked through an attractive pedestrianized section and then continued up the long tree-lined avenue. Past an impressive old cream-coloured building with the words "Court House" clearly emblazoned across its facade – solidly classical, it reminded him of ancient Rome somehow – and next to that… A strange sensation came over him, seeing the blue "Police" sign. It was the Newtown Police Station, should he be going in there? Or running away from it?

At that moment an attractive brunette in tight white pants and a black top – looked French or Italian, with olive skin and curly dark hair – walked out through the front entrance. Mikkel was on the opposite side of the road, but it was only narrow and he must have been staring at her because she caught his look and paused and cast him a curious, half-smiling frown, as if to say "Do I know you?". And then a sudden gust of wind blew something into Mikkel's eye and by the time he'd looked up again with his other eye, she was gone, walking confidently off in the direction of King Street. Mikkel cursed the tree that had just assaulted his vision and could only assume the culprit was a London Plane tree, they were deadly he remembered, from a previous Sydney trip.

But it was all happening, because as soon as he continued his walk up Australia Street, a spectacular bolt of lightning descended from the steely sky ahead of him, followed by a low rumble maybe ten seconds later. Two miles away...

And it came to him. He remembered now, he was still in Broome when the thunderstorm hit. He was in a beer garden, or somewhere more upmarket, some sort of terraced area, with a view of the sea, drinking, with Dean. It wasn't night-time, it was the afternoon. And it wasn't Perth, that wasn't where he'd been drinking with Dean at all. So why were they still in Broome? And when did they return to Perth? he'd definitely arrived in Sydney from Perth. And where did he last see Dean?

He looked at his phone for a clue, but before he even got to check his recent calls, he knew. He knew there'd be nothing from Dean and he knew there'd be no answer if he tried to call him. And a feeling of dread caught in his throat and his map began unfolding some more...

23. The Black Sky

The Cable Beach Club Resort. That's where they'd gone.

Lightning crackled and flashed on the horizon against the black sky, still many kilometres out to sea, but where Mikkel and Dean and Travis were, it was still sunny. They were comfortably seated in cane chairs with leather cushions and they'd just finished lunch in an outdoor eating area overlooking the beach: the restaurant was on a raised deck of polished wood and surrounded by lush resort trees (including, unfortunately, a boab tree) and populated by the usual resort crowd. Beers and steaks and red wine: Mikkel should have been feeling relaxed, like the others obviously were. It was over. Done and dusted.

But something told him it wasn't.

They'd arrived in Broome without incident – they landed at the heliport next to the airport – and had been met by Senior Sergeant Brad Hanson of the Broome police, driving a large, midnight blue Toyota Landcruiser with a double-cab chassis and tray. Their first stop was Broome Hospital, to drop off their "cargo", much to Mikkel's relief. It had been decided by their superiors, given the deterioration of the body and the body parts, that the autopsy and forensic examinations and testing would be conducted in Broome, and that Mikkel and Dean would be relieved by a second team, who were on their way up from Perth. In the circumstances, there was no need for them to hang around, and it being Friday, they were told they only had to report in to Perth base on Monday for a full debriefing.

Brad, the Senior Sergeant, was a fit, self-assured forty-year old with a shaved head and a sense of humour he wore like a suit. He gave Mikkel the feeling there was some practical joke that was being played out, and at any moment it would be revealed. Brad told them after they'd arrived at the police station that the Landcruiser was theirs for the day, all they had to do was leave it in the street out front when they'd finished with it, or even in the main airport car park if that was easier (ignition keys under the seat was fine, no worries). And as far as drinking went, no 'designated driver' was necessary either, because "mate", Brad told them, "this is Broome, not fuckin' Perth". Hence the resort: it was Dean's idea, they could celebrate surviving their desert adventure and catch the 5.15pm flight home.

Despite the jovial air though, Mikkel's bad feeling continued. He could only assume it was due to all the things they'd seen in the previous twenty-four hours.

Mostly they kept the conversation to other things – global politics, national sport, and local women (as in twenty-metre-radius local) – but they were never going to be able to ignore altogether what was really on each of their minds.

'So Deano.' Unbelievably, it was Travis. Starting a conversation. 'Mick reckons you're a bit of an expert on the Golden Age of Sail.'

'Dunno about expert.'

'So this... *Destino*. If it *was* a Spanish galleon... what do you reckon it was carrying? I mean, like... treasure?'

'We didn't see any.'

'No I know, but... half it was buried wasn't it?'

'The ship? Yeah, but I still reckon whatever was in there was probably nicked a long time ago. Centuries.'

'But it *could* be there, right?' They'd never heard Travis as talkative.

'I guess,' Dean shrugged. 'You goin' back there with your shovel, are you Long John?'

They all chuckled, but Mikkel doubted any of them found it all that funny, least of all himself. That ship just reminded him of dead bodies in trees, and body parts in the sand... And to make it worse, he had a strange feeling they were being listened to. He had no evidence of this – call it instinct – but it was an unpleasant sensation.

Nevertheless, he was still able to appreciate the wonderful scenery. Combined with the approaching storm and the sea steadily darkening before their eyes, there was a certain dramatic beauty about it that couldn't fail to move the glummest of the glum. The alcohol didn't hurt either: it was doing what it was paid to do, and he gradually relaxed. Right up until his second trip to the toilets.

Feeling pleasantly light-headed, he passed tables of contented, sun-tanned patrons, and a couple of attractive Euro-types in tiny bikinis. Passed some parked cars. Looking for the sign to the Gents, he happened to notice one of the vehicles, it was hard to miss: a large, red SUV. A Porsche Cayenne with Western Australian plates. Ostentatious. Covered in red dust. Red on red. The red made him think of blood and he stopped himself. And he almost turned away – it must have been such a close thing – when he noticed something else.

The tyres. They were Bridgestones.

And he could have left it there, walked away, but the connections formed in his brain faster than he could consciously keep up and he found himself drawn in for a closer look. At the tyre tread. And it was as though he already knew the result: it was the same as the tyre tread in the tracks at Sandfire, which was the same as what they'd seen at the *Destino*.

Mikkel's first internal response was to tell himself they were over three hundred kilometres from Sandfire – four hundred from the *Destino* – and they were in a busy centre now. There were probably many vehicles in Broome with the same tyres.

Suddenly, he was conscious of being watched and when he turned away from the vehicle to continue to the Gents, he saw the back of a portly man in a short-sleeved, batik shirt quickly retreating into the shadows of the main building.

It hit him when he sat down, rejoining Dean and Travis. He froze. It was like a cold electric shock pulsed through him. He remembered what Rod had said about one of the guests being a Korean or Asian guy who drove "a big flash SUV".

Dean asked Mikkel what was wrong. His face must have told

the story but he smiled and shook his head. And looked around, looked for an Asian face, in the scattered crowd.

He started to feel panicky. Guilty that he'd said nothing at Sandfire about the tyre tracks (if only he hadn't seen them!). And then he started telling himself that maybe he'd been wrong about the tracks at Sandfire: he was tired, he hadn't been himself, he'd been in *shock* for God's sake, still freaked out by the discovery of the naked girl in the boab tree, and the body parts. And anyway, it was too late to say anything now, he'd look like an idiot for keeping quiet about it, it was his *job* to find things like that! Better to leave it, assume he never saw those tracks. And he probably didn't, either. That would explain why he hadn't said anything, or so he'd tell himself.

But… *just* to put his mind at rest…

He decided to ring Rod and find out about the make and colour of the vehicle, and the name of the owner. He excused himself to make a call ("Who is she?" Dean asked) and, just inside the doors to the resort, next to an indoor palm, tried Rod's number, but there was no answer. He left a message and assured himself he'd done what he could. Told himself to relax. There had to be a heap of "flash" SUVs in the Kimberley, and plenty of Asians, so it was all a bit of a long bow, wasn't it?

Of course it was.

Back with the others, and the sun was now obscured from view. The storm was close, the sea had turned from turquoise to gunmetal grey. No white horses yet, but they'd come: the sunbathers had already upped stumps.

'4pm,' said Dean looking at his watch. 'I wouldn't mind checking out Chinatown before we go. Take a look at a couple of those pearl shops. That OK?'

Mikkel and Travis nodded.

'Should still make the five fifteen,' Dean continued, 'but there's always the six fifteen and the seven ten, so it won't be the end of the world if we miss it.'

'Yeah well…' Travis said, downing his beer and looking out to sea. 'As pretty as this little scene is… I for one, have a date tonight. In Perth. And if I'm not on the five fifteen, it *will* be the end of the fuckin' world.'

'Better get cracking, then.'

On their way out, Mikkel noticed the red Porsche Cayenne was still there.

It was a short ten minute drive from the resort, back along Cable Beach Road, past the Broome Crocodile Park and around the airport to the other side of the small peninsula, where the township of Broome backed up against Roebuck Bay. Lightning flashed overhead and thunder rumbled over the town as they parked the Landcruiser on Dampier Terrace, near Johnny Chi Lane, in the heart of Broome's Chinatown.

They took a quick look inside two pearl showrooms, and the third and final one was The Pearl Mermaids, slightly away from the more congested section of Dampier Terrace and just past where they'd parked the Landcruiser. As they approached, Mikkel's heart missed a beat. Parked right next to the Landcruiser, and in a group of about six vehicles in total, was the red Porsche again. It was definitely the same one, same W.A. plates.

He knew it was a small town, but this felt wrong. Was it just a coincidence? Was there really any such thing as a coincidence?

Mikkel felt his throat constricting. He desperately wanted to say something to Dean, but, as before – more so – there was too much that hadn't been said.

'Mick,' Dean said. He and Travis were about to go inside. 'Are you coming or are you just going to admire the view?'

The first drops of rain began to fall on him, as heavy as small pebbles.

'It's OK. I might get some fresh air before the flight.'

'Hope you brought your umbrella,' Dean said and he and Travis vanished into the shop.

Hope you brought your umbrella.

The Pearl Mermaids was the largest pearl showroom in the area, as far as Mikkel could tell, but it also felt like one of the emptiest – from the outside at least. There was no-one around. An enormous mural covered the front wall of the building: three frolicking mermaids with Asian eyes and generous breasts (nipples tactfully concealed by strands of seaweed) were swimming underwater and chasing each other's tails, and underneath them, on the ocean floor, was an open treasure chest overflowing with egg-sized silver pearls.

It was painted in the style of the kind of design you used to find on the side of surfers' panel vans.

This time he took a closer look inside the Porsche but there were no obvious clues: it had the empty look of a hire-car, which could well have been what it was.

He stood under a nearby awning as the rain gradually grew heavier, waiting for the others. The low sky was almost continually lit up and the rain on the tin rooftops gave rise to a steadily building roar that competed with the constant rumbling of thunder. Five minutes became ten.

The startling crack of a lightning bolt sounded like a gun going off.

He looked at his watch: 4.45pm. They were going to miss their flight. He ran across the deserted street in the teeming rain and entered The Pearl Mermaids.

He'd probably been expecting something like a pearling museum, with dark wooden floors and old-fashioned diving suits on the walls, but the room he entered looked more like the waiting room of a doctor's surgery. It was as deserted as the street outside – there was just a Chinese-looking girl with her head buried in some kind of ledger. When Mikkel walked in, she looked up sharply. No friendly smile.

'I'm sorry we closed now,' she said harshly.

'Sorry, I was looking for my friends. Two men...'

She was looking at him blankly.

'They came in here,' Mikkel went on. 'Have you seen them? My friends?'

'Friends? No. Sorry. We closed now.'

'But... They came in here. I've been standing just outside. Two men. You must have...' He trailed off. Conscious of the desperation in his voice.

'No no. No-one.'

Mikkel could see a partly open door, and beyond, the dark interior of a large warehouse, lit in places by low down-lighting.

'Perhaps they went inside,' Mikkel suggested and moved towards the door. That got her going.

'No sir no no sir very sorry you can't go in there.'

'It's OK, let me just stick my head in.'

'Sir!' a man's voice shouted out from behind him. 'Sir! You must leave, we are closed!'

A short Asian man dressed more like a real estate agent than a Broome business manager had come in through the front door. He confirmed he hadn't seen Mikkel's friends and that he, Mikkel, really had to leave. He thought of showing them his badge, but remembered he'd left it in Perth. Anyway, judging by the guy's tone, it was a gun he needed, not a badge.

He left them and tried more of the pearl shops in the vicinity (along Dampier Terrace and up Johnny Chi Lane) but it was the same story: they were either closed or closing and they hadn't seen the two men. It was now after five. Something had gone terribly wrong.

And when he returned to the awning he'd been waiting under earlier, the Landcruiser was gone. Gone! They'd left without him? Surely not. He couldn't believe it, and looked up and down the street. Was this some kind of joke? Left for Perth without him?

The red Porsche was still there, though. It seemed to taunt him. He looked it over again, desperate now for clues, but it was still maddeningly empty. In fact, with its immaculate interior and the rain washing away the red dust and mud, you could have sworn it was brand new and never been driven.

Mikkel called the Broome police station and encountered a jovial receptionist with an English accent called Harriet (and… had she been drinking? had Friday night drinks kicked in already at work?). The Landcruiser had been returned: when Harriet looked out her window, apparently, she could see it parked in the street out front but no, they hadn't seen Dean or Travis. He asked if he could speak to the Senior Sergeant.

Eventually, he heard Brad's voice on the line; Mikkel had been patched through to his mobile. He could hear the telltale sounds of clinking glasses and general hubbub.

'Mate. How's it going.' Brad was slurring his words, just a touch.

'Gedday Brad. Have you seen Dean or Travis?

There was a chuckle at the other end.

'You lost them already? Jeez.' And then a big laugh, a single "Hah!".

'They left the car, the… Landcruiser out front. Of the police station. Which is strange because we were gonna leave it at the airport on our—'

'Mate. This is Broome,' Brad said. 'Listen...' And then he spoke slowly, as if Mikkel's grasp of English was poor:

'There's no—such— thing—as *strange* here. *Strange*—is *normal*—in Broome.'

Mikkel was losing patience with his host.

'Well I don't know where they are, Brad. So we've got a problem.'

'Nuh. *You've* got a problem. As I say, this is Broome. And it's Friday night. Make no mistake: there's a fuckin' *shiteload* of fun to be had here on a Friday night. They ain't goin back to Perth tonight. Trust me.'

'Christ.'

'Hey buddy, I gotta go. There's a, er... a new recruit. Across the room, beckoning me and, er... they need a refill. If you catch my meaning. But listen. Hey this is important. You listenin'? Come and have a drink. While you're waiting for your buddies. Before we hit the town.'

'Yeah maybe. Thanks.'

'You know where we are. And hey. Michael. Whatever you do... have fun, OK? You may as well, 'cause we're all shark bait in the end.'

And Brad was gone. *Shark bait?*

He knew there was no way Dean would have left him – either for the airport or a resort full of honeymooners or even a beer garden full of backpackers.

The rain was roaring at full volume now, crashing down in a solid, endless barrage of water. Visibility was down to metres, like a thick fog. He almost didn't hear his phone ringing. His phone! He didn't recognise the number but knew it was Dean.

But it wasn't Dean, it was Rod. About the vehicle, the SUV. It was red. It was, yes, a Porsche. Yes, W.A. licence plates. And the guest's surname was Song, he couldn't read the first name. Mr Song from Seoul, Korea.

After the call Mikkel just stood there under the awning, a month of rain in one minute, slamming down on the flimsy tin roof above him. He was staring at the red Porsche, semi-visible in the watery gloom. And the image of the girl in the boab tree came to him once more, and at precisely that moment, when that image appeared before his eyes, superimposed on the red car in the rain, he was aware of two Asian men walking towards him from The Pearl Mermaids and there was a clap of thunder or a gunshot or the sound of a meat cleaver hitting wood, he didn't know, but he nearly jumped out of his skin, and then the men were gone and the only sound was the roar of the rain and Dean's comment about the umbrella just gnawed its way into his brain uninvited and kept gnawing...

24. Law Of Probabilities

[Newtown, Sydney, N.S.W. (-33.8959, +151.1780), 19 Oct 2013, 2.02PM]

And that was where the map ceased to unfold. For now, at least, because there was obviously more. Now, as he walked up Australia Street on his way to see his old friend James Lavelle, he could only piece together and guess, from the physical evidence he had with him. From the law of probabilities.

From the fact that the clothes in his bag – his clothes – were wet. This, he assumed, was probably from the rain – he'd probably walked, or run, to the airport, it had been close enough, a kilometre, two at most. The clothes he was wearing he'd probably bought there, at the airport itself.

From the old boarding pass in his bag. He'd probably caught the 7.10pm Qantas flight to Perth. Which would also explain why 1929 was in his head – it wasn't the year, it was the flight number: QF1929. (He could now remember seeing a full moon shining down on monolithic clouds, another snapshot to add to the album.)

But the law of probabilities had nothing to say about why he then boarded a flight to Sydney. And why the hangover. And why he had so much trouble remembering any of this in the first place. Unless something had happened, in Broome or somewhere else, something possibly even worse than what they'd seen in the desert. And unless someone was following him, someone he was trying to lose...

Which is when he suddenly remembered.

Drinking with Brad.

He couldn't put it into context – his memory was just fragments anyway – he couldn't remember where they were, or how he got there, but they were out somewhere, the local pub most likely. He'd probably taken Brad up on that drink after all. But what he could remember was that it was crowded and everyone was drunk. Mikkel, for one, which obviously didn't help the state of his recollection. And Brad's slurring was even worse than before: his sentences were flowing like creeks in the Wet and his mouth was barely moving but somehow, words were still forming. It was as though his mouth was drunker than his brain. His brain though was not at its sharpest, and things were slipping out – words, reactions – that possibly shouldn't have been. Although with Brad, it seemed, you never knew.

Mikkel remembered talking about the *Destino*, and Brad not believing him.

'It was probably just an old shack or a gunyah or something.'

'The *three* of us Brad... We weren't imagining it.'

'Well you know, the desert does fuck people up, fucks with their heads... plays with their brains. Deep fried. And if you go on about it... it might make you look like a bit of dill, mate, so if I was you... you oughta.... you know, I'd keep it a secret if I was you.'

'We are.

'We. Yeah. We are. You're right there.'

Whatever he meant by that. But as soon as Mikkel mentioned the carving they saw in the *Destino*, Brad's face changed; his eyes narrowed and focused on Mikkel and he looked like he was trying to say something. And then he did, and asked Mikkel if they'd taken a photo of it (they hadn't), and how well did he remember it, and could he draw it on a napkin? And then he came over all weird – or weirder – when Mikkel asked him why he was so interested, was he another history nut like Deano, and where the fuck were they by the way.

'Don't worry mate, they'll show up. In one shape or another. This way or that.'

Another memory: Brad trying to talk Mikkel into staying, into not flying back to Perth that night. He was going on, again, about how Broome went off on Friday nights, how it was a target-rich environment with all the backpackers, and there was this woman he knew – called Lena? – some hot Russian, he'd love her, but then almost as soon as he'd mentioned her – when Mikkel asked him something about her – he backpedalled a million miles an hour and changed the subject.

As he did every time Mikkel mentioned the others – Dean and Travis. Changed the subject. It was surreal.

But surreal wasn't the word for it when the man in the batik shirt turned up.

Mikkel remembered noticing him, hovering in the background. He was sure it was the same man he'd seen at the Cable Beach Resort. Stocky, not tall, maybe a little chubby but undoubtedly solid, and he was wearing the same clothes: a short-sleeved, brown and black, Indonesian-style shirt – with a batik design – light grey trousers, and white tennis shoes. On his sizeable right wrist hung a chunky, gold-plated Rolex. This time he could see his face and he was clearly East Asian: Chinese, Japanese… Mikkel couldn't tell. But he definitely could have been Korean.

Was it the owner of the red Porsche with the Bridgestones? That had been parked not just at Cable Beach, but also Sandfire? Was it, as Rod called him, "Mr Song from Seoul, Korea"?

For an instant – and it was only an instant – the Asian stared straight at Mikkel, and it was no accidental glance. It was a stare full of purpose. He had a dark, round face, and mud-brown eyes. And then his lips parted and his teeth appeared, a brilliant white.

'Song!'

It was Brad. It was actually *Brad*, calling out to the guy, and motioning him over.

They – Brad and "Song", presumably the Korean – then had what was blatantly a private conversation, clearly keeping Mikkel out of it.

But he did manage to pick up snippets. Soundbites, uttered by Brad. Two, to be precise, or at least they were the ones he could remember, but two was all it took, and now that they came to him, they shone brightly, rendering all else pale by comparison. They were:

'D'ja deal with them? All fixed?'
and
'One to go. Don't go far.'
And that was enough for Mikkel, he was out of there.

He could vaguely recall leaving – no goodbyes, he just backed away and walked – weaving his way through the sweating, shouting, drunken patrons – tourists and locals – wondering if Brad or Mr Song noticed him leave, wondering if he was being followed, and with two things going round and round in his head: firstly, the terrible realisation that Brad was in on it, whatever 'it' was, and secondly – call it copper's instinct, but he knew this with as much certainty as he knew anything – that this Mr Song was death on legs.

After that, the curtain descended. Another gap.

Although he couldn't recall how he got there, he assumed he must have made a bee-line for the airport. The airport wasn't far – about one and a half kilometres if they'd been near the police station (the Roebuck Bay Hotel, for example) – but he wouldn't have had much time to make the 7.10pm flight to Perth.

Perth.

A final memory 'parcel' arrived. The hangover wasn't simply from his afternoon with Dean and Travis or his drink or drinks with Brad – unless Brad slipped him something? (now there was a thought) – but he remembered now, he'd been drinking in Perth as well. No idea where, either a beer garden, or a nightclub, or both – had someone lent him clothes? – and although he couldn't remember exactly who he was with, he knew there were familiar faces, friends…. And one familiar face who wasn't a friend.

Mr Song. With his batik shirt and his gold Rolex. He was in Perth as well.

Which left little room for doubt, when you looked at all the evidence: he was, most probably, being hunted.

And so that would explain the flight to Sydney. In his, no doubt, alcohol-impaired and freaked-out state of mind, he probably decided to catch the first plane out of there, get away for the weekend, and to that end he probably rang James Lavelle, who probably would have laughed and said something like "yeah, jump on that plane, mate"…

So he was right.
Someone was following him. Someone he was trying to lose.
It was just the law of probabilities.
Hope you brought your umbrella.

Part Four – Dark Oceans

It is an unmistakeable fact that sexuality does not always, like the individual organism's other functions, bring it advantages, but, in return for an unusually high degree of pleasure, brings dangers which threaten the individual's life and often enough destroy it.

Sigmund Freud
from *Introductory Lectures on Psychoanalysis*
Vol. 1, Lecture 26,
"The Libido Theory and Narcissism"

25. <u>16° 43' 9" S 121° 54' 4" E</u> (Indian ocean: off the Kimberley Coast)

11.02am Western Australian Time (03:02 UTC)
Saturday, 19 October

The ocean glider surfaced for the second time in about fourteen hours. The seas were choppy and grey and the 1.8 metre long autonomous craft (which looked like a bright yellow torpedo with wings) was, despite its colour, barely visible. The raised steering fin was probably the most observable feature, occasionally bobbing clear of the wave tops and looking like a person trying to keep their head above water.

Operated by the Australian National Facility for Ocean Gliders (ANFOG), it was meandering its way in a north-westerly direction, collecting ocean data such as water temperature, salinity and dissolved organic matter – information used for research into ocean currents but which was also fed into the world weather communications network. The battery-powered vessel had just about every type of sensory receptor except for eyes (it was blind), and in the usual course of its operation it made its way to a chain of pre-programmed position points. It could also be communicated with by radio or satellite, allowing for a periodic update of navigational instructions and the collection of data. To be able to do this, it needed to surface.

The last time it surfaced – the previous evening – the ocean glider had been positioned approximately twenty-five kilometres to the south-east, just off the Lacepede Islands. On that occasion, the surface of the ocean had been glassy. Glassy, because it had been a lovely, cloudless evening with hardly a breath of wind. Just a risen full moon hanging high in the sky, magnesium bright in the crisp air, illuminating large swathes of the otherwise dark expanse of ocean and turning night into day. When it surfaced, the yellow craft would have been readily obvious to anyone had they been around.

And they had.

Indeed if ocean gliders could see, this one would have observed a yacht only about fifteen metres away, and on the deck of the yacht, a man, staring at it, with large, disbelieving, blood-shot eyes.

26. <u>33° 55' 11" S 18° 25' 11" E</u>
(Cape Town)

5.02am South African Standard Time (03:02 UTC)
Saturday, 19 October

At the same time that Mikkel Backstrom was walking up Australia Street in Newtown, Sydney, and the ocean glider was surfacing in choppy seas off the coast of Western Australia, Ishiko Mizushima woke up suddenly in her hotel room in Cape Town.

It wasn't a pleasant way to wake up: her heart was pumping furiously, she'd gone from being sound asleep to wide awake in an instant. She thought she'd heard something. Or had she dreamt it? It was becoming harder to tell.

Sunrise wasn't for another hour, although outside at least it wasn't dark: the full moon was still burning bright, casting an eerie glow over the city. She usually kept her curtains closed – night and day, as a precaution – but for one night at least, for sanity's sake, she'd made an exception. Even with the moon though, and the open curtains, it was still dark enough in her room, enough to make her nervous, and she quickly flicked the switch on her bedside light.

No-one.

And nothing out of place, as far as she could see. Which was fairly easy to verify, the room was tiny and bare: her grey, logo-free Muji sports bag was sitting zipped up on the floor where she'd left it, there was a small dressing table with a mirror, a phone and a hotel listings folder on it, there was a functional chair, and there was a wardrobe which she always left open, containing a couple of items of clothing which she'd hung up. She always made a habit of leaving the door to the bathroom open as well and she could see in there too, and her modest and neatly stacked collection of toiletries was clearly visible. As for the room itself: there was the same, stained, maroon carpet, blotchy white walls and dirt-smeared window panes overlooking the street, nine floors below. (If she stood in the right spot against the wall beside the window, she could see Table Mountain.)

She looked at the burn wound on her right forearm, it had almost healed. But there'd be a scar. No problem in winter, but annoying in summer. Distinguishing features, never a good thing.

Even at five in the morning there was no shortage of street noise outside – it never let up, the noise – and maybe, probably, that was what she'd heard. But ever since Lüderitz...

27. <u>22° 56' 35" S 14° 30' 9" E</u>
(Walvis Bay, Namibia)

Two months earlier. Wednesday, 14 August

The *Diamond Moon* had been docked in Walvis Bay when Ishiko had executed her chosen course of action. And that was the way she thought of it too – it wasn't killing Bertrand and stealing the Decagon, it was executing the plan. *Her* plan, because she'd been given a choice. She was to do whatever it took to get the Decagon and herself off the *Diamond Moon*, out of Namibia and down to Cape Town in one piece. And "whatever it took", she'd been expressly told, included the elimination of any potential threat to the successful carrying out of her orders. "Elimination" was to be interpreted widely. And she knew these people, her bosses. She had little doubt they'd carried out countless eliminations in their time and that all of them had been carried out for the same purpose, to ensure the success of the operation. And the goal of the operation was never to be questioned. It was a matter of faith, no different from any religion, and she had no problem with that. So if ever she found her mind straying into difficult territory – such as what happened with Bertrand on the boat that day – she'd extract herself, think of something else. She counted herself lucky she was the type of person who could do that. She saw it as a skill. A mental skill, more important to her wellbeing than any physical skill she possessed – there was no doubt about that.

And she had to use all her skills – both mental and physical – from the moment she left the *Diamond Moon*. As soon as her feet touched dry land in the waterfront area of Walvis Bay, with its faceless merchant vessels and its handful of pleasure cruisers, she was working on a calculation of around thirty minutes for the likely time it would take for Drayle to be told Bertrand was missing or dead. Give or take thirty. So she quickly scurried off past the shipping company offices and warehouses and into the streets of the town in search of a taxi. But instead of doing the obvious and heading straight for the airport and boarding the only flight to Cape Town that day (because on her reading of it, doing the obvious would *in all probability* get her killed), she instructed the driver to take her half an hour up the coast to the next town – Swakopmund – and the bus station there.

It was crazy because Swakopmund was in the wrong direction, but being crazy was her only chance. Namibia was an empty, desolate place, hard enough for a lizard to find a place to hide, let alone an orphan girl from Tokyo with an angry team of seasoned criminals on her trail. Hungry too, without their Decagon.

On the way in, they drove through Palm Beach, a name which made Ishiko smile for the first time that day – it was too funny, Palm Beach, here! – even though there were indeed palm trees planted along the seafront, kept alive, presumably, with litres of water and pride. In Swakopmund she boarded a bus that was headed inland, to Namibia's capital, Windhoek. There, after a long and dusty six hour bus journey in a metal coffin on wheels, she got to spend a sleepless night in the cabin of a crane on a building site off Independence Avenue, a name which appealed to her.

The next day, Thursday, she did her next crazy thing, which was board a bus not for the South African border (about twelve hours away) and Cape Town, but rather for Lüderitz, eleven hours drive to the west, back on the coast, well off her quickest escape route.

It would prove to be her first mistake.

28. <u>26° 38' 59" S 15° 9' 8" E</u>
(Lüderitz, Namibia)

Friday, 16 August

Lüderitz was a harbour town about four hundred kilometres (as the seagull flies) south of Walvis Bay. Compared to its competition at least, it was a pretty town, mainly due to an abundance of colonial architecture dating from its diamond rush days in the early 1900s. Ishiko's plan was to lie low there for a week before heading off again, in the hope that it would place her behind the forward momentum of the set of pulsing waves that would inevitably follow the discovery of her escape. As it happened, she didn't last two days there.

On the day after her arrival in Lüderitz she foolishly visited an old church on a hill with a view of the sea. The church was built from the same grey rock of the surrounding landscape. She arrived in the morning and with the August sun in the east coaxing a rich, deep, blue from the ocean backdrop, she was overcome with a feeling of warmth and belonging. A feeling of peace and contentment. She stayed there all morning and into the afternoon, outside the church in the shade of a small tree, staring and lost in thought, and marvelling at the contrasting colours. And when the sun had crossed the sky sufficiently to turn the deep blue of the sea to bright silver, she entered the church and looked around for a time. When she walked out again it was late afternoon and the sun was low over the sea.

And they were waiting for her.

They were just standing there, in front of an imposing, yellow, heavy duty tow truck. There was no-one else around and there was nowhere for her to run. There was nothing to say and nothing was said. There were three of them, three men and not once did they speak. They looked, to Ishiko, like they could have been European, possibly Eastern European, maybe Russian. She expected them to be Russian, given Drayle's connections. But without hearing their voices, there was no way to tell. They frisked her thoroughly, then bundled her into the cabin of their tow truck with her in the middle. They tied her hands to a metal cage behind her head and pulled her jeans down to her ankles as an added precaution. And even though, once they got going, she could tell that one of the men next to her, the short one, was staring at her crotch and growing hard under his trousers, she had no doubt about the singular nature of her intended fate. She knew they were there to kill her, and that she was there to be killed.

She might have been tempted to curse herself for not getting the taxi driver to take her to the airport and for not flying to Cape Town from Walvis Bay instead of this crazy scheme of hers, but she refused to do so and steadfastly kept her mind on the beautiful church in Lüderitz with the deep blue sea behind it which she never would have seen if she had taken that flight, and how thankful she should be, if only for the reason that if life wasn't about those rare and unexpected moments of beauty what *was* it about?

They drove out of town, away from the glistening sea. The colonial buildings disappeared, and then the houses, until eventually there was only desert. After about ten minutes they took a right turn off the bitumen highway onto a dirt road. They passed silently through Kolmanskop, an old mining town now deserted – a ghost truck passing through a ghost town.

They continued on, and the sun disappeared, sinking below the ridgeline to their right. There wasn't a tree in sight – from the look of the landscape they may as well have been in the middle of the driest desert on earth – but it wasn't long before Ishiko caught glimpses of her precious sea again and even though it was now blue-black with the approaching night, the sight of it gladdened her heart. They passed a mountain of sand with a pipeline running from its summit to its base. They passed workers' cabins, apparently empty. They bounced their way ever onwards – first crossing a railway line and then travelling parallel with it – towards what looked like a bay that was opening up ahead. And it was a bay, and it was soon on their left-hand side as they skirted its edges. Past abandoned machinery, and a loading pier with a dormant conveyor belt jutting out into the water where small arcing swell lines gently swept around into the bay and broke along a low rocky shore.

And then, finally, a dead end loomed up ahead, but Ishiko stayed focused on the bay and what sounded like distant booming waves coming from their right, from the other side of the small peninsula.

The rail line ended at the same place as the dirt road, next to the pier and a cluster of demountable metal sheds, and that was where their truck pulled up. The place was obviously some kind of mine site, currently abandoned – although whether this was temporary or permanent, Ishiko couldn't tell.

The driver got out, and when the man on the passenger's side opened his door too, a sea breeze began to whistle through the cabin and with the taste of salt on her tongue and the sudden roaring sound of the nearby Atlantic surf in her ears, Ishiko felt her resources replenishing. And the cawing of a gull! She wondered if it made her crazy, the fact that she could think and feel these things at a time like this. The fact that they'd said nothing to her, asked her nothing about the Decagon, must have meant, she assumed, that they'd found the Decagon in her Lüderitz hotel room and that she was about to die.

The driver – who looked to be about forty and was tall, with a solid build and blond hair, a caesar haircut – unlocked the shed door with a large set of keys and slid it open. The metal rollers clattered and screeched before the door loudly slammed to a halt. The man who'd been sitting on her left, next to the passenger-side door – about forty as well, skinny, wearing too many clothes for the conditions (it may have been the middle of winter, August, but it had to have been at least twenty-five degrees that day) – was by now standing a short distance away, just past the shed and looking out over the bay. The third man, the short one who'd been sitting in the middle and staring at Ishiko's legs, looked about thirty, was round and sweaty and black-haired with a beard, and wore a black t-shirt and cargo pants. With obvious pleasure he removed her jeans from around her ankles and then untied her hands and roughly pulled her out of the cabin. She stood there for a moment, barefoot, wearing only her panties and top, before he guided her and pushed her towards the shed.

The driver didn't follow them, but chose, instead, to walk over to where the skinny man was standing. Ishiko saw that he'd pulled out a handgun and was fondling it as he strolled across the dusty turning circle. It looked like a Sig Mosquito semi-automatic without a noise suppressor (but then who needed to be silent in a place like this?).

As soon as she entered the shed and her eyes adjusted to the gloom inside, she saw a sight that she hadn't been expecting. Slumped against the back wall, gagged and bound, naked and bloodied, with his legs full of bullet holes, was a fellow passenger from the *Diamond Moon*, the dockworker from Marseilles. Arnaud. At first she couldn't tell if he was alive or dead because his eyes were closed and his mouth was open. And then his eyes opened. They were dead eyes (and Ishiko had seen her fair share of them), but after a moment of trying to focus on her, they widened with recognition – just slightly – and they did something else too. It may have been involuntary or it may have been intentional, but his dark eyes darted to the left and back again. Ishiko's eyes followed his, to her right, and there, at the side of the shed, was a narrow opening.

And a narrow opening was exactly what she had.

It was also what the short man had in mind too, by the looks of things, because after checking on Arnaud and then noting that the other two were still outside, he came up to Ishiko, and thrust a thick, hairy hand down the front of her panties. This turned out to be the last thing he ever did and his biggest ever mistake because Ishiko had, moments earlier, picked up an industrial-sized screwdriver that someone had carelessly left lying on the ground. She swiftly plunged it into the neck of her hapless assailant, instantly paralysing him and slowly killing him – with eyes wide open, his compact, hirsute body crumpled to the ground, spasming. Ishiko marvelled at how this man could have been so stupid, turning his back on her with weapons lying around and then attempting to have his clumsy way with her for a bit of quick and pointless gratification, but she concluded it was easy to underestimate people, and everyone makes mistakes, and these mistakes frequently occur at the most disadvantageous of moments.

The chances of her surviving had, however, only improved marginally: in the slow-motion environment that usually took over in these situations, she could see that the skinny man, about forty metres away, had just spotted his colleague with the screwdriver in his neck twitching on the floor of the shed. He was in the process of beginning to run, and at the same time he was alerting the driver, who had been standing facing him with his back to the shed. Time was clearly in short supply. Luckily, Ishiko wasn't scared. She was saving that for later because at this particular moment she had a series of decisions and manoeuvres to accomplish in order to stay alive, none of which could happen if she gave her fear any oxygen.

Instinct was an amazing thing. It allowed for a huge number of experienced-based calculations to be packed into a fraction of a second. If there'd been time to reason it through, Ishiko's thought process would have gone something like this: she'd already seen that the driver was carrying a Sig in his hand, and she had to assume the skinny man had one too. The dying man had no obvious gun for her to grab and she had no time to find out (and it went without saying, she certainly had no time to help Arnaud, let alone the inclination). Her best chance – and, really, her only chance – was to exit the shed through the opening behind her and gamble on the two men outside both coming into the shed through the open door. She knew they wouldn't be able to follow her through the opening and would have to leave the shed again the same way they came in, buying her valuable seconds...

In little more than an instant, she'd slithered out through the slit in the wall like an eel – was there a look of triumph in Arnaud's eyes as she looked back? was there a look of lust still in Shorty's? – and then she scuttled nimbly on all fours over the rocks outside and down to the water's edge like a crab. At this time of year, on this part of the south-west coast of Africa with its cold current, the sea temperature was a chilly fourteen degrees, but she went straight in, sliding into the cold, dark waters of the bay like a returned fish. Ishiko's given name might have meant "little stone", but her surname, Mizushima (水島), meant "water, island" and she'd always seen herself as a sea creature of one type or another. The cold water took her breath away but she ignored it and slipped out of her top and panties. She was now as naked as a fish and she started thinking like one. She'd become a Blacktail. Instead of swimming to the left through the safer waters of the bay and towards the beach about twenty metres away (which was what they'd expect), she swam right, towards the headland, through the churned and restless waters there, and out towards the crashing waves and the heavy swells of the open sea, the mighty Atlantic ocean, coming up for air only when she had to. The surface of the water was windblown enough, the evening dark enough, the whitewater from the surf zone extensive enough, and her lungs big enough for Ishiko the Blacktail to round the rocky point without being spotted.

The last time she looked, the two remaining men were running along the water's edge but in the opposite direction, towards the beach.

She managed to make it around to the ocean side of the headland and find a break in the ten metre cliff wall – a cove protected enough for her to be able to get ashore without being smashed against the rocks. Avoiding, on the way in, some rocks that were jutting out of the water like chimney stacks, the naked girl from Tokyo turned into a land creature again: after waiting for the right moment, she allowed the back of a wave to wash her up onto a rock platform and then she quickly clambered up the cliff face before the next set of waves arrived.

At the top of the cliff there was an abandoned, roofless building and she hid in it while she listened for voices and footsteps and planned her next move.

Her best chance was the highway, but it was probably too far to walk – how long had they been driving? – and anyway, if she started walking there was every chance they'd pick her up on their way back. There was nowhere to hide in this country. There didn't seem to be anyone else around either (although that wasn't necessarily a bad thing: what were the chances of them being well-intentioned? and well-intentioned towards a pale-skinned young woman with no clothes on?) It was Friday evening – almost night, now – and there were, it would seem, only murderers left.

So after satisfying herself the men weren't close by (at one point, despite the overwhelming roar of the ocean, she thought she might have heard distant voices), and that it was dark enough, she left her hiding place. Following a low curving trench which seemed to run roughly parallel with the outer edge of the headland, she cautiously made her way back towards where they'd parked the truck. Towards it, because she had a plan.

It was still there, the large yellow tow truck with its phallic-looking hydraulic boom winch. And just as she remembered, it had a high ground clearance. Plenty of room, in other words, for someone to hide themselves underneath it. She listened for the voices one last time – she needed to know where they were before she ran out into the open. At first she heard nothing, just the sound of the Atlantic surf behind her. But then she heard them again, the voices, more distinct this time, and she thought they sounded Russian (so no surprise there) but she couldn't be sure. They obviously weren't far away, but knowledge was everything and her instinct told her she had time, so she ran across the grey, truck-flattened gravel of the cul-de-sac, feeling no pain now from the sharp stones on the soles of her feet and scrambled under the truck. She thought like an eel again, and found an open cavity with a horizontal metal rod to wrap herself around. And so she curled her small, ivory-coloured body around it, cold skin on cold metal, and clung to it so tightly she as good as tied herself into a knot around it.

A set of footsteps crunched over the gravel towards the truck. At the same time, she heard the sound of the large sliding door clanging shut and being locked – was Arnaud still in there? – and then a second set of footsteps following the first. Nothing was said. The steps were slow but not carefree; she could tell these men were still looking for her...

And then nothing. Just the sound of the sea. If she hadn't wedged herself as high as she could into the bowels of the truck, she guessed she probably could have seen their shoes, because she knew they were *right there*. She didn't breathe, like all hiding prey that knows its life hangs in the balance. The men were metres away, centimetres, looking and listening, but facing which way she didn't know and she hoped they weren't looking at the truck. So she kept holding her breath and imagined she was at the bottom of a very deep, dark ocean. Which in a way, she was.

And then there was movement: footsteps on gravel, into the truck and doors slamming. Then the sound of the engine squealing and turning over, igniting and noisily roaring and revving into life, the whole truck shuddering and shaking like a wet dog. And then, at last, they were off .

It turned out to be harder than she thought – agony in fact, trying to hold on as the truck clattered and bounced and thudded its way back along the dirt road. No view this time, just a close-up of a permanent cloud of blinding dust and sand, and a spray of small stones. The first minute felt like an hour. And it went on. Ishiko would have died if she'd let go or fallen, so she had no choice and kept imagining she was that eel, wrapped around some pylon of a pier deep underwater.

The only factor in her favour was that they were travelling more slowly than they otherwise might have been. They were, in all probability, keeping an eye out for her (lending some support for the well-worn adage that what you're looking for is often right under your nose). She worked out that she'd have to hold on for at least half an hour, and she was counting the seconds in her head, she'd always had a stopwatch in her brain. Half an hour until they reached the bitumen highway and another ten minutes or less into Lüderitz. Which would be tempting (ten minutes versus maybe a cold, dark, two hour walk), except they might not be turning left and going back to Lüderitz but turning right instead. And when the vehicle starting moving into the turn it would be too late to get off – it would be hard enough as it was, getting clear of the vehicle with its large tyres and wide girth when it stopped momentarily (assuming it stopped at all). And hard enough to avoid being seen. In addition, getting off when they stopped in Lüderitz would be almost as hazardous – she didn't want to be anywhere near them when they got out.

It turned out to be academic. By the time they arrived at the critical point, the highway, Ishiko virtually fell off anyway, from exhaustion. The truck almost stopped but not quite – there was no traffic coming – so she had to be quick. She dropped straight to the ground, scraping her bare skin on the gravel but she hardly felt it, such was the pain of having to hold on for so long. As it happened, the truck turned right, to the south and away from Lüderitz. When it rolled on again, she didn't move, just lay there, hoping firstly that the wheels would miss her – which they did, but only just – and then that her skin colour would blend in sufficiently with the dirt of the road, in case either of the men checked their side mirror. She didn't look up again until the truck was at least a couple of hundred metres down the highway, heading off into the night.

She figured it was too risky to hitchhike into town. She would only see headlights and there'd be no way of knowing it wasn't the tow truck returning, still looking for her. And again, there was the fact she was naked, and even more generally, there was the range of types – people and weapons – she could expect to encounter. Even though she was confident she could look after herself in most situations, Namibia wasn't most situations.

With the desert night came the cold. Covered in cuts and scratches, she started walking, and keeping an eye out for headlights. The turn-off where they left her wasn't far from Lüderitz airport – a solitary landing strip but nevertheless capable of generating some traffic. And sure enough, a pair of headlights soon charged over the hill at her and she had to dive into the nearest depression to avoid being seen. It was a sports car as it happened, and what she wouldn't have given for a lift in a car. With a kind man. Or any kind of a man, or woman, other than the kind in that tow truck.

This pattern continued for the next couple of hours: walking briskly, composing music and poems in her head to keep her mind off her aching feet, headlights, diving for cover, watching the disappearing red dots, brushing off the gravel and setting off again.

Eventually she reached the outskirts of Lüderitz. It was only a small town (population 13,000), but she still had an interesting time of it, making her way past warehouses, and then houses and streets and cars, avoiding being seen and creating too much of a sensation.

Luckily the hotel was on the near side of the town. In the final tally only a couple of cars witnessed the extraordinary sight of her, and to her relief neither of the drivers so much as hit their horn, let alone caused her any trouble. And the only people in reception were a speechless couple in their sixties from Stuttgart and the receptionist who immediately handed her a towel to wrap herself in. The receptionist was an understandably concerned-looking white Namibian woman in her forties who Ishiko was able to keep from worrying too much by explaining that she'd been swimming and someone had stolen her clothes and then, of course, she'd managed to trip over in the dark... And yes, the water had been *freezing*, she had no idea what she'd been thinking.

The feelings of deliverance she felt when she entered her room, at last, were almost overwhelming, and certainly confusing, especially for someone in the habit of reducing everything to a calculation.

Furthermore, nothing was disturbed and the Decagon was still in its hiding place. They obviously hadn't tracked her there – hadn't known where she'd been staying. So if they hadn't decided to ransack every hotel room in town by now, she figured they probably weren't about to start. Even so, she took full precautions and kept the lights in her room off. Except for the light in the bathroom after she'd closed the door and where she had the longest bath of her life.

As she lay back in the warm, life-giving water – she could feel it soaking into her skin, her *fish* skin – she thought about the narrowness of her escape (so far) and for the first time since her breakout from the shed in the bay and that last look from him, she thought about Arnaud. She'd always sensed he was on the boat with another purpose – like herself – and she felt a strange, almost troubling sympathy for him. It wasn't enough to affect her plans or disrupt her mission, and even though she decided he was most likely dead by now, for a tiny hesitant moment in time, she wondered what his story was. She pushed it all out of her head though. Because sympathy and empathy were energy and time-wasting emotions. And, of course, she was still in danger.

How to get to Cape Town? She was thinking *this* time she should fly (via Windhoek), partly because a change in her modus operandi seemed a good idea, and partly because she could barely stomach the idea of travelling back along that exposed highway, the chances of being intercepted in the desert were too high. And a plane, a beautiful, sleek, sky-borne machine, banking and soaring like a bird, lifting off and away from that place, Lüderitz, was too wonderful a prospect.

Which was exactly why she decided to go by road. It was too obvious, the flying option, and there could be no more mistakes. Like visiting that church, for instance. (At least she hadn't gone with her initial instinct and brought her things with her, that would have been the end of the Decagon.) As it happened, Ula, the receptionist, who was of German stock and whose parents had moved to Namibia in the seventies, had a relative who could help. Her cousin, forty-three year old Helmut Martin, who ran a tea room in Ula's birthplace, Düsseldorf, was driving to Cape Town the next day, so a bus wouldn't be necessary.

29. <u>26° 41' 32" S 15° 14' 43" E</u> (B4 highway, Namibia)

Saturday, 17 August

They were on the road just after 8am the next morning, the powerful sun rising over the parched hills and distant mountains lining the eastern horizon.

The way Helmut had been looking at her when they packed the car, and the way he still was, when he shot her glances, Ishiko could tell he was attracted to her. She wondered if he'd seen her arriving the previous night, naked. He was powerful-looking and handsome, just what she imagined a dashing U-boat commander might look like. She deserved a little downtime, a little reward, she told herself. Perhaps, she dared to wonder, it might actually be an interesting trip.

As they shot along the bitumen highway though, in Helmut's hire car – a silver Nissan X Trail – back along the path of Ishiko's travails the previous night, a certain level of anxiety on her part was predictable. As was her relief when they passed the turnoff to the airport and she spotted, parked off the airport road and hidden from view to anyone approaching from Lüderitz – clearly positioned to catch her had she decided to leave by plane – the yellow tow truck.

She'd beaten them.

Misinterpreting her facial expression, Helmut asked her what was wrong. Did she wish she was flying to Cape Town? Ishiko smiled – something she rarely did – and it felt like her eyes were sparkling like diamonds when she said no, definitely not. Helmut gave her a grateful look, but said he didn't believe her and set about reassuring her: the desert roads of Namibia were not safe, it was true, but she shouldn't worry, she was safe with him, he'd drive carefully and did she know what the name "Helmut" meant?

'Protector!' he said (in English, for that was the language they were using).

Ishiko frowned, and her sparkling mood left her.

'A name cannot protect anyone out here.'

'Maybe not a name, but a person can. *And...*' He patted the side of his checked, loose-fitting, short-sleeved shirt. '... a gun can as well.'

'A gun. Can I see?'

But Helmut kept his eyes on the road, saying nothing for a moment. 'That may not be a good idea,' he said eventually.

'You do not trust me?'

'Sure, of course. But it's not a toy.'

'I know guns—'

'And anyway, it's a concealed weapon. The idea is you *never* get to see it. Not unless my shirt gets ripped off me for some reason.'

He smiled sheepishly. Ishiko was touched by his 'uncool'. So, not so dashing after all perhaps, but he reminded her of her.

'OK. So... what is the make,' she asked, although it was spoken like a statement.

'The make,' he repeated. Playing for time, as if it were a trick question. 'It's a Glock,' he said finally, not without a certain degree of pride.

'Model.'

'It's a... seventeen I think.'

'Second... third generation.'

'I'm ... not really sure...'

'Staggered column, or double stack magazine.'

'It's um...'

'How many rounds. In the magazine.'

'Ten. It's a ten round magazine. Hey. Ishiko. You really seem to know your—'

'The holster. It is too sweaty?'

'It's OK.'

'You must be careful. Glocks have no… on-off safety.'

Helmut frowned and smiled at the same time. Looked at her. 'No. They don't.' Eyes on the road.

'Which is also… advantage. You can fire…. quickly… without… need to… take off the safety.'

'Exactly,' Helmut said and they both stared straight ahead, with strange, crooked smiles on their faces. Ishiko's eyes were sparkling again.

Her contentment proved short-lived however. She developed an itch on her ankle and she bent down to scratch it. When she straightened up again, her eye caught a glimpse of something yellow in her side mirror. It was the tow truck, about two hundred metres behind them, This time Helmut wouldn't have been wrong about her facial expression, if he'd seen it. This time, it was fear.

She wondered how long it had been there for and whether it was gaining on them. She cursed herself. She must have been careless when they'd passed the airport turn-off. They must have spotted her with binoculars. The highway was straightening out after the earlier curves. The tow truck was growing in size in the mirror at an alarming rate. One hundred and fifty metres.

'You like driving fast?' she asked.

'Are we going too fast?'

'No. Out here, it is OK. You can go… fast. As you want.'

'The police—'

'No problem. Not out here.'

'Why not.'

As they picked up speed and the truck stopped growing – for the moment, although it wasn't shrinking yet either – Ishiko made another one of her quick calculations: her best strategy would be to make sure they stayed ahead of the truck until the next town – it was slightly uphill all the way, so this would be possible – and then slip away from Helmut at a petrol station stop (she'd tell him she needed to use the toilet) and steal a car, get back to Lüderitz… but she didn't have the heart to do it, they would kill or torture Helmut, it was a certainty. If he wasn't aware they were after him, he wouldn't stand a chance.

'Helmut. You see the… yellow truck? Behind us?'

He nodded. 'Mm-hm.'

'The men in that truck want to catch us. To hurt me.'

'What?'

'They tried to kill me. In Lüderitz.'

'Why?'

'You cannot let them catch up. You must stay ahead until the next town and leave the car there.'

'But—'

'Maybe change clothes too. And split up. We should split up. If they do not see us together maybe they will not hurt you.'

'But what is this?'

'There is no time. I am very sorry. I am trying to help you. But you must go faster. Please.'

Helmut appeared to consider the situation for a few moments and then applied more accelerator. He remained like this, staring at the long, arcing road ahead and looking in his rear-view mirror every few seconds.

'I am sorry,' Ishiko said again.

'It's all right. I've got a gun, remember.'

'And they have at least two.'

He thought about this. 'All right. Maybe we can outrun them. All the way.'

'Not after it levels out. Their truck is very powerful.'

Helmut breathed heavily, in and then out, through his nose. He didn't speak again for about a kilometre.

'I'm not deserting you,' he said.

'You must do this. Or they will kill you.'

Another kilometre flashed by. Helmut nodded to himself before he spoke.

'I have a better idea. Next time we get to a bend where we're hidden from view… we do a quick u-turn. They won't be expecting us travelling at them in the opposite direction. Not until it's too late.'

'No. It will not work—'

'We'll make it back to Lüderitz ahead of them. Don't worry, I'm a good driver. In Germany, I do rally driving. I'm a rally driver. Off-road. In the mud, on mountains.'

'No—'

'These roads? By comparison? Easy... what is it? easy peasy.'

'No! Helmut. You *must not do this.*' Ishiko was animated now. And she was never animated, as a rule. 'These men. They are *smarter,* much *smarter* than you think.'

'We'll see, won't we. We'll see how smart these jackasses are.'

Ishiko realised she'd made a mistake. She should never have told him. She'd broken her own rule. "Whatever it took". Always. To eliminate all potential threats.

But she'd allowed herself to *feel*. To feel emotion.

It served her right. She deserved whatever was coming.

They sped on in silence. Helmut, a picture of tight-jawed concentration, extracted every bit of speed he could. They pulled away, the incline was enough. And then, when the truck was about a kilometre behind, he found his corner, where the road curved more sharply around a low hillock of rock and sand. Low, but cover enough.

Just before the road straightened out again he slammed on the brakes and slid to a halt on the gravel shoulder, throwing up a cloud of dust, and then threw a quick u-turn across the bitumen and onto the gravel on the opposite side of the road (and almost leaving it altogether) and they were away again. Back around the hillock. By the time the yellow truck came into view, thundering towards them, the two vehicles were maybe four hundred metres apart and closing fast, the Nissan picking up speed as each critical second ticked by.

'Now, let's see if they're paying attention.'

But they were. The truck hit its own brakes and made an unexpected move: it slid to a skidding halt in the middle of the highway, at the last moment turning *side-on* to the flow of traffic, so it covered both lanes, all of the bitumen, leaving only the gravel shoulders on either side. Helmut's reflexes were good and he swung the wheel to avoid a collision – just enough to miss the truck but not enough to lose control. They flew past the truck on the shoulder and kept going. Helmut whooped with delight and triumph, and with a look of joyful confidence on his face, said something to Ishiko about how it was a common mistake for drivers to try to get off a soft shoulder too quickly, leading to a loss of control and...

'Watch out!'

Ishiko saw it before Helmut, a trench-like depression in the gravel shoulder in front of them. They were still going fast, maybe a hundred and twenty k's and when Helmut swung the wheel to get them back on the road again, the rest happened like a foregone conclusion and seemed to take an eternity: the rear wheels caught the ditch, bounced up and the back of the Nissan slid out and fishtailed and then snapped back in the opposite direction, but on the bitumen this time, and the whole vehicle flipped. Into the air. It was a long, airy somersault... it felt like a triple, but was probably one and a half... before they landed on the road, upside down, and slid off onto the gravel again, right off this time, clipped something, flipped again and then slammed against something impossibly hard.

Ishiko had blacked out. When she came to, they were upright but off the road in a ditch. She wasn't sure how much time had passed. Helmut had already undone his seatbelt. His shirt was ripped almost completely off and he was struggling with his holster, which had twisted around him awkwardly. He finally managed to release the fastener and produce his second generation Glock 17 with its ten round single stack magazine, and just as he twisted his body around and lifted his arm in the general direction of the yellow tow truck which had stopped about fifty metres away, their front windscreen exploded – red and white – as a departing bullet passed through it after crashing through Helmut's skull.

In what must have been one of his final acts, it seemed that Helmut had undone Ishiko's seatbelt for her, so by the time the next bullet slammed into the remains of the windscreen she was already out of its way. She kept her head down as a further pair of bullets hit the driver's side door and buried themselves into the dashboard above her head. Helmut's gun hand had fallen back inside and Ishiko was able to locate the Glock on the floor, next to the accelerator pedal when another bullet hit the vehicle, this time the petrol tank. Everything exploded, flames filled the air...

From the moments that followed, there was one vision in particular that stayed with her, as clear as a photograph: through the veil of flames, the two men, standing on the road between the Nissan and the tow truck, laughing, waiting for her to emerge, each with a gun in his hand, on the left the blond-haired driver in jeans and short sleeves and on the right, the skinny man in trousers and a jacket. At the time a thought flashed through her head, why weren't they worried about the Decagon? Sure it was metal, but even so…

But there'd been no time to pursue this thought. She knew she had a window of seconds. With the gun in her right hand, she pointed it at the driver and with her bare arm in the flames and the smell of her own burning arm hairs filling her nostrils, she fired.

The driver crumpled and stayed down, lifeless, and Ishiko immediately fired a second shot at the skinny man who had jumped far enough to avoid being hit. She fired again and reached over and grabbed her Muji bag on the back seat, pushed herself and her bag over Helmut's shattered face and out the window, and rolled on the ground, the whole time watching where the skinny man was headed. She fired her fourth round just as he was about to jump into the truck. He was forced to dive into a ditch instead. Ishiko did the same just before he fired back, twice, three times. And for the next couple of minutes they exchanged fire until Ishiko calculated that the skinny man had fired his tenth round. She gambled he was using a ten round Sig Mosquito like the one she'd seen the driver with back at the diamond mine and made her move. As she stood up, one more shot rang out (she must have miscounted!) but it missed and kept going, over the rocks and sand, seemingly never touching the ground and on towards the dry, brown hills in the distance. But then he was out, and when she pointed her Glock at him, the skinny man ran, off into the desert, like the bullet he'd just fired but in the opposite direction. He barely touched the ground either. He didn't know she only had one round left and she let him run. In no mood for a jog in the desert, and not wanting to risk wasting her final bullet, she walked over to the blond man's body, took his gun (the correctly identified Sig Mosquito) and fired the remaining five rounds in the skinny man's direction but he was already too far away. She then threw the Sig away, and walked over to the tow truck, jumped in – the driver had thoughtfully left her the keys – and started it up, all the while keeping an eye on the now stationary form of the skinny man, who was standing in the shimmering heat a couple of hundred metres in the distance, watching her departure like a sad lover on a pier.

With a double judder the truck bounced over the driver's body, and back onto the highway, passing the smoking wreck of the Nissan X Trail, with Helmut's charred remains just about visible inside. Despite her painfully burnt right arm, she managed to steer and grind her way through the gears as she headed for Lüderitz airport.

Before she reached the airport turn-off, she realised she'd have to rid herself of any association with the tow truck at the first opportunity, and when she spotted an embankment on the opposite side of the highway, about a kilometre from the airport, she took her chance. She made sure there were no cars coming (she doubted she'd seen more than about three cars all morning) and then slowed right down, got the angle right, steered the truck towards the edge. At the last moment she jumped out, clutching her bag and its precious cargo. Disappointingly, while the truck rolled and the hydraulic boom on the back snapped off like a twig, the vehicle didn't explode but simply came to rest on its side like a tired elephant. It would have to do.

She started walking – it wasn't far. She could see a scattering of buildings in the distance… and a plane! She was in luck, and picked up the pace. Knowing as well as anyone that guns and airports didn't mix, no matter how small the airport, she took the Glock with its one remaining round, found a convenient spot in a roadside ditch, and gave it a shallow grave.

The airport 'terminal' – a small, thirty metre long orange brick building with a slate-coloured roof, stark against the bright sands around it – wasn't far from the turn-off. Maybe a couple of hundred metres. The bitumen approach-road passed through a gate in the middle of a low, bordering fence and ran right up to the side of the building where more fencing, a closed gate and a small sand-drift prevented vehicles from going any further.

There was only one vehicle – a mini-bus – parked nearby. Ishiko dusted herself off as best she could and found a long-sleeved top in her bag to cover the burns to her right forearm. It was painful to wear, but she had little choice.

The aircraft parked on the small square of tarmac closest to the airport building was an Air Namibia Beechcraft 1900 – a twin-engined turboprop aircraft with a passenger capacity of nineteen.

After eyeing it in much the same way a starving man might look at a hot meal, she made her way into the building.

There was one official-looking person behind a makeshift check-in counter, and two groups of tourists sitting chatting in low voices on mismatched seating. Ishiko approached the person at the counter who proved to be bored and unhelpful. As it turned out the plane, which had just flown in from Windhoek, was flying on to Orangemund and Cape Town, but even though it wasn't full, the official told her that she would have to purchase a ticket in town. No amount of pleading was going to help, and the thought did cross her mind she could go back and recover the Glock and make them see things a little differently, but then the pilot walked in – tall, white and blond, and probably South African she thought – and a better plan presented itself.

With a wad of US dollars and, playing a greater role in the transaction, her sweetest smile, she managed to persuade him to take her. In more ways than one as it turned out, although that evening, in the Cape Town hotel room he invited her into, she did manage to retrieve the cash after all had been said and done.

30. <u>33° 55' 11" S 18° 25' 11" E</u> (Cape Town)

5.30am South African Standard Time (03:30 UTC)
Saturday, 19 October

It would soon be dawn and the beginning of a new day. The first rays of the sun would illuminate, to begin with, the top of Table Mountain and then the whole of central Cape Town – the City Bowl area, hemmed in by its amphitheatre of mountains – and the sun's early warmth would caress the pavement below, in Strand Street, easing away the cold of the previous night. And then the hustle and bustle of a city with things to do would start all over again.

But a new day also meant another day. On top of all the others. Two months had gone by and she'd heard nothing. Why hadn't they contacted her? They were supposed to have got a message to her after a month, either through her hotmail address or her fake Facebook page. The endless – and fruitless – visits to internet cafes had already gone beyond tedious and she'd recently had to invest in an iPad.

Most people would go mad in a hotel like the one she was staying in after a week, let alone two months. Recurring words and phrases which appeared in the customer review section of the hotel's TripAdvisor entry (ranked # 114 of 120 hotels in Cape Town Central) included "noisy" and "cockroaches" and "worst experience", but Ishiko didn't mind it. (Sure there were cockroaches, but so what, and anyway cockroaches were animals too, and why else did most people come to Africa but for the animals?) She was used to hardship, and however many complaints were levelled at this particular hotel, it was hardly the "concentration camp" that one of the guests had accused it of being. It was basic, but there was nothing wrong with basic. Not when you'd grown up an orphan in Tokyo, been mistreated and abused in every way for most of your childhood, had 'experience' with one of Japan's most extreme religious groups and settled on a Ukrainian mafia syndicate as your religion of choice. It was all a matter of managing your expectations: she demanded little more than a roof over her head and a door she could lock. She never expected the perks of her job to rival, for example, those of a girl she once knew, Nagisa, who used to review luxury hotels all around the world. Right up until she was raped and murdered on a Mombasa beach. So no, she had no complaints about the hotel.

Money wasn't a problem either. She could easily steal some if she needed to, but for the moment she still had more than enough, even though they'd stopped crediting her account for some reason. They were meant to keep paying her until she handed over the Decagon and that was supposed to have been a month ago. What had happened to them? They couldn't have forgotten about her.

There was one thing that kept her sane (more or less, although she was beginning to have her doubts): ever since her arrival in Cape Town, she'd been making daily trips to the Two Oceans Aquarium. It was a twenty minute brisk walk through a fairly soulless section of Cape Town's waterfront area, but once there, every time without fail, she'd head straight for the Ocean Basket Kelp Forest exhibit and sit and watch the fish swimming between the towering stalks of kelp – their silvery scales twinkling in the patches of underwater sunlight – and dream for an hour or more.

Once, she hired a car and drove as far south as she could go: she made the two and a half hour journey to Cape Agulhas, the southern-most point on the African continent. At the time she imagined it was as far from Tokyo as she could go as well (although she later found out Cape Town was technically further). And near the lighthouse there, she clambered over the rocks – like a crab – and sat, staring out over the vast, cold expanse of this southern ocean, with its white caps stretching all the way to Antarctica.

It never occurred to her to query whether she was on the right team. Her side – the Ukrainians – were involved in a relentless struggle against Drayle's people, the Russians, and that was all that mattered. The Decagon was in fact just one tiny piece of the whole puzzle, and yet the finer points of this overarching battle for supremacy held little interest for Ishiko: she felt no need to know any more than the little she already knew. It was all about faith.

She liked being given orders and she liked following them even more. Her instructions had been to book a diving trip aboard the *Diamond Moon*, wait for the successful recovery of the Isfahan Decagon – in the event it was down there that is, which as it happened, wouldn't you know it, it was (thus ending an otherwise enjoyable diving holiday) – obtain it "at any cost" (and in this regard, as all crew members were in some way connected to the Russians, they were expendable), make her way to Cape Town and wait to be contacted. That was meant to have happened a month ago, where *were* they? And what was she supposed to do now? Without further instructions?

This is what she hated more than anything. The state of being without instructions. The state of being "instructionless".

And now she was worried she was starting to see things, worried she was losing her mind. Three weeks ago she thought she saw the skinny man. In the middle of Cape Town – in Green Market Square, just a five minute walk from the hotel. She didn't think he'd seen her, but it had worried her so much that she took an hour to get back, just to make sure she'd lost him, in case he was following. And then a week later, she was certain she spotted the yellow tow truck. It was crossing an intersection about fifty metres from where she was standing, surfacing from nowhere like a submarine. It slid past, standing out as clear as day – how could you miss it, it was yellow – covered in dents and scratches from its roll down the embankment and still missing its hydraulic boom. And then it vanished again. But worse was to come.

On the day after the tow truck sighting, she saw Bertrand.

She knew it was impossible, that he was dead (and there hadn't been any doubt about that, she'd only made that mistake once and it wasn't a mistake you ever repeated). He was in a fish shop, down on the waterfront, not far from the Two Oceans Aquarium. He was just standing on his own, away from the other customers, staring at one of the fish laid out on the ice. When she saw him she got a shock and even though her head wanted to run, her feet wouldn't let her. So she just stood there watching him, terrified he would turn around and see her. And then he did. He straightened up and turned and looked directly at her, as if he knew all along she was standing there. There was nothing aggressive about his look, but nothing friendly either. He just looked at her, and then calmly turned away and walked off. It was as if he was telling her that she didn't matter, even to him. Even to the person she'd killed. She hadn't wanted to kill him, but how could she not *matter* to him?

She was too shaken to follow him, but after he'd gone, she went over to look at the fish he'd been staring at. It was a Red Kingklip, she knew it well, a local rock fish, prized for its white meat, eel-like in shape, but the most striking about this one was the look on its face. With its open mouth and wide eyes it looked shocked, like it had just been told something too awful to contemplate. As if it had just been informed of its own death. And next to it was a White Stumpnose, silvery and shaped like a bream, with big, beautiful, sad-looking black eyes, and she had the overwhelming feeling that it was her.

She saw Bertrand twice more, both times in the Aquarium, and always staring at fish before looking around at her and then walking off. Apart from anything else he managed to ruin the Kelp Forest for her and she was going to have to cease her daily visits, which constituted, in the circumstances, a serious setback.

Ishiko knew Bertrand was dead and that she was imagining him, so seeing him wasn't as worrying, in a way, as seeing the skinny man or the yellow tow truck. And on top of all that, only the day before, she'd been convinced a man in a grey suit had been following her. In a grey suit, like a shark. Not the skinny man this time, but he kept cropping up the whole day and it had taken all of her skills to finally shake him. Drayle had people all over, and something told her this was one of them. They had a thing about grey suits, she was told, but in a city like Cape Town, if you got jumpy every time you saw a grey suit you'd go crazy.

The sky was growing lighter and Ishiko could already see the Table Cloth – the cloud that often formed over Table Mountain, but as far as she was concerned they were all stupid names – the mountain was more like a coffin and the cloud, a burial shroud.

She was determined to do something that very day. Her life needed change – she could no longer visit the aquarium – and she decided the change would happen before she witnessed another dawn. She'd probably fly somewhere. A big city seemed like a good idea, somewhere bigger than Cape Town. Like London. A place you could, in an instant, with a lazy flick of your tail, switch from easily contactable to anonymous and vice versa. Somewhere she could hide, like a fish in coral and somewhere she could find her people if she had to, if she was desperate. Although she could never imagine herself as ever being truly desperate. Either solutions presented themselves, or you were dead, it was that simple.

She picked the Muji bag up off the floor, put it on the bed and unzipped it. And as she gazed at the cause of all upheaval (as she'd done every day for two months) – as she gazed at the Decagon, with its strange geometric patterns, and its hundred shimmering oceans of precious stones – she wondered why everyone wanted it so much. It was pretty enough (but since when did beauty ever get anyone – or anything – anywhere worth getting?). She supposed it was because it was old, but people really had to make up their minds what it is they wanted to worship: one week it was Youth, and the next it was Age. How was that consistent? It just went to show how foolish people were.

31. <u>26° 38' 59" S 15° 9' 8" E</u>
(Lüderitz, Namibia)

One hour later.
6.30am West Africa Summer Time (04:30 UTC).
Saturday, 19 October

As the full moon was sinking into the Atlantic ocean on the western horizon, the first rays of the sun were, at last, clearing the hills to the east and providing some much needed colour to the drab grey stone of the church walls, lending the building an orange tinge. It was an odd time – and place – for a meeting, here in the town's old church, but after two months in limbo, 'underground' as it were, Gerhard was willing to try anything. It was risky too, but it was a chance he had to take.

He'd been waiting for at least an hour before going inside, told to wait until sunrise *proper*, until the sunshine was actually hitting the church – strange instructions, and what if it had been cloudy? And anyway, was it even going to be open at this hour? Who goes to church at six thirty in the morning? But he supposed that was the point. The sunshine thing though, that was a real mystery.

The waters of the bay were beginning to take on their familiar indigo colour. The night's greys and blacks were giving way to the day's oranges and blues.

Before he attempted to enter, though, he checked himself, and went over it all one more time. Ever since he'd received the anonymous note, he'd been sweating over it: it was written on the back of an old Namibia postcard of a lone baobab tree (and to Gerhard's mind at least, quite phallic). Written in poor English, in almost childlike writing, it had simply said:

> *I know why things are that you are running. I can help you. Meet me inside church on the hill ***Felsenkirche*** at sunrise on Saturday morning. but DO NOT ENTER UNTIL <u>SUN'S RAY IS ON THE CHURCH</u>.*
> *Some ships only sail at night. XX*

Some ships only sail at night? The kisses were a mystery too, he assumed it was from a woman, which was an enticement in itself. Christ knows how long it'd been since he'd had a woman. Even just for company. Which is exactly why the whole thing could be a trap. Probably *was* a trap, when he thought about it like that.

But then again, he couldn't go on like this any longer. Ever since he'd escaped from the *Diamond Moon* in Walvis Bay, not a minute in his waking day had gone by without the thought that Drayle, or one of his men, was behind him, or had him in his sights. In the crosshairs. Ever since Ishiko had run off with the Decagon, Drayle had conducted a de facto 'purge' of the crew of the *Diamond Moon*. Bertrand was already dead, supposedly killed by Ishiko, but then what about Arnaud? Disappeared overnight. And the youngest of the crew members, Philippe, Gerhard was sure he'd seen him being pushed into a cabin before he disappeared: he was probably fish food at the bottom of the harbour by now, a pile of bones in the dark depths...

He'd successfully stayed under the radar for two months now, but he couldn't keep it up for ever. And he knew Drayle. There was every chance he'd have all exits out of Lüderitz covered – airport, highway (there was only one way out by road) and sea (the wharves would be the riskiest of all). And where was he meant to go? His homeland, Germany, was out of bounds for him these days – in fact all of Europe was – and the idea of Africa didn't excite him very much. India was where he wanted to go, or better still, Australia – Perth was his ultimate dream, paradise at the end of the world – but his best chance of doing that was finding the right ship. Which was never going to be easy without physically walking the docks, but he knew that Drayle knew that that was exactly what he'd be wanting to do.

And so, everything considered, the postcard represented a kind of hope. There was something about it, something odd enough to convince him. It was a risk worth taking.

He could hear music now, coming from inside the church.

He decided to get it over and done with and he made his way around to the arched doorway at the northern end of the building, framing two large oak doors. He pushed on one of them. It opened and closed again as he passed inside, swallowing him like a clam.

The interior of the church was all shadow and gloom; the sun had yet to find an easy way in. The organ was playing – this was the music he'd heard from outside – but he couldn't see the organist. Could those things play themselves? There was someone in the pews, though. It appeared to be a woman in a heavy grey dress and wearing a brown scarf. She was kneeling in the front row.

Gerhard made his way slowly down the red carpet of the main aisle, keeping a wary eye on the old woman, and glancing up at the vaulted ceiling and the macabre stained glass windows on either side. And occasionally turning around to see if he couldn't yet see the organist.

When he drew level with the kneeling woman, he'd almost reached the altar, it was directly in front of him. She still had her head down, and he was about to say something when she looked up and began to slowly turn her face towards him. At the same time, her hands separated. Gerhard wasn't sure what it was that he noticed first: the fact that she was not a she at all, but a man, unshaven with blonde eyebrows and blue eyes beneath his brown scarf... or the fact that he, the man, was reaching for something.

Gerhard ran.

He'd glimpsed a side exit and made for it, thundering and sliding over the polished floorboards. He was waiting for the gunshot – and the hot feeling in his chest as the bullet hit him, or the explosion of glass as it whistled inches from his ear and into a crucifixion scene, and the shout of outrage in his head, are they allowed to do this? in a church? – but it never came. No footsteps either, as he reached the wooden door.

Naturally it was locked.

Panicked and pumped full of adrenalin, he dashed down the side aisle, had to get to the main entrance, the way he came in, not stopping to look behind him, no time, his only chance was to get out fast, and there was still no sound, no sign of anything happening there, no gunshots, no shouting, nothing at all...

Nothing until he almost had his hand on the oak door at the entrance. It was the strangest thing, like a tap on the back. A punch almost, but not painful. And he felt sleepy all of a sudden. Impossibly tired. In slow motion, his momentum carried him on, twisting, past the double doors, and down, sliding, under book racks, candle stands, a mess crashing around him, his head cracking into stone and then he seemed to slice *through* the stone and he kept going, or that's what it felt like, forever onwards into the dark night until, at long last, it all slowed down and stopped and he could rest his punished body, eternally grateful for the opportunity to be relieved of the obligation to keep breathing.

32. <u>26° 38' 59" S 15° 9' 8" E</u> (Lüderitz)

Ten minutes later
6.50am West Africa Summer Time (04:50 UTC).
Saturday, 19 October

An old woman of about eighty-five, in a pale blue dress and a black velvet hat, entered the church through the oak doors of the main entrance.

As she went to dip her hand in the holy water, she saw, to her great distress, a tanned man in his fifties, lying on his stomach in a pool of blood on the floor, his neck twisted around at an awkward angle, head jammed against the wall, eyes wide open, and surrounded by a wreckage of candle stands and scattered books. He'd been shot in the back and wasn't breathing. In fact, he was dead.

33. <u>15° 19' 1" S 52° 9' 33" E</u>
(Over the Indian Ocean, east of Madagascar)

7.50am Eastern Africa Time (04:50 UTC)
Saturday, 19 October

It was at precisely the moment the old woman, hand poised over the holy water, caught sight of Gerhard's body just inside the doors of the *Felsenkirche* in Lüderitz, that Commandant Laurent Ruart of the *Préfecture de police de Paris* discovered he was in the process of getting an inopportune and unwanted erection.

Ruart was onboard Air Austral flight 974 from Paris to Saint-Denis, Réunion. He lowered his tray table as a temporary fix, and then opened his window blind, leant forward and looked out. Sunshine and blue ocean, all the way to the horizon. He glanced at his Breitling. They'd been in the air for ten hours. Fifty minutes to go before they landed in Saint-Denis and not a moment too soon. He was getting erections – fine at the right moment, *more* than fine – and his back ached. For a moment he wondered if the girl next to him – in her twenties or thirties, brown hair, quite attractive – clocked his erection or figured out the tray table ruse, and then he wondered that if so, whether it could possibly have turned her on at all, and then he thought of Marine and wondered how she was getting on with Jack.

His wife Marine, that is, and his son Jack. Jack had been out of sorts when Ruart had left their apartment, possibly jealous of his upcoming adventure. Jack was ten. Madeleine, their daughter, had an altogether more passive, accepting nature (amazing for a French girl! he was very proud of her. And Jack, too, of course).

He'd originally been booked to fly to Cape Town which was, up until only two days earlier, the location of the last known sighting of Dominique Drayle. But he'd been forced to change his ticket (at his own expense, this was a private trip after all, not a professional one). A source in Saint-Denis on Réunion island had informed the *Préfecture* that he'd just received information suggesting Drayle's yacht, the *Diamond Moon*, had been seen in early September moored in Le Port, the harbour town about twenty minutes drive out of Saint-Denis. The proper papers hadn't been filled out (in other words, money had passed hands, as usual) so no-one knew exactly where it had come from or was going to or what it was doing there. (And why he was just being told this now, he had no idea). No-one had seen Drayle either. But it was, for the moment, all he had. Or, at least, it was better than the older trail ending in Cape Town. If Réunion drew a blank though, that's where he'd probably have to go next.

If truth be told, he was looking forward to it. To a little spell in tropical Réunion. He'd never been to either place, there or South Africa, but Réunion held a certain exotic appeal for him. And it was, at the same time, French. Not that he minded honing his English skills which were really quite decent, but questioning people in the course of *l'interrogatoire* was always that little bit easier in your own language (although a heavy accent, and the odd feigned misunderstanding could come in quite handy at times). Not to mention the fact that Réunion was officially a region of France and as such used the euro, thus sparing him the nuisance of having to deal in an unfamiliar currency and its awkward mathematics. And what's more – most importantly of all, if he was honest with himself – there were the Réunion *girls* of whom he'd only heard positive things, first and foremost that they were beautiful. Not that he'd ever cheat on Marine, but there wasn't anything wrong with looking at the menu even if you couldn't order from it, no? Ruart, with his black hair, and handsome Gallic looks was, at thirty-six, and always had been, despite his logical brain, a little over-awed by attractive women who paid him even the slightest degree of attention – it was something, the whole process, which never ceased to amaze him. But he'd never cheat on Marine. His colleagues in the *Préfecture* all did that sort of thing – almost to a man – but not Ruart. Not before, not ever.

Flying over a sunny, equatorial ocean made night-time Paris feel like ten light years away, not just ten hours. The day had been grey (it had only been yesterday!) and the night cold, and even the full moon, after the Boeing 777 had pulled clear of the heavy cloud, had looked miserable and frigid. It was the same moon, though, as the one that would have been shining down on them as they crossed the skies of Africa, and if he'd stayed awake long enough, he could have proved it to himself. And perhaps it would have made him feel closer to his children. As it happened, he dozed off over a dark and uninviting Mediterranean Sea.

34. <u>33° 53' 49" S 151° 10' 45" E</u> (Zanzibar Hotel, Newtown, Sydney)

4.45pm Australian Eastern Daylight Time (05:45 UTC). Saturday, 19 October

It had only been three hours since he'd arrived in Newtown. And in that modest timeframe, 'would have' had turned to 'should have'. Because before, it was a question of what had happened, and what he thought he probably *would* have done. And now it was all about what was happening, and what he very, most definitely, *should* have done.

Mikkel was downstairs in the Zanzibar Hotel and just about the worst thing that could have happened, had just happened.

He'd had no luck at James's place, and he'd backtracked down Australia Street to the pub, thinking he'd have a drink – hair of the dog, was his excuse – while he waited to hear from James. And he was still waiting. Countless Coopers Pale Ales later.

He should have sobered up.

He should have gone to a hotel and slept it off.

He should have worked out a plan. He knew it wasn't as simple as contacting Perth, he had to tread carefully. If the Broome police were involved. And who'd believe him now anyway, a forensics officer, sozzled in Sydney?

He should never have bought that last drink. Why?

Because now, on the other side of the room, just arrived and staring at him, was the Korean. His batik-clad, worst nightmare.

Mr Song.

What he *should* do was go over there. Have a little chat. They were in a public place, so what was the guy going to do? But he, Mikkel, was too drunk, so that ruled that out.

What he *should* do was leave. But it was pouring out there, pissing down and yeah, nice one Deano, yeah, I *should* have brought my umbrella, you're right.

I bloody well should have.

35. <u>20° 52' 25" S 55° 26' 48" E</u>
(Saint-Denis, Réunion)

11.10am Réunion Time (07:10 UTC)
Saturday, 19 October

An hour and a half after landing at Roland Garros airport in Saint-Denis, Ruart was standing at the northern end of the island, staring out to sea, and sucking in the warm ocean air. He'd seen the island's black volcanic sands when they landed, so he'd already realized his mistake. When anticipating the tropical delights in store, he'd been thinking not of Réunion but of Mauritius, two hundred kilometres to the east. Mauritius, with its white sands and beautiful women. Ah well, served him right, and it was probably a myth anyway, no? These things usually were.

And anyway, he was here on business.

Of course, there was more to be said for Réunion other than the fact that it was French and used the euro. It was beautiful in its own right – it was spectacular. Ruart, who had already checked into the Austral Hotel (Air Austral, Austral Hotel, everything was "Austral"), had taken a walk through the streets of Saint-Denis and then along the *Sentier Littoral Nord* – the northern coastal path – as far as *le Barachois* and its oceanfront promenade lined with cannons pointing out to sea. In front of him was a dark, rocky beach and the endless ocean. Rearing up behind him, and the town, were the volcanic ridges leading up to the mighty *Piton des Neiges*, the highest peak on the island, rising to over 3,000 metres (which was really something for an island a mere seventy kilometres long). At the other end of the island was the equally imposing *Piton de la Fournaise* which, while not quite as tall as its quiescent brother, was a highly active volcano – one of the most active in the world actually, a real blowhard! The whole island was part of an enormous shield volcano structure rising from the depths of the Indian Ocean, a process which had begun over five million years ago and which was still visibly continuing today, courtesy of the *Piton de la Fournaise*. If nothing else, dramatic scenery made a welcome change from the flatness, the pancake topography, of his home town Paris.

There was one image, though, he couldn't quite get out of his head. When they were flying in, he had a breathtaking view of the island out his side of the plane, and apart from glimpsing the mist-shrouded summit of the *Piton des Neiges*, he could also clearly see the houses hugging the ocean clifftops of La Montagne, just next to Saint-Denis (in fact he could see them now), and in front of one in particular, someone had constructed a swimming pool. It looked unbelievably precarious, hanging as it did over the two hundred metre drop down to the highway and the crashing waves below. Was this really necessary? Was the show-off value of this really worth the risk of a tragic accident? And they were on a volcanic island, it wasn't so smart, surely, to tempt fate by building houses in this way? Or perhaps that was the point? Human negligence, as a rule, tended to make his blood boil, particularly human carelessness and stupidity that led to injury or death. But this house, this pool, it made him think: what was a little negligence next to the overwhelming and unpredictable and violent forces of Nature such as those found on an island like this one?

Not in the mood for commencing his enquiries just yet, he crossed the road and picked out a nearby cafe at random, the first one he came to. (He was more a man of logic than a man of instinct. Given he was in a foreign country and without his guide book, and given he was just as likely to make a bad choice as a good one if he relied on his instinct, he left instinct out of the picture altogether.) He sat down at a table – all the tables were outside, all had a view of the sea. There was no problem finding a place to sit either, although the place wasn't exactly empty: this part of the town had a reputation for good food.

The girl who came over was, he estimated, about twenty-two, with dark brown eyes and an Indian/African look to her which he found interesting. And she had the most spectacular smile. He had difficulty understanding her at first though, as she was speaking a blend of French and Creole in a Réunion accent. He smiled back and ordered some food and drink, really for something to do rather than to stave off that false sense of hunger you get from doing nothing in a plane for half a day. Keeping it local, as was his usual approach, he chose the pork *sarcives* (appetising little pieces of pork and honey on cocktail sticks) and indicated he'd like to wash them down with the local beer, called a *Dodo*.

After watching the girl walk away with his order, he put his Police sunglasses back on (an unfortunate brand name but hey, *c'est la vie*), pulled out a copy of the previous day's *Le Monde* which he'd brought from Paris and began to read it distractedly while also looking about at his surroundings and the people, and just soaking up the rays generally, making the most of his first trip to the tropics in years.

Looking around there were eleven other people outside, at this particular cafe, occupying five tables between them (Ruart was the only one on his own). There was an older sensible-looking grey-haired couple; a young, fat couple, speaking in a harsh language he couldn't quite pick up, the guy's skin as white as snow, just off the plane, possibly German or Austrian; two young guys speaking the local dialect who looked like they were on a lunch break from desk jobs; a middle-aged black man (as in very black, as black and shiny as obsidian) in a purple shirt, talking to an Indian-looking woman; and, furthest away, there was what sounded like an Italian man with a ponytail in a large, green and white Hawaiian shirt (but not large enough to hide his pot belly) who was speaking Italian and English in equal measure and laughing and smoking and showing off in front of two girls who also had a Mediterranean look to them.

Ruart was looking at them, but none of them was looking at him. It actually felt like everyone was making a point of *not* looking at him. Even the plant on his table – a small succulent, with pudgy leaves – gave the impression its attention was elsewhere, on the miniature cactus at the next table possibly – a silly thought, he knew, and from someone who wasn't prone to whimsy. He put it down to jet lag. Not that a person who'd only passed through two time zones had any right to a claim of jet lag, no matter how long the flight...

'Excuse me?'

He turned, in the direction of the voice, and found himself looking into the eyes of a girl – one of the two women who were being entertained by the Italian with the ponytail. She spoke French with an Italian accent. She had a cheeky smile and her eyes were so dark and reflective he could see himself in them, which was, actually, extremely discomfiting to say the least.

'Yes?'

'Do you have a light?'

She was nonchalantly, suggestively, dangling a cigarette in the space – in the maybe thirty centimetres of air – that lay between her lips and his. In the background, the Italian man was looking over, no longer laughing. Was he jealous?

'I'm sorry but no I don't.'

By the time the girl had moved on in search of greener pastures, he discovered his beer had arrived.

A beer had rarely tasted so good.

Later, after he'd polished off the sarcives and the beer, it was time to go. Time to get to work. Before he got up, he looked at the label on his beer bottle with its dodo bird logo. And compared it to an ad for the same beer on a nearby wall: '*Le Dodo Lé La!*' – Creole for "The Dodo Is Here!". Wasn't the dodo from Mauritius? But he guessed that once you'd achieved the dubious honour of becoming extinct, anyone had a right to claim you, it was open slather.

All too often, things are not as they first appear (a fact Ruart was frequently reminded of in his particular line of work), and a quick internet search on his phone revealed that the bird depicted on the beer label was supposedly the *white* dodo, a bird which, until recently, was thought to have once existed on Réunion. It was, however, now considered that such a belief was unfounded: another theory blown, another good story ruined.

Maybe the *Diamond Moon* was another white dodo? Maybe *it* had never been here either?

* * *

A twenty minute, twenty kilometre taxi ride west along the *Route du Littoral*, hugging the island's northern edge, under a long wall of volcanic cliffs (the ones with the pool on them), delivered him to the town of Le Port on the *Pointe des Galets* and the yachting marina there, the *Port de Plaisance*.

The Port Captain's office, with a design supposedly inspired by the Sydney Opera House, was a small, white, sail-shaped building, feebly embraced by a clump of palm trees, along with some casuarinas and screw pines, the latter being ubiquitous on the island. Actually Ruart knew all about the common screw pine because he'd read about it on the plane – it was a type of pandanus (*pandanus utilis*), discovered by a French naturalist, Baron Jean-Baptiste Geneviève Marcellin Bory de Saint-Vincent (1778-1846), who was forced to leave his ship due to illness in Mauritius while sailing with Nicolas Baudin's expedition to Australia in 1801. Bory de Saint-Vincent – who was even at the battle of Austerlitz (1805) – was one of the first naturalists to attempt a biogeographical classification of the oceans.

Ruart loved these kinds of facts, these pieces of pure information, with little if any room for argument. He lapped them up like a thirsty dog at a water bowl. He was frequently accused of being a slave to the facts (by his colleagues at the *Préfecture* and his wife Marine in roughly equal measure), and he always took it as a compliment.

And it wasn't just raw facts he liked, but connections between them. Connections and coincidences. He liked, for example, the Australian connection, such as the marina office being linked to the Sydney Opera House, and the plants near it being first identified by a naturalist on his way there. An insignificant coincidence to most people, but not to him. After all, all coincidences could at least theoretically be explained (they coincided for a reason, even if that reason wasn't always known or even knowable) and all were interesting by the very fact that they were coincidences, that is, there was a link between two apparently unconnected things which was yet to be uncovered. Because you first had to look at what is meant by the word "coincidence" – and the word was the same in French and English (which was no "coincidence" because the English word came directly from the French – this was a perfect example of an apparent coincidence which was not a coincidence at all, once you were equipped with all the facts). A coincidence in the true sense was more than merely a "co-incidence" of events: there was a sense of there being similarities so close to make it all too improbable, too flukey; a sense of there being something mysterious connecting the events which was not yet obvious. According to the dictionary definition, a coincidence was "a chance occurrence of apparently connected events". This was curious to Ruart as in his view there was no such thing as chance: it only looked like "chance" when you didn't understand how it happened. And once you understood that nothing ever happened by chance, that everything happened for one reason or another, then coincidences were merely mysteries to be solved. The real question was never "is this a mere coincidence or is there a link?" but rather "what is the nature of the link between these two events, and is it relevant to anything I want to know about?". And thus, in Ruart's opinion, the true definition of a coincidence was really "the occurrence of two or more apparently connected events, the link between which is yet to be explained". And a coincidence that turned out to be a link that was relevant to an inquiry he was making, Ruart thought of as being "sparky". He was always, in his job, looking for "sparky coincidences".

As it turned out, a sparky coincidence was just around the corner.

Literally. Because as soon as they'd arrived at the marina office, and he'd instructed the driver to wait, and stepped out of the vehicle into the heat, and squinted at the glary tropical sky above and walked around to the front of the building.... there was the guy with the ponytail again, the potbellied Italian in the green and white frangipani shirt. He was walking out of the office building and although he wasn't looking in Ruart's direction at first, at the last possible moment he turned his head and glanced over – it was more of a smirk actually, and was one of those looks that seemed to suggest he knew Ruart was there all along. Coincidence? It was a small island, sure, but not miniscule. Ruart was seeing sparks.

He wiped away a film of sweat that was already beginning to form on his forehead and watched the man as he sauntered off, a spring in his step as he lit a cigarette. He almost expected the guy to launch into an aria, he looked that cheerful. He wondered where his companions were, the two girls, and imagined they were on his yacht – he looked like the yacht-owning type – and Ruart was about to follow discreetly when the guy suddenly stopped and greeted someone who gave the impression of appearing from nowhere.

It was a man in a suit – creased, as though he'd just emerged from a long-haul international flight and he could well have, as Réunion was a long-haul flight away from just about everywhere. He wore clear, rectangular glasses, and there was a certain paleness, and a certain corpulence about him (was he English?). The suit, apart from being creased, was charcoal grey which, frankly, in this climate looked just a little bit ridiculous. A little sad-looking, too: it was cut a fraction too short for its wearer. He was obviously not French: in France, such a fraction was an *in*fraction. The blue and grey checked socks and brown suede shoes most certainly didn't help. At least the man was tieless, his one apparent concession to the tropical climate.

The Italian was animated, even more so now than before, and greeted this non-descript character as though he were his long-lost brother. The man in the suit, though, was far more subdued and didn't even raise a smile, treating the Italian, Ruart thought, like he was a long-lost pain in the neck, and this appeared to have the effect of dousing the Italian's enthusiasm somewhat. At one point it seemed as if they were aware of his presence – the suit looked around in his direction, briefly, before the Italian seemed to subtly manoeuvre him to face the other way again. Was it simply his imagination, this conspiratorial atmosphere, or was there something behind it? When the two men eventually began walking away, the suit turned around one more time. Was it to look at the marina office with its Opera House design, or to look at Ruart, to see if he was following?

The really strange thing was that moments after the man in the suit had disappeared again, he couldn't remember his face. Not at all, not for the life of him. As hard as he tried, nothing. A blank. And of all people, Ruart, a policeman! A facial identification session – had he been conducted through one, even straight afterwards – would have resulted in nothing but embarrassment. He decided to put it down to the heat and jetlag. Or sleep-deprivation, whatever you wanted to call it. He was slipping, though, definitely losing his edge. He promised himself to lift his game from now on. Be more "on the ball" as they say in English.

In any event, he decided to let the two men go, whoever they were. He, for one, was pleased he wasn't in his suit (he hadn't even brought one, this time, it not being an official trip), and he was not at all unhappy with his choice of mustard shorts, black polo shirt and sky blue leather boat shoes. A slight breeze puffed in from the sea and rustled the hairs on his legs as he turned and made his way out of the sun and into the building with the sails - a design that made it look like it could have been a church for those who preferred to worship at the altar of the god of the winds.

Once inside, he removed his sunglasses and ran a hand through his sweat-dampened hair, slicking it down, and in the process inadvertently flashing his Breitling watch (a prized acquisition and his favourite accessory, it was the Superocean 44 model with steel band, black face, automatic and water resistant to two thousand metres). He was greeted by a man who claimed to be the clerk of the Port Captain's Office, a cheerful local who was overflowing with enthusiasm or, as the English would put it, "as keen as mustard" (*moutarde*, like Ruart's shorts), especially after Ruart had indicated he was from the *Préfecture de police* in Paris and was making some discreet inquiries – and of course, a policeman in Paris is a policeman in Réunion, another wonderful thing about this island paradise! Yes, for sure, the smiling clerk was only too willing to help, and yes, he had heard of the *Diamond Moon* or, hang on, wasn't it the *Golden Moon?* but yes, a superyacht had visited recently, yes, maybe a month or two ago. As far as this man could remember though, there hadn't been room in the marina – the yacht had been too big, it was *fifty metres* for the love of God – and it had been moored near the naval base in the commercial section of the harbour, the *Commandant* should make inquiries there.

So it was back in the taxi, and they passed through streets with names such as Rue Walt Disney and Rue Charles Dickens (as if he'd landed in some kind of fantasy land), and as they did, he was doing all he could to not think about his sister Constance and what she had suffered at the hands of Dominique Drayle. But this was impossible, he was only on Réunion to find Drayle, he was thinking about Drayle the whole time, how could he not think about that terrible night the previous April? Palm trees and sun-drenched warehouses were sliding by outside, but the images began again, the cold night-time darkness inside the Paris apartment, the door slamming shut with the violence of an explosion, the screams that caused the neighbours to call the police...

Mercifully, this time, the familiar sequence was cut short as the taxi pulled up outside their destination, a plain brick building painted white, with a small sign outside indicating the harbour master was out between the hours of 1pm and 3pm. His Breitling told him it was still only ten to one. The front door was, however, firmly locked, with no-one visible inside. He grumbled to himself. Clearly these Creoles operated in their own time zone, and a flexible one at that.

36. <u>20° 56' 6" S 55° 17' 4" E</u>
(Le Port, Réunion)

12.55pm Réunion Time (08:55 UTC)
Saturday, 19 October

'The *Diamond Moon*? I'll say! The superyacht, right? Silver. It was here all right, last month. The first *week* of last month. First week of September.'

Ruart had just struck it lucky.

'And how do I know that?' the man continued. 'Because some bastard on that boat stole my coffee machine. A beautiful Marzocco, handmade in Florence.'

After he'd given up on the harbour master, he'd noticed a street vendor just down the road selling coffees and croissants to the passing sailors and tradesmen and office workers. He was working out of a converted Renault Scenic – he'd cut away the back section and substituted a tray holding all his equipment and food – and he'd distributed a number of stools around for people to sit on. It was quite a social scene, the customers looked like they were from the four corners, mostly men but one or two young women: there were Creoles, Africans, Chinese and Europeans, including a couple of French sailors. The host himself looked like a mix of all of them, but spoke perfect French and with a mainland accent too – he could have just arrived from Paris himself. Ruart had got talking with him on the off chance he'd seen anything. Just went to show, it was always worth asking.

'I paid a visit to Théo,' the man was saying, '...that's Théophile, the harbour master... it was for no time, half an hour at the most, and when I came back, it was gone and that stinking boat was sailing out of the port. With my coffee machine! It had to have been them, who else could it have been? And there was no point in telling the police, they're just a bunch of lazy slackers, and it was out of their jurisdiction anyway, and the Navy... They're worse! You'd think I'd be well protected here, next to the base, but no, not at all! No! God help us if there's a war.'

Ruart nodded.

The man's eyes narrowed. 'You're not one of them are you? From the yacht?'

'Laurent Ruart. I work at the *Préfecture de police* in Paris. One of those slackers you mentioned.'

The man ignored the jest and held out his hand. 'Éric.' They shook hands and Éric started making another coffee for a customer, talking to Ruart at the same time. 'So are you chasing them? What are they wanted for?'

'Did you see the crew?' Ruart countered. 'Get a good look at any of them?'

Éric didn't reply, busy with his coffee.

Was he thinking?

'Or... what about where they were headed. The *Diamond Moon*. Do you know its next port?'

The barista still said nothing. Poured out the coffee he was working on, threw a croissant on a china plate, saw off another happy customer, until he finally came over and spoke in a low voice.

'There are many pairs of ears here, my friend. It wouldn't do for me to be known as a talker, you know? You understand? I will tell you what I know, but first, you tell me something Inspector. What's your interest in this?'

'Let's just say we have a particular interest in the man we believe to be the boat's owner. Dominique Drayle.'

'What's he supposed to have done?'

Those images again, flashing into his head. *Constance...*

'We want to question him about a lot of things.'

'Such as?'

Ruart looked at him for a moment. 'Theft, rape, murder, armed insurrection… the questioning won't be short.'

Éric nodded and again looked around to see if anyone was listening. In a slightly exaggerated way, it seemed. Was he for real?

'If we ever find him,' Ruart added.

'OK, well listen.' Éric looked as though he was weighing something in his mind. 'The *Préfecture* in Paris, you say?'

He began making another coffee, although no-one had asked for one. He unhooked the portafilter and belted it down hard on a narrow wooden bin to empty the used coffee. Took a scoop of ground coffee and refilled the portafilter. Packed it down and wiped off the excess. Purged the machine with two short sharp hisses. Reinserted the portafilter.

'First up,' Éric said finally, 'Théo won't help you. The harbour master. He's a stickler that one. Have you got a warrant? Anyway, lips like a clam, he has a strange sense of loyalty to anyone who sails into his port. He'd go to the guillotine before he blabbed. Even if you were to offer him money.'

He cast a little look at Ruart and then retrieved the espresso from the machine and handed it to him. 'On the house.'

Even though the house was a car.

Ruart sipped on his coffee and waited for Éric to continue. Let his eyes follow the line of the side of the mountain in the distance… a ridge rising gradually, and draped in a seemingly innocent meringue of cloud, pretending to be moving along but going nowhere and spreading darkness. And further along, etching a shadow of its own, a jagged crack in the foothills, a crooked valley into the mountainous interior. There was something forbidding about it. A hidden abyss. *Sadak In Search Of The Waters Of Oblivion.*

'The yacht you're after was sold,' Éric said suddenly.

'Sold?'

'While it was here in Réunion. To a man called Bob. An Australian.'

Australian? More sparks.

'Can't remember the surname. Wait…' Éric leaned over the tray of the Renault and pulled out a wooden box full of business cards. Handed one to Ruart. 'That was him. Bob… Walman. Yeah, he was here, ordered about five coffees. Big man. And very happy with his purchase, he was telling everyone.'

The card said "Bob Walman, Executive Chairman, Kensington Mines" followed by his contact details in Perth, Western Australia.

So why hadn't he heard about this sale? The *Préfecture* had their 'man in Saint-Denis' – they were never going to rely on the local police, Éric was right, they were "slackers" – so how had their man missed it? Éric seemed to read his mind.

'They kept it quiet. I am not sure if even Théo knew. It was a quick sale, boom, and then it was gone again. With my Marzocco!'

Ruart looked at the replacement. Looked pretty good, but not, it was true, a Marzocco.

'So Bob stole your coffee machine?'

'No no no. Not Bob. He didn't sail it away. Bob flew back to Australia after the sale. The same people who arrived in the *Diamond Moon* also sailed away in it.'

'Even though the yacht was no longer theirs?'

Éric shrugged. 'I assume Bob paid them for it. Charter basis. He told me he was picking it up again in… now where was it…?'

And again Éric struck a pose, it was one of those exaggerated theatrical gestures – this time it was forefinger to his chin, eyes to the sky, looking like he was thinking. And then a quick look at Ruart to make sure he was catching it. Was he pretending to think? Or did he want Ruart to *know* he was pretending? What game was he playing? Did he want money? He'd already made a reference to it, when he was talking about the harbour master. Was that it?

'Ah yes,' he said finally. 'In Bali. He was going to sail it from there.'

Ruart nodded, looking at this man carefully, trying to deconstruct him. Letting him make the next move, waiting for him to reveal his cards.

'So Inspector…'

And here it was.

'It's always possible that I could find out more. But it *is* a risky business, so…'

So he was asking for money.

'So?'

'Well I'm happy to make some inquiries for you…. Particularly if you get me my Marzocco back…heh heh… But first I, er…'

But first he wanted a little incentive, and Paris could afford it. *Is that what you are thinking, Mister Éric?*

'I will need to know more background,' Éric said. 'More about this… Dominique… Drague.'

'Drayle.'

Why was Éric so determined to know more? Why was it being made a condition for helping? Unless it wasn't a condition at all and this was part of his game? Perhaps he was pretending he didn't know these things when he really did? And if so, why? Because he wanted to find out how much Ruart knew? Why?

Clearly, he was going to have to tread carefully.

Ruart had no intention of bringing up his personal investment in this – what happened to his sister – and there was nothing to be gained by running through the all too extensive list of Drayle's offences committed in the course of cutting his swathe across the globe, even if Éric wasn't testing him and didn't know about them already. They were public knowledge anyway. On the other hand, he decided to feed Éric a few scraps of information about the *Diamond Moon*, and work out for himself whether his new coffee-making friend was what he claimed to be, whether he was being, as the English say, "on the level".

'We know,' Ruart began, choosing his words carefully, 'that the *Diamond Moon* was supposedly running dive tours to shipwrecks off the Namibian coast. Ostensibly for people interested in the historical aspect. And for the pure thrill of wreck diving. All was not as it seemed however.'

Éric's face was a perfect blank. Not a twitch.

'We believe this diving enterprise was merely a front. Drayle and his team were, in fact… running drugs.'

He made this last part up, of course, as a test. He knew drugs had never been Drayle's thing – too plebeian, too vulgar – and that, in fact, he was running an illegal trade in art and ancient artefacts, including the so-called *Isfahan decagon* which the Japanese girl, Ishiko, had stolen and managed to escape with, immediately after killing the dive instructor Bertrand; and he knew Drayle was the boss of a breakaway Russian mafia organisation called Black Star and that Ishiko was acting for a rival one, possibly Ukrainian or Georgian. But he was keeping all this to himself for now. And he certainly wasn't about to tell Éric about the disappearance of Arnaud, his informer on the *Diamond Moon* who'd been posing as a dive tour passenger. Originally a dockworker from Marseilles, Arnaud was tough – an ex-mercenary who'd fought in Chad and the Congo and someone Ruart had thought would have had no trouble looking after himself. And even though it appeared his remains had been discovered in South Africa, their identity was yet to be confirmed – a pendant found nearby was all they had to go on so far – and if there was still a chance he was alive somewhere, still undercover, Ruart didn't want to be the one to endanger him.

'Really,' said Éric. 'So Monsieur Drague is a drug smuggler.'

'Monsieur Drayle is, yes, I'm afraid. But that's not all. He's suspected of being involved in a number of disappearances. People from the yacht.'

'How many?'

'Four.' Ruart knew very well there were five: Bertrand, Ishiko, Arnaud, the navigator Gerhard and another crew member, Philippe. But this was another test. 'There were five, but one of them has turned up alive and actually... I'm hoping they might be able to help us.'

He was hoping Éric might betray a keenness to know which of the five had turned up and was betraying Drayle's side of things, but there was still no reaction, other than a little nodding. And Ruart was not naive: the problem with this approach was that it was unlikely to uncover a professional, a seasoned criminal well-used to police questions and keeping a poker face. It would only succeed if the suspect was an inexperienced associate, so that was about all he could rule out. But then, a little glimmer, an opening:

'Which one?' Éric asked, adding a barely perceptible lift of his eyebrows. Barely, but Ruart caught it. It was enough to convince him that his new best friend was not, after all, being fully frank.

'Which what.'

'Which one was found?'

Ruart stared at him for a moment.

'So you know about the disappearances.'

The briefest of hesitations and then:

'No,' Éric said. 'Not at all. Other than from you. So four people are still missing, huh. That's sounds bad.'

It was enough for Ruart. He decided to close the conversation down without raising any suspicions, and he indicated he had to go. Finished his coffee. Put his cup down. Handed his card to Éric.

'Call me if anything occurs to you. We need to catch this guy.'

'Sure will. Good luck.'

A final thought. 'By the way,' Ruart said before heading off. 'Have you seen an Italian man who seems to hang around here? Hawaiian shirt? Pony tail?'

Éric, with a long, slow shrug, choreographed with a down-turning mouth and a turn of the head, telegraphed that he was claiming he hadn't. It was nothing if not straight off the stage of the *Théâtre de la Huchette*.

'Or a beefy white guy in a charcoal grey suit and glasses?'

Éric slowly shook his head, radiating great regret, sad as a lost puppy. 'I don't think...' he began, but Ruart had already given up on getting anything useful out of this Marcel Marceau of a witness.

'Thanks for the coffee,' Ruart said, already hotfooting it out of there.

'You're welcome. Enjoy your stay.'

Ten metres away, and still not safely clear, when...

'Hey Inspector!' Éric again, in a big voice that made his customers look up. 'If you catch up with them, don't forget my Marzocco!'

37. <u>20° 56' 6" S 55° 17' 4" E</u>
(Le Port, Réunion)

1.15pm Réunion Time (09:15 UTC)
Saturday, 19 October

The Breitling was showing a quarter past one when he left Éric and his mobile café. The harbour master was still out (unsurprisingly), and Ruart was not particularly enthused by the idea of spending an indeterminate period of time hanging around for "clam lips". Of course Éric could have been making it up, been trying to put him off a scent.. and actually, the more he thought about it, the guy most likely *was* making it up. He wondered what the connection was with Drayle – there had to be one, surely – but he decided his best bet was to head back to Saint-Denis and regroup. Order his thoughts. He could always come back later. Anyway, he felt like a swim and he'd stupidly left his swimming gear back in the hotel room. Another fifteen minutes or so past Le Port, and you supposedly reach some of the best beaches on the island. With white sand! What an idiot.

Sitting in the cab on his way back, the dark wall of basalt sliding by outside his window seemed to be telling him the island was a fortress he would never be given access to. A big "who goes there", was what it was telling him.

And he recalled the phone call he'd received the previous night in Paris, just before boarding his plane. It was from the *Préfecture*. As well as the news about Ishiko stealing the *decagon* (a final communiqué from Arnaud it would seem – Ruart felt he was always the last to be informed about these things), they had some new information about the *Prospero's Dancer* and its cargo.

He'd already known a bit about the *Prospero's Dancer*: namely that it was a British clipper originally used for the tea trade with China but had been enlisted into the opium trade (selling Indian opium to the Chinese in exchange for payment in silver and other treasures) and had been coming back from a trip to Macau – it was 1838, just before the beginning of the first opium war – when it struck a reef off the coast of what is now Namibia and sank with the loss of all hands. He knew about the treasures it had been carrying, broadly speaking. Through his man on the *Diamond Moon*, Arnaud, he'd heard about what Drayle called the "Isfahan decagon" although had little information on it. He only knew that Drayle was particularly excited about its recovery.

What had recently been discovered though – in this case by a doctoral student in London working out of a back room in the British Museum and slaving away for years unseen and unrecognised– was that this mysterious *decagon* could well contain value and interest beyond its historical significance. While it wasn't completely clear as yet what this might entail, the records were suggesting that it had embarked upon a truly remarkable journey. If this scholar was right, it originated in Isfahan, Iran in the fifteenth century (circa 1480) and had been crossing the oceans ever since: there was evidence of it having shown up not long afterwards in Moorish Spain, in Granada; and after that, on the other side of the Iberian peninsula in Lisbon; and later again in Macau, China, from as early as the second half of the sixteenth century. Whatever its provenance, its travels had been somewhat curtailed by a reef off the Skeleton Coast, and it had rested on the sea floor there for nearly two centuries. Although now that Drayle had recovered it, and Ishiko stolen it, it seemed that the *decagon* had hit the road once more.

By now the taxi had arrived back in Saint-Denis. They were, in point of fact, only seconds away from the Austral Hotel when Ruart was almost killed.

Another vehicle had come hurtling in from their right, and straight through a red traffic light. Not looking, obviously. If it hadn't been for the taxi driver's quick reflexes, it would have slammed directly into Ruart's passenger side door. As it happened it missed them altogether and kept going. After the shock of it, and then the angry exclamations, and a moment when he almost commandeered the taxi cab and embarked on a dangerous chase on his own, he was forced to quell some separate mixed feelings of anger and sadness. This sort of unbridled, arrogant negligence was always guaranteed to get him going. His older brother, Jérôme, whom he'd idolised as a boy, had been killed when he was just nineteen years old and in the Army: it had happened on French soil, in the Alps, and the brakes on the truck he was driving had failed, he'd gone over a cliff, and all due to the contemptible negligence of the crew responsible for maintenance, the imbeciles known as Army Engineers – and the inquest had been absolutely clear about this: it had been laziness, pure and simple.

He cursed himself for not getting the plates, or even noticing the make of the vehicle. These people had to pay. All he could do was remind himself that it usually caught up with people like this, this kind of behaviour. It came back, like a malevolent boomerang. He didn't like it, doing nothing, but most of the time it was all you could do.

'I hope you got the guy's plate,' he said to the taxi driver, knowing he hadn't.

* * *

About half an hour later, when he was heading out for a walk – he was actually stepping into the street outside the front doors of the hotel – he received a call. It was from the *Préfecture*'s contact in Saint-Denis, their source who'd told them about the *Diamond Moon* sighting. Ruart, who'd put the guy's number in his phone but never spoken to him, knew him only as "Sav". He wasn't an undercover guy, so it wasn't a codename. Was it short for a surname? (it didn't sound like any first name he'd heard of). Savant? Savin? Savarin?

'Yes?' Ruart asked.

There was a strangely long pause.

'Commandant Ruart?'

'That is me.'

Another pause. What was that about?

'This is Sav.'

'OK. Are you in Réunion? You sound distant.'

'Distant and…'

He'd gone. Sigh. Tedious.

'Hello?'

'… do.' Sav was back, although it sounded like he hadn't stopped talking. It was clearly a bad line.

'Listen, er, Sav—'

'… destination.'

'What?'

A pause.

'Hello?' This was madness. It couldn't just be the local phone network could it? Or maybe it could. Blame it on the *infrastructure*. 'Hello Sav.' Ruart decided he'd have to hang up and ring back, and was about to lower his phone.

'What is your destination?' This time, Sav was loud and clear.

'My destination? Now? I'm, er… heading for the *Jardin de L'État*. I'm on foot. Where are you? Sav?'

This time though, Sav had gone for good.

* * *

After the conversation with Sav (if you could call it that), he walked to the *Jardin de L'État* which contained the botanical gardens, as well as the Natural History Museum which was housed in an elegant white colonial building constructed in 1834, four years before the *Prospero's Dancer* and the decagon sank beneath the waves off Namibia. He chose to go there for no particular reason other than to clear his head and make a few calls outside in the fresh air. And for a while there, he was expecting Sav to turn up as well, but nothing doing. Not a sign. The call had probably dropped out before he'd mentioned the *Jardin*, or Sav was a million miles away or who knows. The *Préfecture* could sort it out, it was their problem. Sav hadn't exactly been a runaway success anyway: how come he'd only just managed to find out about the *Diamond Moon*'s visit last month?

A fifty metre silver superyacht? And despite Éric's bullshit *sotto voce* act making it all out to be a big secret, Ruart's guess was the whole town knew about it. Which made Paris a laughing stock. Probably the point. Good for them. But they'd better not be hoping *he* could care less, because he couldn't. The final score was all that mattered and it wasn't even half-time. Not even close.

In the meantime, after a quick look inside the museum, he finally managed to get through to the harbour master in Le Port–Théo – who did indeed turn out to be miserly with the sharing of information. All he could confirm was that the *Diamond Moon* had visited, but no, he was very sorry, but it was not his business to know about any sales and he knew of none.

Ruart also took the opportunity to call Marine. Two hours behind, it would have been 1.45pm, lunchtime in Paris.

'What are you eating?' he asked as soon as she answered.

'Never mind what I'm eating, how is Réunion? Is it beautiful?'

'It has, you know, its beautiful *aspect*, for sure…'

Marine sighed.

Their telephone conversations were mostly the same: they followed roughly the same paradigm almost every time. Ruart would say something irrelevant, Marine would try to home in on a conversational goal of some kind and be thwarted by Ruart's precision and calculated tangents. It almost invariably ended in a sigh. Marine's. The conversation that had just taken place was more concentrated than usual, like a kind of *haiku* version of the paradigm. Most probably due to the distance. It was the distance, for sure…

When he ended his call to Marine – it was brief, they were both tired, and the distance thing was too tough to ignore – he was well and truly in the heart of the *Jardin*, on a winding, shady path with no-one around, not even voices, and surrounded by a rich tropical forest sprinkled with spice trees, orchids and palms. The air was laden with equatorial perfumes. There were mangos and coconuts and poincianas, lemon scented gums and jackfruit, cassias and tamarinds and cuban trumpet trees, golden bamboos and chinese banyans; there was senegal mahogany, and there were giant yuccas with their spineless spikes arrayed like knives, and of course, there were the casuarinas and the screwpines.

And there was an African baobab. Ruart knew this because it stuck in his mind later. That shape, like an enormous beer bottle. He'd been wandering aimlessly and he'd reached a spot on the path where he could see the baobab's trunk through a gap in the foliage. Which was when he suddenly realised he had company.

There were four of them, they were Creoles or sounded like it, locals he guessed. Baseball caps and Réunion t-shirts; baggy jeans and large running shoes. Solid builds, they worked out. That's all he knew, he hardly saw their faces, it was over so quickly.

'Visit the Museum?' the tallest one asked.

'Sure.'

'The Natural History Museum.' It was a statement and the guy enunciated each syllable like he was eating it (*Le...mu...sé...um...d'his...toire...na...tu...relle*). Ruart just nodded, all bad feeling now as the other two smiled at a private joke and circled. They were either simple or looking for trouble. Or worst of all, both. He was wishing he had his gun. The tall one continued:

'See the Dodo?'

'No.'

'No?'

'The Dodo? No.'

'You never seen a Dodo?'

'No.'

'You will.'

'I think that's unlikely—'

'And why?' the guy said. And then looked to the others. 'Because...' and they all joined in, a singsong Creole chorus:

'*Le Dodo Lé... Laaaaaaaaaaaaaaaa!*'

The Dodo is here.

The first kick was to the head. It came from behind him and just about knocked him out cold. He stayed on his feet. Staggered. And like the first drop of rain in a tropical storm, it was followed by a deluge. The kicks showered in from all around. He dropped or fell to the ground, he couldn't remember, as the assault continued to the rhythm of the slogan in the beer ad, like it was some kind of shamanic chant.

'Le... Do... do... Lé... La... Le... Do... do... Lé... La...'

With all his energy directed towards protecting himself from the blows, all he could think was three things, one after the other:

In broad daylight!

And me, a cop, I'm not even in a foreign country, how humiliating.

I may not tell Marine about this.

* * *

He had no idea how long he was out for. He didn't even remember regaining consciousness, or walking back to the hotel. Not until he was almost there. He remembered passing people in the street, and most of them were giving him weird looks. What are *you* staring at? If his head hadn't been as sore as it was, he might have said something.

It was twenty to five, he still had his watch on. Amazing they hadn't stolen it. So what the hell was *their* story?

Up in his room, the mirror showed him why people had been staring: he had a smear of dried blood coming out of his nose like a lava flow. The side of his face was swollen, a nice bruise on the way. His mustard shorts had blood on them too. And his shirt was ripped. Thanks guys, thank you very much. But what did they want?

He decided not to report the incident. For a start, it was embarrassing: a Paris cop beaten up by a bunch of gym boys. And the local police – Éric's "slackers" – were very possibly involved in some way themselves. Why not? It was all a bit too strange, the unexplained intelligence failure regarding the *Diamond Moon*, the fact that everyone seemed to have 'clam lips', Éric's theatrical *tour de force*, the call from Sav which was nothing short of bizarre – and highly suspicious, given the timing – and even the odd characters that kept cropping up including the Italian with the ponytail and the faceless man in the grey suit...

He was convinced the whole business was connected with Drayle in some way. And then he remembered something one of the muggers said, or something he thought they said, he could have dreamt it, but he'd probably been semi-conscious:

'It's a little gift for you.'

It was that same voice, same Creole twang. In his head at least, it was clear as the whistling call of a Réunion Cuckoo-Shrike (which was "near-extinct" actually, like just about everything else around there, including himself on one view of it). But if the words were said, what did they mean? Was it a gift from Drayle? Drayle, though, didn't sound like the sort of person who bothered with gifts, even unsavoury ones.

And then, a text from Paris. It was the *Préfecture*. He'd already told them what Éric had said about the purchaser of the *Diamond Moon* being an Australian called Bob Walman, not really expecting there to be any such person. But they'd just confirmed it. He was indeed a CEO of a mining company over there, just as the card had proclaimed. Walman's office had said he was on a boating holiday in Broome.

So that seemed as good a place as any to go to next (and he definitely had to go somewhere). Broome, he'd read about it. *Broome, a pearl of a town*, or something like that, it was a phrase he'd come across somewhere that had stuck in his head. He might have more luck with the Australians. And he had a feeling about this Bob Walman. Feelings, of course, were not things he usually acted on, not without something more concrete. But Time, as his Breitling continued to remind him, was constantly on the move and rarely on your side. And he may just have run out of his Réunion supply, judging by the welcoming committee back in the *Jardin de L'État*.

So Broome it was, then. The beautiful aspect of Réunion would have to wait.

He was about to get in the shower when he got a call. On his room telephone. It was the woman at reception. (Ruart remembered her: demure-looking, blonde. Slightly downturned mouth perhaps, but unquestionably attractive.)

She informed him that while he was out, someone had dropped in to see him. A male. (Sav, most likely.) He didn't leave a name, or a message, just said he'd be in touch. What did he sound like? He spoke in English. (Not Sav, then.) With an English accent? Or American? She couldn't tell, he could have come from anywhere. Most people spoke English these days, didn't they?

And so what did he look like? Was he European? Ah, well, yes, perhaps, he could have been. He was white, at least. OK, great, anything else? She didn't really know, she couldn't say, she didn't look at him very closely... oh, there was one thing though. Yes?

He was wearing a dark grey suit.

38. <u>17° 57' 34" S 122° 11' 38" E</u> (Broome, Cable Beach mooring: the *Diamond Moon*)

9.10pm Western Australian Time (13:10 UTC)
Saturday, 19 October

As a battered and puzzled Ruart was getting into the shower in his room in the Austral Hotel in Saint-Denis, seven thousand kilometres to the east and looking out over the deep-blue, night-time waters of Cable Beach, Diane heard a scream. And she could have sworn it came from the *Seaking*.

They're back. She'd only just realized. She and Brian were settling in for the night on the *Diamond Moon* – they'd arrived back from the Lacepede Islands that day and Bob and Peta had left straight away for the airport to fly to Perth. Some business meeting or other. Which meant she and Brian had the yacht to themselves (and what a yacht!) – apart from the captain and four crew of course. All of them very nice though, it had to be said, absolutely no complaints on that score: The Australian captain was impeccably charming with his unexpected English accent, the first mate Spanish (and extremely handsome) and the Portuguese cook – Nadine, a lovely, auburn-haired girl of about twenty-five – a barrel of laughs. The two other crew, one from France and one from Denmark, young men – boys really – were well-behaved, cheeky, athletic and went around shirtless for most of the time. So no, not quite to themselves but she wasn't complaining obviously.

And now the *Seaking* was back. Diane wondered if they'd heard the bad news. They must have by now. So what on earth was that scream? The *Seaking* was moored about fifty metres away, she could barely make it out, but there was no-one else in that direction as far as she could tell. Maybe it was Lena and she'd just heard the news about Aleks and Lydia? Oh God, Diane tried not to think about it.

She was pleased they were back though, she'd been wondering where they'd got to – her attempts at contacting them had drawn a blank. She'd actually been thinking about calling the police.

She first heard the news online that very morning. She'd been reading *The West Australian* and it was right up at the top, one of the first news items. There'd been a tiny piece the day before, on Friday morning, reporting that an unnamed couple were missing in the Great Sandy Desert, but she thought they meant way inland, not near the coast, and anyway, she'd been led to believe Aleks and Lydia were in Perth, not venturing off the beaten track in the middle of nowhere. So she didn't for a minute think that it could have been them. But now they were named. She couldn't believe it and had to read their names over and over. Aleks and Lydia! And what had they been doing? What had happened to them?

Everyone had been a bit surprised when they rang to say they wouldn't be coming along. Lena seemed particularly put out. Sure, she and Lydia were – and still are, supposedly – best friends but even so, you would have thought she'd have liked having Roy to herself. She'd certainly been acting like it over the last few days! And anyway, ever since Lydia had started seeing Aleks, Diane had noticed a frostiness that hadn't been there before and cracks in what had once been a seemingly inviolable friendship. You would have expected Lydia's absence to have been a blessing if anything.

There was definitely something about Lena's initial reaction that was puzzling and she couldn't quite put her finger on it. Something weird.

Diane had only met Aleks once. There was a hardness and a kind of distance about him, maybe it was just because he was Russian (or Ukrainian or whatever, same thing). She wasn't sure. Lydia had met him at a resort in eastern Thailand apparently. Lydia herself though, Diane had met quite a few times. Lydia and Lena went way back – to their Moscow student days, supposedly – and they were both really similar. Strange senses of humour but very determined. Pretty too, both of them. Both of them blonde, *Russian* blonde, although Lena was the one with the olive skin. Diane wasn't at all jealous that Brian used to be married to Lena – it'd been ages ago, and they were just good friends now (and good friends with absolutely nothing in common, too), but every now and then... maybe a slight tinge. A slight little stabbing pain, but that was normal wasn't it? She liked Lena, although, again, there was something about her that unnerved her a little. She wasn't sure what.

Speaking of pains, she was feeling the telltale signs of her period starting. She felt her breasts. She wished they were larger. (Should she get implants? A few of her friends in Perth had them and what a difference a bit of silicon made! The way guys looked at you...) But her period was definitely starting, so that'd be that as far as sex with Brian went, for the next few days at least, but it wasn't exactly *Secret Diary of a Callgirl* anyway – she couldn't, now she came to think of it, remember the last time they'd actually done it. Was it her? Or was it Brian? It didn't *feel* like it was her.

She found herself getting the hots for the first mate from "Barthelona" and that wasn't good.

Brian was a lovely guy but not the most exciting in bed, it had to be said. Not that that was everything, but he was no Casanova. At first she wondered if he'd had his eye on Nadine, but about the only thing that had made his eyes widen on this trip had been a Spanish mackerel jumping out of the water (speaking of Spanish). He used to be so passionate for her. For her body, her skin, her lips... and now it was fish.

She sighed.

She wasn't complaining though. She had a kind boyfriend and got to go away on yachts like the *Diamond Moon*. What a treat, it was such a beautiful boat. Everything brand spanking new, or close to it, beautiful decor, beautiful cabins, beautiful galley – which was where Brian was now, she could hear him chatting to one of the crew. Making his hot chocolate "on the Marzocco" as he put it. He was always off to make a hot chocolate or a coffee on the Marzocco, although Diane was more of a tea drinker herself. She'd been trying to convert Brian but there was a way to go yet by the looks.

The evening was heavenly. All the stars were out and there was a lovely light breeze from the west, not even raising a ripple. "Angel's breath" the Captain called it. (Captain Charming she called him. Oh God, she was getting the hots for him now too?) Diane looked to the south towards Gantheaume Point and past the *Seaking*. There were other boats around, she knew, but they were rendered invisible by the dark tropical night. She could only see the *Seaking*. Why hadn't they come across and said hello?

What were they doing in there?

39. <u>17° 57' 35" S 122° 11' 36" E</u> (Broome, Cable Beach mooring: the *Seaking*)

9.10pm Western Australian Time (13:10 UTC)
Saturday, 19 October

Lena screamed out.

Roy had a firm grip on her hair. A great clump of it, the blonde strands bunched together in his fist and sprouting out the top of it, like an eruption of golden silk.

Her clothing had long since been ripped off and he had her pushed down on the bed in their cabin, face first into the cotton lapis lazuli bedspread, and was brutally fucking her from behind. It was virtually rape, she was struggling quite a lot, but then again she always did, and mostly she wanted it, so he was giving himself the benefit of the doubt. Her screams – of pleasure, he was comfortable with assuming – were mostly muffled by the bedspread, but the occasional squeal or shriek still managed to escape. And he was enjoying the way she was bucking and wriggling like she was a fish at the end of a line, trying to get away.

He particularly enjoyed watching his cock sliding into her – he was really ramming it home – and above it, her anus, exposed to the world and mouthing a silent scream to match Lena's vocal one. The last one – really more of a yelp – was loud, that was for sure. He wondered if anyone their side of Réunion Island had missed it.

She gasped and almost shouted out again when he suddenly pulled himself out of her – he loved to surprise her – and then he quickly flipped her over, straddled her, and pushed his cock into her mouth before she had a chance to scream again. He had her pinned, but held her arms down for good measure. She made a series of animal, grunting noises while she sucked him with gusto.

It was the reverse, he was thinking. The reverse of what had happened that morning. When he woke with *her* straddling *him*. He'd been so out of it, he thought he was tied up. Maybe he *had* been, he didn't know anymore. Lena was mad enough. She was a crazy bitch all right – she spun his head around – but when he thought about it, he probably preferred it when the steel-capped boot was on the other foot. He pushed his cock further down her throat until she gagged and thought, no, he *definitely* preferred it.

He let her breathe for a moment then put his hand over her mouth to stop the shrieks and pushed deep inside her, front on, her legs virtually back up over her head. Her blonde hair was splayed out over the vibrant blue bed and looked like a stylized medieval sun with its flaming rays. She fought hard but he pushed down harder, and he pummelled her until he came. She was screaming under his hand by this stage and a final orgasmic groan echoed off the walls, merging with his own, after he slumped down and rolled off her. And all he could think was he was lucky she came, or else she probably would have killed him on the spot.

* * *

Ten minutes later Roy got up and began picking his clothes off the floor. He looked at Lena, still lying there, spread-eagled, exhausted. Her hair was a spectacular golden mess, her olive skin glowed and the "V" of her pubic hair pointed to the scene of the crime. And it was an actual "V" too: the hair had been shaved into the letter. Or rather…

'It's not a "V",' Lena had said when Roy first commented on it. (He'd suggested the "V" for vagina was a good idea, ensuring no mistakes.) 'It's an "L". Obviously.'

A pretty skewed "L" he'd thought at the time, and he was thinking it now. Pretty skewed, just like Lena. Roy didn't usually go for labels but he went for this one. Her labia label. Lena's lewd labia label…

His mind was all over the place. *Still* all over the place. He wasn't sure if he'd quite recovered from the morning. And the previous evening. It was a blur, the moonlight, the creature that had come out of the depths, what was that about, was it real? He'd just taken a few lines of coke, not a tab of acid. Or had he? You could never be completely sure with Lena. It was *always* a blur with her. Christ, when she was asleep it was so fucking peaceful he could cry. Not that he'd give her up. She'd probably give *him* up one of these days – she was the ultimate femme fatale – he was philosophical about that. May as well just enjoy the ride in the meantime. May as well. Roy had not so long ago come out of a ten year marriage, no kids and thank God for that, his viper of an ex sued him for just about everything he had as it was. This was *after* walking out on him one day without warning – gone by the time he'd arrived home from work, no sign, not even a piece of fucking forensic evidence to suggest she'd ever lived there. Did him a favour though: quit his job, bought the yacht, never looked back. You certainly didn't get too much time to do a lot of looking back with Lena around. Speaking of whom...

'You better not have ripped my pants you fucker.' She was awake. Was probably never asleep. Probably watching him through mascaraed eyelashes.

'I did hear something, I thought it was my back.'

'Fucker.'

'You're the one who nearly broke it this morning. Jesus.'

'I didn't hear you complaining.'

It was true. Complaining was not something that had crossed his mind.

'Hey,' Roy said suddenly. 'I can't remember. Was I tied up?'

'Tied up?' Lena did that a lot. Answered a question by repeating the question.

'Yeah, you know. Bound. Secured to the deck. Couldn't move my limbs.'

'Tied up,' she said again – as a statement this time – and smiled. Roy shook his head.

'You were fucked up,' Lena added. 'Well and truly.'

'What did I take?'

'What did you take.'

Lena sat up, stood up, looked about and found her panties which Roy had tossed against the far wall. He loved watching her dressing and especially putting her panties back on. And why was that? Maybe because it reminded him of how he'd be taking them off again before long.

She sighed. Was looking at her white pants and fingering them – obviously a few stitches had come apart in Roy's haste.

He'd only intended to take *her* apart at the seams.

'Fucker,' she said for the third time.

'I don't deny it.'

Lena turned and looked at him. Stared hard, as if attempting to unlock the secrets of his soul. Well I wouldn't be silly enough to keep it just behind my eyes now, would I. But of course, he would. Luckily Lena was slightly long-sighted. Although she was standing across the room…

'And *I* don't deny…' she began.

'What.'

'I don't deny slipping you… something.'

'You *what*?'

'Maybe it was a bit much. A bit too much for—'

'Slipped me what?'

'A bit too much for a poor little boy.'

'What was it? Acid?'

She didn't answer.

'You've got to be kidding me. You are completely insane.' He shook his head. And, although he immediately regretted it, then added 'You *both* are, you *and* Lydia.'

Her face darkened – like the shadow of a cloud passing over the ocean. It was too late to withdraw the remark.

'Sorry.'

They'd heard the news about Aleks and Lydia that morning. Roy was a bit surprised she hadn't been more upset, actually. It was as if she'd already known. Already grieved. Although grieved wasn't the right word was it, it wasn't like a body had been found or anything. They were just missing. Out of their car, though. Not good.

Roy had suggested they call the Broome police, tell them what they knew, check in on progress. Nothing to tell, was Lena's response, they'll call when they want to, and she was probably right, but even so. It was a strange way of dealing with the loss – temporary or otherwise – of your closest friend. Maybe it was the Russian way. Lena had seemed more hurt, in fact, when Lydia had called to say she wouldn't be joining them on the *Seaking*. (Roy had been pretty pleased and was just a tiny bit put out that Lena hadn't been pleased as well, although he sort of understood at the same time.)

He'd even offered to cut the holiday short, take her back to Perth, but again, no thanks. She had some "business" to attend to in Broome, whatever that was. (Lena *always* had "business" to attend to and in this case he suspected it was looking into buying up the Broome pearling industry. She was just that kind of girl!)

If it had been Roy's best friend missing out there, he'd be in his four-wheel drive in a second and off searching. He offered this too, but it was another offer declined. No point, she said. They'd just get in the way. Leave it to the police, They'll show up.

They probably would show up, but in what state?

Out a porthole, he could see the lights of the *Diamond Moon* moored about seventy metres away. He wondered how they were all getting along, they hadn't spoken to them since yesterday. He'd suggested dropping over that evening, but Lena hadn't been keen, despite claiming that she really liked Diane. Maybe it was Brian's presence, her ex, and frankly Roy couldn't have blamed her. Brian was a bit of a loser and Roy had trouble understanding what Lena saw in him in the first place. (She met him in a Perth night club, perhaps she was drunk.) She *married* him for fuck's sake. For his money? She would have been better off going for Bob if money was the goal. Lena and Bob did always seem to get along pretty well now he came to think about it. Not that he was jealous – Roy prided himself in not having a jealous bone in his body. But there looked to be a bit of shared history, or at least a similar view of the world, or something. He couldn't quite place it, but good luck to them was his attitude. The more friends Lena had in Roy's world, the more likely it was she'd hang around. Not that he'd be heartbroken if she didn't. No fear.

The *Diamond Moon* though, what a spectacular vessel. Lucky for Roy that Bob had found it, otherwise Roy'd still be lumbered with his previous boat, sluggish old thing that she was, bless her barnacle-encrusted keel. The *Seaking* was a step up, no doubt about it, but the *Diamond Moon*... it was another proposition altogether. Bob had been a bit cagey about how he'd got it – all Roy knew was he'd had to go to Réunion to collect it and he refused to say who the previous owner was. Why? What was he, a drug baron?

Bob hadn't been as cagey about where he'd got Peta from though – snatched her from the guy who ran West Ocean Metals. Nice one! Roy could never really be sure though which girl was Bob's favourite: Peta or the *Diamond Moon*.

Actually yes he could.

40. <u>23° 15' 15" S 64° 41' 36" E</u> (Over the Indian Ocean, east of Mauritius)

2.30am Mauritius Time (22:30 UTC)
Sunday, 20 October

Ruart was sorry he didn't get to spend even a single night in Saint-Denis.

While he wasn't going to admit to himself the blonde at reception might have contributed to that regret – even if it briefly crossed his mind – on any measure it did seem just a little bit crazy to be jumping on a plane the very evening of the day of his arrival. But he had to remind himself he had a job to do. Not to mention, speaking of receptions, the inexplicably hostile attitude of the locals, acting, as they were, like it was still the nineteenth century. (Acting like Ruart was some despicable colonialist: an officer, perhaps, fresh off the Napoleonic battlefields, exploring the southern oceans, mocking the natives and in need of a good spearing, was that the situation? Was that what it felt like for these unenlightened *retards*?).

So here he was on another plane: this time it was Air Mauritius, an hour out of Sir Seewoosagur Ramgoolam International Airport in Mauritius, and heading for Perth. After that it was on to Broome to see if he could track down this Bob Walman guy and his fancy boat.

He opened his window shade. The lights in the plane's interior had been dimmed for sleep and movies, but there was still almost nothing to see outside. Just the benighted Indian Ocean below, no more welcoming than his friends in the *Jardin de L'État*, spreading out to the forbidding southern extremity of the globe like a creeping, unstoppable spillage of something black and malevolent.

41. <u>31° 58' 44" S 115° 46' 4" E</u>
(Peta's bedroom, Perth)

3.30pm Western Australian Time (07:30 UTC)
Sunday, 20 October

Later that day, when Ruart's Qantas flight to Broome was taxiing down the runway at Perth Airport, about twenty kilometres away Bob was removing Peta's corset and Peta's nextdoor neighbour, Maggie, was feeding celery to her pet rabbit Snowy.

'Ouch!' She grimaced as Bob accidentally pinched the skin on her back.

'Sorry.'

They'd only just returned from their sailing adventure – up the Kimberley coast, and how beautiful was that place? – and Peta had been surprised when Bob suggested they catch up again so soon. Nicely surprised, but, still... yeah, surprised. She hadn't thought he was exactly the type, to be overkeen... not that she was complaining. Anyway, they were meant to be going out to dinner, but Bob had turned up early. *Real* early. He made her get dressed in ten minutes flat, and then what did he do? Make her take it all off again! Still, that was Bob and this was fun.

'I wear this for *you*, you know,' she said.

'I know. Doesn't mean I don't prefer you *out* of it.'

'Out of my clothes? Or pissed?'

Bob just smiled and kept unlacing.

Outside, in the nextdoor backyard, Maggie was making noises that you'd expect a rabbit to make. A *cartoon* rabbit, that is, going *tch, tch, tch, tch* and shaking her head as if she had ears that moved and flopped around. Snowy looked at her nonplussed, his attitude to the celery unchanged.

'Do you ever speak to your neighbour?' Bob asked.

'Maggie? Sometimes. She's very sweet— *ow!*'

'What did I do?'

'That's my sore shoulder.'

'Sorry. The massage will fix that.'

'So you say.'

Finally, the corset fell to the floor. Victory, she supposed. All hail mighty Bob.

'Now lie down,' said Bob. 'On your stomach. Where's the oil?'

'On the bedside table.'

Snowy hopped away – must have been one "tch" too many, had it up to here with the freaky noises and the head shaking – and his little white butt disappeared into a hedge. Before she lay down, Peta caught Bob's smile as he watched Maggie crossly toss the celery aside and stomp off, before turning his attention back to another white butt: the one in the room, on the bed. The one that was all his.

'Does she call in often?' he asked her.

'Who? Maggie? Hardly ever.'

'So I guess you wouldn't get many visitors.'

She turned around to see what expression Bob had on his face, it was an odd statement.

'Face down,' Bob instructed. He was stern. She kind of liked that.

'Liked the dress you had on tonight, by the way.' And with that, Bob began rubbing oil into Peta's back.

'Mmmm. Oh that is so nice. Aaah, just there, ohh...'

Bob applied pressure, gently, to her sore shoulder, and then worked his way down her spine – he had wonderfully strong hands. Then it was back up her sides, lightly touching her breasts in passing, and up to her neck.

'You're good.'

Bob said nothing. He pulled away. She waited for the cold sensation of fresh oil dripping onto the middle of her back, but nothing happened. After about fifteen seconds, she began to twist her neck around to see what Bob was doing, but Bob – a little roughly, she thought – pushed her head back down into the pillow.

'Hey—'

'Don't look.'

'Yeah, but you don't have to be so rough! What are you doing anyway, the crowd's getting restless.'

Bob didn't answer, but Peta could feel him sliding her panties off.

'Oh I get it. One of *those* types of massages.'

Bob again said nothing, but thank heavens, a few seconds later she could feel the cool tingling of the oil as it dribbled down onto her from above – this time onto her buttocks. She almost groaned, no, scratch that, she groaned all right, as those wonderful hands began massaging the oil in, with firm, downward-sweeping strokes, right down into the *crack*, and down to the insides of her upper thighs. She could feel herself getting turned on, becoming wet… my *God*, she was so horny, she didn't see *that* coming!

'You've done this before,' she said, trying her hardest not to moan. But it was hopeless and the whimpers began to flow.

Soon, Bob's hands were going into all *sorts* of places, and she knew she shouldn't, but she let him, and craved more, much more…

And more he gave her. His fingers slid inside her, in and out, rhythmically, like the ocean – that's what it felt like – a restless, pulsing sea, pounding the cliffs, the rocks, the caves of her grateful body, and then steadily, gradually, becoming more insistent, and then impossibly urgent, before that desperately-anticipated, crashing tidal wave of ecstasy overwhelmed her and she yelled out.

It must have been a full minute afterwards before she looked up, and realised there was no-one in the room. Languidly, and serenely comfortable now in her nakedness, she rolled over fully and looked around. Empty, except for…

Except for the open laptop she hadn't noticed before, with its red light, and next to the light, the built-in camera: that unblinking little eye that stared at her and kept staring.

42. <u>7° 59' 49" N 109° 59' 29" E</u> (Uncharted reef, Spratly Islands, South China Sea)

The same time
2.30pm Indochina Time (07:30 UTC)
Sunday, 20 October

The first thing Drayle saw when he woke was a blinking red light next to his face. Just as he had every morning for the previous four weeks. It was a daily reminder of where he was and what had happened. Thank fuck he was out of there today. He'd have to kill someone otherwise. He may anyway.

* * *

Four weeks earlier. Monday, 23 September

It was the morning after he arrived, and the first thing he saw when he woke up was that blinking red light. It was part of the machinery beside his bed. Silent, but making its own brand of noise. And making him realise, like the little aide-mémoire that it was, that the next time he looked in a mirror, he wouldn't recognise the person staring back.

Morning. At least he'd assumed it was morning, but was it afternoon? a.m. or p.m.? antemeridian or postmeridian? His mind was running around trying to catch its tail. He wanted to kick it.

The machine may have been the first thing he saw, but the first person was Laska, the surgeon's assistant, who was suddenly smiling down at him. The surgeon's *beautiful* assistant, it had to be said, with her straight quartz hair and arctic-ice-blue eyes and perfect body, always tightly contained behind one or two thin layers of white cotton. She was smiling too, so he guessed the results must have been at least OK. No disasters, in other words.

'Laska—'

She quietened him immediately, putting a delicate forefinger against his lips.

'Dominique. No speaking, remember? Just nod or shake head. You are feeling good, yes?'

She spoke to him in English. Her voice was crisp and clear. And she always called him Dominique. He loved this. If one of his team ever called him that, he'd have them keelhauled, but from her it was somehow soothing.

He nodded.

'Great. It went… really well. The doctor is very happy, Is very, very happy.'

He was concerned about the repetition, and the extra "very". It was one too many. Something was wrong.

'And I will bet… you are wondering how you look.'

My God how he loved her Russian accent. He nodded again.

'Yes? And so very very soon we are able to show you.' She paused for a moment. It wasn't a natural pause. Something was definitely wrong.

'However.' It was said as a sentence on its own. The cruellest of sentences.

'There will needs to be a little further procedure, so just lie back and relax and…'

Drayle didn't hear the rest. He couldn't exactly lie back any further and relaxing was out of the question. Especially after seeing, in the polished steel of the machine next to his bed, his very *very* unfortunate-looking visage.

* * *

He decided soon afterwards that it was no cause for concern. Admittedly his eyes were closed when he was thinking this, but the machine probably had a slightly undulating surface which skewed the reflection. He had a right to be edgy, though. It was not a minor operation.

Drayle was in a doctor's surgery – a mini-hospital really – that was contained within a structure standing in the middle of the South China Sea, about halfway between Brunei and Vietnam. It was implanted into a reef attached to a section of the Prince Consort Bank, which in turn formed part of the infamous Spratly Islands. Not much bigger than an oil rig in area, the oddly shaped – and even more oddly positioned – structure stood in water only a few metres deep. It was L-shaped: a white building on stilts essentially, crouched over topaz shallows, with a large white sphere perched on the roof at the corner of the "L" (like an oversized globe plucked from a dusty study) and a helipad (Drayle's point of entry) at the other end. The sphere, which housed radar and other 'intelligence' equipment, stood on top of an eight-sided section of the building, five stories high, while the remainder of the structure was of variable height, and housed variously apartments, offices, a gymnasium, a restaurant and, of course, a hospital. There was also a small mooring jetty although larger boats had to anchor beyond the ring of white surf in the distance.

Although the surrounding water was only a few metres deep, you didn't have to travel far before the seabed fell away dramatically, in some places to depths of over two thousand metres. The Spratly Islands were not just a hot spot of simmering international tensions and feuds – the main players being China, Vietnam, the Philippines, Taiwan and Malaysia/Brunei – it was also a notoriously dangerous area for shipping, being near major shipping lanes, with reefs and abruptly variable depths, and frequent typhoons. When Drayle first arrived he couldn't help but admire the skill of the early mariners, including of course the captain of the *Prospero's Dancer* (whose skill though – or was it just luck? – deserted him off Namibia; unlucky for him, lucky for Drayle). Those clippers might have been fast, but they were still just as vulnerable to the perils of nineteenth century shipping. And modern shipping too, it would seem. The reefs were littered with wrecks, although at least one of the rusting remains, he was aware, had been steered there intentionally, for strategic purposes, enabling the country responsible to man the vessel with soldiers and thus occupy the reef in question, in an effort to stave off the relentless advances of the Chinese.

The particular structure that had just become Drayle's temporary home was located in a part of the Spratly Islands occupied by Vietnam, although in this case, the building, the facilities and the personnel were all Russian. Built with the tacit permission of the Vietnamese government (or explicit – money or weapons had no doubt changed ownership at some point), it was a useful (and unpublicised) foothold for the Russians. (And handy for Drayle as well, with all his Russian connections. Many of his 'foot soldiers' were still Russian after all, and he himself was, even now, still treated as an honorary Russian, despite returning to Paris and leaving that snowdome known as Moscow far behind him.) Given it was situated in such a lawless part of the world, it probably suited everyone that the Russians were there. Except perhaps the Chinese who, as everyone knew, had their eyes on total domination of the South China Sea.

It certainly suited Drayle. Not just because it was a perfect 'pit-stop' for whenever things got a little hot – he knew he had a number of agencies on his tail by this point, the latest irritation being a cop from Paris – but also because it provided him with something he needed now more than ever: a facelift. Or rather, not merely a facelift, but a full-blown facial reconstruction. Plastic surgery.

It wasn't that he had a problem with his looks. On the contrary, he'd always been quite pleased with them, although in recent years others may not have agreed. Apart from the distinctive mixture of a double-chin and a severe cleft chin, he had a horizontal scar across his face, halfway up his nose and extending from cheek to cheek, that looked like someone had tried to slit his throat with a large, sharp knife but aimed too high. Distinctive too, and almost as conspicuous, were his curly blond hair and boyish rosy complexion – you wouldn't have picked him for French. More like German. And with his strong build – broad shoulders and narrow waist – you'd have thought him an athlete were it not for the double-chin. None of this bothered him in the slightest. He was actually quite proud of his scar, grown quite fond of it over the years if mainly for its shock value, and he'd always attributed his numerous sexual conquests, at least in part, to his atypical appearance. What did bother him, though, was the fact that his looks made him simply too visible: he was a gift for a police facial composite interviewer and the risk of his being identified at an airport or seaport was now unacceptably high. So plastic surgery it was.

The doctor was, he'd been assured, one of the best. To be enticed to work in such an unusual location required, obviously perhaps, the offer of a sizeable amount of money (and frequent transfers to and from an expensive, state of the art, paid-for apartment in Bangkok). Drayle was willing to trust him. He was hoping though that the North East Monsoon held off, as it was supposed to, and that no late summer typhoons ventured their way. He wouldn't be wanting any slips of the scalpel.

* * *

She'd given him something. She must have. He was slipping in and out of consciousness. And this time, when Laska entered his room, she was naked. When she bent over him, her breasts – her nipples – brushed his bare chest. He tried to move his hands but couldn't. And he couldn't open his eyes either. He knew she was there and he wanted to feel her. To touch her.

And suddenly his eyes were open and he *was* touching her. But it wasn't Laska, it was that woman, the cop's sister. Constance. They were in her Paris apartment, and she was struggling because he had one hand around her neck and the other…

* * *

It must have been days later. Two? Three? Four? He had no idea, every day was the same in that place. Now he knew how prisoners must feel. Another reason to be going through this little version of hell: to ensure that a prisoner was something he would never be.

The doctor was looking down at him. A serious look on his face.
'Dominique.'
You can't call me Dominique.

'Time to wake up. Time to remove some bandages.'

'Did they find Ishiko?' Drayle asked. The obvious question. He'd been told she was speaking to the French police. They had to stop her. Stop her and get that decagon back.

'I beg your pardon?'

'Ishiko. Have we heard anything?'

The doctor wore a crumpled smile, apparently not understanding.

'Never mind,' Drayle said. Realizing he was still not fully 'back'. Realizing he'd have to keep his mouth shut for a while.

The doctor set to work, delicately removing the bandages. His movements were precise, his hands were all expertise and confidence, he was an artist – a painter or a sculptor – and Drayle was his masterpiece, his legacy…

The doctor's eyes, though, they betrayed his hands, because as each bandage fell to the floor, his eyes grew wider. And when he finished, and he donned his doctor's smile, the eyes not only failed to reflect the assurance of his hands, they had a distinct look of panic about them. If there was one thing Drayle could smell a mile off, it was fear.

'All done,' the doctor said. 'It looks good, Dominique.'

'I'll be the judge of that, hand me the mirror.'

'It's… a little early for that really. There are—'

'Hand me the mirror.'

'You must understand Dominique, there is still a lot of swelling, so it really isn't possible to see at this stage—'

'Hand me the fucking mirror *Herr Doktor*, don't make me have to get it myself or you and I, *we'll be swapping places.*'

The ferocity in Drayle's voice gave the doctor no option.

'I have to warn you—' the doctor began, mirror in hand.

Drayle snatched it.

Looked into it.

And nearly died of fright.

43. <u>13° 44' 50" N 100° 31' 37" E</u> (Siam@Siam Design Hotel, Bangkok)

5.00pm Indochina Time (10:00 UTC)
Sunday, 20 October

Later that sultry *Indochine* afternoon, twelve hundred kilometres to the north-west, at 5pm, (almost on the dot), a staff member manning the check-in desk of a particular hotel in central Bangkok – decorated the modern way and designed to appeal to the smartphone+tablet generation – looked up and saw a familiar sight walking towards him. Johnny had been working at the hotel for three years, and he knew the regulars. And Mr Song was definitely a regular.

He was back! Johnny beamed at him, praying he would look in his direction, and come to him and not to his colleague at the other end of the desk. Mr Song always gave a generous tip to whoever checked him in – often in Australian dollars (and sometimes even U.S.). For some reason he was always going to Australia.

Disaster! His angle of trajectory changed at the last possible instant. It had been looking promising initially: from the moment Mr Song had first appeared, he'd been heading straight for Johnny – it was a beeline (although since when did you ever see a bee fly in a straight line?) – but now, all of a sudden he'd done a late, inexplicable swerve, and veered off to the left, towards the most annoying of all his fellow employees. His name was Sum, but Johnny called him Stumpnose for obvious reasons.

Deflated, he listened in to the conversation, and smiled brightly whenever Mr Song looked in his direction. He scored a nod at least, so maybe it meant a slightly larger tip for next time. He watched as Mr Song handed over his passport – always his Korean one, but he knew for a fact that he had others, one of the cleaning girls told him – and chose his moment.

'Hello Mr Song!'

'Hello.' He seemed a little distant, a little more than usual – and that was saying something! – but it never worried Johnny. His generosity made up for it!

'You have a good trip?'

'Yes,' said Mr Song. 'Was good.'

'You just in? This afternoon?'

'Just in,' Mr Song confirmed.

'Australia?'

Mr Song barely answered – it sounded like he said "Sydney" – before giving him a tired half-nod and turning away to pick up his passport and room key.

The cleaning girl – Plarm – told him that he had *twelve* passports including Australian, American, British, you name it. He wasn't sure whether he believed her but there was certainly something very odd about Mr Song. Johnny had no trouble believing he was Korean – he certainly looked like he came from either there or China – but he had a dark aloofness about him, even for a *bibimbap*! Maybe he wasn't Korean after all, maybe Russian? And with so many passports, who knew *what* he was. He probably didn't even know himself!

Not that Johnny would ever say anything (and he'd made sure Plarm wouldn't either) – not with tips like that. He wasn't stupid!

Mr Song was saying thank you to that cretin Sum and Johnny watched as a fifty dollar bill – Australian – slid its way across the counter pinned under Stumpnose's greedy little fist.

'You enjoy your stay Mr Song!' Johnny called out, cutting off Stumpnose's parting remarks, whatever they were. They were bound to have been lame, for sure.

Mr Song just smiled weakly, and turned and set off for the lifts. The weariness in his face was in marked contrast to the crispness of his white shirt and the shine of his light grey suit.

Why, though, when he travelled, did he always choose to wear a suit? He always looked more comfortable in those Indonesian-style, short-sleeved shirts of his. Johnny supposed his job required it, whatever that was.

Maybe he just needed to lighten up a bit. Or consider a career change!

Part Five – Jon

44.

'Bertie saved you, you know!' Alastair bellowed.

Nearly everything Alastair said was bellowed. His conversational volume hovered around the nine mark. Which only left a jump of one – to ten – for emergencies. Jon wasn't completely sure why this was – possibly something to do with boarding school and dinners there. Most things in life – or at least in England – could be traced back to boarding schools and food.

'You're his slave now, you do realise that don't you, his slave for life. Isn't he Bertie darling? He's your slave!'

'That's right,' Jon said to Bertie. 'Your wish is my command. Anything. Anything at all.'

But Bertie just appeared embarrassed and didn't seem to know where to look.

The three of them – Alastair, Jon and Alastair's orange cat Bertie – were sitting in Alastair's musty, chaotic living room. The curtains were open just enough for the weak morning light to seep through and for those inside to be able to see out into the street, but not so wide that anyone outside could see in.

Alastair was Jon's neighbour. Two doors away, in fact. Two doors away from what was now a charred shell of a house that used to be Jon's home. It was Wednesday, and it had already been a week since the fire.

According to Alastair, he'd been sound asleep when Bertie scratched his face and then scarpered, beating a hasty retreat.

Cheeky bugger! was his first thought except when it got to the doorway the cat turned, and put on a 'follow me' face and then vanished down the staircase. Intrigued, Alastair had trundled off after it and found Bertie waiting impatiently by the front door, wanting to be let out. When Alastair opened the door, Bertie shot out of the house and by this time Alastair had noticed that the street outside was bathed in an eerie orange glow. Which was when he realised the house two doors away – Jon's house – was on fire.

He began to debate with himself whether to call the fire brigade (Alastair had an innate distrust of the 'authorities' or any official body whatsoever) when he noticed Bertie was running *towards* the fire. Now this was most unusual. And, of course, worrying. Alastair told Jon how he shouted out '*Bertie*!!' (his register no doubt hit the maximum of ten for the occasion), but even more unusual was seeing Bertie peer inside the front door of the burning house which was inexplicably open (Jon was sure he'd closed it) and look back at Alastair.

(Jon, incidentally, had no reason to disbelieve him about any of this, partly because it was so ludicrous it was probably true, but also because it was the least he could do, this man had saved his life after all.)

Alastair immediately realised that Bertie was trying to tell him there was someone inside the house. He didn't have his mobile phone with him. He knew he probably wouldn't be able to both ring the fire brigade *and* save whoever was inside, and so his dilemma over whether to contact a tentacle of government corruption such as the fire department was solved. For the time being then, the fire brigade – or at least the only one that counted – consisted of Alastair, a fearless Englishman with ginger hair (being genetically Scottish), and Bertie, an indomitable house cat with ginger hair (being genetically orange tabby *Felis Catus*). Brothers in kind if not in species.

And anyway, as Alastair pointed out, his own name was the Gaelic derivation of Alexander, from the Greek, meaning "protector". He did admit however that mostly it was his *own* life and property he concentrated on protecting, and rarely anyone else's. For breaking his usual modus operandi, Jon assured him, he was very grateful.

'Well it was better than waiting for the fucking fire brigade wasn't it. *I'd* have died of boredom and *you'd* have been *toast*!'

Jon remembered very little of his rescue other than two fragments: the first was coughing a lot while being carried over a broad pair of shoulders down a dark staircase; and the second was lying on his back on what he now realised was Alastair's living room floor and having an oxygen mask placed over his face. What Alastair was doing with an oxygen mask was a mystery that only occurred to Jon later and which proved to have no ready solution although Jon suspected it may have had something to do with Alastair's complete lack of faith in the emergency services.

Jon had been pretty much "out of it" for days, according to Alastair, and it was true, Jon could remember virtually nothing of the period between the fire and two days ago, Monday, when he'd finally regained his senses – the four days in between had seemingly vanished. And so when the fog finally lifted, there were a number of things he needed to get clear.

'Why didn't you call the hospital?' Jon had asked. Of course now the answer was obvious. They were all in on it. Another tentacle of the creature coated in venal slime, known as "the government". The "authorities". But there'd been, apparently, another reason.

'If they find out you're alive,' Alastair had told him, 'you're a dead man.'

'What do you mean "if"? You haven't told anyone?'

And this was the nub of it. Apparently Jon was now dead. And Alastair was determined to keep him that way.

'They're as sneaky as hell these people,' Alastair said. 'There wasn't anything reported about a body, but that doesn't mean they didn't actually find one.'

'A body?'

'I saw them remove a body bag! I was watching them out this very window. They're *brazen*. It was broad *daylight*. This happens all the time, you know that don't you. If no-one complains, it's easier not to announce it. There are so many vagrants and illegal immigrants in this city... there are many more murders than you think.'

'Wait a minute. No-one reported I was missing? No-one at all?'

'Well I most certainly did, didn't I! It's bloody typical you know. I told them. I went out there and told them. Said I heard these godawful blood-curdling screams, sounded like a, a what, middle-aged man, young man, my neighbour, I'd forgotten your name of course, but said my barrister chappie neighbour was in there, that was *him*, in that bag you brought out.'

'Why?'

'Why?! Why?! Well so they'd think you were dead of course. And not a moment too soon either. With all these attempts to kill you, someone had to put an end to that ghastly process didn't they, the rogues!'

'I told you about them?'

'You did. After Olivia gave you the kiss of life, you were actually talking some sense for a while there.'

'Who's Olivia?'

'Oxygen! dear boy, the giver of life. Olivia the oxygen mask.'

'Oh, right. So the papers haven't yet mentioned me as—'

'The papers!...'

And in a wild flurry of papers and hands – because he had very large hands – Alastair launched himself into the latest newspaper.

'... I'd forgotten to check today's paper. I've been at them and at them. Check your *facts* man, there was a *barrister* living in that house and they took him out in a *bloody body bag* and no-one's had the ... ah hah... Here it is! Ha ha! Finally. You're dead!'

And sure enough, there it was on page ten. Jon was now officially suspected of being dead. Subject to possible further forensic analysis of course, which apparently was no small task as the body, or what was left of it, had been crushed and charred beyond recognition.

'Fucking *fantastic*!' was Alastair's attitude. 'There are so many advantages in being dead, good *God* I wish I was, the world is your fucking *oyster*! Slurp it up!'

After he'd taken a few moments to accustom himself to his new status, there were still matters that had needed some clarity, still more questions for his life-saving host (who had also, it would seem, just killed him). So many more questions, in fact, that it was beginning to feel like he was doomed to live out the rest of his non-life in a sea of question marks. A drowning man who couldn't drown.

'So whose body was it?'

'It's not hard to work *that* one out. The front door was open remember, but it doesn't mean the perpetrator got out of there alive. Happens all the time, overcome by smoke, hoisted by their own petard, trapped in their own deathtrap. It's an occupational hazard for arsonists, old chap. You're just lucky Bertie could tell you apart...'

'Very.'

'Oh good *lord*!' Alastair had just seen something in the paper. 'Apparently, they think... who are these "they" anyway, that's what I'd like to know... but they think the fire was started by a faulty battery in an *iPad*!'

'I don't even own an iPad.'

'Well of course you don't. Of course you don't. That's the *point*. This is all a *game* to them. The dissemination of untruths is what they do. Protects everyone. Everyone and everything except for the *truth*!'

This, then, had been the gist of Jon's first conversation of substance with Alastair two days earlier. There'd been a number since. One of them for example – later the same day – involved Alastair's suggestion that Jon "lie low" for a few days in Alastair's flat until the activity on the street died down. On no account should he venture outside or let anyone know he was alive. It was his only chance, these people would stop at nothing. As long as they thought he was dead, he was safe.

'But what about my life? I have a practice to run,' Jon complained.

'Dead men don't *have* practices, my boy.'

'And why the hell hasn't anyone apart from you reported me missing?'

His chambers? Sabine? (although her familiarity with the latest news was tenuous at best). And what about Romy? She'd known he was in that house.

'Well it just goes to show you, doesn't it,' Alastair said. 'When we *really* die, we're spared the further pain of finding out just how little all those bastards out there actually miss us!'

So now, two days later, a week had passed since the fire and Jon was still 'lying low', but there was only so much he could take. Of Alastair for one. He was a wonderful man – the heroic rescuer and the intriguer both – but his theories and philosophies were of such epic proportions that Jon's head felt like it was about to explode. If there'd been an air of unreality before the fire, with the series of incidents, there was certainly one now. Unreality, surreality, words didn't seem to quite cover it. But even words were apparently in short supply, because Alastair, the man with all the answers, would become strangely tongue-tied every time Jon attempted to address the questions of why him (and he'd already told Alastair about 'the money'), and who was actually behind all this.

'Who? Don't get me started,' was all he would get by way of a response.

So Jon would lie low no longer. He would come up for air. He would make contact.

He had no phone, though. Alastair had banned him from getting a new one: quickest way to being discovered, let alone the location function, let alone the tracking capabilities, they watch you through the pinhole camera lenses, they watch you as you *eat*! Not to mention a phone was no use when you were doing your best to not exist.

He had no-one's phone number either. He just had addresses in his head. There was still a detailed map of London in there too. So it was decided. He'd give Alastair the slip, make his dash for freedom, and find out what the hell was going on.

His first port of call was Sabine. There was always the remotest of possibilities that she was actually worried. Stranger things had happened.

45.

He waited until after lunch, when Alastair usually went out to the shops, before he made his move. Gave him a good ten minute head start.

Jon left a note (giving no useful details should it be somehow intercepted), essentially telling Alastair he needed to get out – fresh air and all of that – and have a bit of a hunt around, but not to worry, he'd be remaining below the radar. And he thanked his host for his help. He felt a bit guilty running off in Alastair's clothes (suit and tie, and ironed shirt, sorry Alastair!) and with some of his money, but he had little choice. For now. He'd pay him back somehow. He even left him an IOU.

He stepped out the front door and into the street. To the right, the charred ruins of *Qui Vive*, like a victim of a bombing raid, a visible reminder of his life, perhaps, a monument to the catastrophe it had become…

Out of the corner of his eye, he caught a glimpse of something moving stealthily towards him. It was orange.

Bertie. Had he come to say goodbye? From the accusatory look on his face – if such a thing were possible to detect on a cat – it was to scold him. Or was it a warning, advising him not to leave?

Jon turned on his heel and walked quickly away up the street towards the West Kensington station and freedom.

Given he was supposed to be dead, it seemed more appropriate to be underground, so he caught the Tube, not the bus, to Notting Hill. The short walk to the tube station had been wonderful though – it was the first time he'd been outside in a week (even if he could only remember the last two days of it).

On the way there, something that had been bothering him finally surfaced in his thoughts. It was to do with Emerald. Not just why she'd come to visit him that day, or whether it was the same Martin Nevers whose will she had, or even whether there was any connection between her visit and the 'incidents'. It was the mention of something else that seemed to have been lost in all the confusion. He remembered her exact words: "It's about your sister."

As he didn't have a sister, her comment was strange enough. (Of course, it was always possible there was something someone, somewhere along the line, hadn't told him.) But more than that, it was the fact that she'd raised the subject of his family at all. Jon's family had always been a bit of an unknown quantity, and the thought – even the vaguest of possibilities – that they could somehow be connected with any of this he found decidedly unnerving.

The train bounced and rattled through the tunnels, and as it did, he entertained the thought that all these worries and fears would be dislodged, and shaken free, by the time he arrived at his destination. He'd burst out into the sunlight of a new world, into a life he never knew he had.

He almost hired a bicycle when he got to Notting Hill, in Pembridge Road, but realised he didn't have his credit card and that dead men didn't ride bikes anyway, they walked, and so, instead, he made his way on foot along Kensington Park Road and continued on to his and Sabine's flat in Lansdowne Crescent.

Noticing the rusty gate to the basement flat (he couldn't help it, it used to drive him crazy), he walked up to that big black door and pressed the buzzer.

The person who answered wasn't Sabine however. A youngish-sounding male, probably of student age, probably the son of a banker, told him Sabine didn't live there any longer, in fact he'd never met her: she'd moved out earlier than planned, returned to Germany was what he'd been told, sorry.

Returned to Germany? He could hardly believe it. He'd only been speaking to her... when had it been? Tuesday last week, eight days ago. She'd rung about the sheets. There'd never been any mention, or even a hint, of her leaving the country, and she was excited about moving into her new flat (which was now only two weeks away from being vacant), so it didn't make sense: she loved London, she'd always been adamant that she was staying, that she'd never go back.

Jon stood in the street for a moment thinking about his next move. Looking straight ahead he could see, in the distance, the corner of Lansdowne Rise, where the runaway car incident had occurred – the place it all started – two weeks earlier. Had it really only been two weeks?

He wondered why he'd even wanted to visit Sabine in the first place, did he miss her? Romy was more of a friend, he'd have been better off trying her. He would have rung her if he could have remembered the number of the landline there (it might have been his number too – for two and a half years – but numeral recall had never been his thing, a weakness exacerbated by his "rubbish long-term memory" as he'd put it to Emerald). He knew where she lived though: he and Romy were still co-owners in the place – being a "small" (her word) semidetached house with three floors plus a basement and a garden. And because it was in Carlyle Square in Chelsea, and the whole area was a tube station desert, he decided his loan from Alastair could stretch to a taxi.

Carlyle Square, with its Georgian terraces and beautifully maintained central gardens was a welcome sight, but the feeling didn't exactly seem to be mutual. When he pressed the doorbell and the large door eased open, it was Romy, but she looked more horrified than happy to see him. He immediately thought he realised why.

'I'm not dead. As you can see.'

'What are *you* doing here?'

'I would have rung, but...' He shrugged meekly. 'The fire.'

She didn't seem to comprehend.

'I lost everything,' he said.

'What are you talking about?'

'Don't you read the papers?'

'No more than I have to. Writing for them's bad enough.'

'My house burnt down.'

She just looked at him. None of it seemed to register.

'I nearly died,' he added. 'In fact, I'm supposed to *be* dead.'

'Well, dead or not, you can't stay here I'm afraid. Um...' She paused for a moment, apparently framing her next sentence. 'My, er... boyfriend actually, is um... due back.'

'Boyfriend.' There was a childish, mocking tone to his response which he regretted immediately.

She nodded and raised her eyebrows dismissively at the same time. 'Any minute, so you know... I'm thinking um...'

'Does he have a name?'

'... he may not be exactly dying to meet you so...'

'Romy. Social niceties aside for one moment, you do realise my house is a smoking *ruin*?'

'That's awful. Were you insured?'

'I was renting but is that all you can say? Seriously? I've lost virtually everything I own, I've been reported as missing presumed dead and you ask about my insurance?'

'What can I say. I don't know, I'm a journalist. Jon I'm sorry. I'm so stressed at the moment. Work's... And my... But anyway... it's not a good time.'

'And you're pregnant.'

'What?'

'You told me you're pregnant.'

'I did?'

'What happened to you at the end of that call by the way?'

She stared at him, frowning, as if he'd lost his mind. And maybe he had!

'So were you just making it up?' he said. 'About being pregnant?'

'It's... it's a really, really bad time Jonathon.'

'You never call me Jonathon.'

'Don't I?' She frowned again, as if she didn't know what was going on herself. 'I'm sorry. But you're going to... have to... I have to...'

'That's fine, Romy. That's fine. How's our house going by the way?'

'All in one piece, look I really have to go. I'm sorry. And I'm sorry about the house.'

'At least I'm alive though, huh?'

'Yes. God. Yes. Jon I'll ring you OK? But right now...'

'OK. I mean I don't have a phone at the... but I'll be in touch. Oh and Romy. Don't tell anyone you saw me, all right?'

'Who am I going to tell?'

It was said such an odd way – with her mouth turning down at the corners ever so slightly – that he was stuck for words. It may have been rhetorical, but before he could say anything, she quickly added: 'So where will you go?'

'Now? I may go back, I suppose. To West Kensington.'

'I thought you had no house?'

'No but I'm staying with... um... a friend.' He almost told her who, but some deep instinct prevented him.

She nodded and closed the door, with an uncomfortable hand gesture passing as a wave. No kiss. No hug. It was as though she were a different person. As though the real Romy had been stolen. He wondered what was happening in her life that was so transcendent. Or dominant.

He was right, he decided, when he'd told Romy he'd probably head back to West Kensington. It was too hard for now: he'd go back, face the music with Alastair, regroup, and somehow sort out his finances. Not to mention his practice, he'd ring chambers.

It was strange that no-one in his chambers – Tiffany, Ry or any of the others – had told the police early on in the piece that he was missing, but then again, that was typical – barristers lived such disconnected, private lives compared to most people, why *would* chambers run around acting as if they had their collective finger on the pulse of Jonathon Marriner's life?

He decided to proceed on foot – it was only a forty minute walk, it would do him good – and he started off towards Old Brompton Road.

He was almost there – walking north along North End Road in West Kensington – when he was struck by a moment of déjà vu. A girl suddenly appeared in front of him. A red-haired girl in a green dress. For a few moments he didn't register that he'd seen her before, and it felt like the same moment had occurred in the past... then he recalled that he'd seen a similar-looking girl on North End Road a week ago, on the day of the fire, who he'd imagined at the time was the same girl he'd seen walk past him in Notting Hill just prior to the runaway car incident. Could it really have been the same person, and could this be her again? Or was it simply yet another so-called coincidence?

He hadn't seen where she'd come from – possibly out of Tesco – but she was walking ahead of him up North End Road and he decided, out of curiosity, to follow her for a little way.

She had wavy dark red hair that brushed her shoulders as she walked. Her green dress seemed too light for the cool weather they'd been having – it was about knee length and flicked the backs of her legs as she walked. She had pale skin – not quite ivory, but not tanned – and a lithe and graceful figure. She half-turned around every now and then, not in Jon's direction but at the world at large, as if she were expecting to see something extraordinary but had no idea where to look. Her face, side-on at least, was noble and bright and sharp.

She suddenly dashed across the road, through the traffic, and Jon managed to do the same without her seeing him.

She seemed to be heading for the tube station and he was going to let it go at that, but then she turned up the street before it – Beaumont Avenue – and so, at a safe distance, he continued to follow her. Past the computer repair shop on the corner. The street took them away from the traffic of the busy road and ran along beside the train tracks. It was basically a dead end, and so he was confident it wouldn't be a wild goose chase. Sure enough, her destination appeared to be a long, low but imposing, grey building at the end of the street, with the name "Rootstein" emblazoned on its side.

Clearly displayed in the first window he came to was a bald female head, seemingly missing its decapitated body, bringing to mind the days of the French Revolution – *The Terror* – and thus the building's purpose was revealed: it was a workshop, warehouse and display centre for mannequins.

He slowed down as his redhead disappeared into one of its doorways.

A bigger sign on the building read: "ROOTSTEIN Display Mannequins". Below that, there was a large poster of a female model posing in front of a spectacular cloud formation. Approaching as close as he dared, he could see, through the entrance the girl had vanished into, a white-as-snow mannequin striking a pose just inside the glass door, and a back wall crammed with framed photographs.

Was this where she worked? Or even – and his mind was racing ahead of him here – was it a one-off job and was she posing for a sculptor? He didn't even know if that was how it was done or where that thought had come from, but he'd begun, rightly or wrongly, to trust the wilder catches of his imagination.

He turned and headed... not for home exactly, but the closest thing he currently had.

As he walked the well-trodden path back towards Alastair's flat, he had another déjà vu feeling, although this time for no apparent reason. Nothing looked especially familiar – in fact to the contrary, it all looked strangely *un*familiar and foreign. It wasn't, of course. The street hadn't changed and as he walked down the long avenue towards the T-junction where Alastair's building was, he imagined he could see that easily recognizable orange bundle of fur at the end.

And he could. It was Bertie all right, sitting there, waiting patiently, watching the world. Ten metres out however, Bertie stood up suddenly, and for a moment, Jon thought he might be springing forwards to meet him (as out-of-character as that would have been). But he ran off. I've frightened him? ... The moment the thought crossed his mind, a puff of smoke appeared where Bertie had been sitting. Like a cartoon puff when a character speeds off. Although this one was accompanied by a popping noise and the sharp *crack* of a lead projectile hitting cement, and this was no cartoon. Someone was shooting at Bertie! and Jon spun around to witness a man in an unkempt, dark grey suit, baseball cap and dark sunglasses, striding purposefully down the street towards him, gun in hand, silencer rudely attached, straightened arm rising for another shot.

They weren't shooting at Bertie, they were shooting at *him*.

He ran.

The air whistled next to his right ear and masonry exploded in front of him. He only had two choices, left or right, and to the right was a long straight section of road, so he went left.

Which was a dead end.

But it was also where the charred ruins of his former home were and he leapt over the fence and into the gaping space as if he were jumping into a swimming pool.

He landed ten feet below, at basement level, although fortunately on some old cardboard boxes which softened the impact. The irony was, if the building had been intact, and therefore locked, it would have been the end of the road, literally – a dead end in every sense – because out of the corner of his eye, just as he was about to launch himself through the burnt out doorway in front of him, he saw the suited figure appear at the fence railing above him, silhouetted against the sky.

Another popping sound and a shower of masonry erupted behind him. A further shot must have been fired through what used to be the kitchen window (but which was now a gaping hole) because the remnants of the old kitchen table, now looking like a large nugget of coal, spat black splinters into the air just feet away. He stumbled on into the darkness of the collapsed shell of a house. He didn't know if his pursuer had leapt down after him, but he plunged further into the interior anyway, praying he'd find a way out. The place was, still, after a week, heavy with the smell of burnt wood and paper and plastic. And then he remembered there was an exit to the rear laneway, permanently locked in better times, but with a bit of luck, not any longer. He found it fairly easily – there were huge gaping holes in the basement ceiling on the other side of the house and daylight poured in. The exit was on the next level up, on the ground level, but he was able to clamber over and up a collapsed section of ceiling, and then a simple shoulder charge to the exit door not only opened it but sent it flying into the lane outside.

And then he was running again.

Down the lane, towards North End Road, about fifty metres away, which he could see at the end. Waiting for a bullet in his back. Would it hurt? Would he have time to realise he'd been shot? That he had seconds to live? Or would the lights go out instantly?

North End Road, twenty metres away now. It never looked so good. But would it be the last thing he ever saw?

And then he was there. He turned – to gauge how close his stalker was – and he did so just in time to see him, in his baseball cap, only just emerging through the same doorway he had.

The man stopped and looked up in his direction. Gave him a strange look, possibly a frown or a squint. He was a good distance away, and Jon wasn't close enough to get a good look at his facial features, especially under the baseball cap, but he had a pale face and he no longer had his sunglasses on. They could have fallen off in the chase. And then he realised the man wasn't looking directly at him, but was looking around, surveying the scene. And it occurred to him that the sunglasses may have had prescription lenses and that the man was possibly short-sighted.

Jon nimbly dashed across the road, weaving his way, footballer quick, through the traffic. He looked like he was running for a bus, but he ran down North End Road and jumped in the first taxi he saw going in that direction, almost throwing himself on its bonnet in his desperation.

'Fulham Broadway, thanks. And maybe further.'

Clearly, returning to Alastair's was out of the question. He was going to need his ex-neighbour's help though, because it was obvious he'd have to stay underground for a while. Properly underground, until he sorted out what was going on. Contacting chambers was also not an option. He knew Alastair would help him, would be sympathetic. He'd have to get a message to him somehow.

He had a lot to think about in that taxi as they headed south down North End Road, away from the traffic congestion, and the tube station. And away from "Rootstein".

Which got him thinking. Was there a connection? With the girl in the green dress? Or, for that matter Romy, with her weird demeanour? Because he'd either been followed, or someone knew his movements that day.

46.

A fire engine raced by, somewhere.

And then she remembered where she was. In London, not Paris, not anymore. She got confused sometimes. That's what happens when you spend your whole life moving, flat to flat, city to city…

The moonlight shining through the window caused the silhouetted wooden framework to form a pattern of oddly stretched rectangles on the floor. The moon was the same everywhere, but this particular moonbeam, it was just for her…

He may as well have been keeping her locked underground, she had that little contact with the outside world. Felt like he'd been 'keeping' her for years now – decades – yet she knew it had only been five weeks. It was always cold too, there was something wrong with the central heating. She would tell him. She'd already told him, but she'd tell him again.

The sound of a key in the front door. Speak of the devil.

47.

Runion and Bridges. They could have been a firm of solicitors. Partners. They almost were. But for Bridges at least, this latest news was a blow.

Runion was showing Bridges a painting he'd especially wanted him to see – they were in Runion's gallery in Mayfair, Bridges was 'dropping in' on his way back from Paris – and Runion suddenly lowered his voice and muttered something under his breath which Bridges didn't quite catch.

'Sorry?' Bridges asked.

Runion looked around, apparently to make sure no-one was listening.

'*He's* your problem,' he said, more clearly this time.

'Who is?'

Runion indicated the painting in front of him with his finger in a stabbing motion. It was a painting of a mermaid.

'She is?' Bridges said, confused.

'*He* is.'

An extraordinary work of art well ahead of its time, painted in the early sixteenth century. It showed a mermaid sitting on a grim, stony shore and combing her long crimson locks that fell wetly over her breasts, with a dark, moss-coloured sea lapping at the tips of her fishtail. She was casting a sensuous smile in the direction of the observer, presumably the artist himself. *Him*self. It was, in fact, the same artist responsible for a painting Bridges had purchased from Runion's gallery only a month ago.

'The artist?'

Runion nodded.

'How is he my problem?'

'He knows who you are. And me. Which could be a problem. Because—'

'Whoa, whoa, whoa,' Bridges said, completely lost now. 'What are you talking about. The artist died in 1593. And you're saying *he* knows who *I* am?'

'No. I mean yes. The artist does, yes, but...' Runion trailed off.

What was *with* Runion today? Was he drunk? Depressed? Should Bridges be—

'You see, Lawrence...' Runion went on. He looked like he was in pain. Was he dying of something? 'The artist who painted this portrait is not who you think it is.'

'You mean not who you *told* me it is.'

Runion nodded, guiltily, if Bridges was any judge of human body language. Which, he had to admit, he was not.

'Yes Richard,' Bridges said, by now both interested and pissed off in equal measures. 'Do go on. You have my full attention.'

Runion drew a deep breath. 'The man who painted this is alive and well and living in Islington.'

'North London.'

'Well it's not bloody North Paris is it.'

'Hey. Richard. You're the one changing your story here. You're the *art dealer* passing off *forgeries*—'

'Will you keep your *voice* down.'

Runion looked genuinely upset, Bridges observed, but who the bloody hell was the one who'd recently, it would now seem, spent a hundred and twenty K on a Spanish fake?

'Listen. Lawrence. We shouldn't talk about this in here.'

'I'll bet,' Bridges said grumpily. And then he saw something in Runion's eyes that pulled him up. 'I don't like that look. At least tell me... is there some kind of threat?'

Runion nodded.

'Of a... pecuniary nature? Or is it... physical. Pertaining to... one's health.'

'The latter.'

'To *my* health? Am *I* in danger?'

Runion tilted his head from one side to the other – a *maybe-maybe-not*.

'Great—'

'We both could be,' Runion muttered. 'Especially here...'

'What? Speak up.'

'*Especially. Here*. Can you do lunch?'

'When?'

'Tomorrow. Meet me at the club.'

'The Garrick?'

'Yes. No. The Travellers. At shall we say... one?'

The next day, Thursday October 24th, Bridges caught a glimpse of his future while he was waiting for Runion to show up at their rendezvous. It wasn't a person he saw, or anything so literal – it wasn't, for example, the sad old man with a walking stick easing himself into the tired leather armchair in the corner of the reading room – but rather it was the garden. Looking out through the double doors of the reading room – he far preferred the Garrick to these showy clubs on Pall Mall – he could see a garden desperate for a longer summer, tired of the ruthlessness of the English climate, already looking forward to next spring, and no doubt trying not to think about (if plants could think, perhaps they could) the inevitable cold weather on its way. Trying not to feel, if plants could feel, the weight of an evil future about to take its toll.

And that's exactly how Bridges felt as he waited for Runion at the Traveller's Club.

A squirrel gaily bounded across the lawn, pretending to be a gazelle. Was it happy? Happier than I, certainly, he thought. He was probably, in fact, the unhappiest man in London at that precise moment, although he had to concede that one was usually worrying when one shouldn't be, and was usually happy when one shouldn't be as well. Take that squirrel for example. Its future wasn't a pretty one, not on paper at least, it was a grey, and greys were universally hated across the country, regarded as vermin, and just about everyone

Bridges knew had honed their shooting skills on the poor old grey squirrel, so the maths were against it. (Whatever you do, don't go calling them "poor old grey squirrels" over dinner with friends, they'll murder you with their forks). The grey was doomed, all this human fury would catch up with it eventually. Bridges on the other hand was destined for greatness.

Or had been. What now? This latest business sounded bad. What was the latest impediment to Bridge's well-deserved success – and his health! – that his good friend had uncovered this time?

Bridges' confused thoughts were interrupted by a member of staff.

'Mr Bridges, sir? There is a message for you.'

Good grief. Turned out Runion had to move their lunch to the Garrick after all. No explanation given, all very mysterious, but never mind that. The Garrick was a far better choice. One had to be grateful for small mercies.

Bridges, in his pin-striped navy suit, sans overcoat, strolled down Garrick Street in Covent Garden. He refused to rush: whatever the problem was, he wasn't Runion's servant boy. A light, misty rain was falling – if falling was the right word, floating gently downwards would have been a better description – and the stone of the buildings took on an oily sheen.

He threw a sharp right under the monolithic arched entrance, up the four shallow stone steps he knew so well, a sharp push on the polished iron bar and he was through the glass-panelled wooden doors and into the quiet, comforting embrace of the Garrick Club.

48.

Runion was waiting for him in the main sitting room. Bridges gave him a curt smile and joined him. And so there they sat, next to the large window, which at the same time both sucked in and repelled the greyness of the street outside. In no time at all (the staff were excellent here, beyond compare), they were cradling drinks – lemonades for both of them, which indicated the seriousness of the situation better than anything – and occasionally glancing up at the paintings that kept them company, almost every one a portrait from another time. There was no-one else in the room, so only the subjects of the paintings were there to observe them.

'Why the change of venue?' Bridges asked.

'Word reached me about a particular person lunching there today. To do with… all of this. Could have been awkward.'

'Right.'

Bridges waited to see if Runion would be more forthcoming. But nothing came. He continued:

'So come on, tell me. The artist then. It sounds as though I can safely assume it's not Corrientes.'

Runion stared into his drink for a long time. Clinked the ice. Poked at the slice of lemon with his straw.

'It's hard to know where to start,' he eventually said.

'Do your best.'

'Have you heard of Norton Rattatroop?'

'Who?'

'A Venice art dealer, originally Armenian. Norton's anglicized… although you'd think he would have chosen Nick or something, wouldn't you. Anyway, his real name's Nishan. Nishan Rattatroop? No? He recently disappeared. Here in London.'

'That's rotten luck.'

'Wife's just reported him missing.'

'Uh huh.'

'What about Aleksei Denisovsky ?'

'Aleksei…?'

'Denisovsky. Russian. Or Ukrainian, in fact. In the antiquities business. Young and successful. Used to work for a friend of mine in Venice. He rang me a couple of weeks ago, from Perth. Australia. I'm not exactly sure why he was there, and it was a bit out of the blue, I hadn't spoken to him in months. More than a year actually. He was the one, you see…' Runion paused and stared out at veils of drizzle sweeping past beyond the window pane. 'He sold me the painting I sold to you.'

'Here we go.'

'Listen. When I sold it to you, I had no idea it wasn't a Corrientes. I'd swear to that on a stack of King James bibles. It was only since then…'

'When?'

'Not long ago. A few days—'

'You were just about to ring me, obviously.'

Runion smiled grimly at Bridges' sarcasm.

'Anyway,' Bridges said. 'I thought you said he was in the antiquities business.'

'He was. But he handled any art – paintings, jewellery, whatever, as long as it was old. And profitable.'

'And now?'

'Now he doesn't do much.'

'Lucky him.'

'Not really. He's dead.'

'Ah. There's always a catch.'

'Or believed to be dead. Went missing in the desert over there. With his girlfriend. But there's a bit of a smell to it. They weren't sightseeing.'

'What do you mean?'

'It's complicated. And this is where your painting comes into it. There's been a battle for supremacy going on, of late, for control of the black market in art and antiquities. Worldwide. It's always been spread pretty thinly that business – with the exception of the Nazis in the thirties and forties, of course, and the odd foray by the Italian mafia – but lately groups from the old Soviet bloc have been making inroads.'

'What's any of this got to do with my painting?'

'Wait. I'm coming to that. The point is, there's a huge amount of cross-over right now, between art theft, art forgery and the antiquities black market. Which wouldn't matter in itself, except that the people gaining the upper hand are not pleasant people. As in, exceptionally *un*pleasant. To them, human lives are just another currency, slotting in somewhere between the rouble and the rupee, I suspect. A life, to them, is only worth as much as it takes to snuff it out without being caught. In other words, bugger all. Your Corrientes, would, no doubt, be worth more than a dozen lives.

'That's if it weren't a fake, I presume. How many lives would I get for it now?'

'Lawrence, I do believe the bad news concerning the provenance of the painting is blinding you to the gravity of the situation.'

'No doubt, Richard, no doubt.'

Runion sighed, and continued. 'I won't bore you with the finer points of how I came to suspect the forgery—'

'Oh you're not boring me, believe me.'

'And just remember I still own one myself. *La Sirena*, which you saw yesterday. Anyway I got my chap onto this, who managed to track down the forgerer. To Islington, as I said. A very sad little flat I have to say, but there you have it. They usually are.'

'Anyway.'

'Yes, anyway. The reception I received from this Mr Smith as he calls himself... ha ha... It was, shall we say, less than cordial. Made no attempt to deny it, though. He simply said I'd better watch my back... and so had anyone I'd mentioned this to. He has nasty friends. So he said and I believe him.'

'So how did he find out about me?'

'Not through me, I assure you. He seemed to know already. Having said that, I did initially warn him... this was before his counter threat... that I would have to inform anyone I'd already sold a painting to.'

'I can see where this is going,' said Bridges, who was becoming more miserable by the minute. Feeling increasingly squirrel-like.

'It goes without saying that these people won't think twice about causing someone to, um... *disappear* should their operation be endangered. It's a new breed, Lawrence. A new breed.'

'So how was it left? Détente? Or armies amassing at the border? I hope you brought your legendary diplomatic powers of persuasion to bear. Please tell me you did, Richard.'

'An uneasy truce is the highest I could, in all good conscience, put it.'

Bridges took a long slow breath in, and emitted a slow long exhalation.

'So,' continued Runion. 'The first thing is to *not tell a soul* until we manage to sort this out.'

'And how are we going to do that? Sort it out, I mean.'

'Well I have my chap looking into a few aspects, subtly putting out feelers, that kind of thing. Finding out what the upshot of the whole blasted business is likely to be.'

'Sounds like a busy chap, your chap.'

'I do hope so, with the amount I've been forking out.'

'Really? How long have you been—?'

'There is one *very* interesting little piece of information we've found out though. Someone's supposedly recovered the *Isfahan Decagon* from a wreck off Namibia.'

'The Isfahan Decagon? Really? That's a bit of a coincidence isn't it, we were just talking about it... it must have been...'

'Last week, we were. Exactly. Anyway, the *Prospero's Dancer*, heard of it?'

'Vaguely. Wasn't it... one of the... opium—'

'...opium clippers, exactly. It sank off Namibia and that's where the Decagon was recovered. Someone on the *Prospero's Dancer* acquired it in Macau, it seems. This is all according to a PhD student working at the British Museum. The legendary Isfahan

Decagon, can you believe it? Mathematical mysteries bound up in its geometry and all of that, obviously worth an absolute bomb.'

'Exactly,' said Bridges. 'So what's the latest on that again? Why is it different from the other Islamic designs, *girih* designs, made in…. When was it?'

'Late fifteenth. Around 1480. Well. As I understand it, and I'm no expert, but there are three essential differences. Firstly, it employs different underlying shapes in its design… the geometry's more complex in other words. Secondly, its internal patterns and the way the layers relate to each other is different. Stop me if I'm losing you.'

'No I understand, I think.' Bridges, didn't, but he'd google it later. He was impressed enough with himself as it was, for remembering the word *girih*.

'In the case of the Decagon,' Runion went on, 'there is… or there's supposed to be, no-one's seen the bloody thing in five hundred years or whatever… but there's supposedly a subtle and complex inter-relation between the layers in the way they repeat themselves in a fractal manner, but also seem to build in subtle changes as well.'

'Right. And the third thing?'

'The third one's a bit more contentious. There are supposed to be hidden images embedded in its design… at least if you extend the design out far enough. It's a non-repetitive design that can be extended out to infinity, so I'm not sure how far you have to go, but—'

'Images of what?'

'It's unclear. One claim is a portrait of a woman or a goddess… some even say God himself. Or herself.'

'Pffff,' Bridges scoffed. 'Talk about horses for courses.'

'Well yes, because another claim is it contains some kind of map or key to who knows what. But whether you believe those wilder assertions, the general consensus seems to be that the Isfahan Decagon is the first and only one of its kind: perfect tiling with a perfect golden ratio, infinite non-repeating pattern, and a layered shifting geometry unsurpassed even today. As such, it is *most* highly prized, *much* sought after, and *extremely* valuable. So you can imagine why the employers of our friend Mr Smith over in Islington were keen to get their grubby hands on it.'

'They're the ones who salvaged it? Well none of us'll get to see it now.'

'Possibly but it's not as simple as that because... and this is where, I have to say, my chap has done an absolutely stellar job... someone's stolen it. Possibly a member of a rival organisation.'

'Ha! And what's Interpol been doing during all of this? Just playing catch up as usual?'

'I'd like to say they're too busy preventing the sale of forged sixteenth century Spanish paintings, but clearly...'

Runion trailed off as someone else entered the room. He checked to see he didn't know him. Bridges looked around too. A bespectacled, pallid, slightly corpulent man in a charcoal grey suit, wandered over and picked up a copy of *The Times*, nodded to his two fellow members, sat down in the far corner of the room and noisily opened his paper. Runion and Bridges continued their conversation at a lower volume.

'Interpol,' said Runion, 'are about as useful as an umbrella in a hurricane.'

'The Yard?'

'Overrun by politically-correct, pen-pushing philistines who probably think that *Art* is something you put your *'and* on when you swear your daily allegiance to the bloody Queen!'

Runion had presumably raised his voice further than intended and he checked to see that their friend hadn't heard. If he had, the man in the corner wasn't showing it and remained hidden behind a wall of outstretched newspaper. Or almost hidden: his crossed legs could still be seen, the uppermost of which shamelessly flaunted, for all to see, an uninspiring, blue and grey checked sock, and an even more tone-lowering brown suede shoe. The people they allowed into the Garrick these days...

'So those fellows you mentioned earlier,' said Bridges, 'Norton or whatever his name was, and the Russian...?'

'Aleksei Denisovsky. Ukrainian I believe.'

'Right. So are you saying that there's a link? With—'

'Oh there's a link all right,' Runion said, looking around at the newspaper and lowering his voice further. 'The word on the street is that Aleksei has been using his Russian connections on the black market for quite some time. And Norton Rattatroop...' He proceeded to speak in an almost inaudible murmur. 'Norton Rattatroop most *certainly* has been. Interpol have been camped out in front of his gallery, pretty much on a permanent basis. They've never been able to pin anything on him though, the fools. He's hardly going to bring his stolen art in *there*, is he. What's he going to do, have a Stolen Artworks Retrospective? Anyway, I probably shouldn't be talking about him in the present tense.'

'You think he's been...?'

'That or he's decamped to Armenia for the rustic lifestyle. I know which one my money would be on. Oh and the other thing...' Runion checked the room again quickly. 'He's a friend of a member here, Sir Martin Nevers, the judge, so if that's true, this Norton fellow has friends in the right places. Had.'

'Mm. Not enough of them, by the sounds of it.'

'The thorny thing is, Nevers is reputed to have his own line of... *connectivity*, if I can use that word, to the Soviets. Don't ask me how I know that.'

'Sounds like a le Carré novel.'

'Infinitely messier. *Infinitely*. Anyhow, Nevers was the person lunching at the Traveller's today. Thought it might be wise to steer a wide berth on this occasion. You just never know. Right now, any connection's a dangerous connection as far as I'm concerned.'

Bridges nodded, mulling over the phrase "dangerous connection".

There was a sudden rustling in the corner as the man in the grey suit folded his newspaper and put it down on the table in front of him, checked his watch, stood up with a degree of grunting effort and trudged out of the room.

'Any idea who that was?' Runion asked.

Bridges shook his head. 'Why?'

'I've seen him somewhere. Can't quite place him...'

Runion and Bridges shared a miserable moment in their own thoughts.

'So what are we going to do?' Bridges asked eventually.

Runion stared at Bridges for a moment. He appeared to have only half heard the question. 'It's tricky,' was all he said.

It was tricky all right. This situation wouldn't do at all. Bridges hated things being left up in the air. Particularly where his health was concerned.

'Who's this chap of yours anyway, can he help us?' Bridges asked.

'Which chap?'

'*Your* chap. The one who tracked down Mr Smith and who's been putting out feelers. Surely he can do something. Or advise us what to do.'

'Ah yes, my chap. Except it's not a he. My chap happens to be a woman.'

'A woman?'

Runion nodded. 'A private investigator, and a bloody good one. Easy on the eye too, it has to be said, but that's not why I use her. She is, very simply, the best man for the job.'

'I'll bet.'

'No really.'

'Does she have a name?'

'Her name is Emerald Strand. A Danish-Ukrainian... or Ukrainian-Dane, whichever you prefer. Perfect, really, as it turns out, for our current...um... situation. I'd wager she knows a lot of these characters personally. Rather her than me, I might add.'

'How did you find her?'

'Funnily enough it was through Aleksei, but well before any of this began to go pear-shaped. I used her a couple of years ago to track down a Russian who, um, let's say owed me either a painting of mine that he happened to have in his possession, or a hundred thousand pounds, I didn't mind which. After I got Emerald onto him, I ended up with both. The painting *and* the hundred grand. Don't ask me how she did it. But I never saw the Russian again.'

'You don't think she—'

'You never ask questions in this business, Lawrence.'

'No. Right.'

'If there's one thing I've learnt, it's that.'

'Great, so let's get her in. For a three-way. I mean, obviously, a meeting.'

Runion was shaking his head, and as far as Bridges could tell, it wasn't over his choice of words.

'What?' Bridges said. 'I have a right to be involved Richard, after all—'

'Oh I have no problem with you being involved. None at all.'

'Well what, then.'

'There's a little snag.'

'What?'

'Emerald seems to have disappeared herself.'

It was just one thing after the other. Another squirrel down. Bridges could almost feel the crosshairs on him as they sat there in the sitting room of the Garrick club. He stared at Runion for a good ten seconds, blinking. Processing. But there was no answer. Or rather, no answer that was good.

'Fuck,' he said.

'Yes,' Runion replied. 'Fuck.'

49.

It was bang on 3pm and Jon was standing in the crowded circular booking hall of Piccadilly Circus tube station – the proposed rendezvous. He was nervous, there were people everywhere, why had he suggested meeting in Piccadilly Circus? What had he been thinking?

He cast his mind back over the last twenty-four hours...

The previous day, after the shooting incident and while fleeing West Kensington in the taxi, it had dawned on him that he had to find a way of meeting up with Alastair – who had become indispensable, his life preserver – but he knew he couldn't return to Alastair's flat. He also didn't know Alastair's phone number or even, for that matter, his surname. Just his address.

Why didn't he go to the police? It would have been the obvious thing to do, but he was running purely on instinct by this stage, and every electrical connection between every neurone in his brain and every twitching muscle in his body was saying no. There was logic too, behind this decision: if he'd gone to the police they'd have taken a statement, wasted time, and done very little. And his backstory was looking increasingly deranged or at best, hard to explain – the house fire, the week at Alastair's under the radar... Not to mention the fact that going to the police would have immediately announced his movements to all and sundry (and especially the sundry) making him even more of a target than he already was. Rightly or wrongly, he'd made his decision and he had, anyway, perhaps already passed the point of no return.

He still had some cash left, so decided his best option would be to send a registered-post, next-day-delivery letter and pray that Alastair would actually read it. And pray that no-one else intercepted it (in which case, in all likelihood, that would be that – game over, as they say).

He'd jumped out of the cab on King's Road, Chelsea – they'd been stuck in traffic directly in front of the World's End Post Office. It happened to be just up the road from Romy's and was certainly closer to the place of his attempted murder than he would have liked, but he was anxious to get his note off to Alastair.

His note was a wail, followed by a grovel and a plea. It was light on tact and heavy on imploring. He wasn't asking for 'lawyers, guns and money' exactly (he was a lawyer himself and guns weren't his area of expertise), but he *was* asking for money: cash, and as much as Alastair could spare. It was a big ask but he would forever be in his debt. He swore he'd repay him many times over. He then went on to suggest they meet in Piccadilly Circus tube station at 3pm the next day, Thursday 24th.

(Thinking about that suggestion now, of course, it was ludicrous. Piccadilly Circus? Famous for being the place where you'd see everyone you knew if you stayed long enough? And it was hardly all that convenient for Alastair either, who spent most of his time, as far as Jon knew, in West London.)

After dispatching his letter of desperation, and low on cash, he continued on foot towards the West End to see if he could find accommodation for the night. First stop was his old haunt, the Covent Garden Travelodge.

When he arrived though, the staff (as usual) had all changed since the last time he was there and no-one knew him. They couldn't accept his booking without payment up front and he only had about fifty pounds left. Dand everywhere else, it was the same story: the first night's payment was required up front.

It became clear that accommodation would be impossible to secure and that he'd need a plan B. He thought of Heathrow (airport) and then he thought of St. Pancras (station) but as he was at least looking semi-respectable in Alastair's suit (which almost fitted him and was only slightly soiled from his frantic dash through the remains of his burnt-out house), he opted for more comfort and headed for a bar he knew in an expensive hotel near Hyde Park Corner, frequented by rich Russians and high class prostitutes. There were, however, only so many advances from bejewelled, befurred, blonde thirty-year olds with Eastern European accents he could take in one evening – the prostitutes he couldn't afford (not that he was particularly keen to return to Macau, so to speak) and the Ukrainian gold-diggers were a little too much of a loaded question for him. As attractive as it might have been, the thought of a warm bed for the night if he played his cards right, the baggage these women came with had contents he was far better off without.

He didn't want music or alcohol or people around him indulging in either, so that left the twenty-four hour cafes. Bar Italia in Soho fitted the bill for a while with its coffees and hot chocolates until the noise and the late-night/early-morning crowds became too much and he decided to make his way to St. Pancras after all. It was a chilly night – down to six degrees by 6am – and he was sorely tempted to get on a train: a one-way journey on a heated train to anywhere seemed like *just* the ticket except he had a rendezvous, he hoped, to stick to. So in architecturally-inspired, thermally-challenged St. Pancras station he remained, wondering how in the hell homeless people got by. When they did. And it wasn't even winter yet.

In this way, Wednesday blurred into Thursday, the sun reluctantly appeared and slowly rose and the day warmed to a civilised seventeen degrees. It was just about the longest twenty-four hours he'd ever spent.

And now, surrounded by the throngs of tourists and commuters in Piccadilly Circus tube station, he could only dream of a quiet room, a comfortable bed…

Other thoughts continued to bounce around in his head, though. Thoughts that clamoured for attention. Persistent, like the pleading of a young child.

There was no longer any doubt someone was trying to kill him. He no longer had to wonder if he was going crazy. He no longer had to look at the odds or Probability, or the illusion of 'coincidence'. So who was behind all of this? And why? To what end? And most importantly of all, what had any of it to do with him?

Now that he was no longer doubting the connectivity of it all, it drew Emerald back into the frame yet again. She had to be a part of all this. How, though, was the unanswerable question. Nothing she'd brought to him, or said, had made any sense.

A loud, passing group of unchaperoned Italian teenagers startled him for a moment and he felt more exposed than ever. Whoever was trying to kill him was pulling out all stops now. So it would seem. If he was supposed to have died in the fire, he most certainly should have been farewelling the world with a bullet in his back. He looked around at the swirling sea of humanity, faces from every corner of the globe, every nook and cranny: there were Spaniards and Norwegians, Americans and Koreans, Australians and Russians and Indians, and he wondered if any of them was following him. Because that was what must have happened the day before, wasn't it? He had to have been followed. Unless – and this had crossed his mind earlier – someone knew he was returning to West Kensington, knew the timing of his return.

And the only person who knew that was Romy, who he'd just come from seeing.

He kept pushing the thought out of his head, and it kept springing back: it was almost impossible to imagine, but could Romy have been connected with any of this? He had, after all, received her phone call the night of the fire – the phone call, what's more, with its discomposingly abrupt conclusion, nothing more than sinister perhaps, but nothing less than strange.

And then something clicked in his head. It must have been thinking of Emerald and that will, because he was reminded of his own will. He hadn't looked at it in years, and a while back he'd made a mental note to change it (which he still hadn't done), because just prior to his marriage to Romy, he'd altered his will so that everything went to her. Everything, which currently meant the Wiltshire cottage, his half-share of the Chelsea house, the million pounds...

Surely not. Not Romy. She wouldn't... *surely* wouldn't... be capable of such a thing. Nor could she be so stupid that she could possibly think she could get away with it. No. It simply wasn't conceivable...

Suddenly, a man in a dark brown suede coat came charging in from nowhere and bumped into him, hard, and thrust something into his chest. For an instant Jon assumed it was a knife. By the time he realised it was a piece of paper – which reflexively his hands had grabbed, the man was weaving away through the churning crowds and rapidly disappearing from sight. Jon only had a second or two, but it was enough for him to see that the man resembled Alastair, with his indignant ginger hair. He looked cross, too.

Recovering from the fright it gave him, and realising there was no point in chasing him (the man obviously didn't want to be followed), he unfolded the piece of paper. It was a large, sprawling handwritten note, signed "Fond Regards, Alastair". There was no addressee and he wondered if Alastair even knew his name. It began:

Wretchedly <u>harebrained</u> place to meet !! see you in 3 HOURS at BRASSERIE ZEDEL 20 SHERWOOD ST W1 just around the corner couldn't get a booking at this late stage being a thursday night but assured a walk-in table at 6PM will be no problem hope you havent had lunch they do a wonderful andouillette de troyes grillee if youre a tripe man as I am and the profiteroles are absolutely OBLIGATORY in the meantime lie low for God's sake go to HATCHARDS bookshop on piccadilly and read a book these FUCKING CRETINS we are dealing with DONT READ you know that dont you
so youll be safe there
DO NOT FOLLOW ME do not try to find me i will be trying my luck in a building <u>FULL OF PUBLIC SERVANTS</u> (!!!!!!!!!!!!!!!!!!!!!!!!!!!!!) in westminster (the department it houses shall remain nameless) it is the most incomprehensible layout of any building in the country even the AUTOMATONS who work there can't FIND

THEIR OWN WAY AROUND IT without gps so you couldnt find me there anyway just go to hatchards and take deep breaths in the poetry section...

The rest of it was a rant – or rather a continuation of a rant, a rage against the nameless government department in question – and as far as he could tell, contained nothing more of relevance other than a command to destroy the note.

Jon knew Brasserie Zédel well – it was a cavernous, opulent, art-deco French restaurant in the basement of the old Regent Palace Hotel building near Piccadilly Circus. It was vast – with seating for well over two hundred – and he wondered how it was any better a place to meet than where he was standing, given how crowded it was likely to be.

Did the "fucking cretins" not eat as well as not read?

50.

It was a source of irritation.

When it came to catching public transport, Bridges hated catching the Tube and almost always caught a bus when he had a choice. Taxis were a wonderful extravagance, particularly after selling a painting or making his way to a flashy lunch – or, as is often the case, both – but it somehow felt rather wasteful and very much against the spirit and camaraderie of the Blitz (not that he was around then) and everything that was good about being a Londoner. But when it came to travelling like a true (if not necessarily true-blue) Londoner, only when special circumstances warranted it would he revert to the subterranean option, which in his view was only really suited to spelunkers, submariners and Morlocks. And also (funnily enough) tourists from the Mediterranean end of the Continent (who you'd think would be out of their element without the sun, but perhaps had less need for topping up their quota of sunshine).

He was on the deep and dreaded Piccadilly line, surrounded by noisy Spaniards as far as he could tell, who began invading his personal space from the moment he boarded the train at Covent Garden. Normally, after a lunch at the club, he would have caught a bus – the good old number 19, as loyal as a Jack Russell – all the way from Shaftesbury Avenue in Covent Garden to Sloane Square, but as Runion lived near him and was *himself* catching the bus home, the bus option was out.

Bridges liked Runion, and he certainly enjoyed their lunches at the club, but enough was enough and that day's lunch had certainly been enough. He needed some air after their conversation, so when Runion had invited him to join him on a bus home, he'd been forced to quickly invent a need to attend to some local business first. As soon as they'd parted ways on Garrick Street, he'd been forced to follow at a safe distance – feeling a little like a spy – and take a sharply angled dive into the depths when he reached Covent Garden tube station.

As the train pulled into Piccadilly Circus, he was almost tempted to jump out and hop on the number 19 there, and rejoin the sunshine. The chances of ending up on the same bus as Runion were remote and it was a risk he would have taken. If he could have been bothered. But he was feeling distinctly weary, and now that he was on the blasted thing, he decided he may as well stick it out (like a true Londoner). So when the doors opened he stayed where he was, feeling confident it was likely to be the Spaniards' stop anyway (no such luck).

Not long after the doors had closed again and the train began pulling away from the station, he noticed a man sitting at the end of the row of seats opposite him. He couldn't place him for a moment, and then realised it was the man from the club, the man Runion had asked him about. The large fellow in the grey suit and glasses who'd been reading *The Times*. At least that's who it looked like, although you could never be perfectly sure in a city like London, swarming as it was with the flotsam and jetsam of the world. He sometimes felt that everyone probably had their double, somewhere, in a place like London.

The man was a little heftier than Bridges remembered, but he was similar in most other respects. He was wearing the same charcoal suit, severely lined and crushed at his back, as if he'd been sitting down all day without taking his jacket off and had been sweating into it. And there. Confirmation: the blue and grey checked socks with the brown shoes. It had to be the same man.

Although if he had to go on the face alone – the man on the train had small eyes set into a rather full face – Bridges couldn't have been sure. It looked unfamiliar, but then he had no recollection of the face of the man in the club either, despite getting a good look at him. He had the same hair, though: a strange mixture of blond, grey and brown, sparse, but just enough to give one a strong impression of multi-colour. Or no colour. Because there was certainly a blandness about the man that almost compelled you to not remember him. It was difficult to describe: he sucked in attention with his presence, like a politician or an actor – but at the same time there was something about his looks, about the man himself, that was opaque and vague. Nevertheless, Bridges was as certain as he could be that this was the man they saw earlier.

There was, now he thought about it, something familiar about him as well, as though it were someone he knew – Runion had obviously felt the same way – but the harder he tried to place the face, the further away from the front of his brain the memory receded. Overwhelmed, perhaps, by the visual lifelessness.

Bridges must have been staring because the man suddenly returned his gaze. He was blinking a lot, too, and it was a gaze that not only said I know you've been staring at me, but also, I know who you are.

Bridges looked away again – quickly – but the unpleasant sensation of being stared at continued for the remainder of the trip.

51.

He held her close. A moment or two passed. And then: the applause, a little less than he deserved. And a lot less than thunderous.

What an abomination!

'Jessica, my darling Jessica...' he was saying to her as soon as the curtain hit the stage, raising dust.

'Not now Michael. Not now.' She was angry and already storming off.

Michael felt the stabbing pain of the falsely accused and tossed his plastic revolver into the dark. It thudded against the chaise longue.

'Fuck you,' he muttered under his breath. '*Double* fuck you.'

It wasn't MY fucking fault you made me forget my fucking lines.

He barely raised a smile as he walked past the stage manager, Geraldine. He knew she liked him and that she appreciated his regular flirting. There wouldn't be any of that this afternoon though.

Not now, Geraldine. Not now.

An hour later, in a vast underground brassserie off Piccadilly Circus, Michael was sharing an *Entrecôte au Beurre Persillé* and a bottle or two of house pinot noir with the gallery owner Richard Runion, dressed today in a Persian-blue, velvet smoking jacket. Richard was a wanker but a fantastic drinking companion (not that Michael was *drinking* drinking, he had another performance in two hours). Richard saw the humour in everything and his endless stories were genuinely funny. And he liked his wine (as his Burgundy-stained, burgundy tie attested to).

'... So after I'd said all this,' Richard was saying, a grin waiting to burst forth on his gigantic red face as big as Jupiter. '... he just stood there, staring at me and then, all at once, blurted out in that Midlands accent of his: "No no no, oh my God, what I said was, she was havin' a *bath*!".'

And at that, Richard erupted in a barrage of rasping laughter and coughing.

Michael found it funny too although not, evidently, as funny as Richard. He chortled along though, and at the same time glanced over at the table next to them, hoping to catch the admiring glance of a theatre-goer (not that he hadn't appeared in his fair share of films and television episodes) – hoping to spot one of those heartening looks of recognition that kept every actor doing what he did.

No such luck though. Just a wild-looking ginger and his more debonair, dark-haired friend, deep in animated conversation. Both in drab navy suits, one, or both of them reeking of mothballs. Probably accountants. Two men, by the looks of it, who rarely if ever darkened the doors of a theatre.

Turning back to his dinner companion, Michael reminded himself that at least Richard went to see a show occasionally. And as the song advised, if you couldn't be with the one you love: "love the one you're with".

52.

Alastair was in the middle of telling Jon about his earlier adventures in the "Department" – he still wouldn't reveal which one – and Jon was, while not remotely interested in the story itself, grateful for the 'small talk' (although no talk, from Alastair, was ever, in any sense, small). They'd been sitting in Brasserie Zédel for twenty minutes and Alastair had talked solidly for most of it. Jon spent half the time keeping an eye out for suspicious-looking characters loitering on the fringes or sitting at the tables, and in his current state of mind, everybody looked suspicious. While it was unlikely his adversaries would 'take him out' in the middle of a crowded restaurant, they could be there, watching him, ready to follow him into the greater world outside.

At the next table for example, there was a dubious-looking man dressed in black from head to toe (black t-shirt, black trousers, black jacket and shoes) and possibly wearing a small amount of make-up, who kept looking over at Jon every few minutes. Possibly he was gay, or maybe Jon reminded him of an actor, or of someone famous or someone he knew… Jon pretended he hadn't noticed but made a mental note to make sure the guy didn't follow him. And make sure he didn't get anywhere near his food.

Apart from the man in black and his companion (a ruddy-faced statue of a man with an explosive laugh that might have given even Alastair a run for his money), there was no shortage of people to keep an eye on: there would have been two hundred people in the place. It was a big space, all marble and chrome and with the big colour contrasts in the floor and wall tiling typical of the art-deco style. Majestically high ceilings. Jon was grateful to be seated with his back to a large marble pillar, even if the illusion of safety was purely psychological. The hubbub of the crowd was bordering on deafening, and Alastair's booming voice was almost drowned out (but not quite). Jon could see the irony in the fact that he'd been told to 'lie low' and 'go to ground' and here they were, literally underground, and surrounded by a bigger crowd than you'd usually find on the 'surface'.

Finally, Alastair had come to the end of his story. Single-handedly he'd stared down the "Department" and won. Horatius at the bridge. *And* he'd managed to get out of the place alive.

'You're probably wondering what we're doing here,' said Alastair reading his mind, '… shoulder to shoulder with half of London. Well after your… to be perfectly honest with you… absolutely bloody *idiotic* foolishness yesterday, there wasn't much point in keeping you hidden and, frankly… it's a *damn sight* better than a *tube station*. Let alone Piccadilly fucking *Circus*!'

'We're just about in Piccadilly Circus.'

'I doubt very *much*, my dear boy, that these people we're messing with eat *offal*. *No-one* under sixty eats tripe these days, take my word for it, not if you're born west of Vienna. Unless it's a dare. Or you're from Suffolk.'

'What about steak?' said Jon after snatching a look at the next table's meals.

'Anyway, you've been wandering the streets of this great city now for thirty hours or so… Did you go to Hatchards, by the way?'

'I did in fact—'

'And loitering in tube stations, good God, I'd be amazed if someone hadn't spotted you at some point.'

'It's a big city—'

'So we have to *assume* they know you're alive. *Comprenday?* These people have access to CCTV cameras, you do know that don't you.'

'They've infiltrated the constabulary?'

'What do *you* think.'

Jon nodded. It wouldn't, in fact, surprise him.

'You probably think I'm barking *mad*,' Alastair continued. 'But there are things I know…'

Jon wasn't sure if Alastair was lost in thought or had just spotted someone; he had an odd, distant and glazed look in his eyes all of a sudden. Jon turned around to see who he was looking at, but all he saw were just more people.

'What is it?'

'Nothing, It wasn't…' And then, he was back. 'Now tell me. What's happened.'

So Jon told him. He'd already told him about the money appearing in his account two years ago, and about the strange incidents leading up to the fire, including the near accidents and the appearance of Emerald in his chambers and the business with Martin Nevers' will. Now he described his encounters with Romy, and the girl in the green dress again and, of course, the shooting which well and truly confirmed his suspicions that someone was trying to kill him. Alastair maintained a steely gaze throughout the telling, not missing a word. When Jon had finished he kept staring for a few moments. Jon wasn't sure what Alastair found the more shocking – the fact that he, Jon, was almost shot, or that Bertie was.

Eventually Alastair broke his gaze and surveyed the room. Thoroughly, as though he'd just thought of something. When he spoke, the volume of his speech had dropped significantly, so much in fact that Jon actually had trouble hearing him until he moved his chair closer – a sign that the situation was grave, if ever there was one.

'I may have been a little hasty in assuming your pursuer was born west of Vienna. I may be wrong here… and I hope I am, dear *God* I hope I am… but…'

'But what?'

'Never mind. First things first.'

Alastair looked around the room again and then under the table, sat up, and then he pushed at something under his chair with his right hand. He then stared straight at Jon, shooting him a very unusual look. At the same time, Jon could feel something pressing against his left foot.

'Don't look now,' Alastair said, 'but when we leave, you are to take with you the attaché case which I've just pushed against your shoe. Can you feel it?'

'I can feel it.'

'In it you will find a few healthy-sized wads of banknotes which should see you through for a while at least.'

'Alastair, I am…' Jon began, touched by his neighbour's kindness and intending to express his gratitude, before Alastair raised his hand in a traffic policeman's 'stop' gesture.

'I've also included a mobile phone with a pre-paid SIM. Don't worry, I have plenty more. Don't ask me where I got them. But if you ring *me* on it, you're going to have to throw it in the river immediately afterwards, so make sure you've made any necessary further arrangements with me if you do. Why? Because whatever you do, you will keep me out of this… which is also for your benefit. I'm your fullback let's say, and you…'

'You most certainly are.'

'… and you need me in one piece, so I don't want my number in that phone.'

'Of course. But I still don't actually *have* your number, which is why I had to—'

'Why you had to write to me, I know.' Alastair sighed deeply. He thought for a long time before continuing. 'You know the more I think about this, the more I think I'm going to have to give you Lucinda's key.'

'Who?'

'A gorgeous little thing, I'm sure you'll like her. I just hope *she* likes *you*.'

'Who's Lucinda?'

'Lucinda is a house, my dear boy. What's more Lucinda, the little tart, straddles the Prime Meridian. She has one inner thigh in the eastern hemisphere and one in the western.'

'She's… the house is in Greenwich?'

'Peacehaven. In Sussex. All that sea air, it'll do you good. You could almost say she's on the sea. In fact she'll be *in* the sea before too long I'm sure, with all this climate change going on. There's even a boat in the backyard. Or there usually is, it's being repaired.'

'For when the ocean rises.'

'No no. I had a mad idea I'd just sail away one day, into the sunset. Still might happen. Not at the moment though, and certainly not with this storm coming.'

'I suppose not. Storm?'

'Anyway. Lucinda. She'll be a good *safe house* and you, my good man, you indubitably need a house that's safe.'

'That I do and Alastair, this is very kind but I could just go to my cottage in Wiltshire if I—'

'You bloody well can *not* go to your cottage *any*where! I don't care if it's in the Kalahari Desert. Wasn't that bloody butcher with the bazooka *enough* for you?!'

Alastair paused, as if he needed a moment to mentally turn the volume down a couple of notches. When Jon looked down, he noticed that the 'attaché case' which Alastair had transferred to him earlier was in fact a zip-up, retro, BOAC shoulder bag.

'Your cottage…' Alastair said gently, a picture of Buddha-calm, '… is the first place they'll look. They're probably there now, quaffing your best vintages. Now the keys…' and he dug deep into a trouser pocket, wriggled his hands around below the tablecloth and produced a scrunched-up table napkin which he placed, magician-like, on the table between them. 'Take it, and let no-one see what it is. The walls have good eyesight.'

Jon put the napkin ball in his lap and extracted a single, small key, slipping it into his own trouser pocket. 'What about the—'

'*Don't*… even use the word. Begins with an "a" and ends with "s" "s", yes?'

'Ass.'

'If you like. But don't be one. This is no time for schoolboy humour.'

'Sorry.'

'Now you're going to have to memorize it… the "ass", as you so maturely put it… but I'm not going to write it down. Too risky. I'm not even going to say it. Ditto. I will however spell it out for you…'

And he unscrewed the salt shaker and upended half its contents onto the table.

'The advantage of using salt is that no-one else can read it. Not unless they're within close range and leaning over the table. You have to get the light just right.'

Even though the address consisted of just a post code and house number, it took him a few minutes to spell it out in crude lettering, attracting some raised eyebrows from the waiters.

'Now memorize it,' he said when he'd finished. Jon committed the eight letters and digits to memory.

'Done?' Alastair asked, and then, with a swift sweep of his arm, the address disappeared. The salt scattered over the floor, with some of it landing in a woman's shoe. To her obvious annoyance.

'Don't forget it, or you'll be trying that key in every door in Peacehaven. Now I was going to say... contrary to what you may think, it's lucky that you *didn't* have a credit card last night...'

'I would have killed for a bed.'

'*Been* killed you mean. It's lucky because on *no account* should you sign *anything*. On *no account* should you provide *them* with *any* kind of electronic trail whatsoever. I cannot emphasize this enough.

Jon nodded.

'Leave nothing in your handwriting.'

'But Alastair. I'm going to have to access my bank account at some point, to pay you back for one thing—'

'Forget about that for now. But listen to me. You mustn't... must *not*... use any credit cards, Oyster cards, or any plastic whatsoever. You mustn't use electronic banking, or any phone other than the untraceable ones I give you. You certainly mustn't sign anything and it goes without saying you must never... *ever*... give your real name. In fact you should *forget* your real name, we'll think of a new one for you. Show no-one your passport or drivers licence—'

'I don't have them anymore, remember? The fire?'

'Perfect. Watch out for CCTV cameras, they're everywhere these days, the best thing to do is wear a baseball cap with the shade low over the eyes. The cameras are usually placed at height. Other than on ATMs, which you must on *no account* go near. You can guard against drones in the same way.'

'Drones?'

'Drones and for that matter satellites. Don't think for a minute that the detail of the imagery you see on Google Earth is the limit of what *they* get to see. Military satellites are unbelievable these days, they can read the label on your jacket. You need to be careful, too, of… forensic deposits.'

'As in…?'

'As in DNA. Just be aware, that's the most you can do.'

'Can I use the toilet?'

Alastair raised a cautioning finger in response. 'Always flush. Now… and I hardly need to say this, but don't even think about driving any car registered in your name because they'll get you with ANPR every time. Automatic number plate recognition. The same goes for a rental car in your name. Not that you'll be able to hire one as you're not using your licence or signing anything. And I'd advise against driving a stolen car.'

'Good advice.'

'No Facebook or any other social media. You don't use those dating websites do you?'

'No. But I can use the internet?'

'Just make sure you've turned off all location finders in any device you use. And *definitely* no selfies.'

'No problem.'

'So that's about it. Use a false name and date of birth, pay only in cash, don't be photographed, don't write anything down, don't touch anything, don't be seen.'

'That's all?'

'I realise it's a tall order, but I don't see that you have any choice.'

'Or I could go to the police.'

Alastair looked at Jon for a moment, his face reddening, trying by the looks of it to keep something under control. His breathing was heavy. He nodded and then nodded again. Then with a flick of his head he gestured for Jon to lean in. He did the same and spoke in slow, low tones.

'You. do. that. and. you… are *dead*. As dead as that cow.' He was pointing to the steak on the next table. 'It is as simple as that. You go to the police and then they know where you are. They've got you. You're not the PM and you're not one of them so don't go thinking you'll be getting twenty-four hour protection which is the only thing that would keep you safe once you go to the cops. Are we clear on this?'

'Yeah.' Jon nodded slowly. 'I suppose you're right.'

'Don't just suppose, dear boy. Don't just suppose. This is no time for suppositions. We do however need some solid theories to work with. This Emerald for instance. She's obviously a private investigator.'

'You think?'

'That toilet ruse,' said Alastair. 'Oldest trick in the book.'

'What. You mean she…?'

'She meant you to see that will, exactly, while still being able to argue it was an accident. Maintain her integrity and all of that. But unfortunately you didn't read it when you had the chance, so we're still in the dark on that one. More's the pity. We'd be a damn sight better off if we knew what the devil it was she was trying to tell you.'

'And then there's Romy…'

'Romy. Yes. Ex-wives, oh how we love them.'

'I find it very difficult to believe Romy's got anything to do with this but I can't help but think I should be changing my will. I should have done it years ago anyway.'

'You should have, I'm afraid it's too late now. Nothing in writing, remember? Anyway, I suspect things have gone too far for something like that to make a difference.'

'But if anything happens to me, she gets everything.'

'Which means you're dead anyway, don't worry about it. We're working on it not coming to that, remember?'

'Mm.'

'What I'd like to know,' Alastair said, 'is who the rasher of crispy bacon was.'

'Sorry?'

'The contents of the *body bag*.'

'Jesus.'

'The remains, from your house. There's been no news on that front. Or rather, no news they've deigned to *share* with us. It did make me think though. Some art dealer disappeared recently. Called Norton *Rattatroop*, heard of him?'

'Vaguely,' Jon said.

At the same time, he noticed that the man at the next table – not the one dressed all in black but his imperious-looking, red-faced companion – was paying Alastair more than the usual amount of interest. Alastair's voice had risen again, and possibly his "body bag" or his "Rattatroop" had drawn the attention. And even though the man had looked away again immediately, Jon could tell he was all ears.

'Well,' Alastair said, 'he was visiting London. From Venice.'

'Venice. My brother's a painter in Venice.'

'Well if he is, he'd better watch his step or he'll end up in a canal. Rattatroop's disappearance has been linked to a war on the black market which the Russians—'

'Dreadful business.' It was the sanguine diner at the next table. So he had been all ears after all. His friend appeared less than excited about the interruption to their own conversation. 'I'm an art dealer myself and let me tell you, what you read about those people is only the half of it.'

'I don't doubt it for a moment,' Alastair said. 'Not for a moment. Anarchy rules OK, yes?'

'I'll say!' the sanguine man said, before his black-attired friend drew him back into their conversation.

Alastair threw Jon a look which he read as saying "Keep an eye on *that* one". 'But he's right you know,' Alastair said softly. 'It's only the half of it.'

'So do you think it's got something to do with my brother? He'd probably know this Rattatroop chap if he operates out of Venice.'

'Your brother's a painter, you say? What's his name?'

'Adam. Adam Greenbridge, he's my half-brother. Actually he goes by the name Adam Ponteverde, or has done since he moved to Italy.'

'Hah. *Ponte verde*, green bridge, that's good.'

'I'd always assumed it had something to do with the money. The million pounds.'

Alastair was thinking again.

'Put it this way,' he said. 'Rattatroop's Armenian. The Armenians aren't nearly as bad as the Albanians. My first reaction to all this, when you first told me, was it's the work of the Albanians.'

'Really?'

'Terrible race, and as they say, you get the mafia you deserve. The Albanians'll turn your *cat* into a *hat*. It's true. They sell them as wildcat pelts. Just take a walk through the Shepherd's Bush Market if you don't believe me. It's why I always get so bloody worried whenever Bertie goes missing.'

'So you think the Albanians—'

'The *Russians* though, they're even worse. Far worse. The Russians are in a class of their own. They make the Albanians look like *Buddhists*. You get on the wrong side of them… They'll kill your child in front of you and not even blink… and *then* turn your cat into a hat and wear it to the *funeral*!'

The man at the next table was glancing over so often by this point that he may as well have pulled up a chair and joined them. Alastair returned the attention with a polite, slightly forced smile before lowering his voice again.

'We talk about the mob, in Italy say, and it sounds like we're talking about one organization but it never is. And that applies particularly to Russia. And normally these syndicates are at each other's throats, vying for territory etcetera, but at the moment—'

'And you're saying they're involved with Art. Why would that interest them?'

'The money obviously.'

'I wouldn't have thought there was enough in it for them.'

Alastair sighed loudly. 'Just *think* about it. Ninety-nine percent of western wealth is owned by people who like….? What. Ping pong? Curling? No. Art. So there's your money right there.'

'OK.'

'Just because you traffick drugs and extort the innocent, doesn't mean you can't nick a few Picassos on the side. Throw in some kidnapping and you're set.'

'Kidnapping?'

'They can legalize drugs, they're never going to legalize kidnapping are they! So anyway. Where were we.'

'The Russians.'

'Yes! So now the Russians have banded together to snuff out the Ukrainians. Major rumble in the jungle. Fight to the death. Eventually, when the Ukrainians have gone, it'll all settle down again, no doubt. Go back to how it was. But right now, that's how it is. That's the state of play.'

'Did you read this somewhere?'

'I have eyes, my boy. Eyes and ears. And beyond that, like the phones, don't ask.'

'Fair enough.'

'The reach of these people is frightening. No-one is immune. Not the police, not politicians. Not judges.'

'You're thinking of Nevers.'

'I'm thinking of everybody. Because you know what's happening here don't you. In societies... in civilizations that take a downward turn, *everybody* is corruptible. And there are two important points to make about this and don't you forget them. First, we always try to blame it all on a single person, one person becomes the face of evil, whereas the truth is it's nearly always a large number of people who are responsible. And second... crime's fingers always end up extending too far. The real victims are the innocent end-consumers. And most of the time they're women. It's the women who always cop it.'

'And the barristers,' said Jon.

'Yes, kill all the lawyers as Dick the Butcher said. But no. That's not what really happens. It's always the end-consumer who gets nailed, and in our poor excuse for a tribal society, that means women. Women are the innocents.'

'Not the ones I know.'

'And one more thing on the first point, what I was saying about evil being attributed to the one person?... well you've heard of bilocation I presume.'

'Um...well, vaguely. Isn't it when—'

'Like *doppelgängers*. Or *vardogrs* in Scandinavian folklore. Bilocation is the ability to appear in two places at once. Vardogrs are a person's doppelgänger that turns up before the real person does. Similar kind of deal. Various saints have supposedly had the power to bilocate. So when society begins to fall apart...'

'Anti-saints start bilocating?'

'Precisely! Or at least people imagine that they do. I'm obviously not saying there are *really* doppelgängers out there. It's all a question of perception, it's how these people operate, how they convince you you're beaten.'

'And this helps me how?'

'We're talking about what you're up against. What I'm saying is, you have to be careful not to inflate your enemy and assume there is one all-powerful person you're fighting.'

'I'm not sure how assuming there are more of them is terribly comforting.'

'I'm not here to comfort you, old chap. I'm here to help you.'

Their meal arrived. By the time Jon had eaten the last of his steak, the two men at the next table had gone. He never saw them leave.

'The main thing,' Alastair said, after confirming he hadn't seen them leave either, 'is for you to get out of London. Yes? Go to Lucinda. If you need to contact me, my phone number's on the door of the fridge, it's the number for the emergency plumber. OK? Now go there. Will you do that?'

'I suppose so,' Jon said glumly.

'This isn't forever, remember. Just until whatever it is blows over. A bit like this storm on the way.'

'What storm?'

'You haven't read the papers? One of those rogues stomping in off the Atlantic. Due on Monday I think. Do you remember the storm of eighty-seven? The London hurricane? What a lulu.'

53.

The sound of a key in the front door.

He strolled in and threw his keys down on the glass coffee table. Like he did every time, he'd smash it one day. He tore off his overcoat, and came over to her. Gave her a perfunctory kiss. On the lips, but cold, unfeeling, and holding his hand on her head – on her clean red hair – longer than he had any right to.

'Fuck,' he said eventually and he headed out to the kitchen. 'What a day.'

And he was gone again. Unbelievable. She picked up her book and started reading. Or pretended she was reading, she couldn't think anymore, and certainly not with him around. He'll pour himself a drink (ice cubes, Vodka from the freezer, tonic from the fridge), re-enter the room and then slump down opposite her, on the sofa.

She was still wearing her green dress. For him.

He'd told her the apartment was the priciest in the area – not just pricey but top of the pile – and the area was non-negotiable. She couldn't be too far from where he worked and anyway, why would she want to be? All the more time together. But of course he'd stopped the lunchtime look-ins – the "conjugal visits" as he so tactfully called them – they lasted less than a week. But "the area", it's such a wonderful area anyway, why would she want to live anywhere else? What, you mean apart from the rubbish on the streets, and the drug addicts, and the needles and the rapes and the advertising teams having their loud conversations on the footpath like we all want to listen…? It's wonderful darling, you're right! And with the best metro station in all of Paris!

But she wasn't in Paris anymore.

He returned from the kitchen with a drink and sank into the sofa.

'Fuck,' he said again, after he closed his eyes. She wondered if he'd actually *seen* her yet, today. He certainly didn't last night when he left at midnight, didn't turn on a light anywhere, didn't need to, he had the routine down pat by now, didn't he.

She wondered why his wife put up with it. Maybe she had her own thing going on. Or maybe she didn't exist.

'How are you.' It was barely a question.

'Mm,' she said, giving barely an answer. A kind of test.

'What say we go out for dinner for a change.' His eyes were still closed.

'What say you fuck me instead,' she responded, barely audible, but another test. There was a long pause.

'I know this place…' Irwin said eventually.

Three hours earlier, she'd taken off her green dress and she was standing on her own, in a crowded room, naked.

She could feel the gaze of the man near the window and she shuddered. Just slightly. Not enough for any of the other students to notice, but enough, no doubt, for this one.

Most of the time, in these classes, she was only barely aware of the students' presence: as soon as she removed her kimono she entered a world that excluded everyone in the room. Venus. She'd land on the surface: four hundred and fifty degrees, but that was just fine with her. Because under the thick clouds of sulphuric acid, she was hidden from all those prying Earth-bound telescopes. On this particular day however, the man in the dark grey suit and the frameless glasses had also, somehow, entered the Venusian atmosphere, dropped beneath the clouds and planted his flag next to hers.

She had a trick of looking without appearing to (it was a peripheral vision thing). She could watch any of the students drawing her without them knowing it. She didn't need to do it if she was mentally absent – if she was on Venus – but today she found herself putting up the periscope. And she didn't like what she saw.

This man – in her mind he was called N., because he looked like a Neville, in his suit, and his blue-checked socks and brown shoes – he wasn't doing much drawing as far as she could tell. Perhaps some very occasional, desultory scratching movements with his pencil hand, but she doubted there was much to see on his sketchpad. And he was blinking a lot, too. People who blinked a lot were invariably insane, she knew that from experience.

She shuddered again, this time from the cold (and wondered why the hell Andy had to open that fucking window, *he* might've been hot but what about her?).

When the class came to an end, she was relieved to be re-wrapping herself in her kimono, it was a welcome barrier between her and N., that was what it was really about, she never usually cared. There were always horny young males who loved staring at her arse and her breasts and her crotch – especially the slim line of her pubic hair, like a pointing index finger (she kept it clipped that way for their benefit, in fact, as much as anyone else's). They made her laugh (inside, of course), they were harmless, but *this* guy… he was *licking* her. And the looks he was giving her. She felt like a roast ready for carving.

So when she saw N. board her bus on the way home, she was understandably ruffled. He sat down in one of the few rear-facing seats and it was hard to avoid looking at him, there was a clear line of vision. Every time their eyes met – which was almost every time she dared to look up – he didn't react, showed no signs of either recognition or embarrassment. Just allowed his gaze to remain on her for a moment – a split second too long – before slowly, too slowly, shifting his attention elsewhere, as if he hadn't registered her presence.

When she got off at her stop, she could barely bring herself to look around. To her great relief, she got off alone. But when she looked into the bus as it began to move, her eyes irresistibly locked onto N.'s. And this time he was staring at her, staring hard as the bus roared off down the street.

Her body shook as if she'd just been thrust into and pulled out of a glacial lake.

When she got home – back to her flat, her prison – she showered and lay on her bed, still naked but dry and allowed the thoughts of her day to float up and away. She lay on her stomach and did what she always did after days like these: she thought, not of Irwin, but of those young men in the class, and imagined they were drawing her, in theory, but really just eyeing her up, barely looking at their sketchpads, just staring at her beautiful arse. Exposed, just for them.

But this time, N. was there, creeping into every image. Inescapable.

54.

Despite his promise, Jon didn't leave London. Not that evening at least.

After dinner with Alastair, he made his way with his BOAC 'attaché case' to Victoria – so he'd be able to quickly jump on a train to Sussex the next morning at Victoria Station. He checked in to the Victoria Park Plaza Hotel on Vauxhall Bridge Road, putting to good use, in lieu of a credit card, one of the 'wads' Alastair had been talking about.

The BOAC shoulder bag with its wads of cash wasn't all he checked in with. On the way there he'd done some shopping, and apart from two new shirts and a few changes of socks and underwear, he'd also picked up a small laptop. The phone Alastair had left him was anything but 'smart' and Jon needed a good quality screen for what he planned to do. Luckily what Alastair *had* provided him with was a lot of wads. They looked suspiciously grimy, like they'd been dragged through a tunnel but maybe it was another one of those things he wasn't supposed to be asking about. No doubt.

He eventually got the laptop working and despite hanging out for one, he postponed his shower. Because what he had to do more than anything else was skype his half-brother in Venice.

Jon and Adam had the same mother, Alicia, but Adam's father was Charles Greenbridge who was killed in a motor vehicle accident just after Adam was born. Alicia later married Henry Marriner and had Jon, who was two years younger than Adam. Adam had lived in

Venice for most of his adult life and Jon hardly saw him anymore. They were still close though, and Jon would still give him hell over his decision to change his surname from Greenbridge to its Italian equivalent. Just because he was a painter, did he have to be so bloody obvious about it?

As he was setting up Skype on his new laptop, it occurred to him to check his emails. Surprisingly, there weren't many. What's more, most of them were impersonal marketing fluff and spam, almost nothing from friends. There was one from an old university friend that covered just one topic – himself – but other than that, a big zero. Not even from his chambers. He concluded that when people thought you were dead, they didn't waste their time emailing you on the off chance they were mistaken. After all, how would they word it?

Then, while he was at it, he checked his Facebook. While he did, he realised he was doing exactly what Alastair had told him *not* to do – here he was, staying in London, using social media… Again, no messages for him. (Or rather no messages apart from the one clear message he'd already received: namely that if Life was a road trip we all took together, the rest of the world was blithely driving on as if he, Jon, had never existed, without so much as a pit stop to slow it down.) There was the same mildly amusing but essentially meaningless drivel on his newsfeed. Funnily enough, no-one had yet defriended him…

He wondered whether Emerald had a Facebook presence. It occurred to him, if *he* were a private investigator he wouldn't hesitate: it was the perfect tool really, given you didn't need to divulge a single thing about yourself that you didn't want to. He typed "Emerald Strand" into the search box and sure enough, there she was. Emerald Strand, London, United Kingdom, with some sort of church wall backing for her timeline cover photo and, unexpectedly, for her profile picture, a photograph of her in a bikini somewhere tropical, somewhere like Mauritius – it certainly wasn't London. (So there was, at least, one thing that Emerald was choosing to divulge about herself: she had a rather spectacular body. Did that help in the private eye world? Jon was willing to assume that it did.)

He decided to see what happened if he sent her a message:

– Hi Emerald, Jon Marriner here. Can we talk? Btw keep this to yourself.

He sent it and immediately felt foolish adding the rider. But then again, he could imagine Alastair's reaction if he even knew Jon was sending the message at all. It was probably prudent.

Unbelievably, a live chat box appeared almost straight away on his screen. A reply from Emerald:

– Jonathon Marriner the barrister? Thought you were dead

He couldn't think of any reason not to continue the dialogue, so he did.

– A nasty rumour. Don't go disabusing anyone of it though.

She went quiet, there was no response. Was she thinking about it? Looking up "disabuse" in a dictionary? To keep the ball rolling, he added:

– Anyway I'm still dead. But can we meet?

This time, an answer:

– I dont go on dates with dead men Not usually

And before he had a chance to reply, she added:

– Although there have been exceptions
– Great. This is another exception. Can you come here?

There was another lengthy pause, until her reply eventually came up.

– I havent said I am coming anywhere yet So where are you?

Jon began typing "Victoria Park Plaza..." but stopped. Paused, finger tips hovering a millimetre above the keys. He felt weighed down all of a sudden – swamped by a wave of caution. She was acting all coy, maybe it was a pretence? Was her initial hesitation a symptom of her concern that he *wasn't* dead? He had no idea who she was connected with, who was paying her. And until he did... He deleted the words he'd typed and quickly retyped a new sentence. Before he could send it though, another one from Emerald:

– Which graveyard?

Had she sensed his hesitation? And tried to defuse the danger of her previous question? He sent her what he'd typed:

– Why don't we meet in Victoria Station. Tomorrow 10am.

Another long pause. She replied:

– Are you scared of me?
– Of course.

The seconds, and then minutes ticked away again. Why the long pauses? She didn't seem an indecisive person. Was there some way of tracing an internet connection like tracing a call? Finally her answer:

– OK 2moro 10am
– At the newspapers in WHSmith.
– Which one
– Which newspaper?
– Which store theres more than one
– The big one in the middle.
– Surprised you didnt pick a lingerie store
– There aren't any, I checked.
– Ha ok for that you can wait for me in the fishing section
– Perfect.

But who was doing the fishing?

He congratulated himself for picking a crowded meeting place –
and somewhere he could sit at a distance and observe her. And
make a quick getaway if he needed to. He double-checked he had
Lucinda's key and checked online for the train times.

Which is when he realised he'd been putting off skyping Adam.
In fact a simple call would have been sufficient. Was he choosing to
use Skype because there was less chance of getting through to him?
And thus by telling himself he wanted to see him – and needed to
be seen *by* him – was he lying to himself? Or was he, with all this
talk of being dead, beginning to feel like he actually had a foot in
the grave? Or even that he was already there?

He found Adam easily in the Skype directory: *adam.ponteverde*,
listed as being in *Venezia, Italy*. He clicked on the video call icon.
The disappointment he felt when Adam appeared on the screen
answered, he realised, his earlier questions:

'Adam!'

'Jon?'

'What. You didn't think I was dead, did you?'

Adam looked more like he needed to sleep for a day than he'd
just seen a ghost. 'What are you doing...?' He seemed confused.
'Sorry, I was waiting for a call and I thought you were them...'

'Your relief that I'm actually alive is overwhelming me Adam.
It's too much.'

'What are you on about? Was I supposed to have called or
something?'

'You mean... you didn't hear anything? About me being dead.'

'Dead?' He laughed. 'No Jon, I haven't heard about you being
dead. I've been away anyway, beyond Timbuktu, literally, just got
back. If you'd have blown up the Houses of Parliament I wouldn't
have heard about it. So. How did you die? A blaze of glory, I hope.'

'A house fire.'

'Got it in one!'

'I'm being serious. And I'm going to have to ask you to keep this
a bit of a secret. We haven't spoken. I'm still dead.'

'I'm confused. No. *You're* confused. And since when did you
start skyping by the way?'

'Look, it's been a rough week. I'll tell you about it later. I've got to keep my head down for a while. In a couple of words, there's someone after me and I have no idea who.'

'Is this job-related? Because you're starting to sound like one of *my* people. Or as mad as. I may have to buy you a paintbrush and easel at this rate.'

'Which reminds me. Have you heard of a guy called Norton Rattatroop?'

'Yeah. The art dealer?'

'Do you have much to do with him?'

'As a matter of fact I do. His gallery ran an exhibition of mine here last year.'

'Was he involved in any… you know, anything dodgy? Shady?'

Adam stared at Jon, as if he were trying to read the thoughts behind the face behind the screen in front of him. As if he were peering into a deep, dark, troubling pool.'

'Why?' he said eventually.

'Well that's a yes if ever I've heard one.'

Adam sighed heavily. 'Look, not that I know of, all right? But you can never tell with these Armenians, can you. So what's happened?'

'He's been reported as missing. Here in London.'

'Like you apparently. So maybe he's out there somewhere skyping *his* brother.'

'Right. Now what do you really think?'

And just then, Jon caught it – a flicker of annoyance in Adam's eyes. It was almost imperceptible, subliminal. Like a reflex.

'I'm told artists where you live,' Jon added, 'ought to watch their step or end up in a canal.'

'It's not just Venice. There's a lot wrong with the art world these days. It'd take me too long to explain. But there have been some… disappearances. Players getting caught up in bad deals. Deals with players heavier than they realised. And I'll tell you, it's so overwhelmingly… complete…'

'Complete?'

'It's like they've just been… dropped in the sea. Dropped in a very deep ocean somewhere, and they're gone.' Adam became silent – it was as if the screen had frozen for a moment. Maybe it had. 'Poor old Nishan, eh?' he said sadly. And then he brightened. 'But hey, I try to steer clear of that sort of shit. I just paint. That's all I do. Wanna buy a painting?'

'Nowhere to put it at the moment I'm afraid.'

'You look like you've got some space on the walls there.'

'I'm in a hotel room.'

'Whereabouts?'

'I mean it when I say you can't tell anyone.'

'Not even Mum?' Adam asked.

'That's not funny.'

Alicia, who was sixty-six, had been in a home for nearly five years. She never fully recovered from a breakdown she suffered twenty-five years ago and dementia had, now, fully set in. Her life hadn't been easy, losing her first husband when she was still twenty-five, losing her third child, a daughter, Eloise, six years later, separating from her second husband – Henry Marriner, who had since died – and enduring difficult relationships with a number of men while bringing up two boys... And those inner demons. She was one of those people who always seemed to be grappling with so much more than what was really on their plate.

But there was one thing that wasn't a problem and that was the danger of her being told Jon was dead. As far as she was concerned she was still in her twenties and was yet to have children.

'How is she?'

'Same,' said Jon. 'You could see for yourself one of these days. Might be nice.'

'Yeah well. When I sell a few more paintings and can afford to get on one of those shiny things with wings.'

'You managed to get beyond Timbuktu, apparently. Literally.'

Alicia Greenbridge had never forgiven Adam for changing his surname, even if it meant the same thing in translation, and Adam, in turn, had never fully got over the rejection.

'So anyway,' Adam said, 'you're dead, that's terrific, so what are you going to do? I mean... What does one do with oneself when one's dead?'

Jon ignored Adam's half-arsed attempt at sarcasm. 'I really can't say. But I'll let you know. I'll ring you... or skype you or whatever. When all this has blown over.'

'Sure.'

'No I mean it.'

'OK, listen, um, I've got to go. Sorry, but meeting some fancy... whatever. You know.'

Jon laughed. 'No, but... that's—'

'But I'm pleased you're not dead.'

'Yeah, so am I.'

'All right. Be seeing you.'

'OK—'

And with an abrupt "ping", he was gone. Keen to get away, it seemed. And then Jon remembered – hadn't Adam said he'd been waiting for some important call? Load of old cobblers, probably. Made it up, no doubt, much like most things in his life. Typical. Nothing changes, and yet...

Even though Jon had never been especially close to Adam – they were quite different, in many ways – watching his brother vanish into cyberspace like that made him feel inexplicably sad.

55.

The next morning, Friday 25 October, Jon took his position early. The agreed meeting time was 10am, so he made sure he arrived by nine thirty. Slung over his shoulder when he set out was his BOAC bag, now stuffed full of cash and clothes and his new laptop.

On his way into Victoria Station, he'd taken a moment to look up and admire the light-coloured Portland stone and the fine Edwardian craftsmanship. In particular, there was an ocean theme – as the station used to be the main departure point for the Continent – and the two bare-breasted mermaids stretched out suggestively over the entrance caught Jon's attention, just as they would have, no doubt, caught the attention of all upward-looking, appreciative Edwardians in their day.

Instead of standing in W H Smith – in the fishing section as stipulated by Emerald – he bought a coffee and sat down at a table attached to the cafe opposite. It offered a good vantage point – not just for observing the arrival of W H Smith customers, but for more or less the whole of the main hall in Victoria Station. He had no experience with this sort of thing, so did what anybody who'd seen an action film with a climactic scene in a major train station would do: he kept to the fringes, sat down and blended in. He even bought a newspaper – *the Sun* – although with its shouted headline ("GET IN LINE, CHAPS"), he not only felt more conspicuous than he would have liked, but also that he was sending out a not so subtle message to his would-be pursuers (even if it was accompanied by an "historic royal picture" of the Queen and her direct male descendants). On the other hand, every tabloid had a shouted headline and the vast majority of newspaper-reading passengers carried a tabloid.

A tabloid, too, was significantly easier to read one-handed, leaving the other hand free, for example, to pick up and sip from a take-away coffee cup. When Jon's coffee hand wasn't doing just that, it was in his trouser pocket, fingering Lucinda's key.

By 9.50am, he'd stepped up his vigilance levels, and kept a sharper eye on the thronging commuters. He expected her to be punctual, to the point of wanting to arrive a little early, just as he had done.

At around 9.55am, a pair of seaweed-coloured jeans materialised next to his face, at eye-level. Before he had a chance to turn, she said:

'About to head into the fishing section?'

Emerald sat down next to him, coffee in hand. She was wearing a short, lightweight black leather jacket and dark sunglasses. The latter he wished she'd remove – he wanted to see her eyes.

'By the way,' she said. 'I'm dead too, so you keep this to yourself as well.'

'Who killed you?'

'I don't know yet. There's more than one suspect.'

'So you're OK with dating dead men now? After all, it'd be a bit—'

'I've *never* been OK dating *any* men, and this isn't a date.'

'I didn't say it—'

'It was your idea, this meeting, not mine,' she pointed out.

'It was your idea to come into my chambers in the first place. What was that about?'

'I changed my mind.'

'Come on Emerald, you're here now. It's not an act of unmitigated selflessness I presume.'

'You'd be surprised.'

'Well you've come here to tell me *something*, right?'

No answer.

'I want to know about that will.'

She remained silent. She was so still, and with her sunglasses on she could have been asleep, or dead or frozen in time.

'Since I saw you last, I've been nearly choked to death, almost burnt to a handful of cinders and unmistakably, verifiably, shot at. I've had high-velocity lumps of lead grazing my earlobe. I've lost my home, my career's been ruined and my stress levels are through the roof and, you know, if it's OK with you, I'd rather like a bit of information.'

She moved slightly, proving at least she was still alive. Still said nothing.

'I think you're a private eye,' Jon said, slowing it down now, looking for a reaction. 'A private detective. And I think... maybe... this has something to do with Martin Nevers...', still nothing, '... and Norton whatever-his-name-is, the art dealer...', a twitch, '... and the Russians.'

Emerald took a deep breath and then a sip of her coffee. Looked around. And then, without warning, she began talking.

'I doubt we will be able to have any more of these meetings, so listen very closely. Some of this will maybe come as a bit of a shock and it really isn't my place to be telling you, but... doing things the right way isn't a luxury either of us have right now. As we are both dead.'

She tipped her head slightly so that he could see her eyes – just – over the top of her sunglasses. Her radiant green eyes shone like two distant, unfathomable stars, winking in another galaxy.

'Are you with me?' she asked.

'I'm with you.'

'You are correct in assuming I'm a private investigator. That is, I was. Recent events have forced me to, in effect, disappear. After I leave you, I will be vanishing down that subway over there, catching the Tube to another mainline station, and then catching a train to somewhere very far away. You won't be seeing me again.'

'I sincerely hope you're wrong.'

Emerald removed her sunglasses fully and looked at Jon closely.

'You know, I like you Jonathon Marriner barrister-at-law, and I'm not really sure why. But I don't like false sincerity or being patronised.'

'I promise you, I—'

'Anyway,' she said dismissively, putting her sunglasses back on and looking away, ' these things are now out of our control. But contrary to what you might think, I *am* here for your sake, so you'd better listen to all this and not get sleazy.'

'I'm listening.'

'As I said, I am a private investigator. I've been doing some work for a Mayfair gallery owner called Richard Runion. Do you know him?'

Jon shrugged and shook his head.

'He was recently sold two forgeries, held out to be Spanish paintings, sixteenth century, and the guy who forged them is connected to a real bunch of nightmares.'

'Nightmares?'

'Nasty guys. Play *real* dirty. Part of a Russian mafia group with a fondness for grey suits.'

'Grey suits?'

'Or ex-Russian actually, they go by a couple of names: *Draylskaya Bratva* is one. *Black Star* is another. Run by a guy called Dominique Drayle. French, or at least originally. Has cells all over the place but his right-hand man, his 'brigadier' is right here in London. Called "Irwin". He has been known to use the surname "Long" but everyone just refers to him by his first name.'

Irwin. Where had he heard that name before? And then he remembered. It was the name he'd heard Nevers mutter when he passed him in the street that day.

'Following me so far?'

'Complicated cases are what I do.'

'You won't want to do this one. Drayle has other operatives here too. One's even a cop.'

'A *cop?*

'Mm-hm. But Irwin, as I say, is in charge in London. And he appears to have a close connection to a solicitor called Paul Brilling who I—'

'Paul Brilling?'

'... Who I believe you *do* know.'

'Brilling's my solicitor.'

'Yes. And your ex-wife's also, am I right? But what you may not know, is that he's Martin Nevers' solicitor as well.'

'Nevers.'

'Yes, which was how I obtained a copy of his will.'

'So you're checking out Brilling because of… what… some connection to this Russian group—'

'To Irwin and, through him, to Drayle, that's right.'

'So what are you saying, these are the people that are after me? Why?'

'You're jumping too far ahead. This is where things get a little… knotty.'

'Knotty?'

She paused and sipped her coffee. All Jon could do was watch. And wait.

'I went to your chambers to check you out. To see if you were involved with these people. To see if it was more than a coincidence that you and Nevers were using the same solicitor. Both of you had left your wills with him. And the will, Nevers' will, it was a bit of a test I suppose. I thought you'd at least read it when I gave you the chance. But you really didn't, did you.'

'No. I didn't.'

'My God. You barristers are so… by the *book*.'

'So why did you make such a fuss over the will, pretending to be angry that I might have looked through it?'

'It was part of the test.'

'Right. And I'm guessing I passed, yeah? So what's this knotty bit you were talking about?'

'Martin Nevers' will… that you didn't read… bequeaths a substantial portion of his estate to two beneficiaries in particular. You and your sister.'

'Well it can't be me. I keep telling you I don't *have* a sister.'

'You are named in the will. As his son.'

'Exactly. I'm not his son, so…'

Emerald produced the same copy of the will that she'd brought to Jon's chambers that day and pushed it across the table at him. He picked it up and, this time, read quickly through it.

'You will see that it refers to his son, Jonathon Marriner. London barrister—'

'"…a barrister practising in London",' Jon reads, '"who is, in all likelihood, currently, as at the date of this will, unaware of the identity of his biological father".' He stares at the words on the document. 'This is impossible.'

'It also, as I say, mentions a daughter... you will see he uses the words "my daughter, being Jonathon's sister" or something like that... but doesn't actually name her. I'm a little confused, I have to say, as to why she is not more fully identified. Although there does seem to be some suggestion—'

'This is astonishing. This is... And there's no doubt, is there, that this is the same Martin Nevers? Lord Justice of Appeal?'

Emerald shook her head.

'My father?'

'If I were you, I would be having a... quiet word with your mother, and your... Henry is it?... Henry Marriner, and... Martin Nevers. Or maybe not Nevers...'

'My father, Henry Marriner, he's dead, but what are you saying? That Nevers and my mother...?'

'I'm not saying anything. The will is the one talking.'

'And what did you find out about Nevers? Is he associated with these people?'

'I'm... concerned. Put it that way.'

'Concerned.'

'I don't know,' Emerald said. 'There's something going on there. I perhaps should not tell you this but... I followed him one day and he went to Irwin's apartment building, or one of them. In Soho. He didn't go in or anything, but...' She shrugged. 'It's a connection. And then there's the question of what association he's got with Brilling, he uses his services after all.'

'As I do.'

'Which seems just a little bit coincidental to me.'

And to Jon as well. He tried to remember how he ended up using Brilling in the first place. Could Brilling have engineered it? Or Nevers? If Nevers knew – or thought – Jon was his son, would that have been a reason? As a way of keeping an eye on him? And then, possibly, could Brilling have been 'got at'? But the equation was too hard – there were simply too many variables.

'So come on Emerald, give me your best shot, what's going on? I mean with Nevers and... and my involvement. Is it just the fact that

I'm named in a will? That Nevers claims to be my father? What's happening here? And why is someone trying to *kill* me?'

'Honestly, I'm not sure.'

'I don't care about *sure*, just give me a *guess*.'

'The person you should be grilling about this is your ex. Romy Banks.'

'I suppose you know my entire relationship history.'

'I'm sure I've barely touched the surface.'

'You know you're funnier when you're not being funny?'

'And anyway,' she said with a sigh. 'Runion isn't paying me to examine your love life, so don't flatter yourself. But about Ms Banks, there were some documents I found in Brilling's office that suggest there could be some sort of link.'

'Between Romy? and these…?'

'It's hard to believe when it's that close to home, huh? And of course I don't know, but—'

'Without flattering myself I'm guessing you've seen my will?'

'I have had a quick look, yes.'

'So you'll see everything goes to Romy.'

She nodded. 'Not all beneficiaries are murderers. But you certainly have to tread carefully in my opinion. If Romy is involved… these are dangerous people.'

Jon put his head in his hands for a moment. It was a lot to take in. A new father. A sister somewhere. And a big, dark cloud over everyone.

'You don't think… ' he began. Formulating a thought. Emerald watched him with Scandinavian patience.

'I mysteriously received a large sum of money not so long ago… Stop me if you know this… But I still don't know where it came from. You don't think it could be Nevers, do you?'

'Could be. Was it much?'

Jon nodded slowly.

'Lucky you,' she said. 'Nice to have a rich daddy I guess. But tread carefully. If Nevers is involved, it's not going to be money you'll want to be touching. The blood might not be dry for a start.'

'A bit late now. It's well and truly dry I'm afraid.'

'Right. Oh well.'

'OK so leaving aside the "why", what about the "who"? You've gone through a big list, but you still haven't told me who's after me, who exactly it is that's trying to kill me. It's a bit hard when you don't know who you're running from. However many new family members you acquire along the way.'

'I don't know Jonathon. I'm sorry I can't be any more precise. Maybe... I mean, sometimes, I guess, you just have to run. And not look back.'

'Run.'

'You have somewhere to run to?'

'There's a place... yes.'

'Where?'

'It's a house—'

'In Peacehaven.'

Jon looked at her in amazement. 'How did you know—?'

'I know everything. It's my job remember? Don't worry. *They* don't know. I will tell you one thing though.' She pulled out of her bag an iPad. 'Watch out for the bitch with the red hair.'

'What do you mean?'

She opened up her photo albums, swiping her way through a vast array of photographs, angling the device away from Jon. She opened one photo in particular and showed it to him. They were looking at Jon's old house.

'Familiar?'

'Hmm. Looks like someone's been spying on me.'

'*Correct*. Because look.'

That familiar curving road, the usual array of parked cars, even a pedestrian on the footpath...

'Recognise anyone?'

'Her?'

Emerald zoomed in on the figure. It was a female with red hair, wearing light blue jeans and a white t-shirt. A masculine t-shirt too, with a car-maker's logo on the front: Renault. But more importantly, the girl bore a close resemblance to the girl he'd followed to the Rootstein factory in West Kensington two days earlier. And the same girl (maybe) that he'd seen in Notting Hill, in almost the same spot in fact – only about thirty metres away – moments before the runaway car incident.

'You must have seen her, she spent a lot of time in your street,' Emerald said.

'She did?'

'Believe me. And not just the street you lived in.'

Emerald found a second photo and showed him. In this picture the red-haired girl was standing at the edge of a square somewhere. It was the same girl, definitely. She was even wearing the green dress he'd seen her in, in West Kensington and Notting Hill. And there she was, it looked like...

'Lincoln's Inn Fields,' he said. 'On the north side. Just along from our building.'

'Well done. You can work for me any time.'

'So this girl, she's been spying on me? At my home *and* my work?'

'It would seem so. But wait, even better than that...'

Emerald took her iPad back and went into Google maps and found London, then Holborn, then Lincoln's Inn Fields. She went in further, into Streetview, and they were in the square, on the western side this time, near the north-western corner. Emerald rotated the image and then zoomed in on a woman on the pavement who seemed to be looking east, in the direction of Jon's building on the north-east corner. She was standing strangely, stretching her neck, peering around the corner. As if she were hiding from someone, or observing them. As far as he could tell, given the facial blurring you get on Streetview, it was, once again, the girl with the red hair.

'She's even on *Streetview*?'

'Exactly. So it's either a huge coincidence, or she's been spending a hell of a lot of time around *you*.'

'So what's the image date on this...' he said, looking at the Streetview photo. 'June last year. Well anyway, yeah, I'm pretty sure I've seen her. A few times lately, at least. So who is she?'

'Here's a clue.'

Emerald brought up a third photo from her iPad albums. It was the same red-haired girl and she was wearing the same green dress, but this time she was walking through the streets of what was clearly Soho.

'... there. She lives, as far as I can tell, with Irwin. Irwin Long. It's his apartment anyway, I'm not sure if he's there very often.

So it seems to me, for whatever reason, they're keeping a good eye on you.'

'Shit.'

'And yes, you'd have to say, in all likelihood, they… as in the Russians, Drayle's people… are the ones responsible for what's been happening to you lately. It would be a bit too much of a coincidence, I think, if not. Wouldn't you say? I, for one, don't believe in coincidences anyway.'

'Before,' he said. 'When I said I'd been shot at, you didn't so much as blink. You didn't seem surprised. Did you know?'

'No Jonathon, I didn't know, and I'm sorry, but nothing surprises me when it comes to these people. And you have to remember, when you told me, what was it, maybe ten minutes ago, I still wasn't sure you weren't knowingly involved in all of this. With the other side, or even with the Russians themselves. I'm *still* not sure.'

'I don't even know who the "other side" are.'

Emerald sighed.

'There's a Ukrainian gang called *Deep Zone*. Operate out of Odessa, on the Black Sea. One of the most powerful mafia groups in the region. The thing is… this is a war, and specifically, a battle for control of the black market in stolen art. Art and antiquities. I don't suppose you've heard of the *Isfahan Decagon*?'

'The…? No.'

'A priceless, five hundred year old Islamic relic, some sort of geometric sensation… and supposedly a key to untold riches as well, so you can just imagine. Anyway, Drayle managed to recover it, recently, from the ocean off Namibia. Deep Zone were pretty keen to get their hands on it, and it now looks like they've done just that. Somehow, I believe, they found a way to infiltrate Black Star, and I have it on good authority that one of their people has managed to steal it. Steal the Decagon.'

'Off the Russians? Off Drayle?'

'No honesty among thieves, Jonathon, you should know that. Anyway, we'll see where that goes, it's all very complicated and very messy. That's why sometimes running's your best option. It is in my case. I don't know about you, but I want to live. Do you want to live?'

'Sure. Are you inviting me along? For the ride?'

'I told you. No sleaze.'

'I wasn't being... Not really.'

They looked at each other and chuckled. But only for a moment; the smiles vanished and Jon felt an idiot. An idiot because his life was in danger and he'd just made the lamest pass he could ever remember having made, and to a woman who would have heard some pretty lame ones.

He looked at the photo on Streetview again. Something occurred to him. Something that maybe, just maybe, could shed some light on things...

'*Blyat*!' Emerald swore and twisted her body around, to face away from the milling tourists and the criss-crossing commuters. 'Don't look!' she said, almost spitting through clenched teeth. 'Look away!'

He did as instructed. They both pretended to be looking at her iPad. Her home screen was a photograph of a young child – a boy of about four – with a dog. Her child? Or perhaps, more likely, a cover of some kind. For some reason, Jon didn't picture Emerald as a mother.

'Who are we hiding from?'

'Never mind, just keep looking down and talk to me as though we're talking about a riveting business plan.'

All he had to look at was the photograph.

'That your son?'

While Emerald was busy not responding, Jon snatched a glance over the shoulder of his new 'business associate', catching a snapshot of suits and jeans and daypacks.

'You're not paying attention,' she said calmly. 'The contract wasn't signed and in any event this clause here...' she prodded the dog's nose '... is a penalty clause and as such, unenforceable.'

'You'll make a lawyer yet.'

'No thanks.'

'Can I look now?'

'No.'

But she looked around herself. Her gaze steadied and Jon followed its direction. In the flow of people, he saw a grey suit disappearing behind a snack bar and was reminded of his trigger-happy pursuer in West Kensington. With all the grey suits in Victoria Station – in London – the chances of it being the same man were low to non-existent, but it was a nasty thought.

'I'm going,' she said as she packed her iPad away. 'You probably won't hear from me again.'

'Tahiti?'

'Maybe Copenhagen.'

She threw him a brief smile that seemed as if it was meant to indicate she was either being absolutely truthful or completely mendacious.

'Well, I hope we… bump into each other,' he said. 'Somehow.'

'I don't.' She stood up, and looked back in the direction the man in the suit had gone. 'Because if we do, it'll mean one of us is in trouble. Or both.' She checked her phone. 'I'd be heading for that house of yours if I were you.' She was checking for the time? Or for messages. Or an excuse to stall… Was she wanting to tell him something? She looked up and threw him a curt nod. 'Good luck.'

Luck. She may as well have cursed him.

She then turned and walked off quickly, around the corner, following, presumably, the signs to the Underground.

Jon sighed. Alone again, and feeling more vulnerable than ever. He felt the house key in his pocket, and thought about getting on a train, and then thought about Emerald and everything she'd said and decided to get one more coffee. Think for a moment.

No point in jumping if it was straight into the jaws of a shark.

56.

'Tattoo me,' Isla said.

Isla: that wasn't pronounced *eye-la*, by the way, but rather *iss-la* (or *eee-sla* for anyone who wanted to really nail it), as in the Spanish word for *island*. And an island, she certainly felt like these days. Not to mention the fact that *Isla* was a nicer name than *bitch*, and far nicer than *fucking slut*, both of which Irwin seemed to have a fondness for.

So, "tattoo me", it was an odd thing to say, she realised walking into a tattooist's. For an *Iss-la*, or an *Eye-la*, or anyone else. A bit like walking up to an airport check-in counter and saying you wanted to catch a plane. But tattoos were one of Isla's favourite things, and this was her first one. And that command, "tattoo me", it was something she'd always wanted to say.

Tattoos weren't common in her home country, Switzerland – not among the people she grew up with anyway – but that just made them all the more of an attractive proposition. On this particular morning she'd found herself in Brixton, near the markets. She'd hopped off the Tube half an hour earlier and eventually, after sniffing around the butcher shops and Caribbean breakfast joints and tired laneways, she'd come across the tattoo parlour.

She'd come prepared, as well: she was carrying with her a photocopy of exactly the tattoo she wanted – it happened to be both the perfect design and a wonderful act of defiance – so the only question was whether it was indecently early. It was just after 10am. Who gets a tattoo in the morning?

Answer: Isla does.

She ended up walking out of there with a beautifully intricate Islamic design on the smooth rounded protuberance of her right buttock cheek. Her host had excelled himself. Her expectations had been exceeded.

57.

'Tattoo me,' the redhead said after walking in the door.

Ron was manager, business owner and sole occupant. Sole, that is, except when his friends were visiting (which was, admittedly, much of the time, although thankfully not at this precise moment). Seen better days though, *big Thursday night, innit?* as his friends might say. He had grizzle on his grizzle that particular day; his frizzed grey hair, tortured into a ponytail had long since lost the will to live and his mouth was drier than an African desert – he was only fifty-two but looked, and felt, like an abandoned, burnt-out, shell of a car. Still it wasn't all calamity, it was Friday, and even though Saturday morning was still to be endured, he was in a good mood. And that was even *before* this glamour darkened his doorway. Tallish, pale skin, dark red hair and melt-in-your-mouth brown eyes – looked about twenty-five at a guess – he would have picked her as Scottish or Irish or something until she opened that gorgeous mouth of hers. Accent of some kind, almost Swedish or French or something. And that was why he was living in a rat-trap in London bleeding money to a nasty Jewish landlord (OK, not Jewish, but Hungarian so same thing) and not living the kind of life he'd been led to believe was his destiny: lording it up East Yorkshire fashion in a terraced house on one of the many grand boulevards of Goole. Marshfield Avenue, to be precise, three minutes walk from the banks of the mighty Ouse – once the family home, and now the wasted hovel pilfered by his pig-brained brother. He was enduring his leaking, falling-down, poxy basement flat in Slade Green – he called it "the Sinkhole" – and Slade Green by the way (and there was nothing green about it), Slade Green was so far from central London (he walked it once and it took him over eight hours, although the effects of the lager may have, admittedly, added an hour or two)… it was so far, Ron had his doubts it was even legal to call it London… but he was *handling* it for the very simple reason that London was Europe and Europe was the home of flowers like the one standing before him at that very moment.

Ron was unfazed by the naivety of the girl's statement. He'd heard worse. Much, much worse. He just nodded, and said:

'What's it to be.'

The girl put a sheet of paper in front of him. It was a printout of a photograph of some sort of Islamic design. All rhombuses, hexagonals and jagged lines. It was a helluva tangle, but it was doable. In fact as far as Ron was concerned, anything was doable for a fee. And some things were doable for *free*. Such as the redhead standing in his parlour at that very moment, for example. Not that he wouldn't be completely professional about any job. So no problem, in other words.

'No problem.'

'You decide on the colours,' she said. 'You look like a man of taste.'

Now, of course, Ron was flattered, and as doable as his current client was, he had a rule about not tattooing nutters. And this vixen from Scandinavia or wherever she was from was already begging the question. Because no girl ever left it up to a man to choose what colour her tattoo was to be, and he knew for a fact that he didn't look like a man of taste.

'I'm not too fond of decisions, especially in the mornings,' he admitted wearily, but firmly. As nice as it was, her compliment. 'You'll have to help me with that one, luv.'

Isla, pushed her hands up through her red hair and fluffed it out like she was stretching her wings. She looked pensive for a moment. 'OK,' she said. 'I'll help you, but you have to help me too.'

'Sounds fair.'

'I want some blue,' Isla said slowly. 'Mid-blue, Persian blue, you know? Like… lapis lazuli.'

'I think I know what you mean.'

'And some green. Emerald green. How is that for a start.'

'OK. That's good. That's a good start.'

'And no additional… stuff. No grape vines or tigers or French flowers. Nothing like that. Nothing curly, nothing *soft* and nothing *alive*. Just keep to the pattern. Keep it geometric.'

'Geometric, OK. Just the straight lines.'

'Just the straight lines you see before you, yes. And I want it on my backside. My *arse*.'

The whole set-up sounded a bit strange but what the fuck. On her arse, eh? Well why not, the lass may be a bit *radio rental* but she was a cute one, and if she was giving him leave to be a bit creative (on her arse, too), then surely, he should live a bit, take up the challenge.

'Well OK,' he said. 'Sure. But I have to warn you. I'm not cheap.'

'Neither am I. And I never expected you to give me one for free.' She let that last statement hang there for a moment. 'Let's get started before I change my mind.' And she slapped a roll of twenty-pound notes down on the table.

Ron hurriedly wheeled out the patient trolley which a friend had nicked from the hospital up the road in Denmark Hill, lowered the side rails, locked the wheels and had Isla lie down on it, arse up. He reverently raised the right-hand side of her green dress, and then delicately slid the right half of her black lace panties out of the way and into the beckoning crevasse between her buttock cheeks. Which of course, he did his best to ignore. Because he was a professional.

And then he removed his jacket and went to work. On the whole, he maintained the level of professionalism he knew his customer would expect… except, perhaps, for the one occasion when he 'accidentally' slid her panties too far over just for a quick peek. He thought of it as his tip which she'd probably forget to give him, and he doubted she'd noticed, so what you didn't know could never hurt you, right?

The only misfire in an otherwise flawless procedure occurred when a shadow passed across the length of the opaque windows to the passageway outside and Isla turned her head suddenly. Ron almost – but not quite – made a mistake. A reprieve for which he thanked his lucky stars.

58.

When the local police were called in to the Sirens Tattoo Parlour about an hour later – a visiting friend had rung 999 – they were presented with a mystery. They had absolutely nothing to go on except for two things: the first was the blooming, ruby pool of blood on the floor, and the second was the body they'd found lying in the middle of it, being that of the unfortunate – and dead – manager himself, one Ronald Pond, formerly of Goole, East Yorkshire.

59.

When Jon wanted to think about something clearly, objectively, he'd do one of two things. Read or eat. After Emerald left, he did both. After all, he'd just been informed he had a new father, he had a new sister (somewhere), he was probably being pursued by an international crime syndicate, and both his ex-wife and his new father were possibly connected to the whole business. *And* there was some redhead out there who wanted a piece of him as well. A drink was what he really needed, but reading and eating seemed a better choice for a Friday morning. So after touring Victoria station's fast food outlets, including Delice de France, Wasabi Sushi and Mi Casa Burritos, and a browse through the newspaper section of W.H.Smith, he sat down at the same cafe for his third coffee of the day. To take stock.

And as he sipped his cappuccino and looked around at the hurrying commuters, an idea occurred to him. He pulled out his laptop and opened up Google Maps. He found the Streetview photo of the north-western corner of Lincoln's Inn Fields. There she was again, the woman with the red hair, in that peculiar stance, looking every bit the spy. He wondered if she wasn't actually walking though, as opposed to standing in the one spot. He knew that the Streetview photos were taken by a moving car with a camera attached to the roof and that the various images represented a chronological sequence of photographs. You just had to know in which direction the car was travelling.

He moved the viewing position further down the western side of the square and away from the corner, and sure enough, there was the woman, walking in the direction of the corner. So unless she was walking backwards, the car had to be moving in that direction as well. This was corroborated by a tiny antenna which appeared in some of the shots, indicating the rear of the vehicle.

The northern side of Lincoln's Inn Fields was one-way for traffic, and he hoped the car had turned into it on this particular run, to continue the sequence with this woman in it. It had. And the woman, at this point, was still just ahead of it. Moving to the next image, and the woman was still walking – so clearly she'd never stopped. But what was more interesting was the figure the camera car passed, walking ahead of the woman, further along the street. It was almost certainly, despite the interference of some minimal facial blurring, Sir Martin Lemar Nevers.

Coincidence? Or maybe, on this occasion at least, the redhead hadn't been spying on Jon at all, she'd been following Nevers. Although if so, why? Especially if Emerald's instincts were right, and the woman and Nevers were both somehow connected with the Russians and thus, on the same side, as it were.

He had to find out more. About Nevers and about the money too, assuming there was a link. Recalling Emerald's warning about the risks associated with approaching Nevers, he wondered whether he shouldn't give Romy another try. He'd be a bit more forceful this time. If he didn't allow himself to be wrong-footed again, how difficult could it be?

60.

It was just after midday at Victoria Station. Isla decided she'd get a coffee before planning her next move.

Getting the tattoo focussed her mind. She liked her new tattoo, she'd gone into public toilets just to look at it. The skin around it was still reddish but the design was, by any test, beautiful. Modestly proportioned but striking, and just as importantly, hidden away by all but the skimpiest bikini... And hidden from Irwin too. No danger of *him* seeing it these days.

The only sour note had been the shadow at the door. She was convinced it was the man from the life drawing class. Convinced he'd been following her. But why?

And then, in the Brixton underground an hour later. There he was. On the platform. Victoria Line, northbound. She'd done an about face and made straight for the surface. Found herself a hiding spot and waited and watched, to see if he'd followed her up the escalator. He hadn't.

It was possible her flesh-bound artwork had inspired a new sense of determination – or perhaps it was evidence of it – but it was becoming obvious to her that she needed to find the courage to make some changes.

A boyfriend years ago had told her not to do the wrong thing, when she was breaking up from him. He hit a nerve, too, because she'd always been worried about doing the wrong thing. People who knew her a little bit – and even those who knew her well –

might think that was funny, someone as impulsive as her, worried about doing the wrong thing.

The wrong thing.

After almost five years of Irwin, the possibility of doing the wrong thing no longer bothered her. Altering the equation on the other hand – doing the *right* thing – was a far more attractive proposition. But how? How did you alter an equation that had operated for so long? How did you dig yourself out of something that you'd unquestioningly accepted for so many years?

Drastic action was required obviously, but she wasn't sure she had it in her anymore to do anything life-changing. Inertia was a killer. She knew that, of course, but then so does the bird that sees the advancing snake, and nevertheless fails to fly.

Was *she* going to fail to fly?

Something she'd have to ponder, and ponder well. Over that coffee.

61.

Just after midday and he was still at Victoria Station. Jon finished his coffee and made his move.

Following in Emerald's footsteps he headed down to the underground. Moving bodies of every colour shot across the station hall, each on its own straight trajectory, all of them comets of desire. A flash of grey, a snippet of red. A blur of green made him think of the girl with the red hair, and he almost turned around too, just to make sure it wasn't, but time was running out, and everything considered, it was better he kept his head down anyway.

A brisk ten minute walk from South Kensington station, through the backstreets of Chelsea, helped Jon fully clear his head.

The next ten minutes fully did not.

It was 12.28pm when he arrived in Carlyle Square. Not that he wore a watch anymore – not since the fire – but Alastair's phone told him. Telling the time was one of the few things that Alastair's phone actually did.

As he approached Romy's house (*their* house he had to continue to remind himself), he had a strange sensation, like a warning signal, and he slowed down. It was as if his feet, without instructions, had decided to slow down of their own accord.

And then he saw a man walking out the front door. He was about Jon's height, maybe slightly more wiry, but it was a springy, dangerous wiriness – it was *hungry* – and he sported a crew cut of what was probably dark hair, he was slightly unshaven, and he wore a light grey suit and black shoes that sharply clicked the surface of the pavement as he walked. A human scorpion.

But then maybe Jon was a little biased.

He would have been about thirty metres away. Jon hung back and watched the man – who he guessed, by now, was probably Romy's boyfriend – walk down the street away from him, waiting until he was a safe enough distance away before he approached.

He pressed the doorbell for the second time in two days.

This time when the door opened, the action was more tentative. Romy peered out through the narrow opening.

'Jon?'

'Romy. I need to—'

'You can't... I can't talk now.'

'No, listen Romy—'

'No Jon. Please go.'

She tried to close the door but he jammed his foot into the disappearing gap.

'Don't!' she hissed. 'You've got to get out of here. He'll see you.'

'Then let me in.'

'No you can't...'

He forced his way in and slammed the door behind him. Put his bag down.

She spat and snarled at him like a dog; swore like a succubus. He grabbed her by the shoulders and pushed her towards the kitchen at the back of the house. She scratched and she swung. He shoved her against the kitchen table and put a hand over her mouth.

'Shut up Romy. Just fucking... shut... up. You're going to tell me what's happening here. I was nearly *killed* the other day after I saw you. I had a man in a baseball cap *shooting* at me in the burnt-out remains of my *house*. Do you understand that? And I reckon it's got something to do with *you*. So you fucking tell me... *what... is... going... on.*'

Her muscles untensed. Her face crumpled and Romy came the closest to crying Jon had ever seen. She nodded a couple of times and sat down on a chair. Jon chose to remain standing. He was moved by her obvious distress, by her wretchedness, but he was determined to stay angry.

'I don't know...' she began, finally, but couldn't finish.

'I'll help you. Who was that who just left? The boyfriend?'

She nodded.

'Does he have a name?'

She hesitated. And then: 'Irwin.'

Irwin. Emerald had told him about an Irwin.

'Irwin... Long,' Jon said.

She looked at him sharply. He clearly wasn't meant to know that. 'Except it's not Long,' she said. 'He just uses it sometimes.'

'Sometimes. And he's connected with the Russians.'

A look of great pain crossed her face and he knew that worse was to come.

'Romy,' he continued. 'Don't hold out on me. Not anymore. You know... I've been forced to hire a private investigator. And I've found out things. Unpleasant things.'

She nodded, looking like she was freefalling now, deeper into her abjectness.

'Stop me if I'm telling you anything you already know,' he said. 'But two years ago I received a large sum of money, either by mistake or otherwise, from an anonymous benefactor. Or malefactor.' He paused for a moment to check her reaction but she said nothing, kept her head down. 'Funnily enough, I hadn't changed my will leaving everything to you. Still haven't either. That was an oversight.'

She was trembling or sobbing, he couldn't tell which.

'And what a surprise, or strange coincidence, I'm not sure what you'd call it, but suddenly someone's trying to kill me. Do you think there might be a link, Romy? A link between... the money... and you? Think about it carefully because my life, you know... my life kind of—'

And there it was. An audible sob. Romy, toughest journalist in London, was crying. Jesus, she had a heart after all.

For good measure, he rammed the point home just a little more. 'First I find out my father isn't really my father and now, my ex-wife is trying to kill me—'

'I'm *not!!*' she bawled at him, glaring through red eyes. Awash, her face insisted, in oceans of regret. 'I'm *not* trying to kill you Jon, I swear.'

'Well then,' he said quietly. 'Who is?'

And then she told him her story. It was after their separation. She was in financial difficulty and met Irwin around the same time. She had no idea, initially, about his criminal links (she still didn't know for sure) or even any suspect associates. He was just a super-intelligent, suave and charming suitor and she fell for it. She fell under his spell. And this, plus her fiscal worries and her desire to continue to succeed in the rapidly declining world of journalism, led her into being talked into taking part in what she now realised was a money laundering operation. At the time, she probably knew it wasn't legit, but she just thought it was some tax thing and she certainly had no idea about the sums of money they were talking about...

Anyway she was asked for her bank account details and told to say nothing if anything unidentified should come in, just to hold on to it and not to touch it. Trouble was, she'd accidentally given them Jon's account number instead of her own – the account she'd meant to give them wasn't one she used very often, and all her account numbers were still written down at the back of the same diary, still side by side with Jon's account numbers.

She didn't realise any money had been transferred and just assumed they'd had second thoughts, so thought nothing more of it.

And then, recently, they'd come for the money. It was all done through Irwin of course. Was all very 'civil'. So when she realised her mistake – and whose account number she'd given them – the next thing she knew Irwin was asking her all these questions. About Jon and who his solicitor was. Paul Brilling of course, the one they both shared.

'I had no idea you hadn't changed your will, Jon. I promise.'

'But you found out.'

'No. I didn't. But Irwin could have.'

'Brilling could have told him?'

'I expect Brilling could have *showed* him,' she said.

'So why didn't you tell me? About the money?'

'I didn't think it would come to this. Irwin said he'd...' She seemed to lose her train of thought.

'Yes? Get rid of me?'

'No! I thought they were going to set up a meeting with you.'

'A meeting. Yeah, *sort* of.'

'That I'd be the go-between. When the time came.'

'And then the time came.'

'I started becoming suspicious about... what their plan was. And then... that phone call. The night of the fire at your house. Irwin cut the call somehow.'

'I was wondering about that.'

'I was scared, Jon. I was under so much pressure.'

'So was I.'

'I was told to say nothing to you or, basically... I was dead.'

'So why are you still *seeing* him for fuck's sake?'

'I...' She was shaking her head. 'I have no choice.'

'What. He's... raping you is he? I assume you're sleeping with him. You said you were pregnant.'

She started sobbing again.

'Yes,' she said after a while. 'I *was* pregnant. As far as Irwin's concerned I still am.'

They were both silent for a moment. Jon, because he was forcing himself to. Trying to avoid saying something he'd regret later.

Romy was staring out into space – out the kitchen window – when her eyes suddenly widened.

'Oh... God...'

And there, in the back yard, was the man Jon had seen leaving the place earlier. Making his way up from the back fence, and past a neglected rose bush. There, it would seem, was Irwin.

'Run, Jon. *Now.*'

'Is the door locked? The back door?'

Jon's question was answered a moment later though, when the back door clicked open, and the scorpion in the business suit walked in. The time for running had passed.

Irwin just stood there and stared. At Jon. Didn't move a muscle. And then the beginnings of a smile. A fake smile.

'You're Jonathon Marriner,' he said, still smiling. 'Brave man.' He had an indeterminate accent, part Oxbridge possibly, with a touch of Northern or Eastern European (but what would Jon know). His smile erupted, momentarily, into a short laugh.

'*Brainless* man,' he added, and then the smile disappeared altogether. 'What's he doing here?' The question was intended for Romy, but he was still staring at Jon.

'You do know that's burglary,' Jon said. 'You'll get done, one of these days.'

'I *said*...' Irwin maintained his gaze. '... what is he *doing here*.'

'Unless you're not intending to commit an offence, but you're looking a little like you are.'

'Irwin, it's OK,' Romy said. 'He just came around to—'

'Don't tell me it's OK,' Irwin said calmly, this time to Romy directly. 'Don't tell me it's fucking "OK", just tell me *what*... the *fuck*... is he *doing* here.'

'I'm trying to explain. He came about the *money*. OK?'

'Oh did he? And you just let him in here, did you? You stupid, stupid bitch.'

'All right that's enough,' Jon said. 'You don't speak to my ex-wife like that, mate. Leave now or I'm calling the police.'

Irwin laughed. 'Yeah. *Ex*-wife, you'd do well to remember that. And listen to me, you fucking moron. You're the one that forced your way in. So you just sit down and I'll decide what happens next.'

'Sure,' said Jon, pulling his phone out. 'We'll see what the coppers have to say about that then shall we?'

He was in the process of pressing 9-9-9 when Irwin, as quick as a striking snake, slapped the phone out of his hand. It sailed across the kitchen, crashed into a shelf, rattled across the floor. At the same time, Irwin shoved Jon hard into the kitchen table, painfully crushing his hip. Jon then lost his balance and tumbled over onto the floor, trying unsuccessfully to grab hold of the table on his way down.

Irwin reached a hand in under his jacket.

'I didn't want to ever have to do this in front of you.' Irwin was apparently speaking to Romy. 'Business and pleasure and all that.'

He pulled out a handgun and then, separately, a silencer. He began screwing the silencer into the barrel, keeping a steady eye on Jon.

'Irwin,' Romy pleaded. 'What are you doing? No!'

'No? No *what*? You have no idea. This is *your* fuck-up. Your fault. I told you to use your *head*, woman.'

He finished attaching the silencer and released the safety catch. Raised the gun. Jon had barely enough time to get off the floor. It was a summary execution and Irwin obviously wasn't the type for speeches.

Romy screamed. It was ear-piercing and enough to make Irwin hesitate for a split-second. And that split-second was enough to allow Jon, who was already in a crouch, to leap at Irwin, under his raised arm, and put a shoulder into him rugby-style.

He pushed Irwin back, slamming him into the kitchen wall. He thought maybe Irwin had hit his head, not enough to put him out, but enough to give him time to…

'Run!' Romy yelled, as she hurled herself onto Irwin. She was pathetically clutching, reaching up for the gun in Irwin's hand, and Jon caught the look in her eyes, a look of desperation, pleading with him both to run and, at the same time, to help her. Another one of those impossible requests that women had a habit of making of you.

Jon grabbed the nearest weapon he could find which turned out to be a glass blender jug with a handle. It was empty and perfectly positioned for him to pick it up with his right hand and in one continuous movement drag it in a fast arc through the air and across Irwin's crew-cut.

There wasn't the crack that he'd been hoping to hear when the glass came into contact with Irwin's skull, but Irwin went down all the same. He was ready for a second swipe, clenching the jug with a white-knuckled fist, but it wasn't required. Irwin wasn't moving.

'Is he dead?' he asked, picking up the gun.

Romy just shook her head, which he took to mean either no, or she didn't know. Or she couldn't believe this was happening. Jon decided to give Irwin the benefit of the doubt. He kept the gun pointed at Irwin as he retrieved his phone from the other end of the kitchen floor. Miraculously, it appeared unharmed. Alastair's phones may not have been up to much, but they were tough.

'Keep the gun on him,' Romy said. 'I'll check.'

With obvious distaste, she got as close as she dared. 'He's alive.'

Jon knew he shouldn't have been, but he felt strangely relieved. He'd never killed anyone before.

'So who do we ring first,' he said. 'The police or the ambulance.'

'You should get out of here. You're meant to be dead, remember?'

'But Romy, the guy's just tried to—'

'What do you think's going to happen if you go to the police? Do you know how many friends he's got in the ranks? And even apart from that, this problem that you have, and I have, it's not going to go away. Maybe, if we're lucky, the police'll charge him, and lock him up. Maybe he even gets convicted. A year down the track. In the meantime, do you think you'll still be alive to see it? Or me? Irwin's not the only one, so… We have to be cleverer than that and you know it. You've known it for the last week, haven't you? That's why you haven't gone to the police, isn't it?'

He knew she was right.

'If you've got somewhere to go,' she said, 'where no-one'll find you, then go there. Let me deal with this.'

'What will you do?'

'Same as you. I'm out of here. I need to grab some things upstairs first.'

'Well I'll wait while—'

'No! Please, you'll just make it worse. I'm begging you. Leave now. And take the gun.'

It was still in his hand and he looked at it closely for the first time. It was a Beretta. Not only had he never killed anyone before, he'd never fired a handgun either.

'Don't forget to put the safety catch on.'

Was she an expert with guns now, or had she picked that up from the TV? He kept the thought to himself.

He put the safety on, and unscrewed the silencer and put the gun in one coat pocket and the silencer in the other. They were heavy and felt ridiculous. But what choice did he have?

'Are you sure you'll—?'

'Go Jon, *fuck*. The longer you hang around…'

'OK. But give me your phone number. I don't know what this one's is.'

She wrote it down on a tear-off pad and handed it to him. 'Ring me,' she said. 'And then I'll have your number. Now get out of here.'

He picked up his BOAC bag on the way out. It wasn't until he'd reached Fulham Road almost five minutes later that it hit him. What was he thinking of, leaving her with that psychopath? Just because she'd begged him to leave… It was true, he'd as good as reformatted the guy's C-drive with that blender, or it looked like he had, but for how long? And what if he hadn't? He immediately rang her with the number she'd just given him. No answer. *Don't do this to me Romy*. He tried again. Still nothing.

He swore, attracting a few stares from Chelsea pedestrians and did a quick about-face. Walked and almost ran back to the house in Carlyle Square.

When he got there, the front door was ajar. He was certain he'd pulled it shut when he left. Had Romy run off without bothering to close it? He looked up and down the street – no-one – and then, moving close in to the front door, he pulled out from his coat pockets the Beretta and the silencer. Screwed the silencer back into the gun barrel. Released the safety. He didn't know how to check the number of rounds, so had to trust his instincts on that one. He doubted Irwin was the sort who needed to make empty threats.

He eased the door open with his foot, and once inside, he lifted the gun up to shoulder height ready to fire. Crept as silently as he could, through to the kitchen.

The first thing he noticed was that Irwin's body had gone. And there was no sign of Romy.

He checked the whole house, but it was deserted. Including Romy's bedroom which showed worryingly few signs of its occupier having left in a hurry. Had she left already without taking anything? What had she done with Irwin?

On his way out, he checked the kitchen again. And there, sitting on the table where she'd left it, was Romy's mobile phone. And he found her house keys too, in the bowl near the front door where she'd always put them. There was only one plausible explanation.

Irwin had taken her.

62.

The sheet lightning crackled across the sky above the Chelsea streets, lighting up stony-faced gargoyles perched high on the red brick building next to him. It was still only 4pm, but it felt like night. Runion, who minutes ago had emerged from the jaws of the Sloane Square tube station, was almost home. He knew there was a big Atlantic storm on its way, but it wasn't due for at least another couple of days. It had been sunny too, when he'd entered the Underground at Cannon Street. Whatever the cause, he'd been regurgitated into a very dark afternoon indeed.

For some reason, something he'd been wrestling with for the last twenty-four hours suddenly came to him: the identity of the man in the corner at the Garrick Club. Nigel Stephens. Odd chap, no idea what he did for a living. And always in grey suits – what did he have against navy? – and those awful brown shoes. Letting the side down somewhat, in Runion's view. A small effort was called for when visiting the club – not a mammoth one, just a small one. Speaking of mammoth, and this perhaps explained the man's general unkempt appearance, Stephens was not exactly slim. Larger men often had greater difficulty keeping their clothes under control. Nevertheless he wasn't all *that* large and, once again, a small effort was really all that was required.

Speaking of the club, what in the dickens had happened to Bridges? He'd promised to call before the end of the day about their "little problem". It wasn't like him, he was usually so reliable as a rule. Runion hoped nothing untoward had happened.

And then the strangest thing occurred. First, he experienced an overwhelming sensation of being watched. It was so strong that he actually stopped and turned, as if there were someone behind him who needed him. Someone he knew.

And there was. Because when Runion turned around and looked back, towards Sloane Square, towards the station past the end of the street... he was standing there. Stephens. The man himself. In his grey suit and bloody awful brown suede shoes. And was that a crooked smile underneath those glasses? Runion couldn't tell, it may have been more of a grimace. What on earth was he doing?

It was definitely Stephens, though. How extraordinary that he'd just been thinking about him!

The man was certainly behaving oddly. Although Stephens was looking straight at Runion, he wasn't making any attempt to acknowledge him. As Runion didn't want to stare and make a fool of himself, he continued on his way, albeit in a somewhat rather different frame of mind.

A rolling fusillade of thunder interrupted his thoughts – thoughts which had been sombre enough to start with – and he shivered as he imagined, for some reason, one of the gargoyles dislodging and plummeting into his skull.

63.

It was just after 4pm and a stubborn mist was advancing over the sea. There was hardly a breath of wind and Jon's footsteps echoed in the heavy air.

After the shock of the incident at Romy's and his initial panic that Irwin had kidnapped her, he'd decided he was overreacting. There was very little he could do anyway. Something must have happened, that much was clear, but he didn't have to fear the worst. For one thing, Romy had said she was getting out of there herself, and there was still a hope that she'd done just that. Perhaps Irwin had regained consciousness, and she'd made a dash for it. More to the point, there was nothing he could really go to the police with. And the story that he did have, how would it sound? It got worse the more he thought about it.

To straighten his head out as much as anything, he'd resolved that it was as good a time as any to head south, to the sea air and Lucinda. He retraced his steps to Fulham Road and then on to South Kensington where he caught the Tube to Victoria Station. Once there, he booked a seat on the 1.47 to Lewes and for the third time that day he sat down in the main hall for a coffee (his fourth), and waited.

Changing at Lewes, he made it to Newhaven Town station just after three. He chose to walk to Peacehaven, it was a few kilometres but it would do him good. Crossed the river – the Ouse. "Ouse" was a common name for rivers, he knew, although he couldn't remember where any of the others were. Somewhere in his catalogue of useless facts was the snippet that told him "Ouse" was the Celtic word for "water". Something that made sense, at a time when little did.

By the time he'd arrived at Peacehaven and was walking along The Promenade, that mist was already beginning to roll in (it had been sunny when he'd left London, too). Someone had told him (was it Alastair?) that there was a storm on the way, but there was certainly no sign of it yet. The sea – the English Channel – was as flat as a proverbial pancake, almost glassy. The only sound was the gentle lapping of the water and Jon's patient footsteps.

When he reached the corner of the street Lucinda was in – Dorothy Avenue, it was Lucinda in Dorothy, very Alastair when he thought about it – he could see up ahead to what he knew was the Prime Meridian monument.

Lucinda herself was modest and plain – as the nicest girls usually were. She was a small, single-storey, semidetached house made of light, mottled brick and with a white garage door and a dark slate roof. Not a mansion, but as long as Irwin wasn't on the other side of that common wall, Jon didn't care. Lucinda was, maybe a hundred metres from The Promenade and the ocean loomed large at the end of the street.

Inside, and things became even more spartan. Bare brick walls, empty bookshelves (empty apart from a small pile of motoring maps), no pictures other than a torn travel poster in a cracked plastic frame (a picture of a volcano, with the words "Réunion Island"), no carpet (and no television). Through a doorway, a small kitchen with little more than a refrigerator, and with no china except for the one sad "kung fu for idiots" coffee mug. Cutlery consisted of two forks and a spoon. Two bedrooms which looked out onto a bare backyard. On the plus side, there were a number of Persian rugs tossed around the place and, critically, the main bedroom was large and came with a bed (queen-size) with a mattress. There was even – unbelievably – clean linen in the cupboard, and a duvet.

And to his great relief, stuck to the door of the refrigerator as promised, was a list of emergency numbers for various tradesmen including a plumber.

It was when he began to remove his jacket that he realised he still had the gun. He'd totally forgotten about it – despite its weight – sitting there in his left coat pocket, while still in his right, and almost counterbalancing it, was its taciturn companion, the silencer. Not items he'd want to be walking through a security check with (not that he was likely to be using an airport in the foreseeable future). He removed the Beretta and the silencer and buried them at the bottom of his bag, underneath his spare clothes and the remaining wads of banknotes.

The next thing he did was open up his laptop and go online. Absurd, this need, this addiction to being online, being "connected", but it provided a certain degree of comfort, a sense of security. Which was ironic, this feeling of security, with the internet being the home and highway of so much vice – there was little doubt it was fast becoming, if it wasn't already, the primary tool of the modern criminal. All of which Jon knew of course, but he still connected and he still felt better.

And then he noticed he had a Skype message.

It was from Emerald, sent just over an hour earlier. It consisted of two words:

– contact me

He presumed she meant on Skype (he had no other means, he didn't have her phone number), so he replied.

– At your service.

Unlike the previous evening, this time there was no immediate response. He stared at the screen for a while then gave up. He wondered what he'd do next – the whole situation made him feel like he was under house arrest. To rid himself of the sensation he decided to go for a short walk, explore the area, maybe find a shop.

It turned out Lucinda was well-served. There was a Sainsbury's at the end of the street, as well as a few fast-food establishments, so he could breathe just that little bit more easily. Especially as one of them was the *Oriental Taste* ("chinese and peking cuisine to take away"): he could almost be back in Soho. Almost. With a bit of luck though, they'd have Peking Duck. Before ordering, he retraced his steps to the Promenade and sat down for a while in view of the Prime Meridian monument, and looked out over the water and watched the sunless afternoon make way for the night. If there'd been a visible sun, he would have seen it set over the sea as he was sitting there. No such luck.

Her response came just after 7pm, well after he'd returned to the house with a morale-boosting supply of French wine and chinese takeaway. It was a video call this time and he answered it. That beautiful face materialized, and those green eyes. Unsmiling though, she looked stressed. And she looked as though she was trying not to show it.

'Good evening Mr Marriner.'

'Miss Strand.'

'Did you leave London?'

'I'm not sure I should answer that.'

A smile. A sparkle in her eyes. 'OK.'

The mottled brick was visible inside as well as out. And the empty shelves gave the game away all by themselves.

'And what about you, Emerald.'

There was a pause.

'Well I had been thinking about the Black Sea. But then again, I was hoping...' It was a rare hesitation from this most self-assured of women. 'I was wondering if you would like some company. You might be feeling lonely. Now that you're dead.'

'Depends who the company is. Dead is forever, after all.'

Another smile.

'I thought you were hoping you'd never see me again,' he added.

'I'm not sure if I would put it like that, exactly.'

'You did, actually.' He returned the smile.

'Yes, OK,' she said. 'But Jonathon. I think you're being a little bit cruel here.'

He thought for a moment. Considered the situation. He didn't have to think for long.

'Well... You're right. It is a bit lonely here. Just me. And the ocean.'

'I can imagine. So without... naming any *names*...' She left a meaningful pause, so it might sink in. 'Can I just get you to confirm... it's the place we talked about earlier.'

'It is.'

'That's good. I'll be there in...' A grin, and she looked down for a moment, shook her head, as if she were scolding herself. And then she suddenly turned and quickly checked over her shoulder, as if she'd heard something.

'What is it?'

Shook her head. 'I'll be there soon, OK?'

'OK.'

'And you know,' she said quickly, before he had a chance to sign off. 'There's a storm coming. We could maybe sit it out together.'

Whether she was being metaphorical or not, to Jon the words sounded fine either way.

'We could. There's nothing like a good storm. The bigger...' He trailed off.

Emerald was looking over her shoulder again and this time it wasn't fleeting. She continued to look off-camera at something.

'What is it?'

She held up a hand and mouthed the word *Wait*.

He watched as she got up out of her chair and disappeared from view. There was a clicking sound – possibly a door being opened, or closed – and then nothing. He kept watching the screen, wide-eyed, but there was nothing to see. And now, no sound.

Then all of a sudden, there was a loud thud and a crash. A grunt. Someone else was in the room. Horrified, Jon thought he heard a muffled shriek, and then the sound of someone being punched. A curse, and then a cough.

And then bursting across the screen, visible for an instant, was a person, probably a man, in a dark jacket of some kind, with an arm around Emerald's neck, dragging her down. The man – Jon didn't get a chance to see his face – seemed to fall on her, throw himself onto her, and then both the man and Emerald were out of the frame. Furniture was shifting though, as if there was an earthquake. The camera, the picture on his screen, was shaking.

'Emerald!' He couldn't help it. He shouted her name out of pure frustration as much as anything. He felt so utterly helpless. He didn't even know where she was, where this was taking place…

'Emerald!' he shouted again. And even more impotently: 'I'm on my way!'

More struggling, crashing, strangled cries of anguish and, for a moment, silence, and then, from nowhere, a blunt object, like a block of wood or a cricket bat flew at the camera with a terrible suddenness and violence, and the screen went black.

Oh Jesus.

Jon stared at the black screen. His mind was racing though, like a computer turning over, trying to perform an impossible calculation. But there was absolutely nothing he could think of to do. Not a thing.

He waited, it must have been at least five, ten minutes. Eventually, after a small eternity of frozen silence, he hesitantly, reluctantly, switched off his Skype. There was a horrible feeling of finality about it. Somehow, it felt like he'd just turned off a life-support system.

As he sat there, in the pale light, he noticed his hand was trembling. And he began to shake, all over. Like that old song.

Part Six – Dark Oceans

"Before their eyes in sudden view appear
The secrets of the hoary deep, a dark
Illimitable Ocean without bound…"

(from *Paradise Lost* by John Milton)

64. <u>17° 36' 45" S 167° 23' 49" E</u> (New Hebrides Trench, Coral Sea)

5.15am Vanuatu Time (18:15 UTC)
Saturday, 26 October

Synchronously – give or take a few seconds – with Jon clicking out of his Skype screen on his laptop in Peacehaven while sitting discomposed on a chair in a house that (as Alastair put it) straddled the Prime Meridian, on the opposite side of the globe in the Pacific Ocean at the precise point on the Coral Sea corresponding with the geographic co-ordinates <u>17 degrees 36 minutes 45 seconds South, 167 degrees 23 minutes 49 seconds East</u>, the first rays of the rising sun shot out from the eastern horizon and instantaneously made contact with the restless, corrugated waters there. This particular spot on the surface of the ocean, now beginning to scintillate as if bejewelled with a myriad fragments of iridescent-orange Fire Agate, lay just over one thousand three hundred kilometres west of the Prime Meridian's opposite number, the Antimeridian.

If you were on a boat at this spot, you would see no land. You would have to sail east for eighty kilometres or so before you arrived at the first of the Vanuatu islands. Around a hundred kilometres would get you to the capital, Port Vila. And if for any reason you were to go straight down, you would have to descend over six thousand six hundred metres – nearly seven kilometres – before you hit the bottom. Because you would be positioned directly over the New Hebrides Trench.

Indeed if you were to jump in the water and then breathe out and allow yourself to sink straight down, feet first, it would take you, based on an average rate of about three metres a second, over half an hour before you touched the bottom. And assuming you were somehow able to stay alive after the air had been crushed from your lungs and water forced into every orifice and cavity in your body, you would be able to make a handful of noteworthy observations on your way down: you would see daylight petering out after only two hundred metres; you would be able to confirm that the darkness was well and truly absolute at a depth of one thousand metres; below one thousand metres, generally referred to as the aphotic or midnight zone, you would continue to descend through, specifically, the Bathyal Zone (or Bathypelagic layer, between 1000 and 4000 metres), followed by the Abyssal Zone (between 4000 and 6000 metres). Finally, after thirty-three minutes of this rapid plummeting, you would reach the Hadal Zone (a word derived from *Hades*, the underworld – at 6000 metres and below), and then nearly four minutes later, at a depth of 6,648 metres, enjoying a frigid water temperature of around one degree Celsius, a pressure of 6,800 tonnes per square metre and in the darkest dark you had ever or could ever experience, suddenly and without warning you would feel your feet slam into the soft, silty, ocean floor.

Because if you want dark, oceans hold the purest blend.

Now call it a coincidence if you will, but the timing of Jon's mouse-click happened to correspond not just with the first moments of sunrise on the surface, but also with something similar that occurred at this very spot directly beneath it (which of course shared the same GPS coordinates) – here on the seabed, in the Hadal darkness of the lower reaches of the New Hebrides Trench. The lights came on.

How? Because on this particular day, this undersea location had a visitor.

Two days earlier, an unmanned, remote-controlled lander was lowered to this forbidding place by a research vessel on the surface. The lander was essentially a two metre high aluminium tripod attaching an assortment of scientific instruments (designed to withstand the brutal pressure at these depths) including waterproof video cameras with lights, also remotely controlled, as well as bait for attracting fish and other sea-dwellers. The lander was connected to a permanent buoy on the surface by a cable. The buoy transmitted data, including video footage, to the vessel which was to remain in the area for a period of a total of six days. The team, formed as part of an international project run through a small group of universities, managed to set the tripod down at a depth of 6648 metres in a spot they dubbed *Mare Tranquillitatis* – Latin for Sea of Tranquillity and named after the plain on the Moon where the first moon landing took place. Like its namesake on the Moon, here also there was a large, flat area of comparatively darker basaltic sediment. The lights on the platform were set to come on for only five minutes every two hours so as not to interfere with a marine environment accustomed only to complete darkness. And on this day, at 5.15am, the lights sprang on.

There wasn't always someone from the team to monitor the footage as it came in and control the cameras (rotate them, adjust the focus) – in which case the footage would be pored over later – but these guys were early risers and this time the team's sole female, a research scientist from Seattle, was on hand to observe this morning's "lights up".

On this occasion there was plenty of action. The main camera was already pointed at the bait. They'd used a pig carcass – disturbingly human-like in this researcher's opinion – and overnight it had attracted quite a crowd. For these depths anyway. It was covered in a scuttling gang of four, no, five bright prawns – lobster-like in appearance – and about fifty amphipods (smaller, pale-coloured crustaceans, part shrimp, part cockroach) and both the prawns and the amphipods looked to be approaching their task with gusto. And then the researcher noticed something lurking in the background shadows. It was a large, brown cusk-eel (genus *Bassozetus*): an eel-like fish, torpedo-shaped with beady eyes, it looked like a penis (the prototype dickhead, it occurred to her, which was something it had in common with her research partner). The cusk-eel gradually floated into the light. The prawns and amphipods didn't know it was there, or were unconcerned. But they *should* have been concerned, because all of a sudden the cusk-eel's mouth snapped open and in a vacuum manoeuvre sucked one of the larger amphipods into its gullet in little more than an eyeblink.

Life in the depths.

65. <u>17° 44' 31" S 168° 18' 51" E</u> (Grand Hotel and Casino, Port Vila, Vanuatu)

The same time
5.15am Vanuatu Time (18:15 UTC)
Saturday, 26 October

Meanwhile...

In Port Vila, ninety-eight kilometres to the east-south-east, in the direction of the rising sun (which in Port Vila, given its more easterly position, had risen four minutes earlier), Dominique Drayle was staring at himself in the mirror of his hotel room and waiting for a knock on the door.

Out through the glass sliding doors and past the balcony, the previously black sapphire, now Persian-blue waters of Vila Bay were gradually lightening and at the same time divorcing themselves from the dawn sky. Drayle wasn't interested in the view out of his room however – only the one in the mirror.

He was never going to get used to this.

The operation – or operations – had taken place just over a month earlier – over three days, September 22 to 24. The dates he was clear on, if not the events that took place on them, which were still a blur. He'll never forget, though, what happened when he made Dr. Fischer hand over the mirror. The shock of seeing this... thing. This alien. Unrecognizable. Which was the point, *up* to a point, but not this. This was definitely not the plan.

The plan had been, in summary: a chin implant and reshape, removing the cleft and the double-chin in the process; rhinoplasty, to reduce the size of, and reshape, his slightly hooked Roman nose (a "nasal hump excision"); implants to make his cheekbones more prominent; removal of the scar across his face; and a face-lift, pulling the skin back and narrowing his eyes slightly (*slightly*, note). Also, to complement and accentuate the changes, he'd had his curly blond hair straightened and coloured dark brown, almost black (and he'd grown it as well), and he'd been regularly applying serious amounts of fake tan, banishing his natural rosy complexion.

The operation hadn't been a success.

Sure, the cleft chin was gone, and the scar as well (with the help of make-up); and the hair looked sufficiently different, as did his complexion (although the cheap self-tan somehow managed to turn everything he touched orange, like some sort of B-grade Midas touch).

But...

First there was the swelling. A *degree* of swelling was, naturally, always to be expected for a procedure of this nature. Drayle's, though, had been dramatic, frightening even, and although much of it had now settled, there was a degree of permanent residual swelling, especially over his cheekbones. And the facelift was too extreme – the skin had been pulled too tight and his eyes appeared narrower, more elongated. His nose had been made too small – particularly with his new, swollen face and more prominent chin. Even now, his nose was still numb, and he had to take Panadeine Forte constantly for chronic pain. And on top of all that, the combination of the swelling, the tighter skin over his face, the narrower eyes and smaller nose, along with the straight dark hair and darker skin had made him look Asian. His previous Germanic looks (Germanic *good* looks) had, not just partially, but completely disappeared. And last but most certainly not least: the final insult was his new face wasn't even symmetrical! His nose was slightly crooked and one cheekbone was higher than the other. It had been suggested to him his face had been asymmetrical to start with, but we all knew who made that suggestion. And after all, he would, wouldn't he. He would say that. That Herr Doktor Florian Fischer, he was a dead man.

Literally.

After the botched operation, Fischer had scuttled back to Bangkok, the rat, leaving Drayle to recuperate on his own. Albeit in the soft and capable hands of the surgeon's assistant, the impossibly alluring Laska. And out of the public gaze, another plus. But Drayle had just had it confirmed: Florian Fischer would no longer be looking in the mirror admiring *his* Germanic good looks. Drayle had, via the usual channels, notified a certain Korean gentleman (an extremely *un*gentle gentleman, that is) who, conveniently, happened to pass through Bangkok from time to time. According to official sources, Dr. Fischer had fallen prey to a particularly vicious gang of robbers while enjoying a glass of wine in his city apartment. Nothing plastic surgery was ever going to fix. Not plastic surgery nor, as it turned out, the intensive care capabilities of the Bumrungrad International Hospital which was where Florian Fischer spent the last three days of his richly-rewarded, praise-filled life.

The doctor wasn't meant to have been killed, just given a little face-alteration of his own to treasure, to really test his facial reconstruction skills (or those of his colleagues, he could hardly have operated on himself could he, especially without eyes!). But death or disfigurement, it was immaterial now. Nothing that was done to Fischer could make up for what Fischer had done to Drayle's face. True, the point was that he no longer be recognizable (no problem on that score, thank you Dr. Fischer!). But with the swelling and the asymmetry... he looked like a freak.

And *Asian*? Since when was that in the brief? Asian. And now he looked like the Korean.

It was as if Fischer had done it on purpose. And for that – even the suspicion of that, it was what it looked like and that was all you could ever go on, wasn't it? – for that, Fischer had forfeited his life...

One small consolation was his new identity appeared to be 'taking' (to use a medical analogy). He had a shiny new passport displaying his shiny new face (and oh how it was shiny) and a shiny new name too: Edward Lang (they should have made it Lee to complete the joke) – Edward Lang from London, the city that asked no questions.

He swallowed two Panadeine capsules with a glass of water. They helped, although imagining how Fischer died helped more.

The only real issue remaining was whether he was still attractive to women. He certainly hadn't noticed many admiring glances on his way over from Bangkok. One or two if he was lucky, and from freaks, he could safely assume – attracted to pigfaces with squinty eyes and dark hair. Freaks, and now he was one of them.

The knock on the door would provide the first real test (Laska didn't count, given the absence of consent). Would the person doing the knocking change her mind once she laid eyes on him? He knew, despite her circumstances, she would turn up. But would she still love him?

The mirror wasn't so sure.

And then there were two sharp knocks on the door – just as the first sunbeams cleared the low ridge behind his hotel and hit the mirror-like waters of Vila Bay.

66. <u>33° 57' 0" S 151° 10' 37" E /
17° 55' 51" S 122° 13' 2" E</u>
(Sydney Airport / Cable Beach, Broome)

1.15pm Australian Eastern Daylight Time (02:15 UTC)
Saturday, 26 October

The jarring bump and shudder of the landing seemed worse than it was, but only because he'd been deep in thought. They were down. Another runway, another town. He hadn't travelled this much in his life. And Sydney, wasn't that the opposite side of the world to Paris? Its... antimeridian? its antipodes? It had to be close. He could hardly be further away if he tried. In terms of distance from everywhere though, Broome was hard to beat. And it was Broome that he was thinking of when the plane touched down. Because the last six days had been most... educational.

They'd given him a lot to think about. Who? The last six days. And *them*.

* * *

Six days earlier, on Sunday 20 October, Ruart arrived in Broome. He'd chosen to stay at the Blue Seas Resort at Cable Beach, supposedly one of the best, although it had really been the name that had appealed to him. It was only later that he'd seen the baobab trees on the hotel's website – baobabs would forever give him a bad feeling, ever since the incident in the *Jardin de L'État* at least, and if he'd seen the website photos before he'd booked, he would have chosen somewhere else. At the resort's reception, on his arrival, he struck up a conversation with a member of staff – a colourful Australian girl, literally, with flaming red hair, emerald green eyes and heavily freckled skin. She had none of the sophisticated airs of the blonde in Saint-Denis, but she was unbelievably friendly and had one of the loudest, broadest, strangest accents he'd ever come across: she brought to mind some beautiful, screeching, tropical bird.

The plane hadn't landed in Broome until 6pm, just after sunset – fifteen and a half hours after leaving Saint-Denis. Ruart was having some trouble getting his head around the travelling times and distances in this part of the world (it made him even more tired just thinking about it) and so he decided to take it easy that evening and postpone the legwork until the following morning. And enjoy his first night on the "Pearl Coast" as they called it.

He rang his wife Marine. It was odd: he'd only been away two days – less if you took into account the time difference – yet already she was beginning to feel like a stranger. Was it her or was it him? Or was it the distance? Could distance alone do that? This time she didn't ask about where he was at all, not a single question about Broome or Australia. Or perhaps she could tell there was stuff he wasn't telling her (such as the unmentionable incident in Saint-Denis) and she was getting him back? No, he decided, it was simply the distance, it affected everything somehow. There was something Einsteinian about it.

Later, before he got into bed, he was brushing up on his English and glancing through a local paper – it was the previous day's, Saturday. Big local news, it seemed, was the naming of a couple who'd gone missing in the desert: a Russian couple, it was reported, tourists. Aleksei Denisovsky, 37, and his girlfriend Lydia Korolenko, 28.

A warning, as far as he was concerned, not to be a stupid tourist.

The next morning, on the Monday, the first thing he did was establish that the *Diamond Moon* was indeed in Broome; that it was moored just off the ocean side of the peninsula (although not as close as it sounded: the yacht was nearly five kilometres away, as well as being about four hundred metres out from Cable Beach – he actually entertained a very short-lived idea that he might swim out to it). He was told he'd probably be able to hitch a ride out to it in a small boat (an aluminium dinghy or "tinnie" as they called it here).

After a buffet breakfast of satisfying percolated coffee, and pastries that looked deceptively like croissants (he was French, he was not just entitled but obligated to think like this; in fact they were perfectly edible if you thought of them as bagels), he got going. Out into the sunshine and a surprising heat for ten in the morning – the girl from the day before wasn't around, but the trees were full of her kind. He ignored the baobabs and fired up his hire car, a red Hyundai Getz.

First stop was the harbour master's office down on the point. Once there, he managed to get into contact with the *Diamond Moon* over the office radio. He spoke to the yacht's captain who conveyed a jovial friendliness that seemed to belie his English accent. Ruart explained that he was a yacht enthusiast and buyer and was interested in either buying the yacht or at least speaking to someone there about where he might find a similar one. He was told he would be very welcome to come aboard, and he was instructed to make his way to the southern end of Cable Beach where he'd be picked up. The people in this part of the world were all so friendly!

(It now occurred to him, he may have made some mistakes, but if there was one thing on this trip he could congratulate himself over, it was the standard of his English. All those years of hard work – and American DVDs – were paying off.)

Half an hour later he found himself skimming over the cobalt blue waters of the Indian Ocean in a jetboat (the yacht's tender), away from the white sands of Cable Beach and the red sandstone cliffs of the headland. Blue, white and red: a gigantic French flag – a *drapeau tricolore* – and he was in the middle of it. All very appropriate, because the headland was known as Gantheaume Point. He could scarcely believe it when he read the night before that Gantheaume Point, which had been named after the French admiral Joseph Gantheaume, had been given its name by Nicholas Baudin in 1801 – the very same French explorer whose ship had deposited Bory de Sainte-Vincente in Mauritius (on the very same expedition). For Ruart it was another in a series of beautiful connections. Not quite another 'sparky coincidence', but he always knew he was on the right track when these connections began popping up all over the place. He couldn't explain why, but that was the way it always worked.

And there it was at last. The *Diamond Moon*. It was enormous, especially in comparison with the boats around it. Out there on the water, in the tropical sun, its silver paint was dazzling. True to its name, it looked like a gigantic rock of a diamond, jutting out of the ocean. Like the tip of some precious, unmeltable iceberg…

He was welcomed aboard with the same friendliness he was extended over the radio. The captain greeted him – *James Weston, call me Trim* – and he was shown around the yacht. It was about as modern as you could get with sleek, metallic surfaces, flawless wooden decking and three levels: upper deck, lower deck and "down below". "Trim", who turned out to be Australian despite his English accent, was tall – well over 2 metres – and had a lot of ducking to do. On his tour, Ruart came across the other crew: two fit-looking young guys in boardshorts, Benoît and Tomas (who had picked Ruart up in the tender). Benoît, who was French, appeared moody, and despite being Ruart's compatriot, had nothing much to say in *any* language. Tomas, a Dane, made up for Benoît's surly silence with a mouth as big as a shark's (*quelle bouche!*) which he used *à fond*, to the max, with his non-stop chatter. There was Felipe, a Spaniard with a fashionable nine-day growth sculpted around his chin and Nadine, a honey-bronzed Portuguese girl with auburn hair and large breasts. Ruart was able to guess almost straight away – through some pretty obvious body language – that Nadine was having it off with both the captain and Tomas, and that it was no state secret.

In the kitchen, or rather 'the galley', they came across one of the guests. Brian was a tanned, burly, bear of a man with a crew-cut and Popeye-sized forearms. Friendly, though. Like everyone, Ruart observed, except the Frenchman. And he couldn't help but notice the coffee machine Brian was operating: it was a Marzocco.

So there was the Marzocco!

Brian's wife, Diane, joined them. Diane was skinny, elfin and sweet with mousey hair and lovely, light-blue eyes the colour of shallow rock pools. She was wearing a see-through white dress over a black bikini and her skin was pale for someone on a yachting holiday. Ruart wondered if it was because she was spending all of her time in her cabin, but something told him that if she was, it wasn't sex she was sacrificing her tan for. Or at least not sex with Brian.

As for Bob Walman himself: he'd left with his girlfriend for Perth two days earlier. Missed him again.

So Ruart chatted with Trim, the captain, but learnt little that he didn't already know. Walman had bought the *Diamond Moon* in Réunion in early September, but Trim hadn't had anything to do with it until he'd been instructed by Walman to pick it up in Bali and sail it to Broome. That was two weeks ago, he said. Since then they'd been on a trip to the Lacepede Islands – Bob, his girlfriend Peta, Brian and Diane on the *Diamond Moon* with Lena and Roy on the *Seaking*. Who?

Brian piped up and told Ruart about his Russian ex-wife Lena and her boyfriend Roy and how the other couple who were meant to have been with them on the *Seaking* – they were originally supposed to have been a party of eight – had disappeared.

'Disappeared?' Ruart asked.

'Yeah. It's been in all the papers. Lydia and, ah…'

'Yes. Aleksei…'

'Aleks, yeah. You read about it then. A bit of a worry, that. We've all just… been praying they turn up somewhere.'

'I hope so.'

'Tidy little shiner, by the way.'

'Excuse me?'

Brian pointed to the side of his own face. Meaning Ruart's face. The bruise. Ruart had completely forgotten about it. He had his excuse ready, though. 'Yes, it was a, er, small climbing accident, back in—'

'Not one of the local girls, I trust,' Brian said with a smirk.

'Er… no—'

'Don't worry mate, I know you wouldn't tell us if it was!'

'That's true.' Ruart forced a laugh. 'Yes, but, I er, I want to ask about the other boat, about the, er… the er…'

'You mean the *Seaking*? It's Roy's. He bought it from Bob.'

'Ah I see, and Bob. Maybe I can speak to him? Maybe I will go to Perth.'

'Yeah, well, that's where he went. So you're, what, looking to buy yourself?'

Ruart and his bruise flew to Perth that afternoon.

But he couldn't find Bob Walman there either.

He made enquiries at the head office of Kensington Mines Limited, and was told that Walman had just left. He'd been in a board meeting and Ruart had missed him by half an hour. Walman's secretary – or personal assistant – told him he was probably at lunch somewhere and his diary was empty for that afternoon, she wasn't sure what his plans were… But he was the CEO, surely… No, she was very sorry, Mr Walman was a very private person, she could leave a message on his phone, but that was all…

He was starting to wonder if this Bob Walman actually existed, whether he wasn't just a construct – even more so after spending almost two fruitless days in Perth – because by the end of it he'd still drawn a big blank. No-one could tell him whether or not Walman was even in the country.

Two noteworthy things happened however, during his time in Perth.

On Tuesday morning, he noticed an article of interest in the local newspaper. More disappearances. This time it was three police – a pilot and two forensics personnel – who'd vanished in Broome. The mention of the words "disappearance" and "Broome" piqued his interest immediately. And then the clincher: they'd been investigating the disappearance of the couple in the desert…

The connections were pouring in now, thick and fast.

The second noteworthy event was Ruart's phone call to the *Préfecture* on Tuesday evening. He rang early, 6.30pm, which was 12.30pm in Paris – he wanted to get them before the lunchtime diaspora and the inevitable *demis* of Bordeaux. Conversations in the office were never quite as incisive in the afternoons. (Nor in the mornings before 10am for that matter, prior to the pandemic coffee intake.) When he heard what his Parisian colleague had to tell him, it became clear that his effort to ring earlier rather than later had been amply rewarded.

Paris had learnt from the Western Australian police two things that weren't in the papers: the first, connected with the couple's disappearance, was the discovery of an old ship in the desert, a galleon. In the desert! Initially it had been assumed it was Spanish (or a hoax). The name carved into the badly deteriorated wood of the stern appeared to be *Destino En Distancia*, but a more careful examination – in particular of the worn, right-hand side of the letter "n" in "En" – revealed it actually to be *Destino <u>Em</u> Distancia*, the "Em" making it Portuguese. And preliminary investigations suggested it was no hoax. The authorities though were keeping it all a secret for now, they didn't want to attract treasure hunters and it still needed to be authenticated. It was potentially sensational – with current hunches placing it there around 1560, over forty years before the first known European landing in Australia (being by a Dutchman, Janszoon, in 1606).

More important, from Ruart's point of view, was another discovery. Because the second thing the *Préfecture* had gleaned from the WA police was that in the vicinity of the old ship, a body and parts of another body had been found, and that the bodies in question were believed to be those of the missing couple.

And that wasn't all. Ruart's section at the *Préfecture* had obviously been busy (which made for a refreshing change) because they'd also found out more from the scholar at the British Museum. Delia someone or other – a woman, no wonder, women always worked harder. This Delia had, in turn, done a considerable degree of cross-referencing with a separate researcher based in Lisbon. During his phone call with the *Préfecture* Ruart took copious notes, his interest gradually mounting, as he moved from a state of initial indifference tinged with impatience to one of excitement, and finally to one of those "eureka" moments that kept him in his chosen career. To summarize what he was told:

- It was difficult to confirm the existence of a Portuguese ship with the name *Destino Em Distancia* because the Portuguese at the time were extremely secretive about their trade routes and because the vast majority of their records were destroyed in the Lisbon earthquake and tsunami of 1755.

- Recently however (in what some – not Ruart – might call a "fortunate coincidence"), a record of a secret voyage in 1560 by a previously unknown ship, referred to as "the *Destino*", had been unearthed in Lisbon, (literally unearthed, as it had apparently been buried at the time of the earthquake).

- There was no indication of the *Destino*'s fate, but one theory was that if it really had ended up in Western Australia – and in the desert there, possibly along an ancient watercourse – it could well have been on the way to Goa and/or Portugal's recent acquisition (as of 1557), Macau.

- The *Destino*, which appeared to have been under the command of Captain Gaspar Duarte Dourado De Lacerda, may have sailed as far south as it did because it was blown off course, or was on a secret mission, or was simply on a frolic of its own. Perhaps this Gaspar Duarte decided to find the great southern land himself.

- There was reference to an object carrying the ship's instructions, whatever they were. The instructions have since been lost, but the object matched the description of the "decagon" which Drayle had recovered from the *Prospero's Dancer*. Delia was firmly convinced they were one and the same (and, needless to say, the *Préfecture* by now had Ruart's full attention).

- Assuming all this to be the case, it meant that the decagon had somehow made its way from Western Australia in 1560 to Macau (from where the *Prospero's Dancer* sailed with it in 1838). It was entirely conceivable that the shipwrecked sailors themselves, or perhaps local aborigines, carried it part of the way, and that passing sailors carried it the rest, possibly via the outpost of Portuguese Timor and then on through another of Portugal's colonies in the region, Malacca.

- Delia claimed there was evidence the decagon was owned by a Portuguese merchant and his family in Macau for much of the period from the late 1500s to the early 1800s (and used, predominantly, for storing spices). It was traded for opium with the English just prior to the Opium wars.

- Delia also shed light on the possible significance of this "decagon": she believed it to be a relic known as the *Isfahan decagon*, now more than five hundred years old. If so, and if the various historical accounts of it were to be believed, it represented a highpoint of medieval Islamic geometric design and, it would appear, mathematics. The geometry of the "girih" tiles as they were known involved an advanced form of mathematics not discovered by the West until the 1970s, but the decagon took it a step further. Not only was the tiling "non-periodic" (meaning there was no repeating pattern – a pattern of *no* patterns in other words, and thus "chaotic" in one sense), but it was of a far more complex kind, and the design was more intricate than anything yet created. And on top of that, the design, if extended out far enough, was believed, or rumoured, to contain hidden images, including a portrait and even a treasure map. If that were true, the decagon represented not only the first known example of non-periodic tiling containing such images (whatever their nature), but probably also the *only* known example. (And it raised questions such as was its genius essentially mathematical or artistic? Was it encountered by pure luck or by clever, premeditated calculation?)

- Delia doubted whether any of the decagon's possessors – prior to Drayle at least – were aware of its true significance, and surmised they traded it for its face value only: for its craftsmanship and silver and gemstones.

One thing was obvious to Ruart: this decagon was enormously valuable and in the context of Drayle, there was your motive right there.

Another, more tangential, thought occurred to him: if the decagon were human, would you say it had had an unlucky life (having been shipwrecked, traded for opium, sunk and stolen) or a lucky one (with all its narrow escapes)? That was using "luck" in its colloquial sense of course, because as Ruart well knew, there was no such thing as luck. Who we are is simply a result of everything that's ever happened to us. Nothing more, nothing less. You're not lucky or unlucky. You're only ever just the result of a series of events. You're only ever just you.

More importantly though, he now had his 'sparky coincidence'. Drayle, the decagon, the *Destino*, the missing couple presumed murdered… and their friends, up there in Broome. Including one of them in particular. Lena. A Russian…

The connections were too big to ignore and he decided to head back up to Broome the next day.

The next morning, Wednesday, before heading out to the airport to catch yet another flight, he saw in the paper there'd been a further development in the case of the missing police officers.

Mikkel Backstrom, 33, had been found in Sydney the previous day.

Dead.

His body had been discovered in a park, and it was believed he'd died of a drug overdose (technically, he'd drowned in his own vomit). According to the Broome police who were asked to comment, given that the other two police officers were still missing in the area, there was no ascertainable link.

No ascertainable link? Ruart doubted that very much. Of course there was a link.

As far as Ruart was concerned though, the stranger this business got, the more the dogged nose of accusation pointed to one man. Dominique Drayle. And he was going to find Drayle if it was the last thing he did. And as he said it to himself, he meant it. No exaggeration.

That afternoon, up in Broome, he was on the *Diamond Moon* again, on the pretext that he couldn't find Walman (which was true) and that he needed to ask a few more questions about the yacht (preparation for which had, unfortunately, involved more sleep-depriving research the previous night to shore up his cover as a boat broker).

Brian was once again hard at work on the Marzocco, and offered Ruart an espresso (which Ruart silently dedicated to Éric). In fact Brian and Diane were packing up, about to leave and head back to Perth. So Ruart had arrived just in time to learn more about Lena, Brian's ex, and her missing (or rather, as it now looked, dead) friend Lydia. He had to steer the conversation there first, without raising suspicion. Brian made it easy.

'And the other boat, the *Seaking*...' Ruart was saying, '...You said, maybe, that your ex-wife and her, er...'

'Lena,' said Brian, 'is such a piece of work. My God.'

The comment hung there for a moment. Brian looked at Diane, reassuringly Ruart supposed. Ruart looked at Brian, inviting him to expand.

'From Russia,' Brian went on, 'which probably tells you something. From Siberia, there you go. From a place called... what was it?... Nov... Novosibirsk, I think. She and that Lydia are thick as thieves, you know. Lydia, that's the one that's missing.'

Ruart had already decided to say nothing about the discovery of what was probably her body.

'Both Russians so I s'pose it figures,' Brian added.

He and Diane then had an argument about whether Lydia was Ukrainian or Russian. Brian reckoned she came from Kursk, on the Russian side of the border. Diane pointed out that Lydia's boyfriend Aleks was a Ukrainian. Brian said Aleks was a fuckwit.

On his way back to the beach in the tender, Ruart persuaded the endlessly talking Tomas to take a detour via the *Seaking*. No-one was home. He cursed himself for having neglected to follow up this lead earlier. He'd had the occasion to do so on Monday when Brian had effectively let slip the connection between the missing girl – a Russian (or Ukrainian) – and the *Diamond Moon*. He was fixated on trying to find Bob Walman, and now he may have missed his opportunity. That's the thing with coincidences, they're never expected. Which was why, as a cop, if you were any good, you had to ask a lot of stupid, seemingly irrelevant questions. And on this occasion at least, he'd slipped up.

And then the plot "thickened", as the English say.

In the papers the next day, Thursday, it was reported that the bodies of the remaining missing police officers from Perth – Dean Howard, forensics officer, and Travis Seward, police pilot – had been recovered from Roebuck Bay in Broome. According to the Senior Sergeant Brad Hanson of the Broome police, they were participating in a suspected boating adventure involving alcohol – and as some would say, were out on a 'bender' – and there were no suspicious circumstances.

No suspicious circumstances! Well maybe not to them. Not to the Broome police. What sort of people did the police employ in this country? In any event, Ruart decided to give Roy and Lena one last try before he gave up. This time he managed to borrow his own tinnie.

And this time, they were there. As he approached, Roy was scrubbing the deck. And Lena...

Oh la vache.

Lena was sunning herself, topless, rubbing tanning oil into her brown... so *very* brown, beautiful skin.

Ruart felt like some sort of voyeur, as he cut the engine and drifted in. Like he was dropping round for a 'perv' as the Australians seemed to call it. Luckily you could blush as much as you liked in the tropical glare and no-one would ever notice. Which was just as well, because when they invited him on board and he launched into his yachting spiel with Roy, Lena made no attempt to cover up. They didn't make it easy, these girls, for a cop just trying to do his job. Especially a French cop! A French cop who knew his croissants and jam and his breasts and his tanning oil.

Eventually the sailorly chitchat petered out and it was time for him to leave. Lena, finally, put her bikini top on and joined them. Her top was small enough to still cause him problems but it was, literally, better than nothing.

It was now or never.

'Brian, on the *Diamond Moon*, he told me that you know Lydia and Aleksei. Aleks.'

They were looking back at him blankly. Not sadly exactly, but freeze-framed – it was as if someone had just paused the film. He actually had to blink to convince himself that it wasn't his brain that had frozen.

'The missing couple,' he added. 'That must be very... terrible for you. The... lack of... knowledge.'

He looked at Lena, looked into her eyes, but there was nothing. Nothing, that is, but a wall.

'It is,' said Roy, turning to Lena. 'Lydia is Lena's...' Roy seemed to be waiting for her to finish his sentence. Eventually she did.

'She was... She's my best friend, yes, so... I am very worried.'

Was that a mistake? "She was"? Had she heard something the papers hadn't? He made a mental note and pushed it just a little further.

'And the police still have nothing?'

They both shook their heads.

'It is difficult, no?' he went on. 'Wanting to do something but... you do not know what. You must want to drive out there yourself, but I suppose...'

There was an odd silence, again for no obvious reason, then Roy suddenly jumped in, a little defensively he imagined.

'It's certainly a difficult time. And now we have to go to Vanuatu...'

Ruart didn't miss the sharp look from Lena.

'... but at least,' Roy went on, 'you know,... the police, you have to assume, are doing—'

Lena interrupted. 'And of course you cannot interrupt police investigations, you don't want to be getting in the way. But we thank you for your concern, Mr Vincent. It is difficult... For all of us.'

It was the name Ruart had been using all week, the name he always used in such situations. (Réunion was different. It was French, he'd assumed the clout that came with being a Paris cop may have helped him there. Clearly not.) The surname Vincent was common enough to be unmemorable, but not so common as to smack of invention (like Dubois, for example). And Vincent was also a Christian name, which was an advantage: if the surname was interchangeable with the first name, it maximised forgettability.

'Call me *Robert*,' he said, using the French pronunciation.

'You should be more careful,' Lena said, indicating his face.

'Er, yes, I know, it was a little climbing accident.'

'They can be nasty, those little climbing accidents.'

'They can, and I should have been more careful. As you say. OK. So. You're going to Vanuatu? That's so great. Are you sailing there?'

'No no, we're flying,' said Roy. And then another pause, something was out of alignment.

'Well then I had better let you... get on with things then,' said Ruart. 'It's a holiday?'

'Well we had better get on with things, yes' Lena said. 'Nice meeting you, enjoy the rest of your trip. And don't forget to be more careful... *Robert.*'

It was a good attempt at the correct pronunciation, but the look she threw him was one he couldn't decipher. Surely she couldn't have known his real name, he hadn't used it since Réunion. Was she something more than a Russian trophy wife? In the circumstances he had to assume she was. Her connection with this Lydia, the awkward silences, the comments about having to be careful... But either way, she was a mystery. A mystery for sure.

He spent the rest of the day poking around, looking for more clues, more evidence, getting nowhere, wishing he was back on the *Seaking* asking Lena and Roy more questions. He wandered around the town centre, passing endless shops offering tacky souvenirs, Kimberley tours and fishing trips, camel rides... There were pearl traders reminding him that this was indeed the Pearl Coast – the front of one shop was decorated with a gigantic mural depicting naked mermaids prompting distracting visions of Lena and her tanning oil. He bought an orange t-shirt which announced *"Broome: It's One Pearl Of A Town"*, he recognized the slogan, although it didn't occur to him until afterwards that he'd only bought it to help convince Marine that he really had travelled to Broome. Orange wasn't really his colour anyway.

All this foraging, this casting about, was really only his way of killing time before deciding on his next move. Deep down, he knew what to do, but it took him until the next morning to admit it to himself.

He knew the answer as soon as he woke up. There was only one option. The Lena-Lydia thing, it didn't make sense. Something about it. Something about Lena. And as if to shine a spotlight on his suspicions, the morning's paper made it public: a body had been found and it was confirmed to be that of the missing woman, Lydia Korolenko.

It was staring him in the face. Lena had something to do with Lydia's death. And she probably had something to do with Drayle too, given the link between the *Destino* and the *Prospero's Dancer.*

If Lena had gone to Vanuatu, that was where he'd have to go as well. Because that was where he'd stand a chance of finding Drayle or a clue to his whereabouts. It was far from a sure thing, but for the first time in his life, Ruart acted on a gut instinct without running it past his head first. (Was he turning into an instinctive cop at last? Like on all those TV shows?). Because whichever way you looked at it, there were simply too many coincidences.

And these coincidences, they weren't just 'sparky'. They were *incandescent*.

* * *

'Cabin crew disarm doors and cross check.'

It dawned on him, preparing to disembark in Sydney, that this was possibly the very same flight taken by the murdered forensics officer, Mikkel Backstrom, precisely a week earlier. Could Backstrom have been running from someone? From Drayle, or one of his men? And what about the other two dead police officers? Did Drayle's tentacles really spread that far? Across the continents and the oceans? Could Ruart really stop such a man? Trip him up?

But he, Ruart, had come too far to turn back now. He was "in too deep" as the English liked to say. But deep was good. Deep was where you had to be if you wanted to find a man like Drayle. Because men like Drayle, it was what they did, they plumbed the depths. The depths of humanity. And Ruart was more than happy to meet him there, in those depths.

For sure.

67. <u>17° 44' 31" S 168° 18' 51" E</u> (Grand Hotel and Casino, Port Vila)

Ten minutes later
1.30pm Vanuatu Time (02:30 UTC)
Saturday, 26 October

There was something about the noise coming from Room 404 that made him stop. He should never have stopped – just stopped his ears – but then again would it have made any difference? They would have come for him, in all likelihood, whatever he'd done.

Roy was on his way back to their room at the Grand Hotel and Casino after a long, frustrating morning. Frustrating, every second of it, starting with the moment he'd woken up and discovered Lena wasn't there. Not in the bed, not in the bathroom, nowhere, and early morning walks weren't exactly her thing (he'd woken with the sun, just after 5am, so, yes, early was what it was). His first thought was she'd gone over the balcony and he actually went out there and looked over the edge, terrified, truly expecting to see her crumpled, naked body on the pavement below by the pool, and in a bloody pool of her own. But the pavement was bare. All that greeted him was the view. It was a big view, a GoPro, wide angle lens view of the oblivious, preening waters of the brightening bay, but he hardly noticed it.

Even though, as he assured himself, Lena was a curious creature, and there was no shortage of exotic sights and smells nearby (the fish market for example) – exotic, especially for a girl from the frozen Siberian plains – by mid-morning he was worried again, as worried as he'd been when he'd stepped onto the balcony hours earlier. And then he finally got a text message reply. Saying she was shopping. Zipping his fury, he responded politely and spent the rest of the morning wandering, expecting to bump into her and get things 'back on track', get the bad taste out of his mouth. Because there was no doubt about it, Lena had been acting strangely ever since they'd landed in Port Vila the day before. Distracted. She'd never been to Vanuatu and by rights she should have been, if not goggle-eyed, at least a little bit enthusiastic, a touch curious. But it was as if she still hadn't arrived.

He shouldn't have even been on the fourth floor – their room was on the fifth – and he certainly shouldn't have been walking past Room 404. Was it just bad luck? That his preoccupied state had haphazardly led him there? Or, deep down, did he know something he didn't realise he knew?

Sound was easily escaping the room because the door, Roy noticed, hadn't closed properly, obstructed by the end of a towel or bath mat. (Another piece of bad luck, or was this all connected?) The noise itself was barely noticeable, and, at least at first, unrecognizable. Barely human, but possibly a well-disguised sigh or cough. Barely audible. But it stopped him dead in his tracks. And as he stood there, outside Room 404, he heard it again and this time he knew what it was. He had, after all, heard it many times before. Heard Lena grunting into a pillow. On the other occasions though, without exception, he'd been in the same room at the time.

Roy didn't hesitate. He pushed open the door to Room 404, stepped over the damp towel and walked straight in. He didn't have to walk far. After passing a brightly-lit, rumpled bathroom (well-used), the short corridor, in two or three short strides, gave way to the main room, the 'bedroom', and in it, the queen-size bed, and on top of *it*, the throbbing fleshy tangle of arched back and splayed limbs, looking like a multi-legged brown 'thing' dragged up from the ocean depths, writhing on the deck of a boat.

Lena, though, was easily recognizable, despite being on her stomach and partially hidden by the not insignificant mass of flesh crushing down on top of her. Her head was turned in Roy's direction, with the side of her face now pushed into a flattened pillow, the same pillow her mouth had obviously been jammed into moments earlier (a girl had to breathe). Lena was naked of course, and between her well separated legs (she should have been a ballerina), thrusting his clenching buttocks in the forward and back yet circular motion reminiscent of a coupling rod on a steam train was a tanned, thick-set, black-haired man, his triumphant bare arse hungrily grabbing centre stage and his clutching arm muscles pulsing to the rhythm and impressively defined, all *chiaroscuro*, darkness with light – like a painting he was, he was like a painting, this latter-day Caravaggio-comes-to-town…

Lena's eyes widened and then they narrowed, making way for a smile. She actually *smiled*. And as the man on top of her continued to thrust, the rod of his cock unashamed to show itself, reveal its length (and there was that steam train again), Lena just said a barely audible 'OK'.

OK?

And then: 'Roy…'

The man slowed. The train was pulling into the station.

'Roy this is…' But she left the end of her sentences for someone else to finish. 'This is…'

And the man stopped and slowly turned his head. Roy would never forget that face for as long as he lived (*yeah*). Like a pig dog made human – a pig dog man – with small slits for eyes, a broad, dark brown face, mop of black hair like an exploding helmet, shiny skin and a mouth, by degrees, stretching into a grin.

'Edward Lang,' the man said in an unplaceable accent, just whispery, slightly rasping. And with that, still staring at Roy, he started up again. Thrusting. Thrusting his cock into Roy's girl. Thrusting and smiling at the same time.

Roy, naturally enough, resolved to put a stop to things right then and there, and he proceeded to make his move.

68. <u>33° 53' 45" S1 51° 15' 38" E</u> (Over Tamarama Beach, Sydney)

4.05pm Australian Eastern Daylight Time (05:05 UTC)
Saturday, 26 October

Ruart was looking out his window as they took off over Sydney's eastern suburbs, en route to Vanuatu via Brisbane.

(*En route*, it was the same in English. Yet another reminder of how many English words were in fact French. The *Académie française* were beating themselves up over nothing with all their worry over a few English words creeping in here and there. *C'est la vie*! he wanted to say to them. Such a *bourgeois* bunch of *bon vivants* they were anyway. A *clique* if ever he'd seen one. *Provocateurs*. It was, he suspected, more about preserving their own *raison d'être*.)

Below him, the beaches and bays stood out starkly against the dark blue of the ocean. He didn't know the names of any of them, except for Bondi Beach – he could guess which one it was too: the big one, packed with people, its symmetrical curve of sand bringing to mind the hull of a Viking longship. Or an artificial smile.

The one immediately next to it was a smaller, more benign-looking strand, shaped like a horseshoe. The houses seemed to crowd around the tiny beach, seemed to be pushing forwards, straining to get a better view of the beautiful coastline with its sandstone cliffs and jewel sea.

He wondered who they were, those people in their houses and apartments down there, and what sort of luck they had to have to get to live in a place like that.

But then again, he didn't believe in luck, did he. Or, in other words, as some would say, you made your own.

69. <u>22° 36' 37" S 161° 10' 26" E</u> (Over the Coral Sea, 975km north-east of Brisbane)

8.15pm Australian Eastern Standard Time (10:15 UTC)
Saturday, 26 October

Another dark sea. Would he ever be free of them?

Below him, the sheer vastness and desolation of the night-time ocean seemed to rise up and seep through the skin of the aircraft, and fill the cabin, and Ruart, with a mood of deep melancholy. His Air Vanuatu flight had left Brisbane over an hour earlier – night had already fallen by the time they'd taken off – and there was still more than an hour to go before they reached Port Vila, hurtling as they were northeastwards towards the Equator and into the night.

He worked out they would have crossed the Tropic of Capricorn by now. He was back in the tropics.

While in transit in Brisbane, he'd had a chance to call home. It was mid-morning in Paris, and as it was a Saturday, there was every chance Marine was going to be out, taking Madeleine or Jack to dance or football. As it happened she was in, although she'd become so distant now, Ruart found himself wishing he'd got the answering machine instead. It was like phoning someone not just in another country, but in another universe, and not necessarily a parallel one either. The distance thing was taking its toll, clearly. He was in an 'antimeridian' world now and he may as well have been trying to contact her from the Mysterious Beyond, from the world of the dead. And maybe he was? Maybe he'd died in Réunion – in the *Jardin de L'État* for example, which wasn't entirely inconceivable – and everything since then had been a dead man's dream. Who said the dead don't dream? Prove it!

But flying over the Coral Sea, this was no dream.

But... maybe the distance really had changed him somehow. Had it turned him into his own double? His own doppelgänger? And ditched the real Laurent Ruart somewhere? Whatever was going on, his marriage wasn't taking it so well. Another week and Marine would be asking for a divorce. And he hadn't even done anything! No, the sooner he got this over and done with, the better. Go to Vanuatu, do what he had to do (whatever that was) and get out. Go home.

Maybe he was on the wrong flight. Maybe he should have changed his ticket in Brisbane, boarded a plane for Singapore and hotfooted it back to Paris. The thought had crossed his mind. But he was sticking with the decision he made in Broome; he was giving this one final shot. Everything pointed to Drayle being in Vanuatu. He had all the signs, all the indications but no facts, no incontrovertible evidence, but that kind of thing, how often does *that* land in your lap? He was going to have to work with maybes and probablys like everyone else in this miserable world.

Indeed, while in Brisbane, as his call to Marine had been so depressingly short, he'd had a chance to call the *Préfecture* and it turned out they had a couple of items of interest for him.

Apparently the alleged ship in the desert, the *Destino Em Distancia*, if it ever existed, was no more. Or at least the part of it that stuck out of the sand, because according to the Western Australian police, their man in Broome, Brad Hanson (that name again!), told them he'd checked out the site and found nothing but a charred pile of wood. He said that whatever had been there before – possibly the remnants of an old hut, or aboriginal *gunyah* – had been somehow set alight. Hanson thought the deceased officers may have "dreamt the whole ship thing up", and may have been partaking in whatever substances ultimately "led to their demise".

Ruart was annoyed with himself that he hadn't thought about speaking to this Brad Hanson when he'd been in Broome. Another opportunity lost through carelessness.

The other thing was more of a piece of *non*-information, namely that the *Préfecture*'s informant in Port Vila (using the term loosely – informants were supposed to come up with information) had made no sightings of anyone matching Drayle's description. And he was distinctive-looking too, with his bright mop of curly blond hair, cleft chin, and facial scar, so you could hardly miss him. There was, however, a large boat that had recently arrived in Vila Bay – a super- or mega- yacht (their informant was not, apparently, up to providing dimensional estimates, or even a name for that matter). The rumour being bandied about in Port Vila was that it belonged to "the guys from Google", and even though rumours in that town were as quick to combust as wildfires in a Mediterranean summer, according to the *Préfecture* it probably really was them, as they'd been known to hang out there. And there was no evidence that Drayle had invested in another yacht since the sale of the *Diamond Moon*. Still. There was a *smell* in the air.

He looked down at the ocean again: it was as familiar as the last one he'd flown over, yet somehow completely different too, even cloaked in night as it was. There was still no moon, so there were no phosphorescent pillows of cloud to soften the hard, unforgiving darkness below. And below the darkness? More of the same, just the friendless depths of the sea. The thought made him shiver. Imagine falling, dropping, into the ocean down there. In the middle of the night. With, what, one, two, three thousand metres of water beneath your feet and everything that *that* contained...

Thinking of the ocean depths beneath him brought to mind the enigmatic decagon, the riddle of which he decided was probably being unravelled at that very moment in London, in some small, insignificant backroom of the British Museum. By a researcher called Delia.

He thought about Delia. Or, that is, he constructed a 'Delia' in his mind, what he imagined her to be (it was natural to do this, now that Marine was vanishing before his eyes). Delia was tanned and attractive, he decided, and with blonde hair, pulled back... no... with *short* blonde hair: more modern, and all the better for working outside in the hot sun, under hats. He imagined her at a 'dig', the beads of sweat fitfully rolling down her smooth brown neck, and eventually joining forces, collectively plunging downwards through the canyoning "V" of her cleavage...

And he wondered what Delia was wearing right now, in that backroom of the museum, because even though it was Saturday morning in London, those PhDs, they worked hard. For sure they did.

70. <u>51° 31' 06" N 0° 7' 33" W</u> (Footpath outside the British Museum, London)

At the same moment…
11.25am British Summer Time (10:25 UTC)
Saturday, 26 October

The building itself was impressive – it made her feel like she'd somehow stepped clean out of London and into Ancient Rome or Greece – but the pillars lined up along the front of the building were beginning to freak her out a little bit. At the top of each one it looked like there was a pair of eyes perched there, staring at her. No mouth, no ears, just eyes. Together, the pillars were like a row of sentries, all of whom, at the same time, had just spotted her.

Was this woman ever going to show? Maybe they were wrong, or she'd decided not to come in after all.

But wait. There. Heading towards her in the blue dress. Was that her? If it wasn't, that was it. She was giving up.

But it *was* her. At last.

71. <u>51° 31' 05" N 0° 7' 36" W</u> (Footpath outside the British Museum)

11.25am British Summer Time (10:25 UTC)
Saturday, 26 October

Almost there.

Delia was walking along Great Russell Street, and she'd reached the gold-tipped black railings that fenced off the Museum like a prison. It hadn't been the best of days. She'd got off the Tube at Tottenham Court Road which she never did as a rule – she usually stayed on until Holborn, what was she thinking? – and today she was reminded why: the rampaging, jostling throngs of sweaty, loud, young European tourists. And she'd just noticed the grease stain (from that blasted dinner party, she never wanted to go to it in the first place) – it hadn't come out of her blue dress after all. *And* she was tired. And her joints ached. She hadn't been sleeping properly: she spent a significant portion of most nights awake worrying about things that didn't matter (a state of affairs only marginally better than having things that *did* matter to worry about). Of course she knew it as well as anyone: it all came with the territory when you were eighty-two.

And everything suggested eighty-three would involve more of the same, so there was no point in wallowing. You just had to get on with it.

Which is what she was doing with this doctorate. "Almost there" with that one, too. She didn't want to think about how many years it had taken her (her BA in archaeology and art history was, by now, almost ancient history itself), which was why, at the age of eighty-two, she was working like a galley slave to get this thing finished. She was going to get to be "Dr. Lamprey" rather than "poor old Delia" and she was going to do it before she died. Even if it killed her, ha ha.

Hence the extra hours. Hence the coming in on a Saturday morning, and battling her way through the legions of marauding tourists like Boudicca. It was worth it though: she loved her work. The thesis she was working on for her PhD degree at the University of East Anglia was on Ocean Trade – one of the themes the Museum was currently focussing on – and specifically trade between Europe and the Far East in the pre-steamship era from the sixteenth century through to the opening of the Suez Canal in 1869. It was a fascinating period, the "Age of Sail": so many shipwrecks! They were dark times indeed.

The crowds were already beginning to build around the entrance to the Museum, presumably for two exhibitions that had opened recently, "Beyond El Dorado: power and gold in ancient Columbia" and "Shunga: sex and pleasure in Japanese art". Power and gold appealed to her; sex and pleasure she'd leave for the kids.

It hadn't helped that lately, almost daily, she'd had her work interrupted by a series of inquiries from the Frogs... that is, the police in Paris (with the knowledge and approval of their British counterparts, as well as Interpol). All hush-hush too, so in one sense exciting (although not being able to boast about it was rather tiresome), but in another sense it was just a big pain in the behind in terms of what it was doing to her work schedule (speaking of behind). But not really because she had to admit, the unfolding story behind this Dominique Drayle character and his associates was intriguing if a little scary.

In fact they'd even told her to "watch her step". Fancy that! At her age.

At the end of the day though, the most rewarding aspect concerned this artefact, this *Isfahan Decagon*. The latest information the French had gleaned about it really did seem to fill a number of gaps for her, did seem to provide the missing pieces of the jigsaw puzzle as it were, and much of it, if she were honest with herself, was probably helping her with finishing this blasted thesis.

It was, of course, more than just a little bit disconcerting, to think that criminals were using your research (they'd even been *spying* on her!) to further their own selfish goals – in combination no doubt with the multitude of unsavoury and despicable means at their disposal – but as shamed as she was to say it, it was also quite nice to know that someone was paying attention to what you were doing and maybe even proving you right!

Funnily enough, it was just when she started thinking again about the Frogs' warning to take care, and was looking at the faces around her, trying to imagine which one might be the assassin, that the strangest thing happened. One of those very faces was making a beeline for her.

It was a young woman, and she was carrying a large grey sports bag concealing who knows what.

Delia froze, wondering if this was her time and, while she was at it, noting how apposite it would be, were she to be gunned down outside the British Museum, laying down her life for her degree, as it were…

And then the woman said something.

Delia couldn't make out what she was saying, though. It occurred to her she could have been speaking in one of the Eastern Asian tongues, because she looked Japanese or Chinese.

The woman spoke again, more clearly this time.

Delia Lamprey.

'I'm sorry,' Delia said. 'I'm not sure what you…' She was pleased with the way she had so quickly slipped into 'spy' mode, not admitting her identity. Maybe her next career?

'You know about the ……' the woman said, although Delia couldn't understand the last word or words of her sentence. It was put as a statement, she felt, although assumed it was meant as a question. The woman's accent was certainly heavy.

'The… what, I'm sorry?'

'The ……'

No. Still couldn't get it, and Delia shook her head.

And then the woman began unzipping her grey sports bag.

A gun. It was all Delia could think. *Here it comes. She's pulling out a gun.*

But it wasn't a gun. It was a glittering, bejewelled artefact of some kind, a sort of box, with an Islamic design over it, and the box was round... no... it was ten sided. Was it? Could it be? Was it the Isfahan Decagon?

'Is that...?' But Delia had to be careful, she didn't know what or whom she was dealing with. 'What is that?'

But Delia got nothing more out of her because the woman had frozen, was staring at something over Delia's shoulder. She looked like she'd seen a ghost and Delia turned around to see what she was looking at. But there was nothing, just people going about their business. Scurrying every which way like ants. (You couldn't escape the crowds in London, for the simple reason that being in London was like being inside one great ant colony. The sooner she could get away from all these city ants and back to her cottage outside Norwich the better.)

And when she looked back, the woman had gone. Vanished, back into the surrounding swirl of humanity, along with...

Good God, Delia thought. It didn't bear thinking about. But...

Could it have been? Could it really have been?

72. <u>51° 31' 7" N 0° 7' 31" W</u> (Footpath outside the British Museum)

Ishiko was striding out, taking big steps and not looking back.

Whenever something went wrong, there was always a valuable lesson to be learnt. This time it was a simple one: always go with your gut instinct and never allow your head, or logic, to overrule it.

Deep down, she'd known it was a crazy idea to approach this old woman. (Had she really thought Delia was going to happily sacrifice her valuable time and give her, a complete stranger, a personal antiquities lecture? reveal what she hadn't even published herself yet? and not tell anyone about their meeting?) But seeing Bertrand again was the last straw. She hadn't seen him since the aquarium in Cape Town, and maybe it wasn't him – how could *any* of them be him? he was dead! – but the resemblance was just too close to be a coincidence. The guy walking towards them was his *spitting image*: it was Bertrand with a haircut. He stared right back at her too, like he'd planned it, like he was saying to her: I'm going to torture you for the rest of your life.

Ishiko turned the corner: she didn't know the name of the street but she'd check her phone in a minute and make sure she was heading in the right direction. Her original plan (which she should have kept to) had been to just get out of London and head north. To Scotland, to a city called Aberdeen. And she'd still do that: she had even more of a reason to now. The train left from Kings Cross station (she probably wouldn't make the 11.47, she'd have to wait for the next one, the 12.47), so all she had to do was find it, she knew it was nearby.

She turned, risked a quick look. He wasn't immediately behind her at least.

And now she'd gone and revealed herself to that Delia. A Japanese-looking woman asking about the Decagon. And then *pulling it out*. Stupid! What were the chances of her not telling anyone. And Drayle would get to hear about it, somehow, he had people everywhere. Maybe even Delia herself, the more she thought about it. What a fool she was. What a mess she was making of things.

It was all *their* fault. For not contacting her and getting that thing off her hands. Right now she'd sell it if she could, she didn't care anymore. Even throw it in the river, or the ocean, and maybe she'd still do that. Up in Aberdeen, throw it into the North Sea. Get rid of the temptation of trying to find out about it. Maybe it was worthless? Hardly likely though, not if Drayle was after it; it had to be worth a fortune.

There were trees up ahead. That was good. She seemed to recall there was supposed to be a park somewhere along the way.

By the time she'd reached the leafy splendour of Russell Square – a square of fading colours, ahead of the fast approaching northern winter – she had begun to relax a little. Think a little more clearly. One thing was plain: Bertrand or not, there'd been too many ghosts lately. She'd only been in London a week, not even that, and now she'd seen both Bertrand *and* some guy in a grey suit who she was sure she'd seen more than once and could easily have been one of Drayle's men (although, unsurprisingly, London had even more grey suits than Cape Town). At least she hadn't seen the yellow tow truck. Then she really *could* be sure she'd lost her mind!

She'd do anything to be able to turn back the clock, though. Turn it back so that she could decide *not* to kill Bertrand. She should have just abandoned her mission and run away... the price of that couldn't possibly have been as high as the price she was paying now. Because she'd had an awakening. The ghosts of Cape Town (and now London) had taught her a lesson. She didn't care anymore about dying – she knew she deserved to, after what she'd done to Bertrand – but it was strange, something told her she was indestructible. Maybe that was the punishment.

She'd get to Aberdeen and make her decision there; she couldn't concentrate in London, she didn't know why. The place spooked her. So why Aberdeen? She'd chosen it because it came first in an alphabetical list of Scottish cities and because it was on the sea. It was a fishing city, she liked that idea, and also she wanted to flush out anyone following her. Bring things to a head. *And* it was north, and colder. The colder the better, because it meant all the more clothing to cover the scar on her arm from the burns she received: instead of continuing to fade, after more than two months it now it seemed to be, if anything, growing more vivid.

A ruddy-faced man with an orange cat wrapped around his neck like a scarf walked past her as she approached the fountain in the centre of the park. Gave her an odd look. London had a lot of peculiar people in it. It was much weirder than Tokyo, definitely.

73. <u>51° 31' 11" N 0° 7' 32" W</u> (Montague Street, near the British Museum)

11.30am British Summer Time (10:30 UTC)
Saturday, 26 October

That wasn't something that happened every day. Mind you, lately, not much was. (Which was just as well.) All he could hope for was that it wasn't connected with everything else that had been going on. Hope for, but not expect.

Jon had been walking through the streets of Bloomsbury when it happened. Earlier, after catching the 8.05 up from Newhaven, he decided to make his way from Victoria Station on foot, and to stick to the quieter streets where possible. Apart from a marked feeling of overexposure around the clubs of Pall Mall and the crowds and traffic of unavoidable Trafalgar Square, it was a pleasant enough stroll (in the circumstances) at a leisurely pace, taking the best part of an hour, the only negative being the sore hip he'd acquired from his latest encounter with Irwin. His chosen path took him up through Covent Garden and some of his favourite streets – New Row, Garrick (and its imposing club, possibly best given a wide berth now that he belatedly came to think of it), Monmouth – and on into Bloomsbury: ancestral home of the great publishing houses and bookshops, and the British Museum.

When it happened, he'd just come out of Coptic Street onto Great Russell, where the museum was, and crossed the road, admiring the museum's classical, Greek Revivalist facade and its forty-four columns in the Ionic style (lined up, he'd always felt, like a row of lugubrious rams, with their downward-curling horns) all carved from Portland stone, and was continuing to head in the direction of Russell Square, the nominated location of his latest *rendezvous*.

The funny thing was, he was originally intending to avoid Great Russell Street, with its crowds, but something drew him there. It was, he guessed, either a sixth sense – which he didn't believe in – or stupidity.

As he was walking along, he noticed up ahead, not far, perhaps twenty yards or so, a Japanese or Chinese tourist talking to an old woman. Asking for directions most likely, but what drew Jon's attention as he drew closer was her grey sports bag. Again he had no idea where it came from, but he experienced the strange sensation that this girl, or perhaps what she was carrying, was somehow important or relevant to him in some way.

And then, when he was almost upon them, the girl pulled something out of the bag. It looked like a somewhat round jewellery box of some kind, but it was beautiful. It was covered in gemstones and sparkled in the sunlight. The design on it looked Islamic he thought – certainly geometric, with a complex pattern of jagged lines – and while he wasn't the sort of person to notice decoration of *any* kind as a rule, his attention was certainly drawn to this object.

When he glanced up at the girl, though, as he walked slowly past, she was staring at him. Her gaze, in fact, was so intensely focussed on him, that he may as well have been one of the Beatles – and one of the dead ones at that: there was a startling mixture of infatuation and fear in her eyes.

Even if he hadn't been paranoid to start with, and, to put it bluntly and without exaggeration, on the run, it still would have freaked him out. Her expression didn't change and unsurprisingly the old woman turned to see what the girl was staring at. And then the girl just bolted – in a single movement: put the box back in the bag, a quick swivel of her hips, a twist of her shoulders and she was gone. Like a scared fish.

What had that been about? Was his photograph in the newspaper? Or on a *poster* somewhere? This was not good. At the very least, it was a bad omen. It was also, no doubt, the cause of a song lodging itself in his brain – the words, which came to him subliminally, were the words to the Paul McCartney and Wings song "Band On The Run", but with the word "barrister" inserted in place of "band"…

'Watch out old chap!!'

He'd been crossing the road at the corner of Russell Square when two things sped towards him. One of them just missed him – a white delivery van – and the other didn't: the sonic boom from Alastair's bellowed injunction. Some of the vehicles (not the van) actually slowed down. No doubt about it, Alastair's voice was a traffic-stopper.

'That's *twice* I've saved you now!' Alastair said/shouted. He was standing at the entrance gate to the Square, all ginger hair and stained tweed jacket (as well-worn as a favourite rug), and with the same life-and-death expression on his face he always had, whether he was having fun or not.

'I'm sure it's more than that. You're my fullback, remember.'

'Yes. Well. I would have been waiting at our *agreed* meeting point in *there*,' Alastair said with emphasis, indicating the centre of the park, 'except I came out to put Bertie back in the car.'

'You drove in?'

'Luckily it's a Saturday, or I'd be risking the wrath of the powers that be, with that fucking *congestion charge* of theirs! Yet another excuse to keep *tabs* on us. I thought I'd take Bertie for a drive.'

'Since when do cats like drives?'

'Bertie does! Into the big smoke? Wouldn't miss it.'

Jon looked over Alastair's shoulder, trying to spot Alastair's battered old, book-filled, burgundy Volvo, but it was nowhere to be seen.

'So where's your car?'

'There.'

Alastair was pointing at a bright yellow Ford Mustang coupé with twin black racing stripes. There had to be some mistake. But there wasn't. Jon could see a small orange head behind the steering wheel, patiently watching them: Bertie.

'Two thousand and five model,' Alastair said. 'Fifth generation.'

'Since when were you a petrolhead?'

'Won it in a competition. I really have the most amazing luck, you know.'

'Clearly.' Jon noticed the numberplate: MU55 TAN. 'Muss Tan? Sounds like a botched spray-tanning job.'

'All right Bertie darling?!!' Alastair roared. Bertie remained impassive. 'We got here early so I took him for a spin round the park.'

'In the car?'

'Good to see you've still got the attaché case, well done.' Alastair had just noticed the BOAC bag over Jon's shoulder. 'Still got some cash left in there I hope.'

'Pretty much most—'

'Come on!' Alastair was already ushering Jon through the gate into the fenced-off square. 'Into the jungle. Away from *prying eyes*.'

It was hard to imagine a single pair of prying eyes in the vicinity of Russell Square whose attention had not, by now, been well and truly grabbed by a canary yellow sports car and its foghorn-voiced owner with the little orange cat and the amazing luck.

* * *

Alastair had suggested the meeting after Jon had telephoned him early that morning after leaving Lucinda. Jon filled him in on recent 'events'. (He'd phoned him, naturally, on the mobile with the prepaid SIM card provided to him, and conscientiously dumped it immediately after the call, as instructed, in the River Ouse, much to the amazement of a little girl who caught him in the act.)

The business the night before, when he witnessed the assault of Emerald on Skype, had been sufficiently disturbing to compel him to get out of Peacehaven (as counterintuitive as that was). That, together with the Irwin incident at Romy's. He didn't feel he could simply hang around the East Sussex coastline and do nothing. There was that storm on the way too – still due on Monday supposedly – and gales weren't really his thing. He'd detected a note of disappointment in Alastair's voice when he told him, and it occurred to his cynical side that Alastair liked the idea of someone looking after his house when the storm hit.

* * *

At the hub where the radiating paths met in the verdant heart of Russell Square – still green enough, despite autumn having already begun its yearly task of wasting the trees and daubing them yellow – Jon and Alastair were sitting side by side on a wooden seat, facing the central fountain which was blithely bubbling away. Made it difficult for long distance eavesdropping devices. 'Beware the bionic ear,' Alastair had warned.

Londoners and non-Londoners passed before them, each on his or her own private trajectory. Everyone with their own predicament. Surely none of these predicaments was as dire as Jon's? Then again, London was that sort of town; you never knew.

'Well my boy, things do seem to be going from bad to worse for us, don't they...'

The "us" was touching, at least on one view of it.

'... particularly this latest business with Emily.'

'Emerald.'

'There is *nothing* these people won't do.' Alastair was staring fiercely at the fountain's bubbling waters. '*Nothing.*'

'Mm.'

'Bunch of *cut*throat *cat* rapists. There is no more despicable life form on this planet. Every Eden and idyll has its *antimeridian* and that's where you find them, these newt-headed neoplasms. Fucking parasites. They're closing in on us, but I'm not sure it was such a brilliant idea you leaving Lucinda. You're likely to *trip* over them in the West End, it's where they *hang.*'

Jon told him about the Japanese girl.

'A Jap, eh? Figures.' Suddenly a pained look fell across Alastair's face like a dark shadow, and he chewed a nail.

There was a pause in their conversation, and for a peaceful moment, the only sounds were the passing footsteps and the splashing of the fountain.

'You obviously haven't heard the latest,' Alastair said finally. 'A spot of bad news, I'm afraid.'

And he knew as a certainty it was going to be bad.

'They've identified the *body*, you see.'

The body? But his mind had stopped functioning – it had crashed, its files lost, its screen an empty black rectangle save for the solitary cursor, blinking densely. Everything gone in a snap of the fingers, and that included whatever "the body" was that this mouth, in front of him, was going on about.

'And I was right!' Alastair exclaimed. 'Which would've been a stunning achievement if it weren't for the fact that I'd simply been stating the bleeding evident...' He registered Jon's expression. 'The body they found in your *house*, it was the Armenian art dealer all along. Rattatroop! Didn't I tell you?

'Ratta...' The screen blinked back to life.

'Norton bloody Rattatroop!'

'So... What in God's name was he doing in my house?'

'I very much doubt it was in God's name but it probably wasn't by choice either. Obviously he, and by that I mean his body, was *placed* there. Anyway it's been confirmed. Dental records. Just about the only part of him that hadn't melted to a primordial puddle of DNA. His teeth, and his Iron Cross. They say his father personally ripped it off a German general's neck in the middle of the Battle of Stalingrad. So you can see the irony.'

Jon tried to see the irony.

'Fighting with the *Russians*,' Alastair clarified. 'I'm assuming that's who's responsible here. And you can bet your last gazoo they would have pulled his toenails out first, too.'

'Jesus. You weren't joking about the bad news.'

'Bad news for Rattatroop, obviously. But he's dead. It's worse news for you, because now they know it wasn't you in that body bag. Which means you're no longer dead. Which means if you don't watch your step, you very well could be.'

The brutal simplicity of Alastair's logic was hard to argue with.

'Well I'll definitely have to go to the police now. This changes everything... I mean, if they think that I'm—'

'Are you in*sane*?' Alastair was a bright red beacon in a storm. 'Have you not been listening to a single word I've been saying? Do you think you *dreamt* what happened to Romy? *Dreamt* this Irwin character? *Dreamt* that fucking lunatic who nearly shot Bertie?

'And me.'

'The killing of Rattatroop doesn't change anything. Except for Rattatroop of course, but for you, my dear boy, not a thing.'

'Except they're going to think it was me who killed him. It'll be Lord Lucan all over again.'

'Well firstly he *did* kill the nanny and secondly, as everyone knows, John Bingham, the seventh earl of Lucan, is alive and well and living in Africa. In Ouagadougou, apparently. You, on the other hand, will be dead and *un*well if you carry on with this nonsense about handing yourself in. If you want my advice, you could do a lot worse than taking a leaf or two out of Bingham's book.'

'So you're saying I should abscond to Africa.'

'Not unless you like boiled Black Mamba for breakfast. But you do have to remain under the radar at least. For now. Until something *gives*.'

Jon just nodded, waiting for the rest. Alastair looked uncomfortable. There still was more to come, he could tell.

'You're right about one thing though,' Alastair said. 'Because unfortunately, according to the newspaper, you are now officially wanted for questioning.'

'Oh great. Was there a photograph?'

'It was small. Ish.'

Jon groaned. 'Well there you have it. Barrister on the run.'

'On the run? That we *all* are. That we *all* are. You, me... Bertie. We're accomplices, you know. Accomplices and *harbourers*.'

'Yeah,' Jon said. 'Luckily you have an inconspicuous car.'

'If it's my new *coupé* you're referring to, yes, it is what you might call rather *loud*, but it's so blindingly bloody *bright*, it's the last place they'll look. Always place yourself between *them* and the source of the *glare*.'

'As in, beware of the Hun in the sun.'

'Precisely! You're invisible. They're blinded by their own ignorance. Having said that, you're going to have to abjure the joys of the mighty Mustang for a little while, I'm afraid. We need to take care not to be seen together.'

'What about here?' Jon asked, observing two men in navy suits walking past loudly conversing about "the regulator".

'You don't think these wife-butcherers take the time to go to a *park*, do you? Go to a park and admire the trees? Take it from me, if you're not on a road, or a footpath next to a road, you're safe. A park to them is like stairs to a Dalek.'

'I believe Daleks can now fly.'

'Can they? God, what next.'

He'd already given Alastair a potted summary on the phone, but Jon went over in more detail what Emerald had told him in Victoria Station – about the art dealer Richard Runion and the forgeries, about Dominique Drayle and Irwin and Paul Brilling the solicitor, about Martin Nevers and the extraordinary suggestion of paternity (and siblingship) and about "the bitch with the red hair" who'd been following him. None of it seemed to surprise Alastair, he just nodded sagely away, although Jon did spot the beginnings of a frown emerge on his face at the mention of Nevers. Similarly, when he described the business with Irwin at Romy's house – and for Jon, the mere mention of Romy's name was painful – Alastair remained surprisingly composed.

'I don't fancy Romy's chances to be honest,' Alastair said, after a quick shake of the head. 'Unless she was one of *them* all along, and playing you.'

'I doubt it.'

'Well she is a journo. Those female journos... those *stacked hacks* from Grub Street, they can look after themselves at least. In dark alleys and anywhere else you care to name, I dare say.'

'But that Irwin guy—'

'You do *not mess* with these people, it's as simple as that,' Alastair hissed. 'They're snakes all right, of the worst genus. Exceedingly aggressive, and supremely venomous.'

'I won't argue with that. But you know it did occur to me—'

'Black Mambas have nothing on these guys.'

'What Romy said about the money' Jon said. 'It at least explains a lot.'

'Assuming it's true. But since the money really did turn up in your account... it does *in fact* sound like the best explanation. So. What have we got here. They want their money back one must assume. But they haven't exactly included *you* in the transaction, so we can safely assume that offering it back to them... assuming you still can...'

Jon nodded.

'... won't do you any good.'

'It won't?'

'Some might say that money,' said Alastair, 'is the only language these types understand, but I say... and their actions bear this out I would suggest... I say that nothing but blood will satisfy their thirst for blood. You simply know too much I'm afraid old chap. You're in too deep.'

'Deep is a fair description.'

'No we have to find some other way of nipping this thing in the bud.'

'Law in our own hands, that sort of thing?'

'Quite,' said Alastair in thoughtful mode. 'Although a bit of a work in progress that one, I'm afraid. In the meantime, do you have some sort of plan? Where are you going to stay?'

'I can hotel-hop. Courtesy of the money you lent me. I haven't thanked you enough for that, by the way.'

'Think nothing of it. I know you're good for it, with that little stash of yours.' Alastair sees the look on Jon's face. 'Just a little joke, lad, cheer up. But a plan, do you have a plan? I mean, was it wise coming back to London? Until something presents itself. It's easier to lie low in the countryside, no CCTV etcetera, you could do a bunk, and head for... if Peacehaven's not your cup of tea... you could head for somewhere no-one ever goes like... Wales.'

Jon was shaking his head. 'I can't just wait around hoping they won't find me. I need to do something, be proactive.'

'No point in just doing something for the sake of doing something. Look at what happened to Richard Nixon.'

'I've got one lead. There is one thing I can usefully do. Find that redhead.'

'The one who's been following you? She could be the *cause* of all this!'

'Something tells me she's not. And anyway, it's all I've got. I followed her, on Wednesday remember. In West Kensington. She went to that mannequin factory, Rootstein, so I might check that out.'

'Rootstein,' said Alastair, his face even more grave-looking than usual. 'I don't like it. Hell of a risk you'll be taking.'

'I can't just do nothing. And I've supposedly got this mystery family out there, remember. If this woman's right. A sister, and *father*... Sir Martin Nevers of all people, I really don't know if I can believe it. But I suppose...'

Once again, at the mention of Nevers, Jon noticed Alastair wince.

'Yes, well.' Alastair had a pained look on his face. 'There was something else. Bad news, as we all know, always travels in pairs.'

'Only in pairs? Tell me.'

'Well...' Alastair began slowly, as if he were being asked to eat a plate of dead bees. 'Of course we don't know how reliable this Esmeralda is... or...'

'Emerald.'

'... or was... But Nevers is, um... very sadly... Nevers is... *no more.*'

'Nevers is...?'

'He's dead.'

'Dead?'

'It happened yesterday. Heart attack, or that's what it said in the paper, but if you believe that, you'd believe that I'm Mata bloody Hari.'

'Jesus.'

'Listen. It's just as likely everything Emma told you was malarkey twaddle. She may very well have her own agenda. She may be with the Russians herself for that matter. Another cat rapist! The will you saw could have been faked, there's just no way of knowing. Of course if you're a beneficiary under the will... but that's a thought for another time. Right now... we... that's you, me, Bertie... we've somehow landed ourselves in a puzzle, or a chess game, where the players... no, each of the *pieces*... has its own, very different, objective. And the truth is the first casualty in *that* little game let me tell you.'

But Jon's attention had wandered. He felt as though his life were passing before him like a dream. The two of them stared at the water bubbling up, or erupting, in vertical jets, out of the holes in the ground, leaping skywards and falling back again, and evoking, in Jon's mind at least, lava – lava spurting, in great exploding globules, out of a magma lake – reminding him that here he was, at the heart of it all, in the deep vortex of the volcano.

Before they left – Alastair agreed, despite his earlier note of caution, to give Jon a lift to West Kensington in the "Muss Tan" – Alastair handed Jon another phone, and muttered something about the approaching storm. But the only thing that stuck in Jon's mind later was Alastair's comment about the short-sighted assassin who'd fired at Jon three days earlier: what kind of person wore a baseball cap with a suit?... or was that a suit with a baseball cap?

74. <u>51° 31' 54" N 0° 7' 27" W</u> (Kings Cross Station concourse, mezzanine level)

Fifteen minutes later
12.15pm British Summer Time (11:15 UTC)
Saturday, 26 October

Under the elegantly curved, geometrically patterned ceiling of the half-dome roof – which reminded her of the tiling on the Decagon – she watched him as he stood in front of the departures board, taking his time, presumably weighing up the options that were flashing up before his eyes. Might she be going to Newcastle? or Hull? or Cambridge? or Aberdeen? or Leeds? or Peterborough? or York perhaps? or what about Edinburgh? She tried to guess what he was thinking, based on the subtle movements of his head.

She was observing him from the comparative cover of a table at a Mexican restaurant on the mezzanine level, overlooking the concourse. She took the risk of sitting at the glassed-off edge, with a newspaper her only camouflage. At least she had the upper hand finally, and was the one doing the watching for a change. *She* could keep an eye on *him* for once.

The man in the dark grey suit and brown shoes looked familiar. But then everyone was starting to look familiar now and she was starting to not care. Which was deadly, she knew. You could never let your guard down. Ever.

And then, almost as soon as he'd started, the man appeared to give up. Looked at his watch, looked around – but not up, where she was sitting – and left the station.

Ishiko had just over half an hour before her train left. She already had her ticket, she'd leave her dash to the last minute, just in case he was still around, allowing him next to no chance to follow her unnoticed.

And after that, finally, she'd be able to relax, if only for the duration of the eight hour trip to Aberdeen.

There was an expression, 'no rest for the wicked'. Was that her?

75. <u>51° 29' 26" N 0° 12' 19" W</u> (Beaumont Avenue, West Kensington)

12.25pm British Summer Time (11:25 UTC)
Saturday, 26 October

Alastair had just dropped Jon off around the corner in North End Road. A necessary precaution, given the forces they were up against, not to mention the fact that being driven in Alastair's new car was like travelling in a large banana on wheels and just about as conspicuous. Bertie had been in his usual nervous form (hiding away on the floor in the back, which from Jon's perspective didn't seem like such a bad idea, given the car they were in), and showed none of the enthusiasm for city driving tours that Alastair had spoken of. Jon had suggested Alastair not wait, and the idea had been met with absolutely no resistance.

So he was standing, once again, outside the Rootstein building in West Kensington, precisely where he'd stood three days earlier after following the woman in the green dress. The mannequin was still there, inside the glass door at the entrance. This time, no green dress, no redhead. This time though, he went in.

Inside, past the mannequin and next to a wall of framed photographs of models, was a small white desk, and behind that, a girl. With brown hair.

'Hello.' She greeted him with a big smile and an accent too, maybe French?

He explained that he was looking for someone, it was a bit embarrassing because he'd forgotten her name ('must excuse the bloody Alzheimer's' he said with a smile), but she had red hair, was wearing a green dress, was so high, nice figure…

'A lot of girls here has the nice figures as you can see.' (She might have been Russian – accents had never been his strong suit.) She was indicating the photographs on the wall. He noticed she was a little on the plump side, and wondered whether his "nice figure" description had been a mistake, because her smile had all but disappeared. 'But no,' she added. 'I hasn't seen her.'

'Three days ago? Perhaps you weren't here?'

'I was here. But I hasn't seen her. Sorry.'

He cast an eye over the photographs on the wall. And then, yes, success, it was almost certainly her.

'That's her there,' he said.

The photograph had a caption: *Isla*. Was that her name? He asked the receptionist.

'*Eess-la*,' she replied.

'Sorry?'

'You say her name *Eess-la*.'

'Not *Aye-la*? OK. *Iss-la*. Ah yes. *La Isla Bonita*.'

The girl either had no idea what he was talking about (was anyone too young for Madonna, even in 2013?) or she was completely fed up with him, because she didn't even nod. He soldiered on:

'So anyway, her. This Isla, here. You know her name so I'm assuming you've must have seen her?'

'Seen? I don't know,' the French/Russian girl said, before no doubt realising an ambivalent answer might lead to further cross-examination. 'No. I heard her name but I don't think I has seen her. She is maybe last year's.'

She had to leave the room, and after one more 'sorry' she was gone. Jon looked at the photograph of "Isla" again. It showed her from the waist up, and naked, posing, with a mannequin beside her – her *doppelgänger* – being given what looked like some final touches by a bearded sculptor. As he admired the physical beauty of the object of his search , he noticed, out of the corner of his eye, at the end of the corridor off to his left, a woman with red hair flash past. It was only the merest of glimpses, but it looked like her. Was it? Had the girl on the front desk been just a little too dismissive?

As the receptionist was still not back, he took a few steps down the corridor and peered into the first room he came to. It was a room full of mannequins. And every one of them looked like this Isla, or her 'copy'. Someone wasn't telling him something.

And then the girl was back again, and he was in trouble. He knew there was a word for a person who was sexually attracted to statues, like Pygmalion (Pygmalionism?), and whatever it was, he assumed that the girl assumed that he was one of them.

'I am sorry sir, you cannot go to there. Now we are closing, you must to leave please.'

He persisted – 'Are you sure Isla wasn't the model for those mannequins?' / 'Are you absolutely positive Isla hasn't been here recently?' – but no amount of rephrasing the question would induce the girl to give up any further information. He accepted defeat, said goodbye, and made his way out through the glass door. Just as he stepped out onto the pavement, he glanced up and immediately noticed a figure walking in his direction down Beaumont Avenue from North End Road.

He readily recognised the person, despite the fifty or so yards that separated them, with his crewcut and his sharply clicking black shoes: it was the human scorpion. Irwin.

76. <u>51° 29' 25" N 0° 12' 19" W</u> (Rootstein car park, West Kensington)

12.35pm British Summer Time (11:35 UTC)
Saturday, 26 October

As soon as Jon recognised Irwin, he didn't wait for him to return the favour. Next to the Rootstein building was a small parking lot for cars and it currently contained a black van, a black Audi SUV and a silver Mercedes, along with what looked to be either a large rusty building skip or a small rusty shipping container. He walked quickly into the parking lot and stood behind the skip, praying that Irwin hadn't seen him.

So Irwin was alive. And Romy?

Jon kept his head down and pretended to use his phone, but all the while maintained a wary eye on the Rootstein entrance. He was sure that must have been where Irwin was going, the coincidence otherwise would have been too great. Wouldn't it?

The sound of the clicking heels grew louder and then slowed. Stopped. He could now see Irwin standing outside the glass door and he inched further back around behind the skip. He watched as Irwin hesitated for a moment, then pulled out his phone, keyed in a number.

'I'm here,' he could hear him say gruffly. There was a pause, and then: 'Outside. Hurry.' Then Irwin put his phone away and swivelled on his heels, and took in the scene around him as if for the first time.

Jon quickly retreated even further so that he was completely out of sight, and stood with his back to the skip and waited, listening. He heard an impatient sigh, and some pacing, and an angrily muttered 'what the *fuck*'. And then the sound of the glass door opening.

'Come *on*.' It was Irwin's voice again. 'We're late.'

When he heard two pairs of footsteps begin to move off, he dared to steal a peek and it confirmed what he'd already guessed. Following Irwin with obvious reluctance was the redhead, Isla, today in jeans and a dark cotton jacket.

The decision to follow them was an easy one: after everything that had happened (to Romy, to Emerald, to *him*), he had to find out more, and this was simply his only lead – it was his lifeline to a saner existence, or at the very least, the chance of one. It was Saturday the twenty-sixth of October, it had been ten days since the fire, and enough was enough.

So he gave them a head start of forty or fifty yards, then stepped out from behind the skip and began following them back down Beaumont Avenue.

He had a clear view of them: they were walking briskly towards North End Road, with Irwin one pace in front, turning from time to time, motioning, irritably, for Isla to keep up, and to walk faster. Jon wondered how sore Irwin's head was after Jon had 'blendered' it. It was only the day before, but he didn't seem to be showing signs of injury. Tough nut.

Keeping his distance, he followed them to where he'd already suspected they were going – the tube station around the corner – and he watched them as they made their way down onto the eastbound platform. Unfortunately they'd just missed a train, and it wasn't a busy station, so he had to hang back at the top of the stairs, which entailed an undignified (and risky) dash when the next train arrived, and some carriage-hopping to get close enough to keep an eye on them.

He was able to get within one carriage of them, and he managed to maintain a sightline between a blonde head and the shoulder of a biker's jacket and straight on through the window at the end, into the adjoining carriage. Irwin and Isla were standing at an angle to each other, and not talking, as far as Jon could see.

He remembered something, now. It was something Emerald had told him: that Isla lived in one of Irwin's apartments in Soho somewhere. He wondered if that was their destination.

They got off at Embankment and proceeded on foot, with Jon just about managing to keep up, maintaining his regulation forty yard gap. Up Villiers Street, across the Strand, past Trafalgar Square and the National Gallery, and through Leicester Square: the crowds provided him with good cover, although at the pace Irwin and Isla were moving, and the way London's confusion of tourists always seemed to prevent any orderly pedestrian flow, it wasn't easy, and he had been forced to roughly push past and shoulder-jolt a number of these itinerant rubbernecks, leaving in some places a trail of indignation behind him. *Swap places then*, he thought back at them.

They continued up Wardour Street and into the heart of Soho – always seedy, yet always semi-seriously so – and then they suddenly turned into a small side street. He knew he had to be careful at this point, but he sped up in case they vanished into a building before he turned the corner.

The street they'd turned into was Peter Street. On the corner was a burger restaurant, a good cover should he need a doorway to dash into. Using his phone as a camouflaging prop once more, he slowly turned the corner with his head down, as if texting. He was just in time to see Irwin and Isla disappear through a large black door – proclaiming in bright, white lettering *30A* and nothing else – which slammed shut behind them.

Jon kept walking, taking it all in as he went past. The black door was located next to a Ramen bar but seemed unconnected with it. The street itself was narrow and dark, with remnants of sex shops and closed-up adult cinemas – a street in transition, it was fair to say. A quick glance upwards, above the door, suggested the four-level building of red brick (Leicester red clay, by the looks) was probably used mainly for offices, but possibly flats as well.

A little further on, and off to his right, he saw that the Berwick Street market was open for business – the fruit stalls lifted the area's ambience, at least. Straight ahead, he could see a dead end in an amphitheatre of dilapidation and he made a mental note to avoid it.

He decided to retreat to the burger restaurant back on the corner, and formulate a strategy. He realised, now that he had successfully tracked his quarry to its lair, he had no plan.

77. <u>17° 46' 33" S 168° 17' 37" E</u> (Breakas Beach Resort, Port Vila)

At the same moment…
11.20pm Vanuatu Time (12:20 UTC)
Saturday, 26 October

He realised, as he looked in the mirror, there were only two things he lacked: a face that didn't look like it had just emerged from a cage fight, and a sensible plan.

Ruart had just arrived at his Port Vila hotel – a typical resort, they were everywhere, although this one, nestled in a small cove, had a certain charm which included the soothing, never-ending sound of waves gently breaking on the fringing reef maybe a hundred metres out from his beachside bungalow – and he was examining his week-old bruise, which was taking an annoyingly long time to go away. Not a great look. Someone ought to have a 'talk' to those lads, but he knew very well he had more important things to be concerning himself with. He would've arranged for Sav to deal with them if Sav hadn't vanished, God knows what happened to him. Sav may even have been part of the problem, for all he knew. Still, it was important to establish whether there was a link with Drayle and he'd filed a recommendation with the *Préfecture* (which meant, of course, that would be the last he'd hear of the matter).

The second thing he lacked – a sensible plan of action – was a more pressing issue and he'd be settling down to work shortly:

he'd roll up his proverbial sleeves and get cracking, out there on his balcony, a glass in his hand, preferably containing something cold and vodka-based.

* * *

He'd barely had a chance to get to 'work' – he'd settled into his bungalow (laid out his toiletries next to the basin in the bathroom, and hung up his trousers and jacket), aligned the chair on his balcony with the small outside table, sat down facing the dark waters of the Coral Sea streaked with the thin white lines of the waves breaking over the reef, and enjoyed, at most, two sips of his "Island Passion" cocktail delivered by Room Service (vodka, something coconutty, something fruity) – when a call came in from Reception. A message had been left for him earlier, from Paris. Requesting that he contact them. *Incroyable*! He'd never known them to work so hard.

He rang them back and learnt that Delia in London had reported being approached by an East Asian woman who may have been in possession of the decagon. There was some suspicion that it might have been Ishiko and an alert had been put out but, as Delia's description was a little wanting ("Chinese or Japanese appearance, short and slim with black hair"), they had next to no chance of finding her, especially if she was travelling under a false name (which she almost certainly was). Ruart suddenly felt overwhelmed by a world-weariness. Weighed down by *ennui* (another one for the *Académie*). He suddenly felt it was all too hard. What the hell was he doing in Vanuatu? With an "Island Paradise" in his hand? He took another sip. It was too sweet anyway.

Whichever way he turned, and whatever way he looked at things, it felt all wrong. And if that was using his unreliable gut instinct, as opposed to his predictably reliable powers of logical reasoning, then bad luck!

78. <u>17° 56' 24" S 168° 12' 28" E</u> (Coral Sea, about 25km SW of Port Vila)

9am Vanuatu Time (22:00 UTC)
Sunday, 27 October

As soon as he woke up, Roy knew that he was going to be having a bad day. He had a splitting headache and was experiencing a wooziness so intense it felt like the whole room was moving. The room itself was small and airless, and he didn't recognise it. He didn't even know what day it was.

And then, when he sat up and noticed the small round window, he realized the room *was* moving. He was on a boat.

Slowly, flashes of what had happened came back to him. After springing Lena in the middle of her dirty little tryst and going in to sort out that... pigman – who the hell *was* that? – the guy had gone feral (as if Roy had been the one cutting *his* grass), just lost his head like he was Charles fucking Manson or someone, and came at him like a mini-tornado of fists, his whopping great erection flopping everywhere. He'd done a bit of boxing in his time and made a fair job at defending himself until everything had gone inexplicably dark. Lights out.

His head sure hurt. The *back* of it, too. Lena's work? He wouldn't have been surprised, the little Russian whore. She'd pay for this.

He got up, gingerly, although he had to sit down again straight away. What had they given him, for Chrissakes? When he eventually made it to the cabin door, it was locked.

Things were not looking good.

* * *

It must have been about an hour later when two Vanuatuans came in, or Ni-Vans (locals, Melanesians born in Vanuatu). They weren't tall but they were well-built and fit-looking. And they didn't say a word, despite Roy's questions.

'What's going on here? Is Lena here? *Lena?*'

They roughly grabbed his arms and led him out into a narrow passageway and up onto a deck bathed in sunshine. Which was when he discovered he was on a large rusty prawn trawler by the looks of it, or a (cheaply) converted one. Called the *Blue Shefa*. They were in the middle of the ocean, although he could clearly see what he thought was Efate, the island Port Vila was on, in the distance.

Two more Ni-Vans were waiting to 'greet' him on deck (although they too steadfastly remained silent). And then a man of Chinese appearance emerged – in a brown batik shirt and grey trousers, white shoes (tennis shoes) and a gold Rolex. This was no fisherman, Roy knew that much. He barked something, a name Roy didn't pick up. A reply came from somewhere:

'Coming Mr Song!'

Voices other than his own, at least. But what was going on here? When he articulated the question, no-one deigned to provide him with an answer.

And then a fifth Ni-Van appeared, carrying a large coil of nylon rope. This "Mr Song" nodded and the rope-carrier, along with the other two Ni-Vans came over. Four of them pushed him roughly down onto the deck while the rope-carrier began tying the rope around his legs. Roy lacked the strength to put up much of a fight, and there were five of them anyway. Not counting the Chink.

The rope man disappeared for a few moments and returned wheeling what could only be described as a yellow, small but heavy-looking building skip on trolley-wheels. Roy watched with growing apprehension as the guy began tying the other end of the rope to the skip. Why? He was hardly going anywhere, was he. Given where they were, in the middle of the ocean.

And then, to Roy's horror, the same man, the rope man, walked over to the side of the boat and slid open a section of the gunwale, where you would normally board the boat if it was docked. But it wasn't docked.

The rest happened quickly.

Another nod from Mr Song and two of the Ni-Vans pushed the skip through the gap in the gunwale. There was a loud splash as it plunged into the sea. There was a short interval where nothing happened. And then, all of sudden, the rope began rapidly unravelling. Roy, frozen with fear, knew very well what was about to happen. But it couldn't be. It couldn't be happening…

And as the coil melted away in a dizzying whirl of flicking rope, Mr Song finally spoke to him.

'My advice to you, Mr Roy, is to get up and jump now. Otherwise you get hurt. And don't hold your breath. There is no point.'

Roy desperately tried to undo the cord around his legs but there wasn't enough time, not nearly enough.

Mercifully, in a way, the last things he felt were the inevitable, terrible tug on his legs and, an instant later, his head violently slamming into the deck, because after that, everything was night.

79. <u>17° 46' 33" S 168° 17' 40" E</u> (Breakas Beach Resort: hotel pool)

At the same moment…
10.05am Vanuatu Time (23:05 UTC)
Sunday, 27 October

Just over twenty kilometres to the north-east, across the restive waters of the Coral Sea, just past the gently rolling lines of white over the reef there, Ruart lay at the bottom of his hotel pool looking up at the surface, and beyond that, the sky. He was practising holding his breath underwater, and seeing how his ears held up – not well, they were hurting already, even at a depth of just three metres. He was told it was different when you were scuba-diving, your ears equalized, but he was yet to be convinced.

Not that there was going to be any time for scuba-diving.

He pushed back up to the surface and got out of the pool with as much athleticism as he could muster: he was well-aware of the presence of two attractive brunettes in nothing-there bikinis – he just happened to have noticed them when he arrived at the pool, and he'd picked up their sly glances before diving in. He flexed his triceps and sucked his stomach in as he fluently hopped out. But, even if he was the type (and he obviously wasn't), there was no time for that sort of thing either. Because there'd been real progress at last.

Bob Walman had been traced to a nearby resort. Helpful staff there had informed him that Walman had ventured out on a diving tour that morning which was due back at lunchtime. Ruart would be paying him a visit. But that wasn't all. He'd also learned, through the *Préfecture*'s 'people' in Port Vila (not the police) that Lena and Roy were staying at the Grand Hotel and Casino *and* that Lena and an Englishman by the name of Edward Lang had been spotted out at dinner last night in town.

These guys they were using in Vanuatu, they really earned their money! Put his Parisian colleagues to shame, and who would have thought it, here in this beautiful, lazy, tropical paradise?

It was funny how things were never what you expected.

80. <u>51° 30' 46" N 0° 8' 1" W</u>
(Soho Restaurant)

The same time
12.05am British Summer Time (23:05 UTC)
Sunday, 27 October

Just after midnight – or was it? the clocks were supposed to be turned back tonight, or was it forwards? – and Jon was sitting in the restaurant on the corner of Peter Street, just up from 30A, his BOAC bag by his feet, and a glass of wine in front of him, his third. Still no further sightings of Isla, still no plan. Maybe the wines were not such a great idea but what the hell. He didn't care anymore. It was all getting too hard. "Wanted for questioning"! *Christ.* Lord Lucan didn't have these problems. "Inaction" hadn't been in his vocabulary, obviously. Africa was sounding better by the minute.

Outside, a light rain was falling.

Outside, Isla was walking past the restaurant windows. *Isla.*

He prepared himself for a quick departure, and extracted some money to leave on the table, when Isla turned and entered the restaurant. She was still wearing the same jeans and dark cotton jacket, but she looked tired. Exhausted. He watched as she sat down on the other side of the room and ordered a drink. She hadn't seen him yet.

What to do?

He reminded himself he'd already decided what he'd do if he saw her. Sure, she was with Irwin, and sure she'd possibly been following him, and sure she, by dint of Irwin, represented a real threat to Jon's continued existence. On the other hand they were in a public place, he had to do *something*, and he had a curiously compelling instinct about her. *And* she was beautiful (always a bad reason, but there you are).

In for a penny, in for a pound.

So he slung his bag over his shoulder, scooped up his wine, and walked over to her.

Their eyes met before he got there. She just stared: there was no panic, and no aggression. She watched him agape, and looked as if someone she knew had just risen from the dead. Just as the Asian girl had done, in fact, earlier that day.

He didn't ask for permission to join her – he just rested his drink on her table, pulled out the chair opposite and sat down, keeping an eye on the passing pedestrians outside.

'Not expecting anyone I hope?' he asked.

She said nothing. Just looked at him with a fierce intensity through big, expressive brown eyes. Her hair was less red in the poor lighting, but her eyes shone...

'I know about Irwin,' he continued calmly, returning her gaze. 'And I intend to go to the police.'

'That would be a mistake,' she said. Not a trace of anxiety in her voice, which was soft, almost husky, guttural. And the accent, it sounded possibly French or Italian. Or German.

'Who for?'

'You.'

'So is that a kind of... threat?'

She simply shook her head, not as a reply to his question, but a critical assessment of it.

'Why are you following me?' he asked.

A Mona Lisa smile, this time.

'What's happened to Romy?'

The smile disappeared. 'I don't know.'

'I think you do.'

'*I don't.*' Without raising her voice, she spat the words at him. As if she meant them. 'I'm not involved with any of his...' But she didn't finish her sentence.

'He's, what, your boyfriend? Lover? You share him with Romy?'

'You should forget about Irwin. Your bigger problem is a creep named Stephens.'

'Stephen who.'

'*Stephens*. Detective Nigel Stephens. He's a cop, but a very bad one. And by bad, I don't mean incompetent.'

'I don't know him.'

'He knows you. And you *do* know him. You just haven't been introduced yet.'

'Stephens...'

'Likes his grey suits.'

That rang a bell, but he couldn't quite work out where the sound of the bell was coming from...

'Is he connected in some way to Irwin?'

She nodded slowly. 'As I've only just discovered myself.'

'And how do you fit into this? Other than being Irwin's—'

'Money,' she said. 'And blood. Which is appropriate, because money and blood, they're the only currencies these people trade in.'

Money and blood. More or less what Alastair had said.

'And you say you're not one of them?'

'You can't beat these people. You can only endure them.'

'You can fight back.'

She snorted dismissively. Her drink arrived and she took a large swig. 'I only just found out about Detective Stephens myself.' And then another swig; the glass was all but empty. She opened her bag and pulled out a tenner. 'I can't be seen with you.'

'Wait.'

She was getting up.

'Isla.' *Iss-la.*

By the look on her face, he assumed he managed to get the pronunciation right, or at least close enough to impress her. She hesitated.

'Please,' he said. 'You know... you're my only hope of... My only hope. And I *know*... I mean I can tell you're...' He knew he was sounding drunk, and maybe he was drunk. 'Look, can we meet again? Please. Tomorrow, somewhere. Please?'

As she looked into his eyes, he detected a softening. Then she seemed to catch herself and she looked away again, deep in thought.

'What's tomorrow,' she said finally. 'Sunday. He'll be out. We can meet here. At noon.'

* * *

Minutes later, and a mere twenty or thirty paces from the restaurant entrance, Jon stood in the shadows across from 30A Peter Street. After Isla had left, he made a move himself. And now, as he looked up, he could see her at the window. She was looking down in his direction. There was something about her, something almost... *almost* irresistible. Compelling. And there it was again, that word.

Compelling in the sense that he wanted to help her (because he knew she needed help), but was that for her sake or for his? And was that really what it was – a desire to help and be helped – or was it simply raw, bestial attraction? Was it as basic as that? And if it was the latter, if it was something animalistic and wild, might these impulses, counterintuitively, be stronger in us when we were most in danger? Perhaps we felt them more keenly when we were forced to fall back on our full range, our complete arsenal of mammalian intuition? The in-for-a-penny-in-for-a-pound theory of natural inclinations?

And as he watched her looking down at him, he knew she could see him, and he wondered whether her coming to the window was a sign of some kind.

81. <u>51° 29' 27" N 0° 9' 27" W</u> (Bridges' flat, Lower Sloane St, Chelsea)

The same time
12.05am British Summer Time (23:05 UTC)
Sunday, 27 October

When his front door buzzer sounded, Bridges had been asleep on his reading chair, with the floor lamp still on and the Arts section of Saturday's *Guardian* covering his lap like a pensioner's blanket. Not that he could call himself young anymore exactly, and regularly falling asleep while reading was, he had to admit, rather damning evidence indeed.

'Who the bloody hell…?' he muttered to himself, leaping up as a reflex more than anything else. Which did nothing for his bad back (exhibit B). Halfway to the intercom, it occurred to him that it was probably some misguided specimen of Chelsea teenager or a drunken yob (or both, these days), (and complaining about the latest generation: exhibit C), but he answered it anyway.

'Yes hello?'

'Lawrence Bridges?'

'Who wants to know.'

It had to be said, he'd been on edge lately. Because of what Runion had told him at the Garrick, but also because he still hadn't *heard* from the man. Admittedly he'd promised to call Runion later on the Thursday, after their lunch, but he'd needed some thinking time (and a break from Richard, who could be a trifle intense at times). Bridges had rung, eventually, on Friday evening, and then again during the day on Saturday but not a peep. And it wasn't like Runion to fail to return a call at the *best* of times. Let alone the worst, which these were beginning to look like: for grey squirrels and art dealers both.

'Detective Inspector...', the male voice said, Bridges not quite catching the name, '... of the Metropolitan Police. If I might have a quick word. I do apologise for the hour sir, I hope it's not too inconvenient—'

'Well it is, actually.'

'It is rather important I'm afraid. I will only take up a minute of your time, I guarantee it.'

Access to Bridges' penthouse apartment was via a small three person lift and as the doors opened directly into his living room he wasn't about to let a stranger in, alleged policeman or not. And most certainly not in the current situation.

'I'll come down.'

After checking the officer's I.D. through the letter slot, he opened the door and stepped outside. Which is when he recognised him. He recognised the creased charcoal grey suit first. With the brown suede shoes. And the rimless glasses. It was the large man from the club, the one who'd stared at him on the Piccadilly line that afternoon. He'd seen him since then too, he was sure of it. It was strange, though, he didn't look quite as fat as what Bridges had remembered, but it was him all right.

'I remember you. From the Garrick.'

The officer stared back blankly. He was possibly about to reply, but Bridges didn't have all night.

'And the train,' he added. 'Have you been following me?'

He hadn't intended to sound quite so whiny and peevish, but the detective remained unruffled.

'Not at all sir. If it was me, it would have been a coincidence. I assure you.'

'Right. What was your name again?'

'Stephens. Nigel Stephens, sir. I'm a plain clothes detective, with—'

'Plain, yes, I can see that.' *Whoops*, Bridges thought. A bit insulting, but "plain" certainly nailed it.

'Yes, thank you. I'm a detective attached to the Art and Antiquities Unit of the Specialist, Organised and Economic Crime Command. I'm currently heading up an investigation into various possible crimes connected to, and including, the death and possible homicide of an Armenian gentleman by the name of Nishan, otherwise known as Norton, Rattatroop. You've heard of Mr Rattatroop I presume?'

'Vaguely. Not really. You should speak to...' But Bridges trailed off. Had second thoughts about mentioning Runion. A kind of last minute instinctive 'veto', as it were.

But it made no difference.

'Richard Runion?' the detective said. 'You knew... you know him, I understand. You see, unfortunately, we haven't been able to locate him, and that's why I'm here, that's why I've had to come to you at this most ungodly of all ungodly hours.'

'Has something happened to him?'

'I sincerely hope not. But I have reason to believe you should... watch your step, at the moment. If you know what I mean.'

'Really? Yes, I think I do.'

'Would you mind if I came up? I could... fill you in a little further.'

'No, no. Certainly. Come in, come in.'

82. <u>51° 30' 46" N 0° 8' 2" W</u>
(Peter Street Flat, Soho)

1.10am Greenwich Mean Time (01:10 UTC)
Sunday, 27 October

She never should have returned to the flat. Isla knew it when she walked in, almost two hours ago, and she knew it now.

* * *

It had all started going wrong straight away – just after she'd walked over to the window, in fact. She stood there for no particular reason other than to avoid having to look at *him*. At Irwin. Or answer his questions: about where she'd been, or whatever else. When she looked out at a night that reflected how she felt – there was a stifling, cold greyness as relentless legions of feather-light rain showers descended slowly across the city, like thousands of tiny, silent paratroopers – she saw the barrister standing across the road, his BOAC bag over his shoulder, looking up at her. *Get out of here you fool.* And when Irwin had come to the window, she'd watched her streetbound peeping tom slink off into the night.

Which was when the questions started – you could never escape them. Ever since their recent discussion about the detective, Stephens – and now she knew who the weirdo was in her life drawing classes – Irwin had been probing and probing. Convinced she knew things that she didn't. And now he was about to get physical. You could see it coming a mile off.

She never should have returned to the flat.

She was sitting opposite him, in a chair with leather upholstery so soft it felt like it was trying to swallow her up – grope her first, and swallow her whole.

He'd gone quiet, and was just staring at her. Get on with it.

'I feel bad about what happened,' he said finally.

Was he apologising? Surely not.

'What do you mean.'

'I feel bad, and we need to talk about it,' he said.

Isla just stared straight back at him. He'd played this game before. And if there was one thing she was proud of, it was the way she just sat there, looking at him, not saying anything. Making *him* do all the talking. Well handled. Stupid for not leaving earlier and jumping on the next train to Paris, but well handled.

'And I'm pretty fucking certain you know *why* we need to talk.'

He waited for a response, but she held her nerve, kept her cool.

'Maybe things haven't been so easy for you, since we moved here. Maybe we never should have left Paris. Or Zurich, even, but...' There was a pause. 'Are you just going to sit there? Hey. You'll help yourself, you know, if you talk to me.'

'A bit hard to talk, *Irwin*, when you're gagging on someone else's bullshit.'

This time it was Irwin's turn to stare. He turned a couple of shades redder. It was almost funny – and it would have been, if it hadn't led to such a catastrophe.

She watched him thinking, and wondered if he was counting to a hundred or reviewing his strategy in his head. After what seemed like a full sixty seconds, he slowly stood up, brushed some crumbs or lint off his lap (it was funny how you remember these things, the small things, the best), walked around the coffee table, past Isla and switched off the main light, leaving only the light from the lamp in the corner. Interesting, maybe he wants to *kill* me, she thought.

He then drew the curtains. So no-one could see in? And see him... stabbing her and cutting her up and putting the pieces into freezer bags—

Everything suddenly went black and silent for a moment.

Irwin had just slapped her. Hard, across her face.

'*That's* cutting the bullshit, you stupid cow. *That*... is for messing with *my fucking livelihood*.'

Her face burned, she could still see stars in front of her eyes – they looked more like swarming flies – and her hearing seemed muffled in her left ear (he'd managed to hit that too).

Next thing she knew he was shaking a piece of paper in front of her face.

'Is this it?'

After he stopped shaking it around and she was eventually able to focus, she could see it was the design which she'd turned into her tattoo. OK. So he'd found out. (A normal person in a normal relationship would wonder how he found out. But she was dealing with Irwin and nothing ever surprised her.) *Here we go.*

'You thought it was OK to make a copy did you? Without asking me? And you know what else you did you dumb cunt. You left it with your tattooist friend. Luckily we managed to retrieve and destroy it, although... not so lucky for your friend.'

She'd completely forgotten about the photocopy. The one she left at the tattooist's. And now... It was all her fault.

'So where is it?' Irwin asked.

'Where's what.' It was hard to get the words out, after what Irwin had just told her. And after he'd almost broken her jaw.

'The *tattoo*.'

'Nowhere you're ever going to see it.'

'Oh I think I'm going to see it all right.'

Oh no you're not.

'I'm going to see it,' Irwin added, 'because we're getting that tattoo, *wherever* it is, removed in the morning.'

'Like fuck we are.'

And he slapped her again. It was even harder this time. More swarming flies. Longer lingering flies they were too. Friendly or annoying, she couldn't tell...

'You stupid bitch,' he was saying when her hearing kicked in again. 'You still don't get it do you. One copy in the world and this is it. *This*... is *it*.' He was shaking the piece of paper again. 'So yeah. The tattoo goes.'

Well that was fun, she thought. What next.

Rape, that's what was next. The next thing she knew he was raping her. It always followed a pattern (although tonight would be slightly different). The slapping, the tearing off of her clothes (jeans were the hardest), the act of penetration... And tonight she was gifted a soundtrack too.

'And now you're *fucked*,' he rasped between thrusts. 'You're *fucked*... you're *so*... com*plete*... ly *fucked*...'

And then, after he gave up trying to come – not violent enough for him, perhaps – he said to her softly, almost in a whisper, and accompanied with the surprising, tender caresses of the lover he had never been, nor would ever be:

'Isn't it funny how in English, there are two totally different meanings of that word, "fucked", why is that do you think? It's so strange. And look at you now, lying there, your clothes scattered, your legs spread... You are fucked and you are *fucked*. Fucked in every sense of the word, my dear, sweet Isla.'

And that would have been the end of it, but when she began to gather her clothes, he spoke again.

'Suck my cock,' he said, apparently speaking literally. No double-meaning.

She ignored him.

'Suck my cock you Swiss piece of shit, you slut queen of Europe and you get to retain the use of your legs. Pretty useful in your line of work I would have thought.' He laughed after the last remark.

Which is precisely when Irwin crossed some invisible, arbitrary line which even Isla herself wasn't aware of.

She really had nothing at all to say to that and decided to leave. She was halfway out of her chair when he shoved her back down again, back into that perverted accomplice of an armchair.

'Suck my cock and let's get this over with. You might even enjoy it for once.'

From that point on, all she could clearly recall was Irwin trying to push his stupid little prick into her mouth.

* * *

She was enjoying the armchair now, funnily enough, which had somehow turned into her friend – it was as cosy as a warm bath.

Right in front of her, in her direct line of vision, her ex-lover had his most prized possession, a nineteenth century Melanesian carved-bone fishing knife sticking out of his chest just about where you'd have expected his heart to have been if he'd had one. Judging by the small amount of handle showing, it had been pushed so far through, it must have come out the other side, torn through the back of his Boss business shirt and possibly even scratched the varnish on the floorboards beneath the now blood-soaked Persian carpet.

Had she really done that?

She had. In fact for some strange reason she'd checked the time afterwards – possibly out of some sort of defensive reflex, to help with getting her story straight later – and her mobile, which she'd found next to her jeans, had said 1.55am.

It had been her, she'd really done it. So she'd fought back, she'd stopped enduring. She'd taken that Jon Marriner's advice after all.

She got up, and walked over and picked up the piece of paper that Irwin had been waving in her face. Took the lighter on the coffee table and lit the piece of paper. Watched it burn in the ashtray. Stubbed out the ashes.

'See?' she said to Irwin's body. '*Still* one copy.'

She quickly got dressed, realizing that she was in more danger now, rather than less. And a murder charge was the least of her problems.

Clearly, she should never have returned to the flat.

She checked her phone again before she did a quick last minute inspection of the place (there was no chance of her doing anything about the body). She was confused at first: the time was 1.10am. And then she remembered daylight saving ended that night – the clocks had just gone back, at 2am. Back to 1am.

So the whole hour had disappeared. Did that mean the killing had never happened?

83. <u>17° 46' 21" S 168° 18' 39" E</u> (Erakor Island Resort, Port Vila)

At the same moment...
12.10pm Vanuatu Time (01:10 UTC)
Sunday, 27 October

He was getting lazy. Ruart had planted himself on a seat in the covered bar area with a view that took in the bar/restaurant itself, the sunbathers on the beach, and the lagoon, across which an outboard-powered boat provided the sole means of access to the resort. The Erakor Island Resort to be precise, where Bob Walman was staying. He imagined he could almost get away with remaining exactly where he was, and do all his work from the chair he was sitting in, and never have to do anything more than turn around and order another Bikini Martini.

Well his genie must have been working overtime, because no sooner had the thought crossed his mind than one of the hotel's employees informed him that Mr Walman was arriving, and that was him walking up from the jetty right now. Which one? The big man, white shirt.

Walman looked pretty fit for a CEO, if still a little on the predictably heavy side. Wearing a white Lacoste polo shirt, black logo-less cap, blue patterned boardshorts, deck shoes, and a well-seasoned tan, he was definitely the picture of a hard-working exec on holiday.

'Er, Mr Walman?'

'Yes?'

'Robert Vincent. I'm sorry to bother you but I am a yachting broker, and I am—'

'I'm sorry Mr, ah, Vincent, but I'm a little busy.'

'Yes I can see that.' Ruart left just enough of a pause for Walman to get a whiff of sarcasm without being suffocated by it. 'I just wanted to quickly ask you about your boat, the *Diamond Moon*.'

'What about it.' Any hint of potential goodwill had well and truly wafted away on the balmy tropical breeze.

'Well, first, who you bought it from? You see I am looking at possibly—'

'Listen. All I can tell you is I acquired it in Réunion two months ago, but through a maritime agent there, and I doubt I could even recollect his name. OK?'

'And the previous owner? Perhaps you have—

'No idea.'

'Dominique Drayle? You must have spoken with him.'

'Never heard of him.'

'Seriously?'

'Always. Now Mr, ah...'

'Vincent.'

'Mr Vincent, my holiday time is as valuable as my work time, and I doubt very much that someone like you could afford the bill, so if you'll excuse me.'

* * *

So why were they all here, in Vanuatu?

By being as unfriendly and unhelpful as he was, Walman had, Ruart felt, inadvertently nailed his guilty flag to his mast. His lack of cooperation, plus the presence of Lena and Roy in town at the same time, equalled Drayle. That was Ruart's current whiteboard equation anyway and it was staying up there on the board until he had a better one.

And his patience paid off. Because one more Bikini Martini later, Walman was back, meeting friends at the other end of the bar. And guess who was amongst them? Lena. Where had she sprung from? He hadn't seen her arrive. Must have been distracted by the bronzing semi-naked bodies on the beach – one of the obstacles you encounter when attempting any serious detective work in the tropics.

Lena was with a bizarre-looking, black-haired... Westerner or Eurasian, he wasn't quite sure. Could that have been the Englishman seen with Lena last night? Edward Lang? He didn't look very English.

Lena spotted Ruart and stared. Walman caught her look and when he saw who Lena was staring at, he visibly scowled. Lena excused herself from her male companions and came over. Ruart's chair was working wonders. Or was it the Bikini Martinis?

'Monsieur Vincent.' Her French accent was commendable.

'Good memory,' Ruart said, getting up and offering his hand. 'Robert. Have a seat. Please.'

'Robert Vincent,' she said, nodding. 'You needn't get up.'

She neither shook his hand, nor sat down.

'So how are you Lena?'

'You wouldn't be following me, would you?'

'I was, er... pursuing Mr Walman.'

'You've certainly come a long way for such a short conversation.'

'It's OK, I have other business here, in Vanuatu.'

Clearly unconvinced, she simply nodded curtly and smiled. 'Well I hope you enjoy your stay.'

'So do I.' There was a certain impishness in his delivery, but Lena was having none of it and avoided his eyes. She was about to leave when he added: 'Is Roy here?'

'I'm afraid not,' she said after a moment's hesitation. 'He... had business to attend to, in Broome. Last minute drama. Now I have to get back to my friends. I hope we don't keep bumping into each other like this, or I really will start to worry.'

'What about?'

No reaction to that one either let alone a smile, which seemed to be, by now, way too much to ask for. But when she turned and strutted off, she kicked out her saronged hips, and he had the feeling she knew exactly where his eyes were...

So why was she lying about Roy? Was she having an affair? Or was it some kind of cover for something else?

Ruart watched as she returned to her two companions. He could tell she was talking about him – Walman refused to look in his direction but the black-haired man seemed to take a great interest.

* * *

Half an hour later, after he had finished enjoying a light lunch consisting of a BLT and a local beer (Tusker) and was weighing up the pros and cons of ordering a follow-up beer, one for the 'road' so to speak, Lena took a detour via Ruart on her way back to her table.

'Why don't you join us?'

His genie, or his magic chair, had done it again. It did mean getting up, though. A small price to pay, he supposed. But why the change in attitude, he wondered? Only one way to find out.

Walman had gone, but the other guy was still there and Lena introduced him. Edward Lang. No surprises there.

He had to admit, though, everything about this man set his teeth on edge. An uglier man would have been difficult to find – certainly on Erakor Island, and probably on *any* of the eighty-three Vanuatuan islands – but the striking thing was the God's-gift-to-women air about him and the level of arrogance that went with it. He claimed to operate some sort of maritime business in North London and had the strangest English accent Ruart had ever heard (never mind 'mid-Atlantic', try 'Five Eyes', or even 'five oceans'). He had stringy, greasy black hair that had to have been coloured, looked like he'd spent the morning marinating in St Tropez bronzing lotion, and had a Japanese-puffer-fish face with the eyes of a pit bull terrier. Ruart had met his fair share of rough Londoners in his time, but this Edward Lang was in a class of his own.

At one point Ruart made the mistake of querying whether Lang had any "Asian heritage". Lang had frosted over and told him, icily, that his family could be traced back to Mary Queen of Scots. 'I'd be willing to wager a considerable sum,' he said, 'that you have more Algerian blood in you than I have Asian, let me put it that way.' Ruart of course had not a drop of Algerian blood in his ancestral line, but he took the comment for the insult that it was intended to be and said nothing. And fair enough too, he thought, it served him right.

He watched with great interest when, at one point, Lang ordered a glass of water and took what he claimed were two headache tablets. Big night, eh, Mr Lang? Ruart had, in fact, specifically been keeping a close look-out for any sign of affection between Lena and Lang, but they were either keeping it well-hidden, or it was non-existent. Indeed, it wasn't at all clear what their relationship was, although something told him it wasn't purely business. Neither were giving anything much away though, so he thought he'd test the waters.

'So Lena, it's a shame Roy couldn't be here. Such a beautiful place. Do you know Roy, Edward?'

The mouth kept smiling, but a flicker of irritation crossed his pebbly pit-bull eyes before Lena jumped in.

'Roy has probably been here more times than you've had *escargots*.'

'I don't eat them, actually.'

'So, Robert, that's a nice little bruise you have,' Lang said jovially. 'Anything you're not telling us?'

And the conversation bounced along in this way for about ten minutes with Ruart learning absolutely nothing. Other than making the annoyingly inconvenient discovery that he was unequivocally attracted to Lena. Even more so after his third Tusker. How *dare* she be so alluring. Who, or what, was this gorgeous Russian girl with her honey-brown skin and quartz-blonde hair, glowing with obscene health? *Bad news*, is what she so obviously was, he reminded himself. Even so, she was also, as that terrible cliché in English went, quite "easy on the eye", thank you very much.

She was even lightening up towards him, which was fine, it would make his job easier, wouldn't it? One slip from her, he couldn't help but feel, and he'd be able to confirm that she knew where Drayle was. After that – and the third Tusker may, admittedly, have played a role in this conclusion – after that, all it would take would be a little "French persuasion" to reveal everything he needed to know. He wasn't James Bond, for sure not, but he was exponentially better looking than this Edward Lang for a start, and with Roy out of the picture... All bets were off, put it that way.

Where *was* Roy, by the way? Back at the Grand Hotel playing solitaire? Unless Ruart's information had been 'chinese-whispered' somewhere along the way, and it had never been Roy in the first place. Perhaps Lena was telling the truth. He supposed all would be revealed in due course...

It was after he'd paid a visit to the Gents that Lena said precisely what he wanted to hear.

'Robert. Edward and I have a proposition for you.'

'Ah yes?'

'You've heard of the island, Tanna?'

'Of course.'

'And the volcano, Mount Yasur? It is supposed to be very spectacular. Well, tomorrow we're flying there. It's only an hour away. You take a trip to the volcano in the afternoon and you stay there, on the island, overnight. Would you like to join us?'

The sober devil's advocate in Ruart's Tuskered brain put the brakes on a rapid reply. He couldn't trust Lena further than he could throw her (or even her chunky friend). No way, he wasn't kidding himself on that score. On the other hand, she was his best lead yet. And as far as leads went, she was perhaps one of the prettiest he'd laid eyes on for some time...

'Sure,' he said. 'It might be interesting.'

'I guarantee it will be,' Lang said.

Ruart would have preferred the guarantee to have come from Lena, all the same. 'You've seen it?' he said to Lang. 'The volcano?'

'Edward's a bit of a Vanuatu expert,' Lena said. 'Anyway the flight's at eleven-thirty in the morning, there's only one. Book yourself a ticket, and we'll take care of the accommodation. No luggage, just bring a daypack, it's easier. And good walking shoes.'

'Are you sure?' Ruart said. 'That is very generous of you. Oh and... a return flight, I assume, coming back the next—'

'One always hopes so,' said Lang. 'Doesn't one.'

Lena and Lang had some business in town to attend to, so after they left, Ruart sent an urgent message through to the *Préfecture*'s Vanuatu operation to ensure they were followed in case they were meeting Drayle. After he'd done that, and then booked his flights, he finally allowed himself to relax. Given his location, relaxing came easily.

He was certainly feeling pleased with himself: it had been a most productive afternoon. And so he sat back, all the better for fully appreciating various pleasant, alcohol-infused thoughts rolling in and over him in waves, like the breakers over the distant reef, and he watched the golden afternoon sun, like a celestial alchemist, turn one end of the lagoon to shimmering silver and the other, to luminous lapis lazuli.

84. <u>57° 9' 1" N 2° 5' 40" W</u> (Hotel Room, Aberdeen, Scotland)

9.00am Greenwich Mean Time (09:00 UTC)
Sunday, 27 October

The grey was overwhelming. *Everything* was grey. The sky, the sea, and worst of all, the buildings. All of them, the same grey as the sea, sky, rain, cobblestones and everything else.

Ishiko was looking out at all this bleakness and, like the turmoil she pictured out there in the North Sea, beyond the wall of clouds on the close, hemming horizon, her mind too was in a state of great confusion.

She'd just received a message. Finally, which ought to have been a good thing. But there was a lot to worry about.

On the plus side, it was via an email account they'd used before, and the email was addressed to her in the usual way. But it hadn't been signed off the way they normally signed off. Her handler, Aleks, always signed off with "love Aleks xx" (it was his little joke, they'd never met), but this one had no sign-off at all. Not hearing from Aleks for over two months was one thing – he'd always been a little unreliable and disorganized anyway, always losing phones and generally slow to respond at the best of times – but to finally hear in *this* way, without the usual sign-off, was disturbing. Could it simply have been so long he'd forgotten his usual habits on this occasion?

That was the trouble with this kind of set-up. With cells in general, and the sole-point-of-contact rule in particular. If anything out of the ordinary happened (and let's face it, in this business that was basically every operation), there was no easy way to get approval for a change in plan. You had to go out on a limb, and if you succeeded, they still got the credit; if you failed it was all your fault. Sure, they'd given her a special number to contact in case of "extreme emergency" (they called it the Dire Straits number), but her current situation was hardly that. She'd always been told that almost without exception, whenever a problem was encountered they were to just sit tight and wait – up to a year if necessary – and that someone would eventually contact them.

But the message itself: Ishiko was instructed to make her way immediately, with the Decagon, to Port Vila, Vanuatu. Once there, she was to send an email to the new address provided and a meeting would be arranged. And that was it. No "Aleks", no name, nothing.

Vanuatu! That had to be close to the exact opposite side of the world to Aberdeen, hadn't it? Couldn't they have picked somewhere a bit closer? Of course, she had to assume they didn't know where she was. Aleks never used the same email account twice in a row, and she'd always been told not to respond anyway. It was always *her* waiting to hear from *them*.

She was certainly becoming very, very tired of the whole thing, everything. Looking out at the North Sea, she was sorely tempted to hitch a ride out on one of those fishing trawlers – or even better a marine research vessel, it was her dream job – and sail right out, past the North Sea and into the Norwegian Sea, and somewhere out there, at the deepest point, which she knew was almost four thousand metres, she would throw the Decagon over the side when no-one was looking, and to hell with them all, just disappear, and start a new life somewhere.

Maybe she should never have left South Africa. She loved the ocean and down there, they had *two* of them right next to each other.

But there was always the terrible nagging sense of duty. A sense of duty not just to 'them' – she was sick of 'them' – but to herself, to finish what she'd started.

And then she thought of the warm waters of the South Pacific. The Coral Sea, even the sound of the name warmed her body. As opposed to the cold, grey bubble she now found herself in. With all that grey stone that served as a constant reminder of somewhere she didn't need to be reminded of: Lüderitz.

And she thought of another reason to take a chance on Vanuatu: after her stupidity in approaching Delia, the UK authorities could be expected to launch an extensive search for her, once the information had filtered through to the relevant people. They'd start in London, and then follow the inevitable trail to Aberdeen. Maybe she'd already been tracked, or at least spotted on a CCTV camera somewhere. Not to mention that man in the grey suit, whoever he was, how sure could she be that she'd lost him?

But every time she thought of the clear, lapping waters of the Coral Sea, she couldn't help but think that was exactly what they *wanted* her to think. And she couldn't help but think Aleks would have signed off properly. And if it wasn't Aleks, who *was* it?

85. <u>17° 46' 33" S 168° 17' 37" E</u> (Breakas Beach Resort, Port Vila)

11.30pm Vanuatu Time (12:30 UTC)
Sunday, 27 October

Lena

Ruart just liked saying the name, although he wasn't saying it aloud, or he didn't think he was anyway, but maybe

Lena

He was looking down at her, at her blonde hair pooling behind her head like a halo, a framing nest for her angelic face. And she was looking up at him, with those big loving eyes, but was it love? sparkling blue like the effervescent midday sea...

He'd tell her that. Later. If he hadn't already

And now he was looking down at her "L", although it looked more like an arrow, an arrow pointing at his lunging, deep-plunging...

Oh my God. He was so screwed

It didn't stop him though, did it

Was there a creature like her? Anywhere?

Too late to turn back now anyway, too late to turn back, way too late

He was so screwed

How did this happen?

Dinner invitation, and

Edward had a "mild dose of sunstroke"

What else was he going to do?

He did the right thing. He did it for Constance. He was only doing his best, trying to learn as much as he could

She was from Siberia, he found that out, from the frozen wastes... And what a waste if she'd never left it, eh?

He still didn't even know her surname!

The bungalow looked like a Coral Sea cyclone had been through it. Cyclone Lena. (They'd been having some fun)

But how did this happen?

It was so fast... he couldn't even remember who suggested the drinks in his bungalow

What happens when you fall in love with a suspect, a potential accomplice, and you're a cop, right? What happens when you fall in love and you're not involved in any sort of operation? You're on holiday, right? And she's not even an official suspect, she's not even wanted for questioning, it's only *you* who wants her, no-one else, what happens then?

You stay the fuck away, man. You stay right the fuck away unless you can handle the heat. And Commandant Laurent Ruart, can he handle the heat? Oh yeah. So if you're Ruart, what happens?

You're screwed, that's what happens

Marine

How would he deal with that? No point in even beginning to blame the alcohol, that didn't wash these days, never did

But there was no going back now

Lena pushed him out and back onto the bed and cupped him, stuck her finger in at the same time, which was just a *little* too... and then oh God slowly lowered her head down over him, her blonde hair a bridal veil, and her mouth a candle snuffer, embracing the flame, but nothing was being snuffed here, his life maybe, or, rather, his life as he knew it, but that's OK, long live change, without it you die...

Oh my God, her mouth, her tongue, she's a golf ball washer, just a spit and shine and everything's fine! And... Oh whoa my oh my God she was so amazing and he was so completely screwed... But this sort of pleasure... To experience it just once in your life... would make it all... worth... worth...while

No going back

Completely screwed
Don't go
About to come

86. <u>51° 30' 46" N 0° 8' 1" W</u>
(Soho Restaurant)

The same time
12.30pm Greenwich Mean Time (12:30 UTC)
Sunday, 27 October

It was coming all right.

Jon could tell from the breeze that was picking up outside – it was what they used to call a "stiff" breeze. The awning across the street was starting to flap around with each gust. The storm was definitely on its way. And it was going to be worse on the coast, but it was just a storm, it couldn't be helped. Because overnight, he'd had time to think about things (his Bayswater hotel room had been so small, thinking was about all you could do in it), and he'd made up his mind that as he needed Isla's help and she needed his, he'd try to talk her into returning to Alastair's house in Peacehaven with him, and sit out the storm there, figure out their next move. Because that look she gave him last night... she *did* need his help, he was certain of it.

But where was she? It was already twelve thirty, and she'd said noon. Thirty minutes late and she didn't exactly have far to go. Twenty yards, max. She could hardly blame the traffic.

Something had gone wrong.

He thought the thought, and the moment he thought it – as if his mind had created it rather than perceived it – he heard sirens.

He didn't need to wait to find out, he knew they were headed for him. There was a vague notion at the back of his mind that if they were intent on arresting him in this labyrinth of a city, one would expect they'd be more *softly-softly* about it, but when dark thoughts took hold, they were hard to shake.

He quickly grabbed his bag and made a move. As soon as he stepped outside the restaurant entrance he could see them, coming up Wardour Street, lights flashing and sirens heehawing. He turned into Peter Street and kept going, walking as briskly as he could without actually running. When the first police car turned into Peter Street behind him, he readied himself for a dramatic arrest combining the squealing of tyres and the springing of car doors... But they stopped. Well before they got to him.

He kept walking to just past the next corner and turned around. Two vehicles – a marked police car and an unmarked one with a siren planted on its roof – had both wedged themselves at lazy angles about thirty yards behind him. Outside 30A.

At that point, he knew he should have made himself scarce, but curiosity was a strange thing. It made you do things. And all he could think was, *don't tell me*, he'd lost another one: Sabine, Romy, Emerald, Isla... These women, they couldn't *all* vanish on him. Could they?

Three or four policemen jumped out and one of them pressed the buzzer. Someone let them in... Isla? Surely not.

And then, out of the unmarked car, stepped a man in a dark grey suit. He stopped at the doorway, and as if guided by some sixth sense, he looked up in Jon's direction.

For a few moments neither of them moved.

After which everything seemed to unravel at once. The man, who was stocky and wore a badly-fitting dark grey suit and rimless, rectangular glasses, started walking towards him. And Jon thought he recognised him. The large build, the suit, the purposeful stride. It reminded him of the man who'd tried to kill him in West Kensington. And what had Isla said? Look out for Detective Stephens.

Likes his grey suits.

Jon ran.

His instinct was to seek out the crowds. It was Sunday, the Berwick Street market was closed – he'd passed Berwick Street anyway – which meant somehow getting through to Brewer Street running parallel to his left. In the meantime he was banking on not being shot in front of the other police, although maybe they were all inside... No time to look around, but he was certain he could hear a set of running footsteps behind him. Ahead was the derelict dead end that had spooked him earlier – everything about it screamed death, he probably died there in a parallel universe – so thankfully a last chance left turn presented itself, a narrow lane through to Brewer. He knocked over a chair with his foot to a chorus of American *hey buddy*s, shot round the corner and kept running, dodging the lazy, lucky, Sunday amblers.

* * *

An hour and a half later, he was finally on an overland train heading south. He was heading, indirectly, for the only haven currently open to him. He supposed he'd been caught by the odd CCTV camera, so he was taking no chances: he was making his way to Lucinda in what one might call a roundabout fashion. Headed *away* from Victoria first, rather than towards it. And when he eventually arrived in Newhaven, he'd take a few detours there too. All of which might, with any luck, help him sleep a little better that night.

Militating against a good night's sleep however, was his recollection of that terrifying dash through Soho. He didn't look around once, and even though he was no longer sure whether he could hear a pursuer or not, he could certainly *sense* one. Passing through Piccadilly Circus, he ran into the Underground, to make them think he was getting a train there, and then burst out into the fresh air again on Piccadilly, shouldering away whole families at a time, and ran all the way along the crowded footpath to Green Park, where he caught his first of many trains.

Outside, at the green edges of Greater London, light rain showers were sweeping past the window. Wet weather gear would have been useful, but he couldn't think of everything.

How was he going to contact Isla now? Assuming she was still alive. They'd probably missed their chance, he and Isla. He had no contact details for her, and he knew she wouldn't be able to contact him either: he'd taken Alastair's advice and kept his cyberspace profile invisible. He pulled out his laptop anyway, in the hope that an idea might present itself.

He went into the only mail account he now used, an anonymous Google account, and he checked for messages in the vain hope that it had somehow slipped his mind and he'd been clever enough last night to give his account details to Isla.

As it turned out, he *did* have a message waiting, but it wasn't from Isla. It wasn't spam either. Not judging by the specificity of the language. It was from an equally anonymous account – the server was unrecognizable – and it read simply:

```
There is nowhere to run to, Jonathon Marriner.

I will erase you from the whole earth.

I will hunt you to the end of Time.

You will never sleep again. With one exception…
your final sleep, when you never wake up.

One more sleep.
```

87. <u>17° 44' 31" S 168° 18' 51" E</u> (Grand Hotel and Casino, Port Vila, Vanuatu)

9.30am Vanuatu Time (22:30 UTC)
Monday, 28 October

And now it was *no* more sleeps, because she was here!

Or almost. The guest in Room 405 of the Grand Hotel and Casino was in a state of high excitement. His girlfriend was flying in today, the sun was shining, Vila Bay was dazzling and it was difficult to imagine how anything could spoil his day.

Funnily enough, the conversation that he subsequently overheard went some way towards doing just that. It took a lot to spoil Nick's day, though, and a mere conversation was never going to be the thing do it. Unless it was on the floor of Parliament that is, but Canberra was nearly three thousand kilometres away, thank fuck.

Nick was on his balcony soaking up the rays, juice in hand, when he heard a man and a women suddenly emerge onto the balcony of the next room, Room 404. It sounded as though the woman had just arrived. She was saying something in another language, possibly Russian, and the man interrupted her.

'No,' he said. 'Keep it in English.'

'OK.'

'At all times. Just in case.'

'Yes, OK. You're right.'

The accents were hard to pick: the woman's sounded European or Russian; the man's was trickier – European also, maybe French, but there was a hint, too, of educated English. Nick would have loved to have been able to get a look at them – especially after their conversation got going.

'So how was last night?' the man asked, with a sarcastic edge in his voice.

'It was… manageable.'

'I'll bet. You managed to… what… *accommodate* him well enough then?'

'Shut up Dominique. You know I had to do it.'

'No, you had to do *him*.'

Hello. Russian, Nick decided. A Russian prostitute.

There was a pause, some rustling and then

'No,' the woman said.

More rustling, something fell off a table.

'No!'

The movement stopped. Silence.

'Just wait,' she said. 'After, we'll have all the time we want.'

'Sure. Look. Lena. I was only joking before. You and I, we're…'

'I know.'

'You're my… You're my number one. My most trusted. Sometimes… It's true, sometimes… I feel… I feel you're the *only* one I can trust.'

A pause.

'I wouldn't want to lose you,' the man added.

'Don't worry about it Dominique. You won't. They'd have to kill me. I'd die for you, you know. I would.'

Another pause.

'You know Irwin's dead,' the man said.

'What?'

'Just heard. Fuck.'

'How?'

'We think it was that woman he was living with. Isla. And possibly something to do with… Now *there* was another Irwin stuff-up. The million pounds that he lost, that he *somehow* sent to that London barrister. Jonathon Marriner. So it looks like he was involved as well. Marriner. Fucking barristers, eh? *Fuck*. But never mind. Our man in the Met, Stephens, he'll see to him. Nigel never misses.'

Pause.

'Apart from losing my London brigadier,' the man went on, 'you know what else? His apartment was checked out and... no *Destino* photo.'

'The one...? The one Song took of...?'

'The carving. In the Destino.'

'Oh...'

'Nothing there, not in the safe, nowhere. That photo... It could have been enough. I saw them both, the Decagon and the carving. Not at the same time, but I remember... You know, my memory, it hasn't.... My face may have changed, but not inside.'

'I love your face.'

'Liar!'

'It's true,' she said, with a calm voice. 'I do.'

There was a pause, and the man spoke again. 'I'm one hundred percent certain the carving was a copy of the design on the Decagon. Or part of it.'

Nick heard the woman sigh.

'It could have been enough,' the man said.

'Mm.'

'These designs, if you have enough to go on, they draw themselves. You can *extrapolate* them.'

'Mm.'

'Out to infinity. All we needed was enough to start with...'

'Mm. And the carving...'

'So what it *means*.... It's all the more reason we need to *get that Decagon back*.'

Another silence. *What is this "Decagon" they keep mentioning?*

'Don't worry,' the woman said. 'I'll get it.'

The man grunted.

'It's a pity, then, that we got Brad to destroy the old ship,' she said.

'Brad?'

'Hanson. The Broome cop.'

'Oh yeah. Right.'

'We could have got him to take another photo—'

'Anyway,' the man said impatiently. 'We're going to get the Decagon back aren't we? So it won't matter, will it.'

'*Yes*. I'll *get* it.'

It was the man, this time, who sighed deeply.

'Speaking of Song,' he said. 'Have we heard anything?'

'About Roy? Yes. All taken care of. Yesterday morning—'

'Good. Choose more carefully next time, will you?'

'Dominique...' The woman's voice was soft with a hard edge. Or was that hard with a soft edge?

'Song's been doing good work.'

'He has.'

'Where did you find that guy?' the man asked. 'No, don't tell me. But he's good. Bangkok, Sydney. Western Australia, he certainly seems to take... *pleasure* in his work.'

'You mean what he did—'

'I mean all of it' the man interjected.

'...with Lydia and Aleks?'

'With them, and dealing with those nosey forensics guys.'

Western Australia, forensics guys... Nick had read something in the paper back home – it would have been only a couple of days ago – about some forensics officers turning up dead in Broome. Could this be them? This was some serious shit...

'Lydia and Aleks...' the woman said. 'That was partly me. I wanted them to suffer. I wanted them to really pay for their disloyalty. And I told him... I told him he had to make sure that bitch Lydia was totally humiliated.'

'He certainly did that.'

'I can't believe her. After all these years. We were best friends!'

'Well obviously you weren't.'

'We were! And she goes and does that.'

'Hm.'

Silence. The woman sniffed. Or it could have been a snorting laugh. Who *were* these people?

There was a long pause. Nick was wondering whether he shouldn't be trying to record this.

'One thing's for sure,' the man said. 'We wouldn't have got past first base without that British woman's work.'

'Who?'

'At the British Museum. The Brits, for all their cock-ups, they can be useful sometimes.'

There was another pause, and then the man added:

'We have to get that Decagon.'

And there it is again. The "Decagon".

'First things first,' the woman said. 'Right now we have a plane to catch.'

'Yeah. OK.'

There was movement, and Nick listened as the couple retreated into their room and closed the sliding door.

Wow, Nick thought. Jesus Christ.

What do I do? Go to the cops? But where, here or in Australia…?

But hang on, what am I thinking, am I *insane*? *Jenn* is about to arrive you idiot. *Think*. If I were to report this, news of our affair would be all over the papers. And wouldn't they have fun with *that* on the floor of Parliament.

Bad idea. Wake up Nick.

88. <u>50° 47' 25" N 0° 0' 0" E</u> ("Lucinda", Peacehaven, East Sussex)

12.30am Greenwich Mean Time (00:30 UTC)
Monday, 28 October

Jon woke up suddenly – and was immediately grateful for it too, because the dream had been particularly unpleasant, if not particularly unpredictable.

He was being chased by the grey-suited detective, Detective Stephens, through what he'd thought at first was London, but it looked more like Paris. He was running down a deserted cobblestone street with Stephens in hot pursuit, like a lumbering, heavy-pawed lion running down its prey, and then the cobblestones started sinking, as if the road were a marsh, and the stones softened and turned into clumps of clay, until it was all just heavy mud he was trying to run through, and he couldn't pull his feet out... He looked behind to see Stephens, with a big grin on his face, bearing down on him in a small boat with an outboard motor, and he couldn't escape and the boat continued to bear down on him until it hit him, and ran over the top of him, entombing him in the mud and carving him up with its propeller...

Being awake though wasn't such a huge improvement.

Outside, as if mirroring the state of his mind, the night was in turmoil. Heavy rain and gusting winds were making havoc. He always slept with the blinds open and he didn't have to get out of bed to be able to see that someone nextdoor had left the washing on the line in their backyard. The way the clothes flapped around, it looked like there was a man hanging there, frantically waving his arms about, struggling to free himself while being choked by an invisible force.

89. <u>17° 42' 6" S 168° 19' 10" E</u>
(Port Vila Airport)

At the same moment...
11.30am Vanuatu Time (00:30 UTC)
Monday, 28 October

Disturbingly, things were beginning to take on the properties of a dream. Everything was supposed to look different in the daylight, tropical or otherwise, but it was nearly midday and he was still screwed.

Ruart was standing in the modest surrounds of the departure lounge of Port Vila's airport and the previous night's wild excesses were very much in the picture, with Lena, the object of his unbridled carnal desire, sitting opposite him, legs chastely crossed, reading a magazine. The wisdom of taking this trip, even if it was only a night, was beginning to wilt under scrutiny. He was no closer to finding Drayle, or learning anything else about him – this woman was as circumspect as she was titillating – and "only a night" had a hollow ring to it when you looked at how quickly things had changed on the "only a night" that had just passed. With a one night stand, you had a chance of pretending to yourself it never happened, but make it two... There was a reason no-one ever called it a "two-night stand".

What had he been thinking? If you could even call it that. Could he blame the equatorial heat? But he knew what had happened. When he agreed to this trip, he'd been lusting after Lena without being fully conscious of the fact, or of how much it was steering his actions.

Like a puppet on a string.

It was painful to recall now, but after Lena had left his bungalow (and it wasn't clear to him why she couldn't stay, but maybe it was a Roy thing), in his exuberant, post-coital, obsessional mood, he'd thought of that sixties song, "Puppet On A String", and googled it, and sang along to the YouTube clip like the drunken Frenchman on holiday that he was. Now, though, he was starting to see the ugly side. So yes, in that sense, things did look different in the light of the day, cold, warm or temperate.

With these sobering thoughts in his head, Ruart looked up and saw Lang on the other side of the lounge, talking to someone in an animated way. He wondered if it was a friend, but something told him it was business. Maybe because the other man was a severe-looking Asian. And suddenly Ruart had a sense of déjà vu, with this man in a tropical-style short-sleeved shirt and large gold watch appearing from nowhere…

Déjà vu or maybe just dreamt up, because after he looked away for a moment, distracted by an announcement, he looked back again and the man had gone and Lang was browsing the souvenir stand very much on his own.

It was that moment, more than any other, that told Ruart there was definitely something wrong – but if you'd asked him to explain it, he wouldn't have been able to.

90. <u>19° 31' 54" S 169° 26' 49" E</u> (Mount Yasur, Tanna Island, Vanuatu)

5.30pm Vanuatu Time (06:30 UTC)
Monday, 28 October

When they arrived at the rim of the volcano, Mount Yasur, with daypacks on their backs, it was still almost an hour before sunset and Ruart was able to get his first good look into the heart of an active volcano with its lava lake. He also found that his mind was running off on a frolic or two of its own. It was doing some strange things, for sure.

As he stood there on the dark and barren, rock-strewn moonscape, watching the clouds of ash and vapour billow skywards – and listening to the deep, intermittent, explosive booms that echoed around the crater walls, seemingly emanating from the earth's very core itself – he suddenly caught himself imagining a large chunk of molten rock being blasted out of the magma below and landing on Lena.

An uncomfortable dynamic had developed on the way to Mount Yasur. On the flight from Port Vila, and then the hour-and-a-half-long overland journey by four-wheel drive from their resort on the west side of the island (the three of them were sharing a bungalow apparently, which promised to be interesting), through a lush and variable tropical world of plantations, grasslands, rainforest and mountains, Lena had remained steadfastly cold and aloof towards everyone, but towards Ruart in particular. For his part, he'd done nothing. He was convinced that something was going on between

Lena and Lang. Meanwhile, Lang had simply continued with his annoying over-friendliness. As a weapon, he suspected, rather than a shield. And the more he thought about this side-trip to Tanna and his fling with Lena the night before, the more regretful he became. His tank of passion was rapidly emptying and his tank of remorse was overflowing.

And now, a little late perhaps, he was becoming increasingly aware of the danger he'd placed himself in. Not only was there a reasonable chance that Lena was connected to Drayle somehow – and he already had his 'sparky coincidence' with the death of Lena's friend Lydia in Western Australia – but it was beginning to appear highly likely that Lang was connected too. And maybe they "had him sussed" as the expression went; maybe they could see his game. Perhaps, in other words, he'd created a little problem for himself in more ways than one.

Of course, the chances of a rock actually landing on Lena were too remote for serious consideration: he didn't believe in luck, and he'd long ago learnt to discount long shots when you had your evidence sorted and knew the odds. But what was interesting to him wasn't so much the possibility of the rock scenario actually happening, but rather the fact that his mind was going there in the first place.

Because his imagination then threw up another idea: if Lena were to slip – an easy thing to do on this crater rim, there were loose edges and steep precipices everywhere – and if she were to tumble down into the crater and into the roiling lake of magma at the bottom, and if no-one were to see it happen, her body would be engulfed and dissolved in an instant, beyond reach of discovery or recovery or identification. And just as Lena would disappear, never to be found, so would, maybe, Ruart's guilt. His guilt, that is, vis-à-vis Marine. (Whether it was guilt, or a fear of being caught out and other complications, was a question for another time.) A little footnote: as Lang was with them, he would have to fall in with her, for such a clean result (sorry, my friend). There were few people on the volcano that particular day, and of the ones that were, none was on their side of the rim, or even within sight of it, so there'd be no witnesses. Especially not once the sun set. No witnesses, other than Ruart.

For sure, he would never actually *precipitate* such an event – he was no murderer after all – and he wasn't even willing it to happen either, but he couldn't control where his mind went, could he? This was how the criminal mind worked of course, balancing the prize with the risk and eliminating the risk to such an extent that the seeking of the prize became, irresistibly, the only course of action open. And just as the criminal mind worked like this, so did, by force of necessity, the mind of the pursuing detective. Purely as a force for good, naturally. That was the difference between someone like him, and someone like Drayle. Morality versus no morality.

It was, then, pure fantasy on Ruart's part, this scenario. But at the same time, it did make one think. If they both fell in, and there were no witnesses, Ruart could simply walk back to the Landcruiser, tell the driver there was no reason to wait, that he'd seen the other two head off in another vehicle, that they'd be doing their own thing. No-one would be any the wiser. Problem solved. It wouldn't solve his Drayle problem, sure, but his Marine problem would disappear as quickly as a body vaporized in a lake of magma.

In other words, about five seconds. And anyone'd be happy with that.

91. <u>50° 47' 25" N 0° 0' 0" E</u>
("Lucinda", Peacehaven)

The same time
6.30am Greenwich Mean Time (06:30 UTC)
Monday, 28 October

'When I said Lucinda was located on the Prime Meridian,' Alastair had said to Jon two days earlier, 'I should have been more specific. She's voluptuously draped across the *WGS 84* Prime Meridian. This is the prime meridian used by most GPS systems, including Google Earth, which is the one *you'll* be using if you decide to try to join Lord Lucan in Burkina Faso. The Prime Meridian that passes through the Greenwich Observatory is the *Airy* Prime Meridian, which is about a hundred yards west of the WGS 84. But it doesn't end there... because many British monuments and other markers, including the Prime Meridian monument in Peacehaven, are based on the *Bradley* Meridian aren't they. The Bradley's a superseded measurement that is, in turn, six yards to the west of the Airy. Bloody typical, isn't it? Just to confuse us. It helps them, you know. Helps them to keep things slippery. Let's go with *three* Prime Meridians, shall we? Now *there's* an idea!'

Why Jon had that conversation in his head when he woke up was anyone's guess. It was one of those hallucinations you have when you're still half-asleep but have a dream in your head which refuses to leave. They're usually annoying, as this one was. The WGS 84, Airy and Bradley prime meridians were rattling around in there, essentially making nuisances of themselves. Banging around as if questions of geographical accuracy had suddenly become matters of great importance to him. At least it explained one thing, though: why the Prime Meridian monument was further up the road than it should have been, given Lucinda's particular claim to fame.

Finally he shook himself free of the geometry and sat up.

It was almost sunrise and the storm had turned nasty. Not much in the way of rain now, but the wind was howling. Next door's washing was gone – collected by either the neighbour or the tempest – the windowpanes were rattling and the skies were dark and scudding.

What had, in truth, pushed him out of bed wasn't the Prime Meridian, but rather something that had really been bothering him, nagging at him, all night. Stephens was a cop. With all the resources. They would find him. And while Stephens may have been threatening to hunt him "until the end of time", something told him he wouldn't be needing that long. If he stopped, they'd get him, it was as simple as that. He only stood a chance if he kept moving. And if you had to do some serious moving about, what better time to be doing it than at the height of a great storm?

He was still in the clothes he'd been wearing the day before, he'd slept in them – they were the same clothes he'd been wearing for days: old navy suit, blue shirt, black shoes and black university college tie (one of the Oxford colleges, St Peters, had Alastair been to Oxford?) – and all he had to do was slip on his shoes and jacket and grab his faithful BOAC bag. His spare shirt, underwear and socks were all used now anyway – he'd 'rotate' them later. The only reason he wore the tie was to keep his neck warm. His suit was now almost as creased as his harrier's and he knew he must have looked like a homeless person. Of course, he *was* a homeless person, he had to remind himself. Just slightly more cashed up.

Where to now? Sometimes it was better to do the least sensible thing, particularly when you were being chased by someone who knew you were sensible. And the stupidest thing to do, with this storm, seemed to be to catch a ferry to France. Never mind that they'd probably be delayed or cancelled – all the less reason any sane person, with adequate means, would attempt it at short notice. Portsmouth, he thought. Catch a Brittany ferry to St. Malo? Senseless. (Perfect.)

From a window in the living room, he checked the street for unfamiliar vehicles before deciding the coast was clear. He had time to mull over what he assumed was an old pirate's expression, and hoped that for him the coast would indeed be clear as he made his way back along it to Newhaven. He left via the front door and locked it, wondering if he'd ever be back to unlock it again. He had a feeling he wouldn't.

Outside, the wind was coming in hard from the west; it was gusting up to fifty or sixty miles an hour, making walking difficult – he even had to slip the strap of his shoulder bag over his head, to secure it diagonally across his body. There was no-one around but he'd already decided to keep to the smaller front road, The Promenade, for as far as he could. Just in case. He walked down Dorothy Street, buffeted, as though he were constantly being shouldered off the footpath, and when he looked up and straight ahead he could see, beyond The Promenade and the edge of the cliffs there, the troubled, black ocean, mountainous and streaked with white. When he reached the front he turned left, east, and with the wind behind him – a small mercy – he headed for Newhaven.

After walking about forty yards or so he had a strange unshakeable feeling. Didn't know whether it was the half-dream or not, but he stopped and turned around, squinting into the gale and the small, stinging pellets of rain that had just begun to appear again (not "fall", because they were being driven horizontally). He could see the Prime Meridian monument: it would have been about a hundred yards away and the thought did occur that that placed *him* pretty close to squarely over the WGS 84 Prime Meridian (along with Lucinda). Next to the monument though, and thus located on a prime meridian of its own (the Bradley), a car that was parked there, and it was the only one, suddenly switched its lights on. It was a brand new, storm-grey Range Rover.

It was probably an unfortunate coincidence – the synchronicity of the lights being switched on, and his own sudden presence on The Promenade – but he was completely spooked. He turned and walked quickly towards the beach access up ahead.

The access road consisted of a crook-shaped cutting down through the cliffs to the sea defence which doubled as an undercliff walkway. He wasn't sure whether the vehicle had turned off or was hanging back: he couldn't hear it or see its lights, but that proved little, due to the noise of the wind and the curvature of the road. He told himself he was being hyperreactive, and made a mental note to watch it in future if he wanted to avoid drawing attention to himself. For now though, he decided he'd wait at the bottom for a few minutes before heading back up again. Pretend he was just being a storm-watcher.

In better weather, the pathway along the sea defence, being hidden from the road above, would have provided an attractive alternative route for him, for part of the way at least, but not today: the gale-force winds – hurricane-force, probably – were whipping the sea into a foaming frenzy and pushing waves and spray over the sea wall in numerous places turning the path into a dead end.

The beams from the headlights arrived first.

Jon didn't wait around to get a glimpse of who was driving the Range Rover, or whether they were going to get out and follow him. Because he knew. He knew before he heard the door open and he knew before he saw the grey suit.

He ran west along the undercliff path but in that direction it turned out to be "under construction" and he was forced to descend a set of stairs onto the beach there. The beach – consisting of a stretch of rounded stones and pebbles, as all the beaches were in that part of the world – was awash with spray and foam and the last gasp of an occasional rogue wave (although it was more of a grasp than a gasp, if you were unlucky enough to be caught by one) and he found himself clambering and slipping over the smooth wet stones in a kind of living nightmare.

Detective Nigel Stephens, a large man, was probably having more difficulty than Jon, but he kept coming, stumbling onwards with a fearful momentum – an unstoppable juggernaut – and there was nowhere, ultimately, that Jon could go. The beach was finite and the cliffs were unclimbable. And then, to make matters far worse, he lost his footing and fell awkwardly, jamming his shoulder painfully between two rocks and almost knocking his teeth out.

He twisted around onto his back in time to see Stephens, his grey trouser legs dark and wet from the rushing edges of the sea, standing still and reaching into his jacket. Pulled out a handgun, no silencer. Flashes of West Kensington, as Stephens put one leg on a rock to steady himself and raised his arm, and pointed his weapon. Jon froze. He was still wedged between the stones and realized there was nothing he could do to save himself.

Stephens fired.

And missed. Blasted some stones a couple of feet away. He shook his head and wiped the rain from his eyes.

And in the middle of this, all Jon could think was where *was* everyone? Was anyone *seeing* this? He was being executed by a policeman on a public beach in a civilized country, was there really no-one to witness it?

Stephens picked himself up, found his footing again, and began to move in closer, for a better shot Jon supposed. The screaming wind was ferocious now, the shotgun rain was still peppering the air – the wind was equal parts air, rain, spray and foam – and the wave height was increasing if anything, the waves crashing more loudly. It was pretty obvious why Stephens didn't need a silencer...

And straight away Jon remembered the gun at the bottom of his bag. (That he still even *had* the bag, was no doubt due to his having securely strapped it across himself earlier). How could he have forgotten about the gun! Quickly felt for it, pulled it out, safety catch off, and all the while not daring to look up...

But Stephens was still battling the elements and clambering in closer, slipping and staggering in equal measure.

Jon raised his Beretta. Stephens caught what was happening and stopped, but didn't react, just smiled and shook his head. Stumbled slightly and found his footing again. Jon knew he had to shoot, Stephens was, maybe twenty yards away and was unlikely to miss next time.

Like some nineteenth century pistol duel, with Jon still pointing his gun, Stephens raised his own gun again. The one advantage Jon had was that Stephens was to his east. Stephens had the wind and rain in his face and Jon did not.

Jon began squeezing the trigger but found he couldn't do it. It was ridiculous, his life was in danger, but he'd never shot anyone before and it wasn't so easy, even as this person was clearly about to—

Stephens fired. The moment he did, or perhaps an instant beforehand, his foot slipped and the bullet went wildly astray, and buried itself into the cliff face. This time Stephens cursed, and stood upright again, furious with himself.

Jon fired.

First time lucky: Stephens' left shoulder punched backwards, his arms suddenly splayed out like he was directing traffic (or an orchestra) and the big man stumbled backwards towards the waves, and then tripped and keeled over, falling out of sight down the slope of pebbles.

Had he killed him? He didn't hang around to check. He put the gun back in his bag, got up and scrambled over the rocks like a crab, half running, half sliding, not daring to look back until he reached the access road and the Range Rover that was still parked there. From that position, he could see roughly where Stephens had fallen, but as to whether the dark shape he could see was a body or just a rock, and if it was just rock whether the waves had claimed him, God only knew, and there was no time to find out. He ran back up to the road at the top, The Promenade, and then as calmly as he could, walked back to Lucinda. He calculated that if Stephens had known where he was staying he would have shot him in his bed. Far better to lie low for a while than be visible on the streets.

When he arrived, the front door was open. He'd assumed at first that he'd forgotten to close it, and it wasn't until he was safely inside and he'd shut the front door behind him that he recalled, with clarity, locking it when he'd left.

Supporting this conclusion to some extent, was the fact that there was someone else there.

92. <u>19° 31' 46" S 169° 26' 43" E</u> (Mount Yasur, Tanna Island)

At the same moment…
6pm Vanuatu Time (07:00 UTC)
Monday, 28 October

'So,' said Lang. 'I think this is probably the spot. Here.'

They'd been gradually making their way around the crater rim, for better viewing. For sure, the walls of the crater had grown progressively steeper and more vertiginous. The sun had just set and the fireworks display below them was becoming increasingly resplendent and dramatic.

Jagged flakes of tossed-out lava littered the ground around them like broken glass, as sulphurous smoke smeared the darkening sky.

'What spot,' asked Ruart. The viewing didn't look so different to what they'd been exposed to for the last five minutes or so – except the precipice was more sheer – and, more importantly perhaps, there was something in Lang's voice that bothered him. Something about his accent…

'For our little show, Robert,' Lang said.

Yours or the volcano's? he thought. He noticed Lena reaching around for something in her daypack.

'Or should I say Commandant,' said Lang. 'Commandant Laurent Ruart.'

Ruart uttered a silent curse.

'Of the *Préfecture de police* in Paris, no?' Lang said in flawless French. 'Who so *desperately* wants to find his man, this Dominique

Drayle… so desperate he is, that he spends his precious holidays away from his dear wife and children, scouring the great oceans of the world, the Indian, the Pacific… Well. We all know how much a Frenchman likes his family holidays, so we know it must be important to him. Ah, but then one remembers that he is the brother of Constance…'

'In English, Dominique,' said Lena.

Dominique? Ruart looked into Lang's pig eyes and the ugly truth became horribly clear. Lang, or rather Drayle, smiled at the look of understanding and horror that must have crossed his face.

'Precisely,' Lang/Drayle said to him, reverting to English. 'It's your eureka moment, I can tell. That must be satisfying for you, surely? Monsieur le cop? To finally have the answer you've been seeking for so long? Where is this Dominique Drayle? Isn't it so often the case. The answer is right under your big French nose all along.'

He was rapidly calculating his chances of survival, looking for a possible way out, but every model yielded the same result. It was clearly no coincidence – so to speak – that they'd chosen this moment, this place, to reveal the truth. Lang/Drayle would have covered every conceivable response – even the quickest of evasive or offensive manoeuvres would be doomed to failure. Sure enough, when he looked across at Lena, he saw what she'd been reaching for in her daypack: she was training a gun on him – a Sig Mosquito with a silencer. He turned back to Lang/Drayle.

'Dominique Drayle.' It was all he could think of to say (and he had to buy some time somehow, after all). He still couldn't quite believe it, though. The guy looked nothing like his photos – not a single one. 'I'm not sure I really believe you.'

'Of course not. I had a little work done, as they say. Do you think it makes me look younger? OK. Let me see. Proof. Shall I tell you what it was like to fuck your sister, perhaps?'

Ruart came close to charging Drayle and taking them both, him and Drayle, over the edge. Lena wouldn't have had time to react and it would have been all over in the blink of an eye. All over for him, but all over for Drayle too. But Drayle seemed to read his mind and he stepped back away from the brink. *I should have done it when I had the chance.*

'How long have you known?' Ruart asked. He directed the question to both of them, but turned to face Lena. She maintained her cold, steady gaze. A real killer, that one.

'Does it really matter?' Drayle said. 'You could ask a whole lot of questions and I could give you a whole lot of answers, but what would the point of that be? In the circumstances. It'd simply be a waste of everyone's time, wouldn't it. Ours *and* yours.'

There was little doubt what they intended, but hope was a weapon, and he still had a little of it left…

'One or two answers… two minutes to satisfy my curiosity,' he said, doing everything he could to avoid losing it, and to keep at bay thoughts of his family. 'If it's not too much to ask.'

'Well it is, actually. Now here's what's going to happen and I'm afraid it may seem a bit unpalatable at first.'

Now, he thought. Now would be a good time for that piece of molten rock to come hurtling down on top of Lena. He promised the god of good luck that if it did, he'd never doubt his existence again.

'You see that lake down there?' Drayle said. 'We're going to get you to dive into it.'

Dive into it. Into a molten lake of magma.

He looked at Drayle and then Lena. Hoping a last minute stroke of genius would descend upon him. But nothing came.

'Look at it, go on. Turn around. That's an *order*, Commandant.'

He slowly turned and looked over the edge, and down into the depths of the crater. In the pit at the bottom, glowing a brilliant red in the tropical dusk, the magma boiled and popped and churned to an endless soundtrack of booms and roars: the resonant cannonade that filled the air and shook your very soul. The magma itself, with its irregular pattern of almost geometric cracks, reminded him of cobblestones. Massive, shape-shifting cobblestones. It wouldn't be like diving into a lake; it would be like diving into a street.

It was Lena's turn this time to read his mind.

'Imagine you're diving into an ocean,' she said. 'A cool, deep ocean.'

But he didn't have time to imagine for long. Drayle's voice cut in behind him.

'Now put your hands behind your back.'

Ruart turned. Lena was still pointing her gun at him, itching to pull the trigger judging by the look in her eyes.

'Now just stop for a moment and think about this—' he began.

Drayle punched him, hard, under his right eye. It was a swift left hook from nowhere that hit the pause button in his brain. He reeled. Sound and vision took a moment to return.

'... what I say,' Drayle was saying. 'You listen, and you *do*. Or else...' And he indicated Lena's gun.

'It appears I'm going to die anyway.'

'We're all going to die, Ruart. You'll just be heading off a little early. But if you don't want Lena here to blow your kneecaps off, turn around and put your hands behind your back.'

'It's your balls that'll be going first,' said Lena, who'd altered the angle of the gun barrel to match her threat. At the same time, Drayle had produced a set of handcuffs.

'So why the handcuffs. If I am diving.'

'Put it this way. You won't be needing your arms for swimming. Now *turn around.*'

A loose idea began to form in his head, but it wasn't fully formed. Nevertheless, an unformed idea was always better than no idea. He slowly shuffled around until he was facing the precipice again.

'Hands behind your back.'

Ruart offered his left hand first.

'*Both* of them,' Drayle said, cuffing his left wrist.

Luckily Ruart knew a thing or two about handcuffs...

'Hurry up...'

He quickly spun around to his left, making sure he kept Drayle between him and Lena's gun, and managed, in one lightning-fast movement, to both snatch the handcuffs away from Drayle's grasp and cuff Drayle's left wrist. Tying yourself to the dragon: a particularly desperate – and highly unreliable – form of insurance.

From that point, a terrible, close-proximity struggle ensued, the two men handcuffed left wrist to left wrist: Drayle was trying to either knock Ruart out or push him away for Lena to get a cleaner shot; Ruart was attempting to keep Drayle close, and at the same time he was hoping he could steer Drayle away from the crater's edge and towards the volcano's steep outer slope – if he could get him to that, they could roll down the mountain, away from Lena, and maybe Drayle would hit his head, maybe Ruart could somehow stay alive...

But Drayle was too strong, he sensed what Ruart was doing and pulled him back. Tried to head-butt and elbow him. Ruart had his right arm pressed hard against Drayle's throat...

'Shoot him!' Drayle managed to croak at Lena.

Drayle managed to push Ruart out to one side, and Lena took a shot, but she was too cautious and it went wide, raising a puff of ash about five metres behind them. Drayle got his leg under Ruart's and managed to roll him and for an instant there was separation again before Ruart pulled himself up into Drayle's face again like a tango dancer. Again Lena fired a shot and missed.

'For fuck's sake *shoot* him!' Drayle screamed at Lena.

'I'm *trying* to! Where's the key? Get the key!'

'In my pocket but I'm kind of busy right now, fucking just *shoot...arrrgghhh*!'

Ruart had grabbed Drayle between his legs. He had a good handful of penis and testicles and was squeezing as hard as he could...

'*How does it feel to have your*—' Ruart hissed, before Drayle's right fist hit him in the side of the head and the lights went out again. It was only for a second, but it was all Drayle needed – he twisted Ruart around and Lena fired three shots in quick succession and the third one hit him in the stomach.

It felt like he'd been kicked, but he knew what had happened. He didn't wait for the pain to kick in. While the other two hesitated, taking in the changed circumstances, Ruart made one of the fastest and most significant decisions of his life. Knowing there was a good chance he'd bleed to death no matter what happened now, he mustered the last of his strength and sprang with all his might, pushing past Drayle in a twisting motion and plunging over the edge of the precipice.

The dive, just as they asked.

His left arm was almost yanked out of its socket as he slammed into the loose, crumbling rock and ash of the crater wall. Felt a satisfying sliding feeling as Drayle followed him over and down, but then another painful jerk as everything, all movement, abruptly stopped. He was flat against the near-vertical slope – any more sheer and he would have been dangling in space. His feet couldn't have found any purchase on the ash even if he'd wanted it. He and Drayle had stopped falling, and looking up, he could see that Drayle had managed to get a handhold, using his free right arm, on a knob of rock jutting out just below the cliff edge.

'Lena!' Drayle yelled.

From Ruart's angle, he couldn't see Lena – which was possibly a good thing, given her proven willingness to shoot him, although there was hardly any purpose to be served now. From their point of view, Ruart may as well have been dead already: he wasn't moving, not just because he was content to see how this was going to play out, but also because he couldn't. He'd used up the last of his reserves pushing himself and Drayle over the cliff. He was done.

'Lena!' Drayle yelled again. 'Help me!'

'How?' Ruart couldn't see her but he could hear her voice. 'I'd never be able to pull you both up.'

'Well just try!'

'What, and fall in too?'

'Lena you filthy Russian whore, pull me up! Or so help me God I'll—'

'I can't do it, Dominique. I can't, I'm sorry! but it's not possible!'

'*Fuck*! I will fucking *kill* you!'

There was a pause. Then another jerk as Drayle and Ruart slipped down a centimetre, before stopping again. A moan from Drayle.

'Lena! Please…'

He sounded drained. Ruart doubted Drayle could hold on for much longer. As for himself, he could no longer feel his left arm and the pain in his stomach wasn't so bad if he didn't think about it. He could feel the blood flowing down his left leg, and he wondered if it was forming rivulets on the steep wall of ash. The ash and the blood and the magma. All grey and red, red and grey.

He felt as though he was about to faint. He wanted his final thoughts to be about the things that mattered and he focussed on Constance and on Marine and of course Madeleine and dear little Jack. He hoped Jack would be brave, when the time came. He hoped he'd be remembered for his successes and not his failures. He hoped—

They slipped another centimetre. Another snarl of anguish from Drayle. Nothing from Lena.

Looking down, past feet that already looked like they didn't belong to him, there it was, the refulgent lake of magma. Liquid rock, boiling and flipping, cracking, mocking... incandescent manhole to the centre of the earth... coruscating porthole to the limits of the imagination... Just a small, final slip-of-a-grip away from molten consummation—

And there it was.

A final jerk

downwards, a yell and a curse

from Drayle and the slide

began, steadily

at first, and then picking up speed

sliding, bumping,

  bouncing

  flipping—

93. <u>19° 31' 46" S 169° 26' 43" E</u> (Mount Yasur, Tanna Island)

6.10pm Vanuatu Time (07:10 UTC)
Monday, 28 October

'Lena!'

They'd just gone over and Dominique was yelling at her. It had happened so quickly. She had no idea how Ruart had done it. It was a miracle they hadn't kept going. She'd rushed to the edge and there was Dominique's hand: muscular, veins bulging, knuckles white, clasped around the only solid chunk of rock in the area.

'Lena! Help me!

What could she do? She'd never be able to pull Dominique up, let alone the two of them. The moment she grabbed Dominique's hand and he let go of the rock, that would be it.

'How? I'd never be able to pull you both up.'

'Well just try!'

Dominique was red-faced and angry, as furious as a dangerous predator caught in a trap. Which is exactly what he was.

'But I'd fall too.' Dominique, she knew, would have no hesitation in pulling her in with him if it meant there was an outside chance of saving himself. Or even if there wasn't. He'd make sure she went with him.

'Lena will you pull me up! Or God help me!'

'I can't do it, I'm sorry. It simply isn't possible.'

'*Fuck.*'

In fact the more she thought about it, the worse the situation became. She could hardly go for help. And the longer Dominique held on, the greater the chances of them being seen by someone. She'd be almost better off if—

She watched on helplessly with mixed feelings of horror and hope as Dominique's hand slipped down another notch. She couldn't believe he was still holding on. The man was powerful, she'd give him that.

The seconds that ticked by felt more like hours. There was another slip and then, finally, it happened. Dominique's strength gave out at last.

She kept an eye on them as they fell, tied together. First they slid, with Dominique, using his one free hand, desperately grabbing at the loose flakes of lava and rubble and then, where the slope became even steeper, they bounced once, twice, and then cartwheeled, limbs splayed like two rag dolls. They descended into the darkness and into the bright red glow of the magma lake.

By the end, she could barely see them – they were just a cohesive small dark blob, they could have been a rock, bouncing down the slope, and then a small shadow, and then nothing... until a small spot on the surface of a darker section of the lava suddenly flared up.

It reminded her of a fly hitting an electric insect killer, with its triumphant incendiary send-off.

94. <u>50° 47' 25" N 0° 0' 0" E</u>
("Lucinda", Peacehaven)

At the same moment...
7.10am Greenwich Mean Time (07:10 UTC)
Monday, 28 October

Absorbed. He was completely absorbed. Perhaps too much so.

Only ten minutes had passed since he'd arrived back at Lucinda, but it felt more like ten years. The storm outside was at its height, the wind was howling, peeling tiles off roofs, tossing rubbish down the street... and Jon hardly noticed. Because ten minutes ago, when he walked into the living room, he had an uninvited visitor sitting there, waiting for him. Isla.

* * *

He stared at her. It was really her. She was still wearing the same clothes (as was he, of course) – dark blue jeans, tan boots, brown top and a dark green cotton jacket that dampness had turned to virtual black. And it wasn't just the jacket; all of her, she was dripping wet. She looked cold.

'I'm sorry,' she said. 'I broke in.'

'How did you find me?'

She smiled and wiped some of the moisture off her face and pulled back her red hair which, like her jacket, had become several shades darker from the soaking. Her brown eyes, as she looked at him, were several shades warmer.

'The restaurant,' she said. 'I was there.'

'What?' He checked the street through the blinds and made sure no-one could see in.

'What is it?'

He shook his head. 'What do you mean you were there?' He was sounding more unfriendly than he would have liked. But these were difficult times.

'In the restaurant where your friend wrote the address on the table, in salt.'

'You could read that?'

'You could see it a mile off.'

He had to smile at that, at least. 'So why were you following me? In the first place?'

She didn't answer.

A cardboard box bounced down the footpath outside and into the front gate. He looked out again.

'Hey, are you expecting someone?'

'I hope not. You must be freezing, though. There's a tumble dryer here that works I think. If you want, I could...'

'Great. Thanks.' She stood and began removing her jacket.

'You can use the bedroom through there if you like.'

'It's OK. Do you have a bathrobe or a towel?'

By the time he returned to the living room, she was naked. Not a stitch. Stark-naked and completely unconcerned about his presence. She was busy emptying the pockets of her jacket and jeans.

'Thanks,' she said, accepting the overcoat he handed to her.

'It was all I could find.'

She didn't seem to be in any hurry to put it on – in fact she draped it over a chair as she checked her phone. She caught his look. She laughed.

'Oh sorry.' She went back to scrolling through her messages. 'I hope I'm not... um... offending you. I do this for a living... Life modelling... And, you know... I always forget it's not so... normal. For other people.'

She finished with her phone and put it down.

'No, it's fine,' he said. Her body was what was fine. She had creamy skin – English skin – and a perfect figure, in his eyes at least.

Champagne glass breasts (saucer not flute) and fruit-shaped buttocks (pear not peach). He tried not to stare, not to look at all, but—

'Are you admiring my tattoo? Or do you hate it?'

He could hardly have missed it. On her right buttock, there was an eye-catching geometric pattern, maybe two or three inches across, in blue and red and green that looked, to him, slightly Islamic. He told her. It even looked a bit familiar...

'So what is it? It looks—'

'It's a long story.'

And she finally put the coat on – much to Jon's relief, in a way – and then he gave her a brief summary of what had just happened to him on the beach.

* * *

He was beginning to doubt his own words, doubt that it had really happened. He could tell, though, that Isla had no such problem.

'I still can't believe the way he came after me. No questions, not a word. Like an executioner. I think at one point he was actually *smiling*.'

'It's called sadism. I told you to watch out for Detective Stephens. How sure are you that you killed him?'

'I'm not. I mean he went down. And he didn't get up, or not that I saw. No-one followed me back. I'm sure he doesn't know about this house.'

'You'd better hope so.' She checked the street, just as he had earlier. '*We'd* better hope so. These men... Have you still got your gun?'

He nodded and walked over to his BOAC bag. Pulled out the Beretta.

'Recognise it?' he said. 'It's your boyfriend's.'

She ignored the barb. 'Is it loaded?'

'It was, at least. Obviously.' He fiddled with the magazine until it released. Noticed Isla had her hands over her ears. Not engendering confidence, then. 'I haven't fired one before. Hadn't.'

'And floored a cop with your first shot. Very impressive.'

'So he was really a detective, that guy?'

She nodded. 'And as you just found out, completely psychotic. Well-connected though, knows all the right people. Meaning all the wrong ones.'

The thought of Stephens, dead or alive, seemed to draw a cold fog into the room.

'So where's Irwin?' he asked, as much to break the silence as anything else. In a way, he didn't want to know.

She stared at him for a moment, with wide brown eyes. He almost turned around, to see what she was looking at. And then he wondered if she'd fallen into a trance.

'I killed him.'

It was his turn to stare.

'You...?' He wanted to ask how, but there were too many questions. 'Well we're a couple of killers then, aren't we.'

'At least I'm not a cop killer.'

She threw him an uneven smile that was soft and apologetic and heart-warming in a way he didn't fully understand. And he thought how easy it would have been for him to have walked over to her at that moment – and it was ludicrous, crazy, he'd just killed a man, a *cop*, of all the moments – but he could have walked over and put his hands around her shoulders and pulled her up, overcoat and all, and kissed her, kissed those vowelly, red-brown lips, and pushed his hands up and through her thickly tangled wet hair...

He shook the image free and chose the moment to excuse himself, and put her clothes in the dryer.

'I think...' he said, when he returned to the living room. 'I think you need to explain to me why you were following me in the first place. And following the judge, Martin Nevers, I know about that too. What's he got to do with any of this?'

Isla looked down for a moment, then stood up, wrapped her arms about her as if she were suddenly cold and peered out through the blinds. Turned back and sat down. Sighed, and eventually spoke.

'I grew up in Switzerland. I was adopted. By a Spanish couple. For some reason they decided I was the independent type and called me Isla, Spanish for "island". They got that right I suppose. Unless we follow our names, I can never decide which it is. Anyway, we moved from Spain to Switzerland when I was two.'

'You don't look very Spanish, did they adopt you there?'

'In London.'

'Ah, well that...'

She frowned, deep in thought, before continuing. 'In Zurich I got mixed up with a bit of a rich crowd, kids of European... captains of industry, that kind of thing, and I... I went off the rails a little. And later... when I was old enough to know better, I met Irwin in a bar and... He was the finance world's golden boy back then. At least in Zurich. I really had no idea what I was dealing with. I *did* know that he was married though. So no excuses. I was a bored, naive... or foolish... excitement-seeking young girl in a Big Money town. We moved to Paris... well, *he* did, he and his wife, and I followed... I think it was in Paris that he met Dominique Drayle... You won't have heard of him, but—'

'I have, actually. Russian mafia. Right?'

'How did you...?'

'A little private detective told me.'

She looked at him for a moment. 'You're not quite what I was expecting.'

'Neither are you.'

She shook her head as if she couldn't quite believe she was there, in that house, with him. Or that's the way Jon saw it. And he'd been wrong before, but Isla seemed different...

'Then my life started to unravel,' she went on. 'I mean, *really* unravel. At the seams. Irwin began to... treat me badly. Physically, you know? And I began to have my suspicions about... not just the people he was meeting with, but his wife... She was some mouse, you see, from Prague. She just... faded from view. But he kept up the pretence about his marriage so he could take other mistresses. He'd tell them, when he was running to me, that I was his wife, and vice versa. As a method of juggling affairs, it sure was a solid business model.'

'And you *killed* him.'

Pause.

'Fishing knife, since you asked.'

'When?'

'It was a tribal... a traditional knife. From the South Pacific. When? The night before last, the night I saw you. In that flat.

He was trying to…' She shook her head. 'That was the flat we moved to, after Paris. Everything became clearer, after we moved to London. I was doing my own… research, you see. Which was when I found out about things. About Drayle and that crooked cop Stephens, and what they do. About Irwin's double-life with his mistresses. Everything Irwin touched turned to… not gold but you know, the opposite. It turned to shit. The stuff these people are into. I overheard a conversation recently, about someone having to travel up to Scotland and dumping someone – dumping *him*, whoever *he* was, dumping the *bag* in a deep, dark loch. I wanted to believe Irwin was talking about someone else, nothing to do with him, maybe something he'd heard about or read, but I came to realise I was kidding myself. So you know. I knew, sooner or later, that was going to be me, in that bag in the loch. Nessie… that's her name, isn't it?… Nessie food.'

'Hang on.' Any mention of Stephens gave him a sick feeling in his stomach and he went to double-check the front door was locked. There was always the prospect that he hadn't actually killed him, despite what his gut instinct was telling him. And even dead, Stephens was still a formidable proposition somehow – Jon wouldn't have put it past his *ghost* to do something. He shook these meandering thoughts from his head. A slide into insanity, at this point, would have been unhelpful.

'So anyway,' Isla said when he was back in the room, 'it was in the course of my investigations that I was following *you*.'

'Why me?'

'I first learnt about your wife… your ex-wife, sorry, Romy…'

'God. Romy.'

'… it was just after she'd become Irwin's other mistress. This was when we were still in Paris.'

'Are you sure Irwin didn't say anything about her?'

She shook her head. 'I promise you. He's never even mentioned her name. Not to me. But I found out about her, and recently I came across an email that referred to the money that went into your account by mistake. Romy's mistake. You were obviously in danger, and I wanted to find out exactly what was going on. So… I spied on you.' And she shrugged, as if apologizing.

His brain was trying to process this new information.

'I was there when Stephens found Irwin's body I think,' he said, 'In Soho… yesterday? What day is it?'

'That would have made him mad. Not so long ago… it was around the time I was checking up on Irwin and planning my escape… I realized I was being followed by him. By Stephens. He even came to my life modelling classes, he was really brazen about it. At first I just thought he was some kind of old pervert.'

Both of them sat there, lost in their thoughts for a moment as the wind continued to throw its skull-clattering tantrum outside. A car approached, drove past… and kept going.

'Funnily enough,' Isla said suddenly, once it was just them and the wind again, 'ironically… it was my fault you ever had anything to do with Irwin. You *or* Romy. Because it was when Irwin was checking up on *me*… investigating *my* background, that he found out about Nevers, and I think he must have started blackmailing him or something. And then… this is the bit that's not clear to me… but there was some connection between Nevers and Romy, they used the same solicitor I think—'

'Brilling,' he said. 'Paul Brilling, that's right. He was my solicitor, that's why Romy used him.'

'Right. So that's how Irwin met Romy, probably, through that connection, and then everything flowed from that, all the business with the money into the wrong account and so on.'

'So Nevers' death… Was that Irwin's doing, do you think?'

He'd assumed that Isla didn't know about the will, and about Nevers supposedly being his father, but at the mention of Nevers' death, she looked almost more upset than he was. He could have sworn there was a watery glaze over her eyes. Was it only just sinking in, perhaps, that she'd killed someone? She could hardly have been missing Irwin, from what she'd told him. It was probably all just catching up with her. And him, too, for that matter.

She slowly shook her head. 'Nothing would surprise me with these animals,' she said in a low-toned voice.

No, he thought. Nothing would surprise him either. He thought about Nevers, and Romy and Emerald. And Detective Nigel Stephens trying to kill him on the beach. But something else was bothering him. Something that was just hovering there in the wings of his mind, waiting its turn on the stage...

He was distracted as another car drove past.

But it didn't. It was pulling up outside, and with a short, braking squeal, it stopped altogether and the engine cut.

'That's here,' he said.

95. <u>50° 47' 25" N 0° 0' 0" E</u>
("Lucinda", Peacehaven)

7.20am Greenwich Mean Time (07:20 UTC)
Monday, 28 October

'Quickly,' Jon said. 'There's a way out the... Stay away from the window!'

'Didn't you say his car was grey? Stephens's?' She joined him in the hall. 'This one's yellow.'

'This way. Grey, yeah, but he may have friends, wouldn't you think?'

They were in the kitchen, at the rear door of the house.

'Hold on. Yellow?'

There was the sound of a key rattling in the front door lock, and a curse, and the sound of the door opening.

'Bertie!!' Alastair's voice echoed through the house. 'Will you *get* in*side*!'

Jon breathed out. 'Thank God. It's Alastair.'

'Who's Alastair?'

Alastair was standing in the doorway, wearing an army-green, all-weather jacket with the hood up. He barely raised an eyebrow when he saw Jon, who'd just returned to the front hall.

'Ah. So you *are* here. I thought you were still up in London. It's this bloody storm... oh hello there.'

'Alastair... Isla. Isla, Alastair.'

'Hello,' she said.

'Wonderful, well I don't want to get in the way, if I'd known you two love birds were here keeping an eye on things, I wouldn't have needed to drag *both* of us out of bed at robinfart, would I Bertie. Everything OK?'

'Fine other than—'

'Bertie! Will you kindly bloody well get *in* here, how many times do I have to ask politely?! Unbelievable. He's fascinated by storms. Probably because dogs hate them so much. My-enemy's-enemy way of thinking. *BERTIE!!*'

Bertie came trotting on through, past the guard of honour in the hallway…

'Hello Bertie,' Jon offered.

… and straight on to ensure all was in order in the kitchen.

Looking over Alastair's shoulder, Jon could see the Mustang – out there in all that greyness and gloom, it was like a little portable burst of sunshine.

Once Alastair had settled in and recounted, in some detail, his own dramas, including having to deal with the "wind-blown tarpaulins, downed plane trees and toppled cranes" – in fact, it was, according to Alastair, nothing short of a miracle he and Bertie made it out of London alive – Jon was able to give him a potted version of recent events.

'So in a nutshell,' Jon said, after he'd finished, 'there are now bodies all over the place, and Isla and I are most definitely going to be "wanted for questioning", so not an ideal situation.'

'I know *exactly* how you must feel, dear boy. Well that won't do at all, will it. You know, keep this to yourselves, but the word on the street is that our good old MI5 has been following this Russian crowd for a while and they're well aware the Met's been infiltrated.'

'Word on the street?' Isla said, with a mischievous glint in her eye. 'Or maybe you're one of them yourself. An *MI5*.'

'So the best thing,' Alastair went on, after a small hesitation, but otherwise ignoring the interjection. 'The best thing I think, at least until they sort this godawful business out, is for the two of you to skedaddle.'

'Skedaddle. Skedaddle how?' Jon asked.

'Let me think, let me think.' And in a matter of seconds, and with a big frown and a contorted face, he managed to squeeze out an idea. 'I've got it. I have a fisherman friend in Rye. Mad as a cut snake (speaking of Black Mambas). I'd lay odds he'd be willing to take you out. For the right fee.'

'Take us out?'

'Out there!' said Alastair pointing seaward.

'Where to? Africa?'

'Not exactly, but you're warm.'

Alastair decided they had to get as far away as possible and as quickly as possible – an uncontroversial proposition in itself – and the airports were out ("quickest way to get yourselves caught"). The only thing for it was to catch a fishing trawler to France, and to make their own way through Spain to Morocco ("basically you'll be reverse-refugees… anti-refugees if you like… going against the flow of traffic, it's the *only* way to travel"), and *only* once they'd set foot on the African continent should they allow themselves the luxury of going to an airport and travelling by air. They'd have to split up after they arrived in France of course, they'd be way too conspicuous as a couple. And then, in Africa, they'd be well-advised to head for Honiara.

'Honiara?' asked Jon.

'The Solomon Islands, East of New Guinea, North-east of Australia. Middle of the South Pacific.'

'Why?'

'Because like Wales, no-one goes there, and because *un*like Wales, it's on the other side of the bloody world. And it's beautiful. Did you know it's only twenty-five miles across, and ninety miles long, this is the main island, Guadalcanal, and it has a mountain that's higher than the highest mountain in Australia? Nearly eight thousand feet? Turquoise waters, tropical bloody… God! *I'll* go there if you don't! Anyway I have contacts there. But first things first. We have to get you out of bloody England.'

'You mean go out in *that*?' Isla asked. 'But it's a big storm.'

'It'll be a bit bumpy I expect, that is true my dear. In fact this will interest you. I just received a text from a friend of mine…' Alastair fumbled around for his phone. 'Here it is. From *Nazaré* in Portugal, don't ask me where that is, but some chap there has just surfed the largest wave ever surfed. This morning! Half an hour ago! A hundred bloody feet high! So yes, it won't exactly be smooth sailing so to speak, but Alan's an absolutely five star skipper, and if anyone can get you to a sleepy little seaside village in Brittany, unscathed and unarrested, it's Alan. He could do it drunk with his eyes closed... in fact I suspect that's how he *does* do it. But he's a good one, isn't he Bertie. We went on a fishing trip once with Alan, didn't we. Bertie thought all his Christmases had come at once, with all those fish jumping around on the deck. Cat heaven, wasn't it.' Alastair suddenly donned his serious mask. 'It's not ideal, I know, but there's no other way. And it's so bloody mad...'

'They won't think to look for us there,' said Jon.

'Exactly!'

'At the bottom of the Channel,' said Isla.

Before they sat down to nut out some details, Jon couldn't resist commenting on something that had come up earlier.

'So Alastair. How do you know all this stuff. Did Isla nail it? Are you MI5? Is this one of your safe-houses?'

'MI5? Me? My dear boy, can you seriously imagine me as a *spy*? Ha! Now where were we...'

* * *

And thus plans were drawn up, and arrangements made for Jon and Isla to leave Lucinda, and Alastair and Bertie, and England. Effective immediately.

And the sooner the better, too. There was no telling what would happen once Stephens' body was found – *if* he was even dead of course, and *if* the sea hadn't, in its fury, whisked him away. Jon was itching to check, to see if there was a body there, but it was too risky for him, or for either of the others, to go anywhere near it.

It was a good plan, Jon had to admit. Radical, but preferable to the alternatives. And he was with Isla too, if only for a short time, so that was a plus. Things could be far worse. And he could... should, by rights... have been dead by now, so all of this was really a bonus. Still, and despite owning a plethora of reasons to be feeling insecure, he couldn't shake an uneasy feeling he was missing something, and wondered if it wasn't that thing at the back of his mind that refused to reveal itself. Something to do with Isla, he felt.

He'd have to leave those worries aside for the moment though, because it was time to pack for France, for Africa, for the South Pacific.

96. <u>17° 42' 5" S 168° 19' 11" E</u> (Port Vila Airport)

2.15pm Vanuatu Time (03:15 UTC)
Tuesday, 29 October

She was finally off the plane. It was nearly thirty-two hours since she'd boarded the first one – in Aberdeen, Scotland – and if it proved one thing, it was that she could never be an astronaut, or a cosmonaut. Packed into a small space like that for so long... she might have been a fish, but she was no sardine.

The black tarmac shimmered as it radiated waves of heat skywards, back to the source. And walking across it, Ishiko made her way towards the airport terminal. Surrounded by the wildly green, tropical hills, she should have been elated, at least after the million greys of Aberdeen. The *Coral Sea*. The fish! But the enthusiasm just wasn't materializing.

She hoisted the strap of her stone-grey Muji bag and swapped shoulders. *That* was the problem. What the bag contained. The Decagon, it was like a bad luck charm, it had only brought her problems. Including the scar on her forearm, which meant she had to wear a long-sleeved top, even in this heat. The Decagon had done that.

It had also made her doubt everything about her life that she'd taken for granted. All that she'd taken as certain. Maybe that was a good thing, but why didn't she feel any happier, then? She was definitely doubting her job, if you could even call it that, and the people she worked for. Well not for much longer. She'd get rid of this thing and get rid of this job. And then she'd be free. As free as the fish in the sea.

She could go somewhere and start living a normal life. Put an end to her solitary existence. Find a lover. Like Bertrand, for example, the man she'd killed.

She knew the truth of it, though. She'd killed her soulmate. Her instincts told her that then, and they were telling her that now.

And the Decagon had done that too.

* * *

An hour later, in her room, she used her laptop to connect to the hotel's Wi-Fi. She sent a message to say she'd arrived and received a quick response. Again, there was no sign-off (just a smiley-face, even worse), but something told her it was written by a male. She hoped it was Aleks but accepted it probably wasn't. She didn't care, just wanted to get this over and done with. They could take their Decagon and leave her alone.

The message read:

```
Welcome to Vanuatu.

Meet tomorrow morning at 9.00 a.m. at the
Nambawan Cafe in Port Vila. It's in town, on
the water.

Bring your things. Including the thing.    : )
```

97. <u>17° 44' 14" S 168° 18' 44" E</u> (Nambawan Cafe, Port Vila)

9am Vanuatu Time (22:00 UTC)
Wednesday, 30 October

The Nambawan cafe was located in the centre of town, and right on the edge of Vila Bay. Partly undercover, partly outdoors, it was full of backpackers and travellers from around the globe. Eating their Big Fella baguettes and drinking their fruit smoothies and mega mugs of Tanna coffee. The cafe sat near the end of a row of dive shops, and restaurants and tourist-targeted clothing stalls stretching along a section of the waterfront. And the view was sunny, and watery and warm. Mainstays clinked, boats bobbed about, outboard motors growled around.

Ishiko was right on time – she wanted to impress on her final job – and chose a table in the shade. She was wearing black shorts and a black, long-sleeved top – not a great choice for the tropics (she'd buy something more colourful at one of the stalls) – as well as flip-flops, a navy New York Yankees baseball cap and large, dark sunglasses. Put her Muji bag down on the chair next to her and looked around. Not that she knew who she was looking for.

She didn't have to wait long. Disappointingly, it wasn't a man who approached her, but a woman. Maybe twenty-five or thirty, medium height, wearing a flimsy plum-brown dress, pink floral Haviana flip-flops and a white cap. Like Ishiko, she wore sunglasses, but unlike Ishiko she had ice-blonde hair spilling down from under her cap, which stood out starkly against the jubilant deep browns of her tanned olive skin and her dress. She guessed, or maybe hoped, she was Ukrainian. Maybe one of *the* Ukrainians.

'Ishiko?'

'Yes.'

'Good,' the blonde said, and stared at the grey Muji bag. 'Do you have everything with you?' Her accent was consistent with Ishiko's guess.

'Yes.'

'*All* your things?'

'Yes.'

'And the...' The woman let the gap speak for itself.

'Yes.'

'OK. Good. Follow me.'

'Where are we going?'

'You'll see.'

She followed the blonde woman to the water's edge and along the main path there. She hadn't seen the woman's eyes – which was annoying, although she could hardly complain, she was wearing sunglasses herself – but she guessed her eyes were blue. She'd put money on it.

They came to a jetty where a dark-skinned local man, a Melanesian, was waiting in a small runabout. The engine was running. The blonde indicated to her to go ahead.

'Where are we going?' she asked for a second time. 'I thought... I only... hand it over, that is all?'

'Oh but he wants to *thank* you, Ishiko. You *must* come. It's not far, the boat's moored just around by that island over there.'

She stepped into the runabout, followed by the woman, and the three of them roared off, bouncing over the glittering waters.

'What... is... your... name?!' Ishiko had to shout to be heard.

The woman looked at her for a moment. She was either scrutinizing her, or making up a name, or thinking of something else, Ishiko couldn't tell under the sunglasses. She may not have even been looking at her. 'Lena!' she shouted back eventually.

Lena. Could easily be Ukrainian, she thought, although it was probably made up, too.

They rounded the island – Iririki Island, which sat in the bay just out from the town centre – and eventually came to what looked like a badly-neglected fishing trawler, covered in rust. She saw the name: *Blue Shefa*. She'd been expecting a luxury yacht, something more like the *Diamond Moon*. It didn't feel quite right, but she wasn't really worried. They had their Decagon, why would they want to see her if not to thank her? And anyway, the first sign of trouble and she'd dive overboard and swim away like a fish. She'd done it before after all. Swim away and leave them with their precious artefact.

There were more local men on board, and one of them helped her up and onto the boat, which looked even more dilapidated up close.

Lena followed her on board as the runabout sped off. And then, almost straight away, the *Blue Shefa*'s engines fired up.

Ishiko turned to Lena. 'Are we going somewhere?'

Which was the last thing she remembered.

98. <u>17° 36' 45" S 167° 23' 49" E</u> (Coral Sea, about 100km W of Port Vila)

2.30pm Vanuatu Time (03:30 UTC)
Wednesday, 30 October

When she next opened her eyes, Ishiko had no idea how long she'd been 'out' for. She had more pressing concerns anyway.

She was lying on the deck of the *Blue Shefa* and the sun was shining down onto her face. Her neck hurt, and she had a splitting headache. Worse, a Melanesian man was tying her legs together at the ankles with a rope. Two others, she couldn't see who exactly, but they had large black leathery hands, were holding her arms. Standing off to one side, next to Lena (who was still in her brown dress, and her white cap and sunglasses) was an evil-looking Asian man, possibly Chinese or Korean, in a short-sleeved batik shirt and wearing the biggest gold watch she'd ever seen.

'So you're awake,' Lena said. 'Just in time. Did you have a nice sleep?'

She said nothing.

'You're probably wondering where you are, are you?'

She had no intention of speaking to this woman.

'We're over the New Hebrides Trench.' Lena was looking at a GPS device in her hand. 'And right here... the depth is... six thousand six hundred and forty-eight metres.' She looked up again and unhunched her shoulders. 'Which answers your earlier question about where you're going. Actually... you asked where *we're* going. *We're* going that way.' She was pointing out to sea, to the north-west. And then she pointed to the deck. 'You're going that way.'

And then, in an instant, her demeanour changed. She was a snarling beast, hissing like a snake, like an evil spirit. 'What did you *expect*, Ishiko? A *medal*? You *retard*. You stupid little *cunt*. And so, yes, this is what happens when you fuck with people like *Mr Drayle*.'

And then, in a calmer, lower voice, she said: 'This is what happens when you fuck with people like *me*.'

Lena picked up the Muji bag which was sitting on the deck beside her. Pulled out the Decagon. Its silver and speckled gems glinted in the sun.

'A lot of good it did you. You really must be a little bit backward. You probably have no idea how much this is worth, do you.'

There was something about the way Lena was holding the artefact, showing it off, and gloating, that made Ishiko, suddenly, very angry. It made her realise that perhaps, yes, they had become friends after all, she and her notorious companion, the Decagon.

'I know... what it is worth,' Ishiko said. 'It is worth... shoving up your asshole.'

Lena snorted.

'Thanks for the special delivery, by the way. It's especially lucky for us. You see, we realised how valuable the geometry in the design was. Although I'll bet you didn't, did you. But we did, and we *thought* we were being smart by making sure there were no other copies out there. So no-one was even allowed to take a photograph of it. And then after you stole it, as it happened, we miraculously stumbled upon... oh sorry, your late friend *Aleks* helped us to stumble upon a copy of the design in the form of a wooden carving in the Western Australian desert. So we took a photo of it. And then, somehow, we lost it! Stupid, weren't we? But not as stupid as you, because now you've given us back the original. The beautiful, perfect original. Look at it. Take a last look at what could have been yours. Not only the greatest mathematical secret in the world, but possibly also the key to unimaginable treasures. Poor Ishiko. Poor, stupid Ishiko. Anything you want to say? On second thoughts, keep it to yourself because nobody… and I mean, *nobody* could give a shit.'

She then put the Decagon back in the bag and turned to the Korean man. 'Get rid of the dumb bitch', Ishiko heard her say quietly.

One of the Melanesians slid open a section of the side railing of the boat, and then pushed up to the gap what looked to be a small, yellow building skip. (It brought to mind the yellow tow-truck that had haunted her for so long.) She could now see that the rope she was tied with and which was coiled on the deck was attached, at its other end, to the skip. The man then pushed the skip overboard. There was a splash.

Everyone watched the coil of rope, which had stopped unravelling.

'Don't worry,' Lena said to her. 'Those things sink fast when they get going. You'll see.'

Ishiko was calm again. None of this surprised her. She knew she deserved it. If anything, she was surprised it hadn't happened sooner. That she'd survived, kept going, for as long as she had.

And the gods, had they been watching? Did they forgive her? Did they understand? These questions flashed up in her mind and dissolved again straight away. Because she was a creature of the sea, and that was that, and right now the sea was where she was headed. Nothing else mattered, really. Except… she did wonder whether she might not smell the flowers, so to speak, along the way…

The rope started moving, slowly at first, and then at a ferocious speed, until it was flying. And then *everything* unravelled quickly.

Ishiko swiftly looped a section of the cord around a thick T-shaped iron bollard that was sticking out of the deck near the railing opening. The Korean was quick: he was there immediately, but she was quick too, and before he was able to release it she pushed him hard with her legs, and he may have tripped as well, but he didn't get his arms up in time and went flying face-first into one of the protruding arms of the bollard. There was a satisfying crunch as his skull made contact – deep contact – and he went down in a spray of blood and brain matter – batik shirt, gold watch and all – collapsing in a motionless heap on the deck. One of the

Melanesians pushed her away and quickly released the rope again, keeping a wary eye on the vanishing coil.

Not much time left now.

She had been pushed back over to within reach of the Muji bag with the Decagon in it. She grabbed the bag and slung it over her shoulder. With a little cry, Lena lunged at the bag, and as she did so, Ishiko threw a loop of the remaining rope around Lena's neck. Twice. Lena panicked and clutched uselessly at the cord which Ishiko pulled tight. The Melanesians, seeing the coil of rope almost gone now, stood back stunned, in a state of indecision. Lena, realizing what was about to happen, let out a scream, a scream that was silenced almost as soon as it started when the rope snapped taut and sliced her head clean off, which bounced once on the deck and then into the sea.

Ishiko leapt over the side at the same time in a kangaroo hop, before the last of coil of the rope disappeared. As she did so, she twisted in mid-air and looked back and was left with a parting snapshot: a tableau of the horrified Melanesians, the slumped, faceless body in the batik shirt, the headless torso in the brown dress and the rusty old *Blue Shefa* itself...

And before she hit the water, she caught a glimpse of Lena's floating head in its saucer of blonde hair. The head still had its white cap on, but without the sunglasses, and Ishiko finally got to see her eyes – her arctic-blue, wide-open eyes...

She was dragged downwards with a terrible speed. Let go of the Muji bag. Tried to undo the cord around her legs, but it was tied so tightly...

And the surface was becoming so far away...

She would become a fish. A fish of the Coral Sea. A Grey reef shark, or a Black and White Seaperch, or a Greenlip Parrotfish, or a Silver Sweeper, or a Gold-Spotted Trevally, or a Red Emperor, or a Blue Devil, or even a Yellow Cusk-Eel...

The water grew colder and darker as she slipped down, down like a stone, no, down like a Yellow Cusk-Eel, and she wondered how deep they could go...

Don't forget, she told herself, to think like an eel. Do not forget...

I am an eel.

99. <u>50° 2' 28" N 1° 44' 52" W</u>
(The English Channel)

4.15am Greenwich Mean Time (04:15 UTC)
Wednesday, 30 October

They pounded into another trough, digging deep. Were drenched in spray. He looked down, stared at the obsidian sea flowing past the side of the boat. It was still dark – well before dawn, the sun was barely even a memory – and the large swells were amorphous black beasts, coming at them in their unstoppable legions. The wind had fallen off, in the main, but the black beasts, thumping into the hull… they just kept coming.

It was now Wednesday. And so it was now two weeks since the day Jon had been sitting in his chambers – in a previous life – and staring at his desk calendar. The day of the fire, the fire that had set his life alight.

Back then, he'd been asking himself what had begun. Been telling himself he didn't believe in fate, or luck. And now, was he any clearer? About what had happened, or was happening? Maybe a little, but there was one thing he was sure of: he now most definitely believed in luck. Because all it was, believing in luck, was accepting that things were not in your control. What fool could ever believe they were? And who truly still wanted all of the things they first thought they wanted anyway? Would anyone have chosen their current life, given the choice to have any life they wanted? And yet how many people would give it all up, everything, now that they had it? How many things do we have in our lives that we never would have dreamed of asking for in the first place, but which now, to us, are irreplaceable?

As a result of the big seas, Jon and Isla had had to spend Monday night in Peacehaven and most of the following day. There'd been nothing on the news about a body being found. Was it still there? Or had it been washed away? Or had Stephens survived, and managed to save himself? Jon assumed the latter was unlikely – there'd have been something on the news, he thought, and signs of a manhunt, too – but with someone like Stephens you could never be sure. All you could do was play the odds.

They eventually got away late Tuesday night – last night – but it had been slow-going, pushing into the heavy swell, and they were still many hours away from their destination.

And right now, Isla was standing next to him, staring wide-eyed into the night.

Once, it would have occurred to him there was a chance she might try to push him overboard, given the right opportunity. Not now, though. Certainly not now. Now, fully conscious of the quantum physics universe in which he existed, he knew that nothing was exactly where you expected it to be.

Her eyes shone in the Stygian gloom, collecting light from the heavens, somehow – drawing it out of the atmosphere. And her smile, it shone too.

It had been a strange night, the night before, in Peacehaven.

* * *

While Jon's saviour, Bertie, lay curled up in front of the heater, pricking up his little ears every now and then to a noise that bothered him, his other saviour, Alastair, was on and off the phone for much of the evening, organizing their "Channel cruise" for them. And when he wasn't on the phone, he was passing on his latest piece of news – "intel" as he put it, all of which he swore was true, and if Jon had ever doubted him before, he certainly wasn't doubting him now. Alastair assured them they were making the right decision, and told them not to worry, that this would all blow over, but in the meantime he'd make sure they'd be as unfindable as if "dropped to the bottom of a deep ocean trench".

Jon was reminded of this as he looked down, now, at the surface of the dark sea below.

It just went to show you, Alastair had said, all of this, that in spite of their "brilliant work getting rid of those two clowns and, who knows, possibly their whole London operation", the "doppelgangers and bilocators" were on our proverbial doorstep, there was a "whole bloody horde of them out there" and you had to remain vigilant, although Jon wasn't quite sure what he meant, other than what he'd said earlier about it never being just one person who was responsible for an evil turn of events, it was usually a large number.

But there were two conversations in particular that stuck out in his mind.

The first involved Isla's tattoo.

Jon told her that when he saw it, he thought it looked familiar, and that now he knew why.

'I've seen that design before,' he said.

'Islamic, you mean.'

'No I mean that exact design. It sounds crazy, I know. But it's got quite a distinctive pattern, and… well for some reason it stuck in my head.'

'So where did you see it?'

'In the street, actually. In fact… it was outside the British Museum, of all places. And it gets crazier. This girl, Japanese tourist she looked like, pulled something out of her bag to show another woman, and—'

'Japanese?'

'Or Chinese. Or, I don't know, East Asian anyway, but she pulled out this round box thing, all silver, and gemstones, and with a kind of intricate, lined pattern on it, like… What?'

Isla was looking at him wide-eyed. 'It sounds like…'

'What?'

'Wouldn't it be amazing. Because Ishiko, the girl who stole the Decagon…'

'The Decagon?'

'... she was Japanese.'

'Wait, wait. The Decagon?'

'You've heard of it?'

'The... Isfahan...?'

'Yes! The Isfahan Decagon.'

'That's right,' he said. 'Emerald mentioned it. It's some sort of ancient relic?'

'Five hundred years old. It's an Islamic artefact that Drayle recovered off Africa a couple of months ago. With the most extraordinary geometry, with supposedly amazing properties. Mathematical and whatever. But that's why I chose it, because my tattoo, you see, is a copy of a carving that, in turn, is supposed to be a copy of the design on the Decagon. Or part of it anyway. Irwin was given the job of looking after it.'

'The carving?'

'A *photograph* of the carving. The carving was found recently in an old ship in the desert.'

'In the desert.'

She nodded. 'In Western Australia. And anyway I... found it, the carving photograph, and liked the design, and used it for my tattoo. It's funny because... the Decagon was stolen before anyone had had the chance to photograph it. And after they found the carving, the photograph they took of it became the only evidence Drayle had of what the Decagon's geometry looked like. And so he went and issued strict instructions that no copies be kept on anyone's phone, that Irwin print it out and keep the only copy. To preserve it's value. And when I killed Irwin, I destroyed his copy, so...'

'So your tattoo is the only copy left.'

'Apart from the Decagon itself, of course. And who knows where that is. Probably being sold to a private collector somewhere.'

'So Drayle hasn't been able to get it back?'

'Last I heard,' Isla said, 'they're still looking for the girl. For Ishiko.'

'Ishiko. Huh. So you've gone and got yourself quite a tattoo then. If this geometry really is so special... you know you're going to have a thousand mathematicians flocking to see it.'

She laughed. 'Yeah. To see my arse.'

'Exactly. At least until the real thing… the Decagon… shows up.'

'Well that's another thing. The tattoo doesn't contain the whole Decagon design… there was always a question about whether the carving contained enough of the Decagon's geometry to reveal all its secrets. So I guess… that'll be up to the thousand mathematicians.'

'It could make your life-modelling classes interesting.'

'My life-modelling classes are always interesting. But you're right. I think those days might be over somehow.'

And that, by implicit, mutual consent, was where they left it.

The second conversation that stuck out in Jon's mind took place about an hour later. This one stuck out even more, in a way – in one very major way – but partly because what had been bothering him had finally revealed itself, had come to him at last. He was in the kitchen at the time, with Isla, when he thought of it.

'I have to ask you something,' he said.

'Sure.'

'You said it was when Irwin was checking you out, that he found out about Nevers. What was there to find about Nevers, that he had to find out through you?'

She looked puzzled, for a moment, by the question.

'Oh,' she said. Looked at him in a matter-of-fact way. 'Just that he found out about Nevers being my… biological father.'

He felt woozy. Things clicked and unclicked in his brain. Isla was Nevers' daughter, the one referred to in the will but not identified. Which meant—

'Didn't I say that?' she said, seeing the look on his face. 'So, yeah. He adopted me out. You look shocked.'

'How long have you known? About Nevers being your father?'

'Not so long. Since Irwin uncovered it. They have the… resources, if you know what I mean.'

'What about your mother?'

She shrugged. Told him it was enough, for the moment, to deal with losing a father she'd only just found. His death, she told him, had been creeping up on her ever since she heard. Was only just hitting her now.

When he told her about Nevers supposedly being *his* father, she went as pale as he felt. Of course Emerald, who was his sole source of information, might have got it wrong. Might have made it up, about Nevers being his father. The will itself, or Nevers, might have had it wrong. He and Isla could be siblings, or half-siblings, or neither.

And then Isla, at the time, in the kitchen, with the colour returned to her face , beamed at him, warmly, and lifted a soft hand and stroked his cheek.

'Well I think it's lovely,' she said. 'Whatever is the truth of it. You can be my brother any time.'

* * *

And maybe they'd find out one day, Jon thought now, in the middle of the night, halfway across the English Channel. In the meantime, in the greater scheme of things, where did this information fit in? Who knew what tomorrow would bring? For now, couldn't possibly this be more than enough? Wasn't being alive and having a little bit of love all you could ever really ask for?

He looked down again into the inky-black waters as they rose and fell against the side of the boat, and wondered what lay beneath. And it occurred to him, it made a good metaphor for Life.

There is so much, so close, that we don't understand.

100. <u>17° 40' 15" S 167° 20' 25" E</u> (Coral Sea, Over the New Hebrides Trench)

The same time
3.15pm Vanuatu Time (04:15 UTC)
Wednesday, 30 October

It was her last go at the monitor before they packed up, and the marine biologist from Seattle was feeling like she probably ought to make the most of it. The timer had just switched on the lights down there, on the same section of ocean floor they'd been staring at for six days – approximately ten kilometres north-east and seven straight down – and she could see already there was the usual array of bright red prawns and pale-white amphipods. Come on, she thought, surprise me. It was her last chance to make her name. A new species of fish, for example, or a fish never before spotted at that depth.

'OK guys let's move it out!' someone yelled in the corridor outside, while clapping loudly. One of the other Americans. 'Pack up your toys, we're out of here! Pina coladas in Vila, *yeeeeeaaaahhh*! *WooooOOO!*'

It was always bittersweet, packing up. Saying goodbye to your deep-sea cousins. You often saw the same individuals, and they became kind of like friends. (Better than the ones on the ship, who were only slightly better-looking). Time to rejoin civilisation though, and get away from her colleagues if nothing else.

Without turning off the monitor itself, she turned off the video recording equipment, unhooked it, and took it with her as she stood up and left the compartment.

If she'd stayed for just a few seconds longer, she would have seen an extraordinary sight. Because there, on the monitor in the now empty compartment, past the prawns and their pig carcass, in the grainy background darkness, a large yellow skip thudded down into the silt of the seabed. Following it, coil upon coil of rope fell, and continued to fall, and settle around it. And then, most unusually of all, in the foreground, and almost landing on the pig carcass itself, and certainly startling one or two of the amphipods, an intricately patterned silver container inlaid with hundreds of tiny gemstones, red and green, blue and white, descended into view and landed on the ocean floor in a small puff of silt and then just stood there, next to the carcass with its crowd of sea creatures, sparkling in the camera lights.

One of the pale amphipods seemed to sniff it, before returning its attention to the carcass.

And in the background, the last of the rope hit the floor, with nothing on the other end except for a knot and an empty loop.

For a couple more minutes the lights stayed on, and the latest visitor continued to glint and shimmer in the imperceptibly shifting current before, all of a sudden, without warning...

Darkness. The purest blend.

Afterword

Thank you for reading *Dark Oceans*.

I appreciate your valuable time and I hope you enjoyed it. It's taken six years to conceive the beginnings of, research, write, and redraft this book, but the next one – I have good reason to believe – is just around the corner.

So if you feel like staying in touch, you can sign up for my newsletter directly at http://eepurl.com/dwrRc1

or visit my website at markmacrossan.com

In the meantime, to everyone who bought this, my first novel, thank you!

Φ

Acknowledgments

First and foremost I want to thank my honorary muse Lisa Tyson, without whose constant input, advice, encouragement and inspiration, this book could never have been written.

I also owe a great debt to my other first readers for their time and invaluable assistance: Jeremy Johnson, Glen Woodward, Jackie O'Sullivan, Katri Skala, Marjorie Solomon, Peter Keel, Ross Wilson, and my very wise and well-read mother, Margery Macrossan.

I'd especially like to thank the author Sue Woolfe, who not only provided feedback on the manuscript, but whose inspirational postgraduate classes over six years ago in the English Department at Sydney University helped shape my approach to the writing of this novel and indeed provided the fertile soil from which the first seeds of this story sprouted.

Special thanks must also go to editor and publisher Linda Funnell, who provided the structural editing: her vital contribution to the ultimate shape of this book cannot be overstated.

And to Nicola Atkinson, who provided the line editing, and whose many helpful comments along the way have proved to be 'on the money' and indispensable.

Thanks also to others for their various much-appreciated contributions: to Frank Russo for his early encouragement regarding the novel's form; to the New South Wales Writers' Centre for all the help they provided along the way; to Judith Beveridge, whose instruction on the art of the appreciation and writing of poetry has had a profound effect on my writing; and to the cover designer,

Jonathon Eadie, whose wonderful artistic instincts are, allow me to suggest, clearly in evidence.

And a big thank you to my publishing consultant Joel Naoum of Critical Mass who guided the manuscript so expertly through to publication.

Finally I'd like to thank my late father, John Macrossan, who continues to be a shining light in my life.

Φ

www.ingramcontent.com/pod-product-compliance
Lightning Source LLC
Chambersburg PA
CBHW020647110726
47901CB00001B/78